The Bones and the Book

Jane Isenberg

To Reva, I hope this is worth the wait – Thank you for your patience and support. Fondly, Jane Isenberg 10/21/12

Oconee Spirit Press, Waverly, TN www.oconeespirit.com
978-0-9840109-2-9

Library of Congress Cataloging-in-Publication Data
Isenberg, Jane. The Bones and the Book
p.cm.

This is a work of fiction. All of the characters, organizations, and events portrayed in this novel are either products of the author's imagination or are used fictitiously.

1.Historical fiction. 2. Seattle (Wash.) – Fiction. 3. Jews – Fiction. 4. Jews – Seattle (Wash.) – Fiction.

The text paper is SFI certified. The Sustainable Forestry Initiative® program promotes sustainable forest management.

Cover design by Kaitlyn Tucker. Image © Mikle 15.

Dedicated to the memory of Pam Waechter who was shot and killed on July 28, 2006, during an attack on Seattle's Jewish Federation where she directed the annual fundraising campaign and to Layla Bush, Carol Goldman, Dayna Klein, Christina Rexroad, and Cheryl Stumbo, Federation employees badly wounded in the same attack.

And for Jordan, Lucas, Levi, Malcolm, and Zev

"There's the scarlet thread of murder running through the colorless skein of life, and our duty is to unravel it, and isolate it, and expose every inch of it."

Sir Arthur Conan Doyle, *The Scarlet Ruse*

". . . bring my bones up from this place."

Joseph, *Genesis* 50:25

Prologue

Harry Mazursky strode along Seattle's First Avenue on the way to work that April day in 1965 in a state of post-coital euphoria so great that he was actually trying to compose a poem. But Harry was an insurance salesman, not a poet, and he couldn't think of a single word to rhyme with Enovid. Harry's poem would have been a paean to the Food and Drug Administration for approving Enovid for contraceptive use just a few years back. When his forty-five-year-old former schoolteacher wife, a veteran of too many miscarriages, a woman convinced that every penetration led to pregnancy, started taking the Pill, things changed. "No more with the trampoline for midgets," she said, tossing her diaphragm into the wastebasket. "No more with the *capotes*," she sang, flipping his rubbers in after it. Thanks to Enovid, Rachel electrified their marriage bed with the same high-voltage passion with which she revved up their fights. And just last September things got even better. That was when Marsha, their only child, went east to college in spite of her father's objections. Although it upset Harry that his "baby girl" would be so far from home, Marsha's departure left him secure in the knowledge that there would be no adolescent ear in the next room overhearing his groans of pleasure.

Harry expected Marsha's leave-taking to bring discord after he nixed her mother's return to the budding teaching career she'd had to abandon when the school board found out she was pregnant. That really pissed Rachel off, because she had loved teaching history. When she wasn't talking about her classes, she was reading textbooks, planning lessons, and pasting her pupils' papers into those damn scrapbooks she was always making.

But Rachel left the classroom twenty years ago, and Seattle's schools had changed. Harry figured his bookworm wife would never be able to handle the Negro toughs now overrunning some of the Queen City's schools. He read the papers. And he'd seen for himself all Marsha's colored classmates at her graduation from Garfield High last year. Marsha didn't want him to say *Negro* or *colored* anymore, or even *shvartz*, Yiddish for black. No, Marsha wanted him to call them *black*. Harry smiled. "I call a spade a spade," he punned whenever his daughter critiqued his word choice.

Anyway, there was no need for Rachel to work. Wasn't he the family bread winner? And a pretty good one, too. Harry knew he could sell life insurance to a corpse. So he'd known how to handle his restless wife. When he laid down the law to her, he'd said, "Suppose you really could get a teaching job at your age. You'll earn chickenfeed and push us into a higher tax bracket with nothing to show. Forget it." But even this dismissive prohibition had not dampened Rachel's sexual ardor, and now, with Marsha's freshman year nearly over, his wife still wanted him with the same urgency. That very morning it had been Rachel who moved over him while he slept, so that for a moment his dream became flesh.

Then, because he had reached the office building where his prospective clients, three young associates in a prestigious law firm, waited, Harry tried to focus on the upcoming meeting. He'd been gratified when they agreed to see him. It was important to make the sale. The commissions would help him pay for last week's screw-up so Rachel wouldn't have to know about it and get that long nose of hers out of joint. And maybe there'd be a bonus. The partners in the company he worked for could get generous at Christmas.

Harry straightened his tie and, still struggling to clear his mind of the memory of Rachel astride him, he reached for the door handle. At the precise instant that he adjusted his tie, the tectonic plates forty miles beneath the Puget Sound shifted. The resulting temblor dislodged a challah-sized chunk of cornice high on the building's facade. It landed on Harry, crushing his skull, killing him instantly.

Chapter 1

Kook nisht azoy oometik . . . **Don't look so sad . . .**

Thanks to Jackie Kennedy I got through Harry's funeral dry-eyed and without a cigarette. That morning while I was wedging myself into a borrowed black sheath, I pictured the black-veiled and straight-backed widow holding her two little ones by the hand beside that flag-draped coffin. Like me, Jackie had been catapulted into bereavement, yet that day she stood tall for her children and for us all, a saint in a pillbox hat. I wanted to be strong like her for my own daughter. I focused on Jackie's dignity and decorum when she laid her Jack to rest.

After my mother died, I was strong. Manya's struggle with cancer had served as a cruel luxury, her year of suffering giving me time to prepare myself for what, until then, had seemed unthinkable: my fierce fighter of a mother would die soon, would never even know her grandchild. And that's what happened. Mere months after Manya's death, I gave birth to Marsha. I told myself this twisted version of Godly giving and taking meant that the Deity somehow knew what He was doing. I diffused my grief changing diapers, warming bottles, and nagging God to come up with a surefire colic remedy.

But for Harry, death gave no advance notice. One morning he left for work and never came home. Incredulous and red-eyed, Marsha flew back from New York to sob in my arms. But at the end of the mourning period, she was ready to return to her job and her friends. Thank God, Marsha had her own life, would not be eating dinner alone every evening.

But I would, and I'd be sleeping alone too. From where I tossed and turned in too much space, it seemed that this time God had got the giving and taking completely wrong. I'd been raised to be a wife and mother but then, poof! I had no husband and a daughter nearly grown and gone. Only a month had passed since the disaster, the funeral, the prescribed seven days of mourning, and I was still struggling to accept the sudden and unexpected death of my husband of twenty years.

Harry, may he rest in peace, wasn't perfect. He was 4F, not a war hero like Jack Kennedy, and Harry could be stubborn, especially about Marsha going east to college and about me going back to teaching. But he was a hard worker, a steady provider. Marsha's college money was in the bank and, of course, Harry had plenty of life insurance. He used to tell potential clients, "This policy is so good I bought one myself to protect my wife and daughter when I'm gone." In fact, Harry was going to see a prospective client when he died. He was so proud of his salesmanship. He always said, "If I weren't Jewish, I'd have been made a partner at Pratt and Pringle years ago."

With my dead husband's words echoing in my head, I opened the *Seattle Times*. Every single day of the four weeks since the cataclysm claimed Harry, I examined the paper for further revelations about it. Even during the week of mourning when family and friends crowded our little house, I pored over the *Times* in search of quake-related items. I knew all about the other poor soul who, like Harry, died when he got hit by debris, and I cut out his obituary too and pasted it and the articles detailing the extent of the damage and the cleanup effort into one of Marsha's old three-ring binders.

I had binders bulging with articles about the Internment, the Holocaust, and cancer. Harry never understood how cutting, ordering, pasting, and labeling helped me cope with the catastrophes that comprise human history, but it made sense to me that after the earthquake, I was, once again, trying to constrain chaos within the covers of a binder. By confronting and cataloguing reporters' accounts of the seismic shudder that took Harry, I hoped to make his disappearance manageable.

For the same reason I walked past downtown sites that were hardest hit. But a month had passed. Clean up crews had hosed Harry's blood off the square of sidewalk where he died, carted away the rubble, and repaired damaged masonry. The earthquake was no longer news. That's why I didn't really expect to find it headlining a prominent article on page one.

Quake Bares Bones Under Pioneer Square

Yiddish Book Uncovered With Human Remains

Two Cleveland High School seniors Saturday stumbled onto a collection of human bones alongside a handwritten book in the subterranean streets below Pioneer Square. The students, Royal Townsend and Jennifer Larson, are members of Linda Thurman's journalism class. The class had volunteered to help clear out earthquake debris so the historic underground streets could be reopened for tourist expeditions.

Miss Larson said they found a knotted brown leather sack in a metal container. "I untied the knot, and then Royal pointed his flashlight inside. That's when we saw the skull—and the book. I ran and got Miss Thurman."

Miss Thurman continued the story. "Jennifer was talking so fast I could hardly understand her. But when I saw what was in that bag, I suggested we all go outside for a break, and I called the police from a pay phone." Police collected the bones and book for investigation.

Detective Louis Lombardi said the book was written in a foreign language, and he thought some letters resembled those on the old synagogues in Seattle's Central District. "I took the book over to the rabbi at the University of Washington's Hillel. The rabbi said the writing was Yiddish, using the Hebrew alphabet. The dates in the book go back to the 1880s. We're not interested in remains that old, so we turned the bones and book over to the Department of Anthropology at the University of Washington."

Timothy Hunter, UW professor of physical anthropology, said he and his graduate students will study the bones. "Maybe the little book will help us determine whose bones we've got," Hunter said. "But I'm not making any promises."

My mother, may she rest in peace, would have said it was *bashert* or fated that the same damn tectonic twitch that took my Harry also turned up a book handwritten in Yiddish. Maybe she was right, because after I read the article I felt compelled, driven almost, to seek out that exhumed book. I needed a project to distract me from my grief. But my compulsion was further fueled by my belief that if Jews really were God's chosen people, what He chose us for was to take notes, write down what happens, write history. What if nobody wrote down what happened in Egypt? At Sinai? Torah exists because a few people bothered to jot down what went on. I wanted to read that Yiddish book unearthed downtown.

So I didn't paste the article about the bones and the book in my binder. I put it in my purse and called information to get the phone number of that anthropology prof with the WASPy name. I suspected there was no one he knew at the University except Hillel's Rabbi Yosl Moscowitz who could read enough Yiddish to translate the book. But Rabbi Moscowitz was too busy arranging kosher meals, planning mixers, and conducting religious services for Jewish students to take on another project. Professor Timothy Hunter didn't know it yet, but he needed me. This realization gave me poise and new purpose. The Anthropology Department secretary connected me right away.

"Tim Hunter." Even in those three syllables I heard his lazy southern drawl.

"Hello, Professor. My name is Rachel Mazursky."

"Mazursky? I know that name. Have we met?"

"No, but my husband died in the earthquake. Our name was in the paper."

"I'm so sorry, ma'am, for your loss."

Loss? Did he think I misplaced my husband of twenty years? "Thank you. I'm calling about the book the detective brought you, the book found underground with the bones. I'd like to look at it, perhaps translate it for you." I was a little taken aback when I heard myself blurt out this offer, but I persisted. "I don't suppose you found someone to do that yet."

"No, I just got the bones and the book yesterday. Rabbi Moscowitz doesn't have time to work on it, but he said he'd try to find somebody. Did he call you?"

"No. I read the article in the newspaper." That I took the initiative to contact the professor must mean I was beginning to recover, was acting more myself. "I've had lots of experience translating Yiddish, and the book interests me."

"Your services could be useful, maybe tell us whose bones we've got." He hesitated and then, newly brusque, added, "We can't pay much." This distasteful practicality out of the way, the professor was once again cordial. "But why don't you come and take a look at the book and we can talk?"

"I could stop by this afternoon." If I put off this appointment, I was afraid my interest would give way to the misery that made me shrink from lunches with well-meaning friends and meetings of the Jewish women's groups that crowded my calendar before Harry died.

"Terrific. I've got no conferences scheduled until three."

"And don't worry about paying me. If I can translate the book, I'll do it as a *mitzvah*." Figuring Professor Hunter wouldn't understand the Hebrew word, I translated, albeit roughly, "A good deed."

Later that day I was miffed when the Anthropology Department's secretary hustled me down a long hall saying, "Professor Hunter's meeting with the Dean, but he asked me to unlock his office and let you in. He said the book's on his desk. Said to tell you to be really careful with it." She left, pulling the door shut behind her.

At the sight of the small mottled brown volume, my pique gave way to curiosity and something stronger. Emboldened, I went around the desk and sank into the professor's chair. Carefully I turned the book over so the spine was on the right, gingerly gripped the cover between thumb and forefinger, lifted it, and inhaled deeply, as if to literally take in what I saw. On the brittle flyleaf were the five printed Hebrew consonants— *ayin*, *lamed*, *yod*, *zayin*, and *hei*— the alert detective had noticed. He couldn't have missed them. Each block letter was nearly half an inch high and the quintet marched right to left across the page. These letters, innocent of vowels, were exuberantly if inexpertly printed in bold black ink that appeared to have faded only a little. Aliza. A woman. Who knew?

When I turned the page and saw the Yiddish script, my heart was home. I could have been looking at one of my mother's scrawled grocery lists or, for that matter, the receipts my father used to write. There were the familiar characters, looking like loops and knots of dark blue thread. Wayward strands occasionally arched above and below, perhaps seeking guidelines that weren't there. For these characters were strung across small unlined pages at a slant, their progress only occasionally interrupted by a period strewn in their midst like an errant poppy seed. Hebrew favored no character above any other, so there were no capital letters. Aliza evidenced no fondness for paragraphs either. And words were often blurred, misspelled, crossed out. Taking another deep breath, I gave myself over to my mother tongue, my own dead mother's language.

At the start, my reunion with the vernacular of my forebearers was awkward, but I persisted, translating in my head. The first line appeared to be a heading of sorts, one that was repeated often:

the ______ of aliza rudinsk nyzhni sady 5 august 1889

I assumed the faded word was *journal* or *diary* as it was on subsequent pages and I knew Nyzhni Sady to have been a town in the Ukraine. Adjusting for syntactical differences, I divined the first complete thought to read in part:

If this is not so, let the most high _____my tongue and freeze my arms and legs . . .

After making a grammatical reversal, I determined that the apparently absent antecedent for *this* wasn't absent at all, just perverse. It appeared after the pronoun, not before. The antecedent was Aliza's story, the one she was about to write. And I knew *the Most High* to be an archaic phrase once used by pious Jews to avoid naming the Deity. I wasn't sure about updating the quaint moniker by replacing it with *God*, so I didn't.

The tangle of illegible squiggles that followed could spell either *freeze* or *amputate*. When I compared it to the more legibly written *freeze* later in the sentence, I opted for that word, favoring the rhythm of repetition over the gore of dismemberment. Then I decided that the punishment Aliza was willing to endure if she were writing lies had less to do with temperature than with immobility. With that mix of trepidation and chutzpah familiar to even the most practiced translators, I replaced both *freezes* with *paralyze*.

But I would have no qualms about reversing the day and month in her dates to conform to our American style or about supplying capital letters and punctuation. On the contrary, I savored the prospect of dividing Aliza's strings of Yiddish words into English sentences and grouping those into paragraphs. Reading on, I interpreted, guessed, and assumed as is the way of translators. My efforts were rewarded when, after only a few pages, I began to hear Aliza speaking to me in what sounded like her own spirited voice.

Aliza's Diary, Nyzhni Sady, the Ukraine, August 5, 1889

If what I write is a lie, may the Most High make me speechless and paralyze my arms and legs. Meier Horowitz himself put this beautiful diary into my hand! This morning I was alone in the sewing room stitching the last of the rosettes to the waist of his sister's bridal gown. Mama and Papa would not like that I was alone with him, that he touched me. But, may I be forgiven, I thank the Most Holy for sending Meier to me.

Tomorrow he returns to his studies in Kiev. I will never forget his words. "Goodbye, little Aliza. Don't look so sad. I have another sister as yet unmarried, and she will need these magic fingers of yours to make her wedding dress." Then he lifted my hand that was holding the fabric. He actually took my hand in his. He leaned over and brushed my knuckles with his lips! I swear as I am a Jew that is what he did. Like I was a fine lady in one of those forbidden foreign books he was always telling me about. Then with my hand still in his he said, "So perhaps next summer Hanele will bring you here for a third time. Until then, here is a diary like my own. Record your thoughts and the new words you learn." Then he turned my hand over and put this book into it. My legs felt weak! They shook like the legs of Papa's newborn calf shook when the creature struggled to its feet. Before I could unlock my tongue to thank him, Meier ran out of the sewing room like he thought a peasant with vodka on his breath was chasing him.

Meier taught me many new words this summer like *capitalist*, *socialist*, *Charles Darwin* and more. Meier's tongue never tires of these words. But he does not say them in front of his father. Why in such a big house is there not room for all the words? Our house is small. We have space for only our family, our horse and cow, and for the Most Holy and words about the Most Holy.

Aliza's Diary, Gnilsk, the Ukraine, August 8, 1889

The Rabbi says only the Most High can know all our thoughts. That is why on my last night at Meier's house I had to push this diary under my bedding so that no one would find it. I do not want anyone to read my thoughts. In Gnilsk I do not have to fear because Papa reads only Hebrew and Mama does not read at all. But little Yitzak would chew on the pretty leather cover. That is why I stash it in my apron pocket all day and at night under the bedding it goes. It is the Sabbath now, so, may the Most High forgive me, I write in the privy with the spiders who cannot read.

Papa was in Nyzhni Sady yesterday like always selling prayer shawls and *Kiddush* cups. He brought me and Hanele back to Gnilsk in the wagon. His shoulders hunched over the reins more than I remember. It was not the season of the gentile Easter when priests say that Jews use the blood of Christian children to make matzah for Passover. But Papa kept looking over his shoulder like he was expecting any moment a mob of crazed peasants. He shortened the journey by telling stories of his travels. He can make the sale of a prayer shawl to a baker into an adventure.

Mama limped to meet the wagon. She laughed away the ache in her knees and held me tight. She covered my face with kisses. Little Yitzak greeted me with jumping up and down and waving his skinny arms. Tonight Mama will light and bless the Sabbath candles. She promised to put an extra meat bone in the soup.

Aliza's Diary, Gnilsk, August 28, 1889

May the Almighty forgive me for being ungrateful. Last night, with little Yitzak dreaming beside me, I buried my face in the quilt and wept. Mama and Papa were in their bed making their own Sabbath sounds, so they would not have heard me. But I did not wish to waken my little brother. . . .

Chapter 2

Was it late? I glanced at my watch. I'd been waiting almost an hour, completely absorbed by the diarist's outpourings. And even though I hadn't met Professor Hunter, I knew making Aliza's diary comprehensible to a WASPy Southerner, a man to boot, would take some doing. The physical anthropologist would surely find the Orthodox Jewish girl's bones more accessible than her account of prayer shawls, Sabbath sounds, and *Kiddush* cups. Good thing I'd grabbed my parents' copy of Harkavy's *Verterbukh* on my way out of the house. I ran my fingers over the tattered and soup-stained pages of the old Yiddish-English-Hebrew dictionary.

The small pages of the diary itself were flimsy as insect wings, their edges ragged, and the scripted letters necessarily cramped. I'd need a magnifying glass. Some pages had been torn out, while others stuck to one another. I'd have to heat the tea kettle and steam them apart. It would be hard, slow work, but I knew I could do it. But should I? How would Aliza have felt about a total stranger reading her secrets? Translating them for others to read? I hated it when Bobby Gradstein grabbed my diary and read my teenaged rants. Marsha would kill me if I ever opened the red leather journal Harry and I gave her for her fifteenth birthday. I reminded myself that unlike Marsha, Aliza, so alive on the page, was most likely long dead, resting in peace I hoped. She'd never know I was reading her private writings.

No sooner had I laid those doubts to rest than another one, a darker one, took its familiar place in my head. How did I, Rachel Mazursky, a modern American woman, an educated and assimilated Jew, feel about exposing this girl's unlettered expressions, her foreignness, her Orthodoxy —let's face it, her Jewishness— to readers of English? What readers? Who would actually read my translation of the diary?

Again I imagined Professor Hunter perusing my translation of Aliza's account. Although Seattle's gentiles neither killed nor expelled the Jews in their midst, they knew precious little about us. Most of us lived in a bubble in the Central District, an area unrestricted by exclusionary housing ordinances. There we formed our own organizations and pursued our own activities parallel to the social, civic, and political ones we were barred from.

But we attended public schools, so by second grade I'd memorized *The Lord's Prayer* and all the verses to most Christmas carols and learned that Catholic kids ate tuna fish sandwiches on Fridays. And it was there I'd realized that my teachers and classmates had little knowledge of and less interest in Jewish folkways. That's why, when I composed notes for my mother to sign explaining my absence on our important holidays, I wrote that Rachel had suffered an upset stomach or a cold, not that her parents had kept her out of school to pray, starve, and contemplate her childish sins.

So for Professor Hunter I'd have to carefully decode the girl's Yiddish, Anglicizing and updating at least some of her archaic idioms. It would take time, but with no husband and daughter to cook and launder for and pick up after, I had time, and I really wanted to do it. Gently I closed the little volume and turned it over so it lay as I found it. I stretched, stood, and walked around the professor's desk to one of the chairs in front of it.

On that side of the desk, I became a college student again. I'd felt at home at the U even though, as a commuter, I'd never spent a night in a dorm, and in 1940 I'd been one of only eight women in my class. But going to public school in Seattle had inured me to feeling different. Not yellow-star different, just lips-together-during-*The-Lord's-Prayer* different. And growing up Orthodox in Seattle had hardened me to *being* different. Not forever branded different like the concentration camp survivors I knew, but rather set apart by our family's unfathomable avoidance of bacon and lack of a Christmas tree.

Maybe that's why I fell for Heschel Mazursky, a lonely, intense transfer student, an outsider even among outsiders. When he took a seat next to me that day in the Husky Stadium, he said he recognized me from Hillel meetings and explained that only a back injury had prevented him from enlisting. Hip to hip we watched a simulated gas attack and rescue. When he offered me a swig of coffee from his thermos, I refused, explaining that I kept kosher. A salesman even then, Harry introduced himself as the son of Spokane's kosher slaughterer and vouched for the integrity of his thermos. I took a swig and that was it. There in Professor Hunter's office, tears welled, so I gnawed hard on my lower lip.

Just before I drew blood, the professor came in. "Sorry to have kept you waiting, Mrs. Mazursky, but when the Dean summons . . . ." Shrugging at the tyranny of deans, Professor Hunter smiled down at me and shut the door behind him. That boyish smile did not disguise his crow's feet or the graying temples framing his face. I figured him to be about my age. In his rumpled tan corduroy jacket with suede-patched elbows, he looked predictably professorial. He seated himself behind his desk, and his cordial smile of welcome widened to the grin of a coconspirator.

"Thank you for coming, for your interest in this project, Mrs. Mazursky. Shall I have Roberta bring coffee?" I shook my head. "I see you came prepared. Is that a Yiddish dictionary?"

I nodded. If I didn't say something soon, the man would think I was a mute.

"May I see it?"

"Sure." His unexpected curiosity piqued my own. Intrigued, I passed him the *Harkavy's*.

He held it in one hand and thumbed through it with the other. "It reads from right to left."

"I should have warned you about that."

He shrugged, flipped the dictionary, and resumed thumbing. "Interesting. The letters here do look like the ones at what I realize now is the front of the book." He nodded in the direction of the diary. "But Rabbi Moscowitz insists Yiddish isn't Hebrew. Does it predate Hebrew? Is it a dialect?"

Was Professor Hunter just being polite, making conversation? It didn't matter. "Yiddish is only a thousand years old. It's the vernacular language of

Eastern European Jews. Hebrew's the language we use in synagogue." Still thumbing through the dictionary, he glanced up at me and nodded but didn't speak. I took his silence as an invitation to say more. "Jewish women weren't taught Hebrew and spoke only Yiddish, so Yiddish became known as our mothers' tongue." The *mamaloshen.* I'd been mortified by my mother's kvetchy Cassandra-like admonitions barked in Yiddish, often in public. "Yiddish has some Hebrew influences, but it's definitely not a dialect."

When the professor leaned forward to pass the dictionary back to me, I figured I'd satisfied his polite curiosity, so I was surprised when he asked, "How did Yiddish come into being?"

His questions, perfunctory though they may have been, made me feel like an ambassador from an exotic nation and the teacher I used to be, rather than the middle-aged widowed Jewish housewife and mother I really was. It was exciting. "French Jews migrated to German-speaking countries in the tenth and eleventh centuries and used the Hebrew alphabet to write the Germans' vernacular language phonetically."

"Too bad those Hebrews didn't pick up some Latin while they were in France. I can still read a little Latin."

The professor's remark was as ridiculous as his use of the word *Hebrews.* Would I alienate him if I told him so? Who knew? I'd never had a conversation of this sort with a non-Jew. I forced my eyes to meet his and tried not to sound accusatory. "Jews associated Latin with Christianity and Christianity with pogroms."

"Of course." Unruffled, he fired another question at me. "So what country do they speak Yiddish in now?"

"Brooklyn." This flip answer flew out of my mouth before I could censor it.

The professor smiled. But before replying he checked his watch. "The rest of my questions will have to wait. You've had a chance to look at the book?"

"Yes. It's a diary." No need to tell him more yet.

"A diary, eh? Interesting. That's what Rabbi Moscowitz thought. On the phone you said you had experience translating."

"As a child, I translated for my parents." It was years before their accented and inflected English became good enough to use with doctors, teachers, clerks, and customers. "We spoke Yiddish at home."

"But you have no accent. Were you born here?"

"Yes. I left my accent at the door to kindergarten." I'd discarded Yiddish like a used Kleenex or an empty candy wrapper.

"Have you done any other translating?"

"Years ago I interviewed several elderly Yiddish-speaking Holocaust survivors who relocated here. I taped, translated, and transcribed their stories."

"Holocaust survivors, eh? That must have been fascinating work."

"It was. It was important to get them to tell their stories before they died. I majored in history right here at the U." Accounts of bloody battles and intrepid pioneers offered an escape from my parents' anxious preoccupation with "The Situation" in Europe. "So I'm very interested in this book." I pointed at Aliza's diary.

When the professor spoke next, I knew I had passed muster. "Well, then, as you know, old human bones turned up downtown under Pioneer Square." I pictured Tim Hunter in front of a class. He wasn't handsome, but he had an easy way about him, as if he belonged wherever he happened to be. "And this was with them." He waved his hand at the little brown volume. "Anyway, the detective couldn't make out anything but the dates. The earliest of those is in the 1880s." The professor stopped professing just long enough to draw breath.

"When the police encounter remains that have been around that long, they send them here for us to study. We try to identify them. It's a useful experience for my physical anthropology grad students. The bones and the book were in a leather sack, and, of course, the flesh decomposed." He paused. "Or, if the sack, which I haven't examined, has a hole in it, rats and other animals feasted on the flesh."

"Animals?"

"Sure. Back then there were cougars right here in town. And coyotes and other smaller carnivores also feed on corpses. Critters often move body parts too. That's one reason finding an old and possibly complete skeleton like this one is unusual. I'm eager to set my students to work reassembling the bones."

"Professor, maybe the diary didn't belong to the person whose bones are in that bag." I doubted that the bones in the leather sack in Seattle could be those of the diarist, a pious teenage girl pouring her Jewish heart out in a Ukrainian outhouse. "Maybe the diary was stolen. I kept a diary in high school and somebody stole it."

"Well I can understand that. Who wouldn't want to know your innermost thoughts?"

Caught off guard, I bristled at the man's nerve. Or was I still mad at Bobby Gradstein? Before I could explain that Bobby hadn't given a damn about my innermost thoughts, the phone rang. While the professor talked, I remembered.

When Bobby and I were growing up, the Gradsteins and the Wilenskis were like family. And, like blood siblings, Bobby and I ignored one another in school except when he tried to cheat off me. But when Mo and Harriet Gradstein got together of an evening with Sam and Manya Wilenski, Bobby and I played hide and seek and cowboys and Indians and later Hearts, Slapjack, and Monopoly in each other's rooms until adolescence. Then, if we were in my house, I sprawled on my white chenille bedspread and did homework while Bobby read Superman comics on the floor. But if we were in his room, with Hammerin' Hank Greenberg at bat on every wall, Bobby perused his secret stash of two well-thumbed girlie magazines.

The professor was shaking his head as he put down the phone. "The Dean again. Sorry for the interruption. I was saying I could understand why someone would want to know what was in your diary."

"The kid who stole it was angry because I wouldn't let him cheat off me, Professor."

"Tim, please."

Those two words and his blue eyes gleaming at me across the desk were an invitation to further intimacy. I focused on the bones. I decided against informing Tim that some Jews, like my mother, may she rest in peace, believed the soul of a person buried in unconsecrated ground would not be taken up to heaven by the Messiah. Instead I answered politely. "Rachel."

"Rachel." He breathed rather than spoke my name. "The beautiful sister, the one Jacob really desired." This time there was no deflecting the compliment or come-on. I twisted my wedding ring and lowered my eyes, but not before I spotted the plain gold band on Tim Hunter's finger. "You see, Rachel, I'm not altogether ignorant of your people's history."

I was relieved when Tim resumed discussing the bones. "Apparently the sack was buried downtown in one of the retaining walls below ground. You know about those downtown streets that were rebuilt after the fire of '89?" I nodded. I'd taught a course in Seattle history. "Well, some wacky preservationist wants to make an underground tourist attraction out of them." Tim smirked at the folly of this idea. "My grad students will start reassembling the bones this week." He looked at his watch again. "Speaking of students, I've got one coming in for a conference in a few minutes." He stood. "So, Rachel, if you'd like to translate the diary . . ."

"I'd like very much to work on it." Even if I hadn't desperately needed a project to distract me from my grief, I'd want to find out why that spirited young girl was crying herself to sleep.

"Good. Here, I'll rewrap it for you. It's quite fragile. Try to keep it out of the sun. Treat it like a newborn." He swaddled the little book in the square of beige flannel that lay beneath it, slipped the bundle into a small white box, secured a rubber band around that, and handed me the package.

I thought I'd be relieved when our tète-á-tète ended, but instead I found myself looking forward to meeting with the professor again. Back in the car, I purged the glove compartment of papers and junk, lined it with the sweater I kept in the back seat, and carefully stowed the box containing Aliza's leather book in the resulting Orlon nest.

Chapter 3

***. . . fardorbener klain shtetl . . .* . . . wretched little village . . .**

. . . but I did not wish to waken my little brother this late. Home again for the Sabbath with my beloved Mama and Papa and sweet little Yitzak, what for do I have to sob into my pillow? Here is what for. Nyzhni Sady is a real town with shops and paved streets and a school. Gnilsk is a wretched little village, nothing but mud streets and dead cold in the winter with flies that make you be their lunch in the summer. In Meier's family's big house I slept in a bed of my own with my own wash bowl. My home in Gnilsk is a hovel with dirt floors and only the water that Mama and I haul from the village well or the rain barrel. It was kind of Meier's sister Tamara to give me one of her outgrown dresses and loan me several books. In Gnilsk we girls read only a little Torah translated into Yiddish and our Yiddish prayer books.

Hanele's shop is my school. When Mama's friend saw I was good with my hands, she put me to work for her. I did not have to tend to her old mother or run errands like the other apprentice. Hanele had me sewing right away. She is a stern teacher. From the beginning she gave me what for when I made a crooked seam or wasted thread or cloth, but she also gives me extra bread and soup and never keeps me at her house after dark. She soon paid me as much as she paid the older women who also sewed for her.

And I am the one Hanele took with her to Meier's house for two summers. There I helped her make bridal gowns for his sisters and fancy dresses for their mother. At Hanele's shop we make all day dark and heavy pants, coats, and dresses. The work is always the same for six years, every day but the Sabbath, since I was nine.

In Gnilsk, there is no Meier. Meier is different from the boys here. In the school he attends in Kiev, he does not study only Torah but learns about the whole world. He knows Yiddish, Hebrew, Ukrainian, and Russian. And Meier does not shy away from talking to a girl like she will bite him. He even kissed my hand without fear that I might be unclean! He teases his sisters and makes jokes with me. I think he is handsome. So does the poor orphan girl whose job it is to wash the clothes and linens. She is always staring at him and turning red, but I think he prefers me. I will never be educated, but I am not a servant either. I am a seamstress. I hope Meier does not forget me when he returns to school.

Feigele's Diary, December 5, 1889

So much has happened since I sat in the privy in Gnilsk writing my thoughts. Now I am Feigele Lindner. But oh how I wish I was still Aliza and back there, back with the spiders and the rain barrel and sharing the Sabbath with Mama, Papa, and little Yitzak instead of on the deck of this rolling ship day and night, a ghost among strangers.

It is all because of that busybody Hanele, may her wagging tongue fall into her soup, that I, Aliza, am now Feigele and that I am here. One evening Hanele came to see Papa and Mama and they whispered around the table for a long time. From my bed on the other side of the room I could hear Mama crying. Papa was not saying much. It was mostly Hanele's voice that was keeping me awake. I caught only some of her words: *Gitl Lindner, America, Feigele Lindner, may she rest in peace, papers, pogroms, freedom, fast learner, work, send for you,* and my name, *Aliza*, over and over.

By the next morning everything was decided. Maybe it had all been decided in the summer when two more Jews were beaten on their way to Kiev. Or maybe the idea came to Hanele on the day her widowed cousin Gitl Lindner's daughter, Feigele, may she rest in peace, went swimming in the river and drowned. Poor Gitl already had the papers to bring herself and her Feigele to America, but Feigele was gone. It was Hanele who talked her cousin into giving those papers to me and taking me with her to New York in place of her dead daughter. It was Hanele, whispering in the dark, who convinced Mama and Papa to send me to America.

Hanele had it all figured out. When I get to New York, Papa's friend's son, Herman, who used to live in Gnilsk, will meet me at the boat, and I will pay to live with him and his wife Chaya. This Herman will find me work sewing. Soon I will earn enough money to send for Mama, Papa, and little Yitzak. Then we will all be together again and safe. Faster than Mama's challah disappears on the Sabbath, the money I earned that would have been my dowry went to buy my ticket on this boat. Papa also sold a lot of *Kiddush* cups to buy me passage to America.

ꝏ

That Aliza went to America made it more likely that the bones in the bag were hers, and this bothered me. When Tim Hunter called to say his students had finished assembling these bones, I went to see them. The Department secretary directed me to a well-lit room where drawings of skeletons lined the walls. Hunkered down over an array of bones on a table, the professor straightened as I entered. "Good morning, Rachel. Good of you to come."

I'd expected the bones to be long and white, but they were small and brownish gray, the color of driftwood. The aspiring anthropologists had arranged them to form what appeared to be a complete skeleton, a Halloween jigsaw. I made my way slowly around the table appraising the macabre configuration until I was again at Tim's side. "He's so short. Could he have been a child?" I reached to stroke the gray fissured skull. Quick as a striking snake, Tim grabbed my wrist in a grip that felt like a handcuff. I snatched my arm back, rubbing the place where his fingers had marked me. "Sorry."

"Didn't mean to hurt you. Just can't let you handle the bones. They're fragile."

"Right. Sorry."

"To answer your question, she was an adult." My eyes widened at the information that made it even harder to keep telling myself that the bones on the table weren't Aliza's. I recalled learning in a long-ago anatomy class that female pelvic bones differed from those of males. "And remember, she lived before Wheaties, vitamins, and pasteurized milk turned us into giants."

As Tim spoke, he let his glance travel the full height of my frame so that, when he finished his explanation, he was looking into my eyes.

I broke what threatened to become a charged silence. "So what makes you think this woman is Jewish and not, say, Duwamish or Japanese?" Once out of my mouth, my own question alarmed me. What if the anthropologist cited some Nazi-inspired formula for identifying Jews?

"Her skull is shaped like a garbanzo bean. Also her nasal aperture is long and the nasal sills are sharp. Those features are all European, not American-Indian or Asian."

European was okay. I was relieved and enlightened but still curious. "What are nasal sills?"

"The lower borders of the nostrils. Right here." Tim drew his index finger lightly along the base of my nose.

Oy. His touch, sure and perilously close to my upper lip, felt like a caress. I tried to keep my voice neutral, as if married WASPs I hardly knew stroked my upper lip all the time. "Okay. I see how you could tell that she was of European descent."

"I also think she was murdered." Tim's tone was matter of fact.

"Murdered?" Astonishment made my own voice shrill.

"Yup. See that crack across the top of the skull? That crack is probably the result of a blow, a blow that killed her." I knew that gentiles, except for Catholics, had a propensity for understatement, but this guy made murder sound routine.

"You really think somebody hit her over the head and murdered her?" I tried to match Tim's matter of fact tone but managed only to sound angry.

"I do. Look at the dent on this side of the crack." He pointed at a circular depression the size of a man's shirt button in the skull. "I suspect that whatever she was hit with left this indentation."

"So you think somebody hit her over the head, stuffed her body into a leather sack, brought it down below Pioneer Square, dug a hole and shoved the sack in?" I tried to be civil in my disbelief. "Couldn't her killer have been a grave robber? Maybe the poor woman was buried in a cemetery and a thief looted her grave for jewelry . . ." I still hoped that at one time the dead woman had been properly buried.

"It's possible that she was murdered elsewhere. I don't know." Tim stroked his chin. "But regardless, that underground maze would have been a relatively safe place for the killer to hide the body. If not for the latest quake she'd still be there." And Harry would still be here. I shivered. "You'll see. I'm arranging a tour of the site for my students. I'll let you know when. You should join us."

I nodded but still didn't speak, so Tim went on. "A mistake the killer made was using a leather sack. Leather resists decomposition, so that sack preserved the bones and protected them from moisture, soil erosion, and exposure. If her murderer had known that would happen, he probably would have buried her in something else because I suspect he hoped the sack and the body, including the bones, would decompose."

"Do you have any idea why she was killed?" I couldn't imagine anyone wanting to kill the pious youngster whose biggest sin was writing in her diary on the Sabbath.

"You're the one reading the book found with her, Rachel. That's where you might find the answer to that question. I can only guess." He paused. "You mentioned a grave robber before. I suspect her killer was just a regular garden variety robber."

"What makes you think she was robbed?"

Tim's wordless reply was more upsetting than his allusions to the earthquake or even his murder scenario. He pointed to the skeleton's left hand. The ring finger bones were missing. I hadn't noticed. My gasp was audible. With my right hand I shielded the plain wedding band Harry gave me.

Then I looked at the array on the table again to see what else I hadn't paid attention to. "What about those bones over there?" I pointed to an assemblage of dirty-white bones, each about eight inches long, and lying like curved pick-up sticks near the feet of the skeleton.

"Whalebone. From her corset probably. I'll bag them with the artifacts the police are sending over. I'll let you know when those get here." Tim looked at his watch. "Seen enough?"

"But if this poor woman was robbed and murdered, why aren't the police investigating?"

"You know the dates of the diary entries. As the detective said, there's too much time gone by. What would be the point?" He shrugged. "Have you read anything that might tell us something about who this was?" He jerked his head in the direction of the bones.

Put off by his dismissive shrug, I kept my answer simple. "The diarist was a girl, a teenager named Aliza Rudinsk from the Ukraine. But she sailed to New York under the name Feigele Lindner. She was an Orthodox Jew and a seamstress. I assume she would have been buried in a Jewish cemetery, probably in New York."

"And her relatives would come and put stones on her tombstone so the Recording Angel would know they visited and add their names to some list, right? I forget where the list is."

"In The Book of Life. How do you know about that?" Tim's familiarity with Jewish burial rituals surprised me.

"*A Stone for Danny Fisher.* That custom was interesting. It stuck with me."

I wasn't sure how I felt about the pulpy page-turner being Tim Hunter's window into Jewish life, but I nodded. "Anyway, now that you've reassembled the bones, what will you do with them?"

"Not sure yet. After so long, I doubt anyone will claim them. They'll probably end up in a cabinet on the fourth floor with the rest of our unclaimed remains."

"She deserves a decent burial."

"A burial. Hmmm. We have no precedent or budget line for burials, but I'll look into it." The grin he flashed was conspiratorial as it had been when we met. "Is it too late for us to leave stones at her grave? I wouldn't mind making it into The Book of Life." Before I could answer, he added, "I'd like you to have a look at the artifacts that also turned up in the bag. Somehow they got separated from the bones and the book." Tim shook his head at the carelessness of the cops. "I'll let you know when the police get around to dropping them off." It was clear our meeting was over.

After learning that the bones very likely were Aliza's and that the poor girl was murdered, I was eager to resume translating. I was distressed by the police's dismissal of her murder as unsolvable and by the way the professor literally shrugged it off. Maybe Aliza's scribbles held clues to her killer.

ഇ

I have heard a lot about America. There Jews are free to pray to the Most High without fear, even at Easter. We can also go to real schools and earn a living and buy property. Hanele's nephew has his own bakery even. He owns it. He has learned some English. Hanele said she would go herself but for her old mother.

When I told Mama Hanele was a meddling old woman who should mind her own business, Mama reminded me that Hanele has no children and has always treated me like a daughter. If it were not for Hanele I would never have traveled to Nyzhni Sady, learned to write, or slept in a room all my own. I would not have met Meier.

But now, thanks to this same Hanele, I, who have never traveled beyond Nyzhni Sady, am traveling alone all the way to New York. Papa said I would not be alone because Gitl is going with me to join her older daughter who is already there and because the Most High will watch over me. But how can the Most Holy watch over me if I am no longer myself, Aliza? If I am making this long journey into the unknown as Feigele Lindner, a drowned girl, a ghost? It is her papers that I carry. But Papa said the Almighty is smarter than the officials and knows who I am even though I do not travel as Aliza. I pray Papa is right. But I fear that *Aliza* has become a ghost too.

Also Papa does not know what I know in my heart and can say only here. The Most High has exiled me to America as punishment for envy and ingratitude. Also for my fond thoughts of Meier Horowitz. And now I will never see Meier again. And the Creator is also punishing me for writing in my diary on the Sabbath even though I prayed for forgiveness.

Another thing Papa does not know is that I also give thanks to the Almighty. It is true that in America there will be no Aliza, no Mama, Papa, little Yitzak, and no Meier, but there will be no Yekel either. This Yekel has hands roughened like the leather he works. This Yekel never spoke but stared at me with his narrow eyes like I was a challah warm from the oven. The matchmaker already talked to Papa about him. But now this Yekel will marry someone else. When I am missing Mama most, I stop myself from crying by remembering this Yekel and his hungry eyes.

Feigele's Diary, December 6, 1889

The next weeks were all preparations and goodbyes with no time to record my thoughts, my fears. Every night after sewing on the machine at Hanele's and helping Mama with the chores, I stitched by hand at home by candlelight to make myself another dress. Even though her hands hurt a lot, Mama made me new underwear. Hanele herself made me a warm coat on the Singer. Papa gave his finest prayer shawl and his most fancy Kiddush cup to the cobbler in exchange for new shoes and boots for me. Mama gave me the silver thimble that once belonged to her mother, Aliza, for whom I am named. May she rest in peace and may she never know of my betrayal, that I gave up our shared name for a piece of paper. Mama gave me also her own locket holding one of little Yitzak's dark baby curls entwined in a braid with one of my own copper colored ones. And Mama packed bread and herring for my journey so I would not have to eat non-kosher food on this ship.

At the station, Mama, weeping herself, had to pry little Yitzak from my arms. Then Gitl yanked me up the stairs onto the train, and Papa pushed my trunk up behind me. At that moment I swore that, as I am a Jew, I will sew until my fingers fall off to earn enough money to send for them.

Now I must go below and tend to Gitl. The Most High may be watching over me, but He has neglected poor Gitl who is very sick.

Feigele's Diary, December 7, 1889

All of us up here prefer the cold wind to the stink and crowding in steerage. Poor Gitl is still down there retching after every scrap of bread I share with her. I pray that she survives this voyage. I think she would feel better up here, but she says she is too weak to sit up let alone walk. Down there is like one big privy but with rats instead of spiders. Down there the ship's engine bellows louder than a cow giving birth.

I give thanks to the Most High that I learned from Meier and his sisters how to write. I already wrote a letter to Mama and Papa to mail when I get to America. Hanele will read my letter to them. May the Almighty forgive me, but I did not write about the stench or the rats or Gitl's sickness. I signed my letter Feigele, but Mama and Papa will know who I am.

Feigele's Diary, December 8, 1889

May the Almighty forgive me but I am, as usual, on deck gaping at all the people babbling in many tongues. This morning Gitl still lies below but she is much better and sleeps peacefully. Maybe later she will join me up here. Earlier my eye lingered on an older woman in a black cloak reading the palm of another passenger. Because the Most High is the only one who can know our future, such fortune telling is forbidden. So I had thought she was not a Jew and had not dared to address her. But the palmist noticed me eyeing her and spoke to me in Yiddish. When Yiddish words came out of her mouth, I answered her.

She told me her name was Lottie and that she was from a small town near Kiev. I could not any longer contain my concern about Gitl. Lottie, may the Almighty bless her with a long and happy life, reached into her pocket and extracted a small vial containing a powder. She told me to mix this powder with a little water and give it to Gitl. When I offered to pay, Lottie, may she marry a good man and bear him many sons, refused my coins. I went below and mixed the powder with water and helped Gitl to swallow it. In a few minutes Gilt smiled at me for the first time since we left the shore, and then she slept. I forced myself to stay with her in that hole that reeks worse than a privy in summer until she awakened. Then I gave her a bit of bread and she did not retch, but ate it and slept again.

When I returned to the deck I found Lottie where I had left her, reading the palm of a woman with two little girls clinging to her. When Lottie finished, the woman groped in her pocket for a coin which she pressed into Lottie's hand. To earn coins, I stitch until my eyes blur and my fingers burn, but Lottie earns coins by merely examining the hand of another for a few moments. May the Most High forgive me yet again, for I envy Lottie her gift. I thanked her one more time for the powder that had helped poor Gitl, and then Lottie offered to look into my hand and tell me what lies ahead for me on the golden streets of America.

Instead, may the Almighty forgive me for both my envy and my disobedience, I asked her to teach me how to find a person's future in his hand. Lottie looked deep into my eyes and nodded. When she spoke, she smiled at me. "Feigele, I suspect you will be a good pupil and that the Almighty will forgive us both." Then she held up my hand. "First, do you remember with what care your mama inspects all parts of a carp at the market before she pays money for it? That is how carefully you must look at the hands people bring you . . ." And my lessons began.

Feigele's Diary, December 14, 1889

Thanks to Meier and the Most Holy that I have this diary for putting down my thoughts. Without it here in New York I would die of loneliness even in the midst of so many people. I did not expect America to be so crowded, just like the boat but not rolling. That boat brought us all to Castle Garden, a huge round fortress. Gitl and I clung to each other in the crowd. It was in that swarming mob that I lost sight of Lottie, may the Almighty bless her with a good life in America.

Many from the boat and all the trunks and bundles we brought with us were crawling with vermin. Babies and children bawled from itching and hunger. Thanks to the Most High we did not have to wait there long before Papa's friend Herman and Gitl's son-in-law came together to take us away. I will write more tonight when everyone in my new home has gone to sleep and maybe the table in the kitchen is free. There is only one privy here in the yard for many families, and someone bangs at the door.

Feigele's Diary, New York, December 19, 1889

I prayed to the Almighty to dry up my tears as Herman and I trudged through streets filled with still more people and the racket they made. The streets are lined with buildings as tall as the trees in the forest around Gnilsk. What do they have all those tall buildings for if everybody is outside? Herman pushed the wheelbarrow with my trunk in it to another treeless street called Orchard Street. After we entered one of the tall buildings and climbed many stairs, I saw my new home. Herman, his wife Chaya, and their two little girls, Mimi and Shula, and Chaya's widowed cousin, Dora, live here all together. To huddle in these three tiny, dingy rooms they came to America?

Chaya explained that Dora shared Mimi and Shula's bed, so I would have one of my own. I looked around the tiny room for the other bed. I swear as I am a Jew here is what happened next. Chaya pulled in two chairs from the kitchen and Herman placed some pieces of wood between them. Then Chaya dumped some bedding on the wood. That is the moment I learned from Herman my first two English words. He said that the English word for a piece of wood is *board*, so in English a paying lodger like me is a *boarder*. He laughed hard at his joke. Three dollars a week is what I must give Herman and Chaya for my board. I go now to try to sleep on it.

Chapter 4

It was late when I finished recording my translation of the diary's first few entries on a yellow legal pad. I did a verbatim translation and then edited it, working to make the girl's stream of thoughts grammatical and completely clear to, say, Tim Hunter. To that end I translated any words that I would have transliterated, like *Shabbos* for *Sabbath*, if I were anticipating only Jewish readers. But still I worried. This murdered diarist was no Anne Frank. Unlike the literate and relatively worldly Anne, Aliza was unschooled and Orthodox to boot, too Jewish, too provincial, too poor.

That night I slept a few hours, longer than I had any night since Harry died. This was good because Bruce Freidman, friend and lawyer, was stopping by with something for me to sign. Bruce and I grew up in the Central District and went to Garfield High and the U together. I dusted, made a fresh pot of Maxwell House, and put a Sara Lee pecan coffeecake in the oven. At the sound of the doorbell, I shed my apron.

Bruce gave me a hug and followed me into the living room. "On my way here, I passed your dad's store. Hard to believe he's still on Jackson Street."

I shrugged. Sam Wilenski spent his days behind the counter of that damn store, the last Jewish business in the now mostly black neighborhood. "He's still in the house on 29th Avenue too. Harry and I begged him to come and live with us after Marsha left for college, but he wouldn't budge. Maybe now I can get him to move in with me."

"I don't see why he wouldn't. Montlake's not far from the Central District. And it's not like he needs to be within walking distance of a synagogue anymore." Our parents' Orthodoxy had mandated that they live within blocks of their synagogues so they could walk to Sabbath services. For decades exclusionary housing ordinances had conspired with Orthodox taboos to pen several generations of Seattle Jews and other immigrants into a kind of American ghetto.

When I brought out the coffee, my old friend was all business. "Have a seat, Rachel. Let's talk a little more about Harry's legacy." Avoiding my eyes, he helped himself to sugar. "As we discussed, Harry left you a life insurance policy and the money in Marsha's college account and, of course, the house and car, but . . ." Bruce stirred his coffee. "He also left a couple of debts that I suspect you didn't know about. I didn't." The lawyer persisted. "Rachel, did you know Harry played poker? For pretty high stakes?"

I shook my head. "I know he played poker with you and Morty and Paul occasionally, but he said that game was for pennies."

"It is. But apparently he also played for higher stakes fairly often with a couple of his clients and their associates. Rachel, the thing is, shortly before he died he lost. A lot."

The sweet buttery confection I'd been savoring became dry and tasteless, a mouthful of matzah meal.

"If things had been different, Harry, may he rest in peace, might have been able to pay this back, but . . ." The lawyer shook his head at the quake. "This notice was hand delivered to me at the office. The signature is notarized. It's a valid legal document." He placed the IOU on the table.

I felt the blood leave my face as I read the number over my dead husband's scrawl, took in the crimson seal below it. Nine thousand dollars. A fortune. I took out a Salem and bent my head over the light Bruce offered.

When I didn't say anything, Bruce pointed at the IOU. "I contacted the lawyer whose office this came from, and he says his client will turn it over to a collection agency unless he gets paid right away. The interest would be high and add up. You have enough in the savings account to cover this, so I strongly advise you to sign the withdrawal slip I brought."

Bruce referred to Marsha's college account as a savings account, as if it were not earmarked for her tuition. But since Marsha's birth, every penny in that account was put there to fund her college education. A few years ago when she begged to use some of it to pay for a nose job, the two men vetoed it. "Already she's beautiful, like her mother and her grandmother," my father insisted.

"My daughter shouldn't have to work her way through college like I did," was the two cents her father put in. How could Harry have played poker with Marsha's tuition?

My belly cramps reminded me of why years ago my father dubbed Marsha's college account "*kishke-gelt*," money you hocked your guts to get. Although we didn't actually pawn our intestines, we gladly made certain sacrifices. I collected S and H Green Stamps, shopped at sales and thrift shops, and wore my cousin's hand-me-downs. I cleaned our home myself and, after my mother took ill, I cleaned Sam's too. When Harry and I moved out of the Central District to Montlake, a "better" neighborhood, we bought a modest house without a lake view or a dishwasher. We shared the '61 Chevy Biscayne. We never set foot in Israel or even San Francisco or New York.

"I'll get the cash withdrawn as a money order and get that to the lawyer this came from." Bruce pointed to the IOU and then shook his head. "But paying this debt is going to leave you a little strapped, and the life insurance policy . . ." He hesitated.

I took a deep drag on my cigarette and held my breath.

"After I saw this IOU, I called one of Harry's colleagues to check on that policy. He said Harry borrowed heavily against it, so it's close to worthless." Bruce lowered his head apologetically, as if he were to blame for the news he brought. When I finally exhaled, I slumped in my chair until the fishhook jabbing my gut forced me to straighten up. "Rachel, I want you to know you can come to me and Rona . . ."

"Thanks, Bruce, but we'll be fine." To utter this lie, I had to speak over my cramps. "I hope to go back to teaching. I called the School Board for an application last week. It came yesterday." This at least was true.

"Good idea. Rachel, what's it costing to send Marsha to Vassar?"

"Her tuition, room and board, and flying back and forth for vacations, it all comes to just under four thousand dollars a year." Bruce and I both knew a teacher earned little more and that I needed money to live on as well as money to replace the *kishke-gelt*.

"Maybe your dad has a few bucks squirreled away."

"He put whatever he could into Marsha's college account. But if he sells his house and store and moves in with me . . ."

"The houses and shops in the Central District that our parents moved into are old, and the latest crop of newcomers is dirt poor." That was a nice way of saying that blacks had moved into the neighborhood.

"I know, but I don't need a real estate bonanza." I tried to keep the impatience out of my voice. "My father's store and house together just might bring in the twelve thousand dollars it'll take to get Marsha through Vassar."

"You're right, Rachel. And you don't have to decide anything today. All you have to do today is sign this." He handed me his fountain pen. I complied, my fingers numb. "Do you want me to talk to your dad about selling the store and moving?"

"Thanks, Bruce, but I need to figure out how to approach him without telling him about Harry's gambling. I don't want to upset him. Or Marsha. This is not how I want her to remember her father."

"She's a big girl now, Rachel. She can live at home and finish up at the U for about six hundred bucks a year. The U was plenty good enough for you and Harry and the rest of us." I knew what was coming. Bruce never missed a chance to revisit our bright college years. "We had good times there, right? Got a good education. We started our own frats and sororities. We even got Hillel going. Marsha could do a lot worse than transfer there."

Bruce hadn't seen the tears of joy streaking Marsha's cheeks when she opened her letter of acceptance from Vassar. But Harry knew what Vassar meant to Marsha. How could he have gambled away his daughter's dream? His recklessness made me furious. And his deception hurt. If he were still around, I'd bitch like hell. But Harry had been struck dead, and that punishment seemed more than enough.

I wanted my old friend to leave, to just get up and go. But all I said was, "Marsha really wanted to go east to college." The lawyer nodded, but he didn't get up. "She thinks Seattle's still a frontier town full of bigots and materialists. She says in New York Jews write plays and songs and books and found hospitals. In Seattle all we do, all anybody does, is make money." I shrugged. "You know how the kids are today, Bruce." I stared at the front door, willing him to stand and walk through it.

He nodded again but still made no move. "Well, Rachel, call me prejudiced, and I don't want to worry you, but I'm not sure your dad's safe in his store anymore. That neighborhood's just not the same now. It's not even like he's in Kosher Canyon." I tried to smile at Bruce's reference to a section of Cherry Street where lots of Jewish tradesmen set up shop as their customer base moved south and north. "And even the Canyon's changing now."

"Tell my father that. He goes about his business as if nothing's changed. He sees the Jews leaving the Central District as some kind of doomed Diaspora." I stood, hoping Bruce would take the hint. He must have, because finally he was on his feet saying goodbye.

By the time I heard his car start, I was seated once again at the dining room table filling out the application from the Board of Education. As I wrote, one of my mother's Yiddish-inflected mantras sounded its familiar drumbeat in my head. "Teaching you can always fall back on." Manya's career advice had proved prophetic.

But what if I couldn't get a teaching position? What would I, a two-fingered typist, fall back on then? The question was purely rhetorical. I'd helped out in my father's store since I was tall enough to dust and old enough to make correct change. I could get a sales job. And I would, at least for the summer. As soon as I put the application for a teaching position in the mail box, I headed downtown.

On the Frederick & Nelson application, I slightly embellished my experience selling china, silver, furniture, and antiques in my father's shop and the woman who interviewed me hired me on the spot. At least I didn't have to buy any clothes. Saleswomen at Seattle's fancy department store wear navy, brown, or black dresses or skirts, so we older ones all look like widows or nuns while the younger ones come off more like Catholic schoolgirls. My

New York cousin's city-dark hand-me-downs and my French twist were perfect. I started work the next day.

My first customer was a large woman whose white hair edged a florid round face, like cream cheese framing lox on a bagel. "Perhaps you'd like to consider something a little more ornate?" I bent over the display case and carefully extracted yet another silver water pitcher, this one with a handle supported by a winged cherub.

"That's more like what I had in mind. It's a retirement gift for a colleague of my husband's, a judge." Each time the bagel spoke, I reminded myself to answer her politely. "He's being honored at the Cascadia Club." It wouldn't do to let on how impatient I was catering to the whims of the snooty kid-gloved customer whose expensive purchase made me acutely aware of my own sudden plunge into poverty.

After I made the sale, I returned the eight rejected silver pitchers to the display case and scanned the aisles for another customer. If one didn't materialize, I'd have to resume the endless polishing that kept the silver gleaming and the saleswomen from succumbing to "idleness," a condition forbidden to Frederick & Nelson employees. This job would pay my living expenses until I could get a teaching position, but it wouldn't cover Marsha's education.

I had to figure out how to recoup the *kishke-gelt.* How could I get my father to agree to sell his precious house and store without telling him about Harry's gambling? Silver cloth in hand, I rubbed tarnish off a Sterling flask, wishing a genie would pop out of the damn thing.

Chapter 5

With no help from a genie, I figured out how to approach my father about selling his house and shop. It came to me while I was showing Sterling serving spoons to Sylvia Kronman whose husband Morris does our income taxes. During my break, I called my dad and invited him to dinner on the first evening I wasn't scheduled to work.

By the time I got home, late on the appointed afternoon, my feet were killing me and my father was pacing back and forth in my living room. Time had whitened his hair and reduced it to three tufts, one sprouting above his round face and the other two on either side. He looked like a geriatric Kewpie doll. "I was beginning to worry." Since my mother's death almost twenty years before, Sam worried about me all the time, so he never really had to begin. I worried about him too especially after he started marching and rallying like a kid, like my kid. Harry thought my dad was crazy. "Your father never laid eyes on a *schvartze* until he got to this country. All of a sudden he's their best friend?"

Unbeknownst to Harry, on the same day Martin Luther King led the March for Jobs and Freedom in our nation's capital, our own beatnik daughter and my do-gooder dad joined other activists in Seattle and marched to the Federal Courthouse downtown. And with Marsha and her friends from the Id Bookstore Sam went to a huge rally at Garfield High to try to get the City Council to adopt an open housing ordinance. Harry didn't know that his "baby girl" hung out at the Id with University students reading SDS pamphlets, and I didn't tell him. I figured there were worse places for a kid to spend time than a bookstore or even a rally. Besides if Marsha didn't go to the rallies, who would keep an eye on her grandfather?

I planted a kiss on Sam's fleshy neck just above his frayed shirt collar. Even before taking off my pumps, I slid the meat loaf and potatoes out of the refrigerator and into the oven.

"Scotch?" Sam was getting glasses out of the cabinet.

I nodded and opened a package of frozen peas, dropped the solid square mass into a CorningWare pan, and held it under the tap for a second or two. Sam handed me an old fashioned glass filled with ice, Cutty Sark, and a splash of water. "Working at that store's making you a boozehound." Ignoring his dig, I raised my glass to meet his. "*L'chaim*," he said. "To life." Finally seated, I lit a Salem, inhaled, and, this time ignoring his scowl, kicked off my pumps. "I don't see why you gotta work in that store. It's too much for you."

"It's good for me. It takes my mind off things. Anyway, if I get a teaching job, I'll quit the store in the fall." To rechannel our conversation, I added, "Tomorrow I go to work late. I'll be able to spend more time translating the diary."

"The Yid in the bag. All bones. I saw it in the *Transcript*." In the sanctuary of his store, surrounded by his hoard of cast-off goods, Sam sipped Sanka, skimmed newspapers, and chatted with the occasional customer or crony who wandered in. He handed me a folded copy of *The Transcript*, the bi-monthly tabloid chronicling the doings of Washington's few and far between Jews. "It's old now. I saved it for you."

Quake Unearths Jewish Remains Buried with Yiddish Book Hillel's Rabbi Moscowitz Confirms Hebrew Letters

By Jacob Heller

According to Hillel's Rabbi Yosl Moscowitz, the bones in the bag discovered last week in Seattle beneath Pioneer Square are most likely those of a Jew. The Rabbi says he read just enough to confirm that the book found with the bones was handwritten in Yiddish by a Jewish girl and that it is a diary. "Detective Lombardi was smart to recognize those letters from the walls of our old synagogues. The officer with him thought the letters were Chinese. I told them there have been Jews in Seattle for about a hundred years. Even so, I don't understand how those bones and that book ended up down there. I told the detective we bury our dead in cemeteries. . . ."

Even as I read, Sam began to talk. "So Jake Heller's gonna call you. He's a nice guy. His wife's dead ten years now." Like I could forget how Blema Heller's kids found her body in the shower where, at forty, she'd died of a brain aneurysm.

I'd last seen Jake when he paid a condolence call bearing a box of rugelach. He'd stuck a scrawled note between an apricot and a prune pastry. It read, "I've been down the road you're on. I know all the potholes. Call me when you feel like talking." Jake's a nice guy, but my father's very premature attempt at matchmaking ticked me off. Fortunately the scotch burning through me blunted my annoyance. To distract him, I asked, "Would you like to see the diary?"

When Sam nodded, I placed the little book in his hands. Sam had seen his share of old books in the store and handled them with appropriate reverence. He opened it and ran his eyes down a page. "I can't read much Yiddish no more. Hebrew either." He shrugged off his linguistic losses. "But I bet if you read it aloud to me, I'd be able to follow it. Better yet, you should do like they do in the Reform prayer book with Hebrew. Write the Yiddish in English letters."

"Good idea. I bet a lot of people are in the same boat you are. They can understand spoken Yiddish, but they can't read it." Right then I resolved to transliterate the diary as I translated. It wouldn't be hard and would make Aliza's own distinctive voice accessible to those who understood spoken Yiddish but couldn't read it.

When he returned the diary to me, his voice was dismissive. "Those bones can't be from a Jew. We say *Kaddish* over our dead and, like Moscowitz says in the paper, we bury them in cemeteries." He was right. When a

Jew died, saying *Kaddish,* the misnamed Mourning Prayer that makes no mention of the deceased but praises God, was something we did —even those who didn't believe, even those who never entered a synagogue at any other time, even those who, like me, bitched at God and feasted on shellfish. At Reform Temple de Hirsch, even women could chant the prayer. "Bobby Gradstein came all the way from New York to say *Kaddish* for Mo, remember?"

I remembered. Right after our high school graduation and his eighteenth birthday, Bobby enlisted in the Army and went off to fight the Nazis. I worried when he stopped answering my letters, but he returned from Europe unscathed. He just didn't return to Seattle except to say *Kaddish* for his father and, again, to go to our twentieth Garfield High reunion. He got so drunk there that when Harry and I gave him a ride back to his mom's house, he puked all over the back seat of our car.

Sam's voice was Scotch-strong. "But may that poor soul in the bag, whoever he was, rest in peace."

"But Dad, the bones just may belong to the diarist, and the diarist was a girl. She was younger than Marsha."

"A young girl, eh? Like Anne Frank."

"Well, not exactly. She was poor and uneducated. She was a seamstress in Gnilsk before she immigrated."

"What the hell is the diary of a dead Gnilski doing in a hole in the ground in Seattle?"

"I'm not sure yet, but get this." I paused to give my revelation the drama and suspense it deserved. "Professor Hunter told me that assuming the bones are hers, which he does, she was murdered here." Filling Sam in on Tim Hunter's reasoning made for unusually lively dinner conversation.

"So was she murdered? Didn't you read ahead and find out? Maybe there's a hint."

"I thought about skipping ahead. But it's funny. I want to know what happened to her but I also just want to keep on reading." When Sam's brow lines collided over his nose, I explained. "You know how we both hate it when the lights go on at the end of a good movie?" My father nodded. "Well it's like that. I don't want this diary to end, especially since I learned that the girl who wrote it was murdered." Sam nodded again. "As long as I keep reading, she's alive, at least to me." Satisfied with my explanation, Sam helped himself to a second slab of meat loaf.

After we finished eating, I launched into my carefully scripted pitch. "Dad, when are you going to get sensible and retire?"

He groaned at the familiar nudge. "You want I should close the store?"

"Yes. And I want you sell your house, move in here with me."

"You want me to leave your mother's garden." I winced. Manya had literally put roots down in Seattle where the temperate, wet winters, rich, dark earth, and lack of homicidal anti-Semitism encouraged her to dig in. She raked, mulched, seeded, and weeded the tiny yard behind their house into a verdant Eden of flowers, fruit, vegetables, and vines. "You want I should move into this house where I don't know nobody and die of boredom, right?" No Jew fleeing Babylon after the destruction of the Temple sounded more miserable.

"Right." I was relieved that I didn't have to spell things out for him, but, predictably, his martyred addendum to my wish list infuriated me. "Frankly, I'd rather you die of boredom than at the hands of a thief with a knife. I worry about you in the store. You're seventy-two, not twenty-two." Sam sipped his drink and said nothing. Maybe he was going to be reasonable. I lit another cigarette, leaned back, and inhaled.

"On you the Surgeon General is wasting his breath, right?"

I persisted, finally offering up the half-truths I'd been honing all week. "Here's the thing. There are some back taxes I didn't know about. With Harry gone, I could use a little help. If you sell the store and your house and move in with me, you'll have extra money that I can borrow. And now that I'm working, I can pay you back a little at a time."

Defiance jutted his chin out when I began, but as my meaning sank in I was surprised to see it lower to meet his chest. "The *kishke-gelt*? It's not enough?" His shoulders sagged and tears brightened his eyes. I felt bamboozled. I'd been prepared to counter Sam's obstinacy, his refusal to admit his aging, his accusations of racism, but I hadn't imagined watching my father deflate into a weepy sad sack.

I made myself go on. "No, the savings account is not enough. I talked with Bruce Freidman about the taxes. He advised paying them promptly, so I did. There's not much left."

Sam's response flabbergasted me. "But the store and the house, I don't got them no more." He put down his drink and raised his hands palms up as if he had once held a building in each of them. "*Gornisht.*" Nothing. It was a familiar performance. Sam used to delight me, and later Marsha, by displaying his empty palms, and exclaiming, "*Gornisht.*" Then he'd produce a coin from behind his ear.

His voice was husky and his eyes were on his glass as if he were directing his words to the scotch. "I borrowed on the store for your wedding. Your mother and me, we didn't get married under a *chuppa.*" I hoped Sam wouldn't repeat the oft-told story of my parents'canopyless wedding. "For us there was no *chuppa*, no dowry, no rabbi even. Between us we had *bubkes*, goat shit. Your mother wanted your wedding it should be different." For a moment we both sat in silence, remembering the scores of guests, the catered kosher food, the musicians, and my gown, a confection of tulle and lace. I felt sick.

"And your house? What made you borrow on that?"

"The house I borrowed on to pay for your mother when she was, you know, in the hospital and, you know, later." His hand swept across his chest and his eyebrows, whorls of white beneath the creases on his forehead, lifted. I winced at the familiar mime. These gestures had served my father to explain and define my mother's malignancy, mastectomy, and eventual death. As far as I knew, Sam had never uttered the words *breast cancer.* "We didn't have no money for all that. I'm sorry, sweetheart." Sam's eyes stayed on his scotch which he began to stir with his finger.

Something was missing, didn't make sense. "Dad, you must have paid back the loans. Otherwise the bank would have taken the house and the store."

"I didn't borrow from a bank." Sam's voice was stronger now.

"Did you go to a loan shark?" A sense of menace prompted the too familiar twisting in my belly.

"Crazy, I'm not." Sam knew what I was thinking. "And I wasn't then either. I went to a customer." He hesitated. "Someone I trust, a friend more like."

"Who?" I barked the question. I knew most of his customers and all of his friends, had known them for years. There was not one among them I could imagine lending Sam that kind of money on such odd terms without my hearing about it.

"Her name is Yetta Solomon."

"Who on earth is Yetta Solomon? You don't have a girlfriend, do you?" My second question was so ludicrous that as it left my lips I blew it away with smoke.

"I told you. She's a customer and a friend, a good friend."

"I'd like to know how some good friend I never heard of got a hold of your store and your house."

"Let me have a refill." I poured his drink. "It started back when you were just a kid, maybe 1931-32. Those were hard times." I braced for another one of Sam's stories about the Depression, but he was headed in another direction. "Yetta came into the store wanting me to do some upholstery work for her. She seen my ad." He paused. "She was moving from Canada, starting a business here. She was furnishing a place downtown, in the Garden Court Apartments. On Stewart Street it was." He hesitated. "Anyway, she wanted some antique chairs and a sofa reupholstered, so?" He answered his own question. "So I picked them up and did the work.

"I hauled a helluva lot of beat up furniture and junk out of that building for her too." Sam looked up as if he could see truckloads of stuff on the ceiling. "Yetta was always dressed nice, wearing fancy hats and real pearls." He knew jewelry because occasionally a valuable bracelet or brooch turned up in the store. "So I charged her the full price for the reupholstering, and she paid on the spot in cash."

I leaned closer because his voice was getting lower again. "Couple a years later she opened a hotel at First and Virginia, near the Market. Yetta really liked my work. And, you know, I think also she wanted to do business with a Jew. Yetta was a customer, a good customer." He took a deep breath. "Anyway she bought a bigger place down there on Pike Street. So she needed me again. Like I said, her hotels were classy, good furniture, nice decorations, the works."

Had Sam cheated on Manya? It was inconceivable. But my mother had been alive and well up until the forties. "Did Mama ever meet her?"

"Yeah. They met. Your mama didn't think much of her, but . . ." Sam shrugged. "Business is business."

"Why didn't Mama think much of her? What synagogue did she belong to?" I was accustomed to Manya's disdain for those who deviated from the Orthodoxy she favored.

"Yetta is not a religious woman."

That declaration answered both my questions. "Okay, so go ahead. Tell me how this woman got ahold of the only two things you owned." I heard the scotch talking and regretted my sarcasm.

"When you and Harry got engaged was about the time your mama first got sick. She wanted we should make you a classy wedding." He shrugged at the absurdity of denying what he must have suspected had been his wife's last wish. "So Yetta and I made a deal."

"You gave this Yetta the store in return for the money to pay for Harry's and my wedding?"

"You got it. Yetta said she'd give me what money I needed in exchange for the deed to the store. She'd pay the taxes but I could stay there, keep it up, work in it, as long as I wanted, and whatever I earned was mine. The business is still mine." Sam's level, satisfied tone implied that this arrangement that had made him into a kind of Jewish sharecropper still seemed sensible to him. "But then after your mother got even sicker, the bills started coming. It was like I was drowning. Yetta come into the store and right away she saw what was with me. So she made me another deal for the house. She gave me what I needed in exchange for the deed and she paid what was left of the mortgage and the taxes. And I can live there until I croak."

There were more questions I wanted to ask, but two decades had gone by since my father had, in my misery-muddled mind, given away the store. And the house. But Sam was aware of my unasked queries. "I didn't see much chance of paying back a bank loan with what I was making in the store. I figured if I borrowed from a bank I'd lose the building and my business."

Sam smiled, again satisfied that he'd made savvy deals. I wanted to ask if he still saw this Yetta, if she still ran her hotel, but I didn't. And I didn't argue when my father said, "So, I'm staying put, but I'm sorry about the *kishke-gelt.* I figured Harry, may he rest in peace, was such a go-getter you'd never have to worry about money." He shook his head. "Who knew from the IRS?"

Chapter 6

***. . . Ich feel vee ah shade.* . . . I feel like a ghost.**

Even telling God off for taking the two buildings from my hapless father didn't help. Lying wide-eyed in the dark, I recalled my mother kvetching at God, giving Him what for in the guttural syllables and jagged cadences of her own dead mother. Inspired, I let Him have it again in Yiddish, and only then did I drift off for just a few hours before Marsha phoned the next morning. Since she got back to New York, she called a few times a week, mostly to see if I was okay. She was relieved that I was finally making like a good widow, "getting out" to work and "keeping busy" translating.

ꙮ

Feigele's Diary, New York, February 23, 1890

There is no time for writing thoughts in America or for going to the school they have here at night. I have no time to try to make a few extra pennies reading palms either. Besides, Herman and Chaya would not like that. Chaya is big with another child, and Herman says if I help her with the chores I can pay one dollar a week less for board. He says it's not like being a servant, but like being a member of the family. So after hurrying up for ten hours at the shop where I sew for Herman's friend Boris Lipschitz from Gnilsk, I hurry up home and hurry up to wash clothes in the yard and hurry up to haul water up the stairs for washing dishes so I can sleep a few hours before it is time to get up. I am grateful to the Almighty for giving us a day of rest. In America the Sabbath is truly a gift from the Most High.

Except for the Sabbath my life is all work. I may be free here, but I am still poor. I may make more money than I did at Hanele's, but I must pay Herman, and I am trying to save for Mama, Papa, and little Yitzak's tickets on the boat. Even though there is much to buy here from the shops and peddlers, I do not buy, but save my dollars in the envelope with the letter Hanele wrote for Mama.

Mama wrote that she misses me. She said that little Yitzak is very smart and that by the time the boy is old enough to begin his studies, she and Papa hope they will all be here, and then I can help pay for my brother to study Torah. And she said when they arrive Papa will find a good husband for me. Mama did not mention the pain in her knees or how few people are buying Papa's Kiddush cups just like I do not write to her how I sleep on a board and work for a mean man or how I feel like a ghost.

I want to learn English before they come. That way when they get here I won't be a greenhorn. I can be their interpreter, can teach them English. Without English in America a person stays a greenhorn. Every night I ask the Most High for time to study and someone to teach me. And may my pen turn into a needle and prick my finger if what I write next did not happen.

Yesterday I passed a peddler selling Yiddish-English dictionaries and eye glasses and medicine. I have seen him on my way home before. He has eyes that smile like Meier's. And he speaks English as well as Yiddish! I have heard him. Yesterday when I saw him I decided the Most High kept putting him in my path for a reason, and this thought made me bold. I made like I was thinking of buying a book, but then I offered to read the peddler's palm instead of paying him. Now I have a dictionary and he has visions of a happy future owning a store of his own.

This book is the only book besides a prayer book that I have ever owned and even that prayer book I shared with Mama. But this dictionary is brand new and it is mine alone. It is large with a somber dark cover, small letters, and many, many pages. There are no pictures. The pages are thinner than the silk Hanele and I used to line the bodices of bridal gowns. And even the Hebrew letters of my own language, look formal and foreign, but at least I can make them out. The American letters are like marks scratched in the dirt by a chicken. Maybe only another chicken can understand them. So even though I treasure my new book, I am glad I did not pay money for it. Without someone to teach me and time to study, this book is as useless as the milk that comes to the grieving mother of a stillborn. If I meet up with my smiling-eyed peddler again, I will ask him where he studied English.

Feigele's Diary, New York, March 18, 1890

Winter here is not as cold as in Gnilsk and the snow does not stay white. Darkness comes early so the days seem shorter, but the number of coat sleeves to finish sewing doesn't change. My heart is glad, though, because I have found a way to go to the class for English! My smiling peddler who speaks English like a native told me he studies still in such a class and he accompanied me there one evening. May the Most High forgive me, but I told Herman and Chaya I am working late the night of the class. And I told Boris I am needed at home. The classroom is crowded and the teacher is old and cranky, but I am learning how to say the days of the week in English and to count and ask the time.

Even if lying is wrong, I don't mind lying to Boris. He is a liar too. But I am not lying now. In fact, may I swallow my own tongue if what I am writing here is not the truth. Boris turns the clock back when he thinks we aren't looking, so we work longer every day for the same little money. His shop is a small room where a few old men from Gnilsk and I make coats. Boris gets paid by how many coats we make in a day. We get paid by how much Boris gets. So Boris is always yelling "hurry." I think it is the only English word he knows. While the men are working they sing, talk, smoke, eat, and drink whiskey. Sometimes a peddler comes in selling rolls and brandy. All the time the men make jokes about what married people do. Their jokes make me ashamed. I am not used to the company of so many men.

I liked working for Hanele even though she had only the one Singer and three other workers, all of us women. We got along and helped each other, taught each other. Hanele herself taught me to use the Singer. We talked a lot, too, and even sang when we were tired to help us keep alert. Hanele taught us a song that I can hear in my head even now. "Seamstress am I, the needle's my possession. I need no longer worry for the coming days." I always thought of the dowry I was earning and felt good when we sang this song. Sometimes now I sing it to myself while I am working, but it doesn't sound right in my head, especially while my head is in Boris's nasty sweatshop.

The sweatshop is nasty because Boris is nasty. I am the only person there except Boris who can make a garment from start to finish, so I sometimes work as finisher and sew together the parts the others make. For this job, Boris should pay me more than he pays the others, but I don't think he does. And even worse, he is always grabbing at my hair or my arm with his cane. As a joke, Boris calls his cane Ari or lion, then he roars like a lion and pulls me over to him with it and grabs at my chest and puts his hand up my skirt. I try to move away. The other men see and yet they do nothing but laugh. Boris and the rest of them make me have bad dreams and cry at night. Boris gave me my pay this week after he gave all the others theirs. That's when he said if I wasn't nice to him, he would fire me. The only good thing about this place is that it is closed on the Sabbath. . . .

Grateful for the Sabbath? The girl's appreciation for the holiday caught me up short, and I stopped reading. I hadn't refrained from work on a Saturday since my mother died. With Manya gone, Saturdays soon found Sam behind the counter in the store, Harry hawking insurance door to door, and me cleaning, cooking, shopping, and devising lesson plans. Back then I felt liberated from what seemed like just another outdated set of Orthodox old-country constraints. I was certain that the God I prayed to and argued with was modern and American. He too was Reformed, had assimilated, understood English.

But over the years I learned that an observant upbringing, like any other, remains a first response, a frame of reference forever. I'd spent more than half of my forty-five years observing the Sabbath. Now that I was older and on my feet for hours every day behind a counter at Frederick & Nelson, I found myself missing that day of peace and rest. On Friday nights and Saturdays my customers seemed harder to please, my pumps tighter, the tarnish on the silver more resistant, and the hands on the clock slower.

I pushed the little book away and lit a cigarette. To Feigele's credit, she'd contrived a way to get to those English classes. But Boris, the horny sweatshop owner, literally had her cornered. Sighing, I realized some things don't change. Harry used to talk about how one of the partners at Pratt and Pringle, a hardnosed old curmudgeon, was sleeping with his "stacked" secretary, the very same young woman he sent to Frederick & Nelson to buy birthday and Christmas gifts for his wife. Harry also reported that several of the other agents were always groping the younger women in the office and that the firm's annual Christmas party was a drunken orgy. "I leave as soon as I get my bonus check. It's all downhill after that."

Were Marsha's bosses and co-workers at the Strand chasing her through the store's labyrinth stacks? Oh God. Before I went off the deep end, I reminded myself that, unlike Feigele's co-workers, Marsha's young colleagues were more likely to be planning protests with her. Anyway, in a few weeks she would leave her job to cloister herself once again at Vassar. But to keep her there, I had to find Yetta Solomon and get back our property.

I spent a sleepless night pondering who the hell Yetta Solomon could be and how to find her. Poking around Pike Place querying desk clerks at the tawdry rooming houses there about a woman who wasn't even listed in the phone book would be a last resort. I didn't want to ask the Sephardic fish monger at the Market if he knew the name either or, God forbid, the gypsy woman who, like a modern-day Feigele, told fortunes there. I had no intention of explaining my quest to anyone.

Finally dawn brightened the sky so that I could see the leaves filigreed outside my bedroom window. Blinking at the leafy lattice work, I remembered that God brought forth the sun on the fourth day of Creation. According to at least one Reform rabbi, this was neither the powerful deity of pagans nor the fiery orb of astronomers. Rather it was the light of consciousness, enabling us to see the possibilities of the world around us.

As if responding to this cosmic cue, a corresponding light went on in my head. The transfer of the titles to Sam's store and house would have been registered with the City. And these papers had to be available for inspection by anyone with the stamina to search for them in the dusty files of Seattle's Municipal Building, a blue and gray behemoth, located on Fourth Avenue.

I spent the morning hunched over musty drawers containing yellowed titles, deeds, and land tracts until I located a file for the store property. In it I recognized the title Sam had signed when he bought the building and another with his name as the seller and that of a person named Edna Douglas listed as the buyer. Who on earth was Edna Douglas? Douglas wasn't a Jewish name. At the desk I asked to look at a phone book and found an E. Douglas listed in Alki or West Seattle. I wasn't sure this E. Douglas was Yetta Solomon, but there was a good chance of it.

Yetta Solomon wouldn't be the first American Jew to shed the telltale name of a biblical or genetic ancestor for that of an innocuous and unrelated Anglo-Saxon. Hadn't Bob Dylan, one of Marsha's idols, been a Zimmerman before he took the name of a Welsh poet? And how many foreigners had their names reconfigured when immigration authorities couldn't spell or pronounce them? Feigele had taken on a new name even before she left the Ukraine. Changing your name was a rite of passage for many American Jews.

I didn't want to phone Edna Douglas, to give the woman, if she was Yetta Solomon, a chance to refuse to see me or to report my call to Sam. I preferred to beard the witch, as I now thought of my father's friend, in her cairn, to surprise her. I wasn't sure what I would say or do once I was face to face with my quarry, but I assumed inspiration would come. Rushing to work, I resolved that somehow I would figure out a way to make Yetta Solomon return Sam's property.

The next afternoon, I drove through heavy traffic across the Spokane Street Bridge to Alki. Lying west of Seattle, the wild peninsula had been slow to attract white settlers. According to the Indians, who'd lived there since the sixth century, it was shaped like a bear's head, so they'd named it accordingly in their language. But a few of the pioneers, perhaps those looking behind them with regret, renamed it New York, the hometown of one of their group. Those looking ahead added "*Al-ki*," Chinook for "*by and by*." And as these forward thinking settlers envisioned, the place ultimately drew many inhabitants and on that day, just over a century later, had the traffic to prove it. Cursing the lines of cars and slow-moving trucks and the sudden cloudburst that made the drive even longer than it should have been, I finally pulled over and parked across the street from my destination.

The house was on the corner of 63rd Street and Alki Avenue and had a stunning view of the Sound. But like those pioneer wives of 1851 who disembarked on the slim strip of windswept pebbles below the heavily forested palisade and burst into tears, I wanted to bawl. The pioneer women were unhinged by the prospect of homesteading on the desolate strand between the waves and the wilderness. I was just frustrated. Yetta Solomon's place was more fortress than home.

Looking up at the floodlights fringing the top of the ten-foot tall chain-link fence and the high thorn-spiked holly hedges, I thought about remaining in my dry car and heading home to change for work. Instead I reached for the umbrella I kept in the back seat of the Chevy and braved the familiar downpour. A gust of wind off the Sound inverted the umbrella, turning it into a useless handful of stems and silk. By the time I crossed the street, I was soaked. I approached the front gate, and peered into the yard. The only thing missing was a vicious guard dog. Relieved at the absence of a slavering canine, I shook the chains that secured the padlock as hard as I could while hollering, "Hello! Hello! Anybody home?" I felt like an ass.

The curtained windows and windowless door remained opaque. It did not occur to me for even a second that Yetta Solomon might be out. I'd gone to too much trouble locating the woman to turn back. I would not leave without trying to get her to pay for Marsha's diploma. Once again, I rattled the chains on the padlock and yelled.

When no one showed up, I walked around the corner to the back gate adjacent to the garage and repeated my performance. I figured my luck had changed when the side door opened. A tiny old woman emerged followed by a tall muscular man of about sixty holding an umbrella over them both. Could this shriveled gnome be Yetta Solomon, shady banker to an aging Jewish junk dealer? But no, I recognized the woman! She was Tzipporah

Salazar, an ancient Sephardic crone who was an occasional customer of Sam's. They went back many years. In fact, I remembered Sam bringing Tzipporah, whom Seattle's old-time Sephardic Jews believed to have healing powers, to visit Manya near the end.

Before I recovered from recognizing Tzipporah, the man opened the gate and ushered her out. He accompanied her, locking the gate behind him and pocketing the key. "What do you want? Who are you?" He took in the strands of wet hair streaking my face, my sodden denim skirt, the crippled umbrella, and scowled. Unlike her escort, Tzipporah, her wrinkles rearranged into a beatific smile, appeared delighted to see me. Leaving the haven of the umbrella, she approached with her arms open, ready to hug her old friend's dripping daughter.

Taken aback, I allowed the hug, returned it. Tzipporah radiated an aroma that was pleasantly pungent, familiar. It was the same scent that permeated Manya's bedroom after Tzipporah's visit. The healer had sprinkled crushed cloves over Manya's scarred, cancer-ridden body in the hope of exorcising whatever malevolent forces were destroying it. Then she set the powdered spice aflame in a metal brazier. All these years later, I breathed deeply, drawing strength from the pungent aroma, from the memory of Tzipporah's tender ministrations, her gift of hope.

I spotted the curtains of a front window part for an instant, bringing me back to the present. Extricating myself from Tzipporah's embrace, I maneuvered the tiny figure back under the umbrella. Then I addressed the man in my school teacher voice. "I'm Sam Wilenski's daughter, Rachel Mazursky. I need to see Edna Douglas. Please let me in. It's important."

"She's not expecting you." I couldn't tell if the man was a servant or a relative. He wore a nicely cut dark suit.

I changed my tone from imperious to imploring. "Please. Tell her I'm Sam Wilenski's daughter, please. I won't take much of her time."

"Wait here." He gestured to Tzipporah to wait also. Handing me the umbrella, he unlocked the gate and dashed back into the house.

Tzipporah and I stood in silence. Unlike their men, Seattle's first wave of immigrant Sephardic women stayed close to home and socialized mostly with other Ladino-speakers, so few among them learned English and none of them knew Yiddish. It was as if these women, whose ancestors fled the Inquisitors in Spain and Portugal and who themselves had fled poverty or persecution in the Ottoman Empire, arrived here too tired to learn yet another language, yet another set of customs. Holed up in the comfort of their kitchens, they had kept America outside while they rested and recovered. Standing there in the rain, I pictured myself explaining the Sephardics to an attentive Tim Hunter.

The rain stopped, so I shook out the umbrella, folded it, and leaned it against the fence which I'd come to think of as a chain-link web woven by an arachnid-like creature waiting within to trap victims and divest them of their property. When the man finally emerged, he closed the door behind him, dashing my hopes for an audience.

He didn't open the gate again, but addressed me from behind the damn fence. "She'll see you tomorrow at eleven. Meanwhile, she'd appreciate it if you'd drive this lady back where she came from. Here's the address." He handed me a slip of paper with an address in Seward Park printed in block letters. "It'll save me a trip." He turned abruptly and left us standing there just as the rain began to fall once more.

Traffic was even heavier on the way home, and I tensed as I maneuvered the Chevy through windborne sheets of water across the crowded eastbound bridge. With water on all sides and below, I felt like a salmon struggling upstream en route to its birthplace. I tried to share this thought with my passenger to make conversation, but deafness and a paucity of English vocabulary prevented her from understanding. She seemed tired and content to sit quietly. I'd get no information from Tzipporah about the woman in the brick bunker. All the way home I wondered about her. Who was she really? Where was she from? Where did she get her money? What drove her to live in barricaded seclusion?

Chapter 7

Ich feel nisht vee ah shade. **. . . . . I do not feel like a ghost . . .**

I slept fitfully. When I awakened, more pointed questions about my father's mysterious friend still preoccupied me. How the hell was I going to get this Edna Douglas, née Yetta Solomon, to return the deeds to Sam's store and house? What had brought Tzipporah Salazar all the way to Alki? Was Yetta sick like my mother had been? Dying perhaps? And if so, what about Marsha's money? I drove towards the bridge, the sky bright and blue. Ahead in the distance the snow-capped Olympic Mountains peaked, a row of celestial sundaes dripping with marshmallow sauce.

When I pulled up in front of the house, the place appeared as well defended as it had the day before. The padlock securing the gate in the fence had not been unlocked in anticipation of my prearranged visit. Then, just as I approached the fence resigned to shaking it and hollering again, I saw a shade blink in the front upstairs window. In a moment, the front door opened and a dark-skinned older woman in a gray uniform and white apron strode down the steps toward me, a key in her hand. Edna Douglas could afford a maid.

Her nod, unaccompanied by even a hint of a smile, was more an acknowledgement of my presence than a greeting. The silent servant unlocked the gate, let me in, and indicated with a tilt of her head that I should walk towards the house while she secured the gate behind us. The bastion barricaded once more, the dour welcoming committee followed me along the short walkway and up the few steps to the front door. She pushed it open and closed it after us. I heard the deadbolt click into place, locking the world out and me in. Finally, as we stood in the barely lit vestibule, my escort spoke. "I'll tell her you're here." There was no trace of the South or the field in her unaccented and grammatical speech. She wasn't one of the recent waves of blacks to move to Seattle in search of work, but was probably a native of the Northwest like me. "Wait." Standing there, I wondered again why Yetta Solomon lived in such a well-fortified place. Who was she afraid of?

In seconds the maid was back. "Follow me." We entered a room shrouded in curtains, dim as the cave of a nocturnal animal. But this lair didn't smell of carrion, musk, or scat. Rather, the scent of crushed cloves lingered in the shadows. I heard Yetta Solomon before I saw her. Tapping that got louder and louder heralded her entrance. As my eyes adapted to the lack of light, I saw my silhouetted hostess sink into a chair and hook the cane she had used to feel her way across the room over the back of it. "Hello, Rachel. I was saddened to learn of your husband's death. Please accept my deepest sympathy." She was certainly civil. And her voice was ordinary, her diction as uninflected as her maid's.

"Thank you." But Yetta Solomon had more to offer than civility and sympathy. She empathized. "Your poor husband's fate was my worst nightmare. I'm terrified of earthquakes. I used to own a hotel on the bluff next to Pike Place Market, The La Salle, and I was there during the quake of '49. The whole building shook. I could still see then, and I remember looking out those huge windows and imagining the entire place pitching into the Sound." She paused. "After that I never felt safe there, so I sold the building and moved." She paused again and then, remembering her duty as hostess, she asked, "Tea or coffee?"

"Coffee, thank you." I fondled the cigarettes in my skirt pocket.

"Two coffees and some cookies, please, Bess. Have a seat, Rachel. You may smoke if you like, although it's breaking your father's heart." I snapped to attention. That guilt-inducing clause appended to the woman's permission like the sharp stick stuck in a marshmallow about to be toasted could only, as far as I knew, come from a Jew. "Edna Douglas" was an alias.

"So you're Yetta Solomon." I scrutinized the figure across the table as best I could in the limited light. She was petite, and with that rounded profile she didn't look Jewish. In the forgiving semi-darkness I pegged her at fifty-five, a number I later learned was off by at least ten years.

"Yes, I am, sometimes, to friends. I'm also Edna Douglas and Nellie Curtis." She stopped speaking, perhaps waiting for a reaction, but that last name meant nothing to me. I knew several Jews who'd changed their names for business purposes. Even Feigele was Fanny on one side of her business card. But I knew no one who went by more than one Anglo alias at a time. "In business it's sometimes advisable to use different names. It was enterprising of you to find me."

"I was highly motivated." I was also wary of flattery.

"How can I help you, Rachel? Did your father send you? Sam hasn't mentioned this visit to me. Does he know you're here?"

I answered the last question first. "My father doesn't know I'm here unless you told him I was coming."

"I did not."

"Good. And you can help me." I inhaled deeply. "My daughter is getting cheated out of her college education." I paused. Yetta remained silent, her eyes shuttered by the dark glasses. Discomfited, I repeated myself. "You certainly can help." I rattled on. "Return to my father the titles to his store and his house. We'll sell the buildings and pay you back what we owe after Marsha finishes Vassar. I'm applying for a teaching job."

I was unprepared for Yetta's snort. Like Harry, she clearly saw teaching as so poorly paid that it was not worth doing. I felt like leaving until I remembered Marsha opening her letter of acceptance from Vassar and weeping with happiness. I would persist. Bess returned with a silver tray bearing coffee, cream and sugar, cookies, and linen napkins. She filled the coffee cups and poured cream into Yetta's.

"Thank you." I tried to keep my tone civil, but it was hard. I'd made my pitch, and now I was being stonewalled.

Yetta resumed the conversation as the maid withdrew from the room. "Now, Rachel, let's get down to business. Why would I renege on the arrangement I made with your father? It was in both of our best interests.

He got the money he needed when he needed it and retains use of both buildings during his lifetime. He got to keep his store and his home. In return for those titles, I got to give him about twelve thousand dollars and pay off the remaining mortgage on one property and annual taxes and insurance on both."

I replied in a firm voice, a tone appropriate to protest. "But it's not fair. It's usury. The buildings have to be worth more now."

"An interesting interpretation. I had each of the properties appraised at the time I considered taking possession. As I recall, neither of them was worth more than about six thousand dollars then. I have the paperwork on file somewhere." She waved an arm into the space around us where shadows of furniture loomed. "Given the changes in the Central District, I doubt if they've appreciated very much, if at all. Your father's house isn't that far from what some people call "Coon Hollow," right?"

Cringing at Yetta's use of the crude epithet for the strip of streets between two hills, I spoke before I thought. "What if they'd called Cherry Street "Kike Canyon" instead of "Kosher Canyon"?

"They probably do," said Yetta, not at all disturbed or surprised by my rebuke, "just not to our faces. What I'm trying to get across to you is that Sam's store is one of the few retail businesses remaining in an area that has lost its appeal to many shoppers. In return for the deed to his store, I gave your father the money he needed to pay for your mother's surgery and her hospitalization, not to mention her funeral. You can see the paperwork if you'd like. He didn't have to ask for anything from anybody else. He wanted to make a deal, not get a handout."

She was right. My father, a notoriously poor businessman, would have hated to acknowledge that he lacked the means to care for his wife, to bury her, would have hated to become an object of pity and charity, his paltry worth parsed by well-meaning peers at Temple committee meetings. I didn't blame him. I was glad the room's dimness hid my reddened face.

"We made a similar arrangement when you got married. It pleased your parents to give you away in style. Your wedding was really your father's last gift to your mother. He told me it was the wedding they never had."

If Yetta Solomon didn't feel she owed Sam anything, how could I recoup the *kishke-gelt*? Desperate, I figured maybe I should follow Sam's example and try to borrow money from Yetta using my own house as collateral. I lit another cigarette. "Okay. I'm sorry. I guess you and my dad do have a fair arrangement. Could I make a similar one with you?" I spoke faster, my voice tremulous. Harry, not I, had been the salesman in our family. "I own a house, too, in a different neighborhood. It's in Montlake, and it's mostly paid for. My husband and I bought it for about eight thousand dollars fifteen years ago. It's got to be worth more now. Could I borrow twelve thousand dollars from you, using my house as collateral? I'll bank the money for Marsha's college expenses, and then work to pay off the loan with interest."

Yetta didn't answer right away, but when she finally spoke, I couldn't tell if her voice was mocking or polite. "The value of your property has decreased since the Expressway went through Montlake two years ago." How did this blind lady living way out on Alki know about that? "I'm sorry, Rachel. But as you can see, I'm not a young woman, and I'm not in good health." Yetta drained her coffee cup and put it down tentatively until the well of the saucer cradled it. "Do you know how your father and I became friends? Why I do business with him?"

"He upholstered furniture for you, and you liked his work, so you gave him more and more work." I resented what I heard as a digression and spoke as if I were reciting a lesson.

"That's how we met all right, why I do business with him." She paused. "My hotel near the Market, the La Salle, was a brothel." My jaw dropped, nearly dislodging my cigarette. "When I sold it, I bought another hotel in Aberdeen and named it The Curtis. That, too, was a brothel, a whorehouse. Because of my health, I've had to sell that building as well. I'm a retired madam."

The smoke I inhaled went down the wrong way, choking me. I coughed until I could breathe. Even then I didn't try to talk. I was speechless at the news that Yetta Solomon, a Jew, a friend of my do-gooder father's yet, had been a madam. How many of the six hundred and thirteen commandments did she break every day? How many of Marsha's Vassar classmates had relatives in hock to a madam? How many applicants for teaching positions in Seattle consorted with whoremongers? What if someone from Seattle's Board of Education learned of my association with Yetta?

But curiosity trumped both my distaste and my anxiety, so I listened as Yetta continued. "Your father was also a little surprised when he came the first time to pick up a sofa and some chairs at the place I ran when I came to town. It was in the Garden Court Apartments, and it was another whoreh-ouse. But Sam treated me like I was the queen of England." Yetta sighed. "When I was still new in town and starting my business, he gave me the lowdown on all the local politicians. The man is a walking *Who's Who.* I needed that information to keep my business running smoothly." I made out Yetta's hand moving, pictured her rubbing her thumb across her first two fingers, perhaps to indicate that she paid off the local politicians Sam informed her about.

"Then when my eyes started to go, your father called me every day to tell me what was in the paper. Even now he calls me with updates." That would explain how she knew about the freeway. "And before his arthritis, he was the best upholsterer I ever had. So that's why I do business with him. Now do you want to hear why I agreed to, shall we say, "loan" him money, at considerable loss, I might add?"

"Yes." My interest in what Yetta had to say about Sam had been revived by the woman's revelation. Who knew madams drank coffee out of cups made of china thin as paper?

"Your father was in the La Salle picking up a chair. Martin, the man you met yesterday, was out, and one of the girls upstairs, a little Chink she was, started yelling. We heard banging, too. Your father dropped the chair and ran up the steps and into her room. A big logger, drunk as a skunk, was holding her by the neck up against the wall and hitting her, punching her in the face." I could make out Yetta's head shaking at the memory.

"Your father charged in and took on that john who was three times Sam's size and blind drunk, a real bully. It was like David and Goliath, only I'm not one to wait for God to help. And I didn't want any cops." Yetta sighed as if the very thought of the police depressed her. "So I ran and got two other johns to pull that son of a bitch off your father."

I vaguely remembered a day many years ago when Sam came home with bruised eyes, a cut on his cheek, and an injured arm. He said that while walking uphill carrying a carton of china from a failed restaurant, he slipped on the black ice that in winter can coat Seattle sidewalks like a second skin. "Think I look bad? You shoulda seen them dishes," he quipped. Even with my own memory corroborating Yetta's story, it was hard for me to imagine Sam fist-fighting.

"So that's why I'm friends with your father. He doesn't know what's good for him. He just knows what's right. And he may know who's who, but he doesn't always know what's what when it comes to business. He needs somebody to look out for him, watch his back." She reached for the plate, felt for a cookie, and lifted it to her mouth. "And apparently, so do you. You don't have much head for business either." Harry had told me the same thing many times. But look what he'd gone and done. "So, for Sam, I'm going to watch your back too."

I was trying my best to imagine a blind madam, no matter how rich, in the role of guardian angel when Yetta asked, "You want to work?"

I nodded and then, remembering the futility of gesturing, murmured a yes.

"Well, I have work for you, probably a summer's worth. I'll pay you well, say eight thousand dollars."

The relief I felt at this news dissipated into discomfort when Yetta added, "That's about ten times what you're making at Frederick & Nelson."

I hadn't mentioned working at the department store. Just what kind of task did this woman, who could see little but knew everything, have in mind?

My neck muscles tightened. Keeping my voice even, I asked, "What is it you would pay me so much to do?"

"I need your eyes now." Yetta adjusted the frames of her dark glasses on the bridge of her nose. "And your brains and your energy. Your father's always bragging about how smart you are. I need you to organize my files." She gestured at shadows I took to be file cabinets lining the wall across the room.

I was relieved. Filing was boring, but doable, like housework. But I still didn't trust my good fortune, didn't trust Yetta. "Surely you could get someone else to do this work just as well for a lot less money."

"Believe me, Rachel, you're a bargain." I couldn't imagine any service costing thousands of dollars as a bargain. "You're Sam Wilenski's daughter. I don't have to worry about you cheating me or stealing the silverware or yapping about my personal business. The files with the receipts for purchases I've made are a mess. Records of loans I've made are a mess. Legal documents and hotel records are a mess. And all this mess is a problem now because the goddamn IRS is after me."

Her voice faltered for a moment and then grew steady again as she continued. "But I can't let just anybody go through my records. And my lawyer or my accountant would charge an arm and a leg. Like I said, Rachel, you're a bargain."

Yetta turned her head, as if the thieves and bigmouths she feared were lurking in the hall and as if she could see them. "I've got a lot of valuable stuff here." She hesitated. "And some cash." Then I understood why Yetta's otherwise unassuming brick house was so well fortified. Her tone turned urgent, harsh even. "So, Rachel, I expect you to keep quiet about what you see and do here." But her voice softened a little when she added, "I don't want to wake up some night to face a burglar. I'm not a good shot anymore."

I reached over and gently patted my unlikely benefactor's hand. "Thank you for your trust. I'll do my best, and I'll keep what I see to myself. I promise." Then I remembered Frederick & Nelson and Feigele. How would I have time for everything?

As if she could read my thoughts, Yetta had the last word. "I know you're busy, so don't worry. You come here whenever you want, days, nights, weekends. Just call first so I can have Bess let you in."

Now that I had a way to replace most of the *kishke-gelt*, I felt relieved, although the fact that I'd signed on to work for a madam, even a retired one, bothered me. But, as the saying goes, "Beggars can't be choosers." Instead of thinking of myself as helping a madam delude the IRS, I'd focus on the fact that I was helping a blind and sickly old woman, a good friend of my dad's. It was the least I could do, practically a *mitzvah.* When I got home from work that night, I opened Feigele's diary with a lighter heart than usual.

Feigele's Diary, New York, September 2, 1891

Bernie Olafsky, my peddler with the smiling eyes, is my only real friend in America besides Gitl who I hardly ever visit because I am almost always working. When I am with Bernie, I do not feel like a ghost. Bernie speaks English like he was born here. Someday children of mine will be born here, will be American citizens, and will speak English like Bernie Olafsky. Their lives will be easy, and only after I am dead and they read this little book, will they learn of my struggles. Bernie does not seem to struggle. He is at ease, and he dresses nice. Bernie shares a room in a boarding house with his brother Jake.

Tonight, on the way back from the English class, Bernie and I visited a café and sat at a table in the back out of sight of passersby who might recognize me and tell Herman and Chaya what I am up to. Then Bernie distributed to the other customers a card he had printed about me in two languages! On one side in English the card says *Madame Fanny Lindner, World Famous Palmist recently arrived from Europe! Tells the past, present, and future! Gives advice on Business, Journeys, Law Suits, Love, Sickness, Family affairs, etc.* All the people in the café were speaking Yiddish, but Bernie says that the card is for the future too. He took my hand in his and pretended to see there what the future holds for me. "Under the name of Fanny, you will soon read palms in English and earn many dollars." He sounded so certain. On the other side of the card is printed the same thing in Yiddish, and there I am still Feigele.

My first customer was a greenhorn girl like I was before. She was worried about her mother who is sick and her sweetheart who is waiting for her far away. I told her to care for her mother before joining her sweetheart. I said that if he really loves her, he will wait. She cried and thanked me for my words. It was a good beginning. People started coming over to our table to have their palms read. I charged each one fifteen cents, but if the customer was well dressed, Bernie said I should charge more. I gave Bernie half the money because he had the cards made and took them around to the people at other tables. I saved my half of the money to pay for Mama and Papa and little Yitzak's tickets. With the extra money I earn telling fortunes, I can bring them here sooner. I made a promise to the Almighty that when Mama, Papa, and the little *pisher* get here, I will no longer read palms in violation of His will.

Feigele's Diary, New York, January 25, 1892

For months I have been unable to write my thoughts because since October when the letter came, my thoughts have been too dark to put on paper. But maybe if I put down what happened that night it will be easier to bear. May lightning strike me if I lie, but, fortuneteller that I am, I knew. As soon as I reached the top of the stairs and saw the pale and tearstained face of poor Gitl there in the kitchen with Herman, Chaya, and Dora, I knew. I swear I knew even before I saw the piece of paper Gitl held in her hand and before she read to me from it.

The paper was a letter from Hanele who wrote how in Gnilsk there had been a pogrom. Most homes and the synagogue were torched in the night. The people who awoke and tried to escape were beaten and some were forced back into the burning buildings. There were many dead, among them, Mama, Papa, and even that little *pisher* Yitzak, may they rest in peace.

On that night, Hanele had been in Nyzhni Sady making a dress for Mrs. Horowitz to wear to her cousin's daughter's wedding. Dear Hanele escaped the flames. But her old mother died when the house around her burned. Even the cobbler and his son Yekel are dead. The rabbi and his family are also gone, their ashes mingling with those of the Torah scrolls. Before Gitl could say "May they all rest in peace," I snatched the letter away from her and crumpled it in my fist. When Gitl pried it out of my hand and took it back, the paper was as wrinkled as the face of Chaya's newborn when the midwife pulled her from the womb.

As I moaned and tore at my dress, all I could think of was that Papa was named Moishe. Like the other Moishe, my Papa would not come to the Promised Land. Sweet Mama and little Yitzak neither. And Mama will never hold you, my little ones, sing you to sleep. After Gitl left, Chaya rocked me in her arms for a long time crooning to me as she does to her infant. Dora set a bowl of soup on the table and tried to spoon some into my mouth. I could not eat.

If the Most High stayed Abraham's hand as it was poised to slay his Yitzak, why had the Almighty not quenched the flames that consumed my own sweet little brother and Mama and Papa? On that night my orphaned heart became hard and empty like a stale American bagel, the kind bakers take from the oven and string on a broom handle to carry to the street to sell. That broom hole in my stale bagel heart is where God used to be. My dreams are filled with fire.

Feigele's Diary, New York, January 26, 1892

Because I must work to earn my livelihood, the Rabbi said I needed to mourn at home for only three days instead of the usual seven. Boris Lipschitz came to Herman and Chaya's apartment to say *Kaddish* every morning and evening during those three days so we would have the ten men needed to make a *minyan*. Daughters do not say this prayer, but the Rabbi let me because no son survived. I made the words with my lips only, as I have no heart now for praising God.

Bernie did not come, because I have not yet introduced him to Herman, Chaya and Dora. They would not like that I have made friends with a man I met on the street, a man they do not know, a man who says, "In America the Most High is everywhere. He does not hide Himself only in synagogues." And Herman speaks ill of peddlers, calls them thieves, even though he knows my own Papa was a peddler with a wagon instead of a pack. They would not understand about Bernie.

But Bernie understands how I feel. Like poor Gitl who still grieves for her daughter, Bernie does not say that in time I will recover from my sorrow. He knows from sorrow. He too is an orphan. His mother, may she rest in peace, died when his brother was born and their father brought them both to this country a few years ago. His papa found work as a presser in a factory where he got a sickness of the lungs and died. May he too rest in peace. Bernie and Jake have been on their own since then. I hope someday to meet this Jake. I am ashamed to say I envy Bernie because he has one relative still alive.

Chapter 8

. . . dee gantze veg adurch Amereeka tzoo ah shtot vos hayst Seattle. . .

. . . all the way across America to a city called Seattle . . .

Before I read about how all her dear ones were killed, I pitied the girl, uprooted and alone in a strange country. But after reading of the fiery pogrom, I saw her as rootless and alone in the whole world, except for Bernie, a new acquaintance. I thanked God that my Marsha had not lost both her parents, was not alone in New York, but living with her cousin, aunt, and uncle and a million other Jews safe on the Upper West Side. I told myself that Feigele, too, would be safe in America where anti-Semitism, although a fact of life, was rarely a cause of death. But according to Tim Hunter, poor Feigele was killed in America, probably in Seattle. Who would hurt this orphaned girl?

That evening Tim called to remind me about the next day's field trip to the streets beneath Pioneer Square. I was eager to see Feigele's makeshift grave for myself, but I was also anxious because I had yet to tell Tim Hunter I was reneging on my offer to translate for free. On my way downtown, I stopped for gas and so arrived breathless to find Tim waiting for me. "So sorry I'm late."

"You're worth waiting for. Take it easy. My students and our guide are down below." I followed him down the steep narrow steps. Towards the bottom, the stairwell grew darker than even Yetta Solomon's shuttered house. I didn't protest when the professor turned and offered his hand. His grip tightened, and with that slight pressure, my breath came even faster.

At the foot of the stairs Tim held onto my hand and turned to face me. "That's the last step. Too bad." This man, standing so close I could smell the Colgate minting his breath, was married. While I was betraying only the memory of Harry, Tim was betraying a woman still living and breathing and fixing him breakfast. I retrieved my hand.

Over Tim's shoulder, the glow of flashlights beckoned me to venture further into the subterranean gloom. They say the ghost of Chief Sealth's daughter, Princess Angelina, haunts this cavern. I moved away from the professor toward the students standing in clusters, the beams from their upturned flashlights grouped like constellations of battery-generated stars.

Illuminated in the glow, was our guide, his hair a mop like the Beatles.' He wore dungarees and a Seattle World's Fair tee-shirt emblazoned with a rendering of the Space Needle and carried a large lantern which he handed to Tim. "Take it away, Professor."

Tim took the lantern and ambled over to the nearby wall. When he began to speak, his voice echoed slightly, and I was charmed to hear his drawled syllables reverberate. "This is what we came down here to see. Here's where those bones were buried before the quake." He raised the lantern to illuminate a waist-high square opening in the retaining wall behind him. It was about two feet wide and two feet long, the size of four of the stones that comprised the rest of the wall. "As I told you in class, the quake of '49 loosened the cement around the stones and then this year's quake finished the job. Popped them right on out. Come up here and see the grave for yourselves."

I chafed at the word "grave." The recessed pit we were looking at wasn't what I thought of as a grave. The students filed past, probing the hollow in the wall with their flashlights. When it was my turn, I blinked into the blackness and pictured Feigele's killer cramming a sack rounded by the curves of her corpse into the square hole.

Tim had repositioned himself a few feet away and was pointing his flashlight towards the floor. "Here's the bathtub the kid tripped over, where the quake flipped the bones." I took in the metal tub, grayish in the lantern light. "Pete moved it so we could get a close look at the grave, but when the boy fell in, the tub was in front of it. The quake loosened the stones in the wall, and a couple of them landed in the tub first with a lot of dirt. That dirt cushioned the bones.

"Pete tells me they're keeping this tub on the tour." Tim reached down and patted it affectionately, like the Lone Ranger patting Silver's flank. The drumbeat of hand on metal echoed. "Tourists will want to know that during Prohibition, bootleggers appropriated this tub from the hotel up above and brought it down here to make moonshine in. And they sold their likker straight out of the tub, right Pete?" Tim returned the lantern and ceded the floor to the guide.

Pete's voice was tinny, a boyish squawk compared to Tim's. "You bet, Professor. And for sure those tourists will dig knowing about a corpse turning up down here too." Tim, no longer constrained by the obligation to teach, moved to stand next to me. Pete was lecturing, but with Tim again so close, concentrating required an act of will.

"Over 25 square blocks of downtown Seattle were completely destroyed by that fire. Why?" Pete didn't wait for a reply. "Because all the buildings were wooden." His voice lowered as if he were sharing a secret. "But not one single person died in the blaze. So maybe that fire wasn't such a bad thing." Another pause. "Why? Well, it gave the town a chance to start over, do it right. So when the City and the merchants rebuilt, they used brick and stone. They raised the level of the streets and sidewalks and widened them.

"But the whole regrade took decades. And the merchants and hoteliers were in a rush to rebuild and reopen, so they built in the depressions and then had to construct stairs leading from the new raised sidewalks down here to the entrances and window displays of their businesses. Customers had to clamber down the same steps you just came down. Imagine these shoppers lugging their purchases back up those stairs." I remembered navigating those steps hand in hand with Tim. "There were injuries and protests. Eventually street level entrances were built."

Pete's next words refocused my attention. "Once these streets down here were no longer in use by the general public, Seattle's gamblers, prostitutes, and bootleggers took them over. City officials didn't do anything to stop the lowlifes from carrying on down here, but folks were in for a surprise." Sotto voce, he proclaimed, "Some of those lowlifes were rats." A few students looked down as if the offending rodents might still be scampering at our feet. Pete's voice lowered again. "The place was still a tidal flat, really. So rats came in on the cargo ships from Asia, and found a home down here in the mud. And back then, where there were rats, there was what?" Again our guide answered his own question, his voice raised to a portentous boom. "Bubonic Plague! In 1907, right here in Seattle."

"That's when our City Fathers put in the cement floor and closed the whole place off. It's been closed ever since— except to bootleggers and ghosts and to whoever buried those bones." Pete's voice was a whisper. Picturing Feigele's killer thrusting her body into that hole, I shuddered.

"Cold?" Tim murmured his query into my ear.

Before I could reply, his arm was around me. I had to get out of there, go to work. I turned away from Tim as if we had been dancing and the music stopped. I spoke quickly, primly. "I've got to run now. Thanks for including me, and please thank our guide for me." I retreated back up the stairs, eager to breathe fresh air in the bright and specterless summer sunshine, relieved to be out of Tim Hunter's disturbing orbit, craving a cigarette. I didn't realize I'd forgotten to tell Tim I wanted to be paid for translating until that night when I opened the diary.

Feigele's Diary, New York, January 30, 1892

Yesterday I went back to work and Boris and the others were taking away the clothes and work tables, everything, and moving them to a new shop around the corner. Boris said it was a bigger shop, but it isn't. May my body be invaded by a dybbuk if what I write next did not happen. Last night there was a big fire in the building where Boris's shop used to be. The whole building went up in smoke and flames like the synagogue in Gnilsk. An old lady home alone in one of the apartments broke her leg jumping out. I went to see the smoking ruin. It looked like the pyres I see in my nightmares now, except in those nightmares there are people screaming and bodies roasting like the chestnuts the peddlers sell here. There on the street I shivered all over.

ഇ

Feigele's Diary, New York, February 3, 1892

I wonder how Boris knew to get all the clothes, fabric, tables, and machines out of the old shop before the fire. Bernie says the owner probably paid Boris to move and then had it torched. Maybe the owner paid Boris to torch it and Boris will go to jail. Bernie says there is a gang of men who make money emptying buildings and setting them on fire so the owners can collect the insurance. Some of these fire setters are Jews with no work. This makes me afraid. In Gnislk it was the gentiles who started fires, not the Jews. Since the pogrom and the shop fire, Boris is a little nicer to me, but if Bernie is right, Boris is a criminal. And I cannot forget how mean he was before.

ഇ

Feigele's Diary, New York, April 16, 1892

Herman and Chaya say I should marry Boris. The money I was saving for tickets on the boat for Mama, Papa, and little Yitzak, may they rest in peace, could be my dowry. Herman said Boris has his own shop now and Boris likes me. But if Boris likes me, why was he so nasty to me for so long? Why does he still turn back the clock when he thinks no one is looking so that I have to stitch so fast my fingers feel like they are on fire and my back aches? No. I did not say much to Herman, but I do not think Boris would be a good husband or father.

When I told Bernie of Boris's interest, Bernie got angry. He said I should leave Boris's sweatshop, because after I refuse his marriage offer the old troll will probably fire me. Besides, Boris's stinking shop still has only Gnilskis there drinking beer, smoking cigars and cigarettes, and talking nasty in Yiddish. Bernie says it isn't the real America. So without letting on to Herman or Chaya, I looked for work somewhere else.

I sew now in a dress factory way uptown on Broadway near 14th Street where Bernie sometimes sells dictionaries and eyeglasses to the workers. I make sleeves on the machine and earn 10 dollars a week. Bernie says uptown on 14th Street is where the real Americans are. A rich German-

Jew named Greenberg owns the factory, and there is a foreman named Joseph. Joseph makes us work hard, and I must do the same thing over and over, but he doesn't move the clock hands or touch me and the other girls. We are mostly Jewish girls, but there are also a few others.

During my break yesterday, I tried speaking some English with an Irish girl. Bridget O'Malley is her name. She wears a silver cross around her neck, but she is nice, not like the murderous peasants of the Ukraine. I can learn a lot from speaking with her. She and her friend Sean go out walking together. They are saving to get married. At lunch Bridget shared with me some bread she brought from home. I know it was not kosher, but ever since the letter came I have not been eating much, and I brought no lunch of my own. I felt weak from hunger, and the bread from my kind new friend tasted good.

At the factory I have to work on Saturday, but this is America, and the Sabbath is on Sunday here. I know Herman thinks I am ungrateful for leaving Boris's sweatshop and even worse for working on the Sabbath because when I told him and Chaya about the factory job, that's when Herman said I had to pay more for board. So I told him that with Chaya no longer pregnant and with me paying more, I would not do chores. He gave me one of his looks, but I just walked away.

I did not come to America to be a servant. Here I am free to learn, to work on Saturdays, and to eat what I want and where I want. I do not want to eat with Herman and his family every night. Instead, after work I will go to English classes with Bernie and then read palms at the café and have a little food there. My palm reading pays for my meal! Bernie told me last night that I am getting very good at predicting futures and giving advice. He says I have a gift. I still haven't introduced Bernie to Herman and Chaya or Dora or even Gitl, but they are not my real family. I have freedom in America, but still no family. Freedom without Mama, Papa, and little Yitzak sometimes makes me afraid.

Feigele's Diary Seattle, Washington, May 4, 1893

I write now sitting in my seat on a new fast moving train. So much has happened in the four years since since my first train trip across Europe to

Hamburg to board the steamship to America with Gitl. Now I am crossing all of America with my fiancé Bernie Olafsky! But this morning when we boarded this train in New York, there was no one at the station to say goodbye to us and wish us well.

Herman, Chaya, Dora, and even sweet Gitl, would not like it that I am going with Bernie before our wedding so I did not tell them. I have not introduced them to my fiancé because, since I left the job with Boris, Herman has acted mean to me. Besides Herman would say Bernie is a nogoodnik. Herman and Chaya and Gitl too would say Bernie and I are crazy to leave New York and go all the way across America to a city called Seattle in a state called Washington. But Herman is not my papa, so I do not care what he thinks.

Besides, the teacher in my night school class told us that an American President named Washington is the man who said in a letter that Jews could stay in America in peace. Bernie and I will be happy in a state named after such a man. And in his state we will be married! In his state our children will be born.

The couple's departure from New York for Washington dashed the slim hope I still entertained that the bones might not prove to be Feigele's. I had hoped the diarist, who protested so often that she was telling the truth, had embellished her humdrum immigrant existence with tales of arson and romance. After all, she was a fortuneteller, paid to weave the lines and lumps of people's palms into credible forecasts. But the sweatshop Cinderella and her peddler prince really did schlep all the way out west to marry and live happily ever after, only for her to be murdered. If there was a record of her presence here, I wanted to find it.

Chapter 9

. . . Doo vos kumpt noch meer, vet kaya mohl nisht visen foom mayn shverikayt . . .

. . . you who come after me will never know of my struggle . . .

The next morning I drove downtown to the library. Feigele just might have been counted in Seattle's 1900 census, but, according to the reference librarian, those records won't be available until 1972. Instead, she directed me to the library's collection of Polk's Seattle City Directories. I was pleased when I found the one for 1893. I took the bulky volume to a nearby table where I searched the alphabetical list for Feigele Olafsky. When I couldn't find her, I tried Fanny Olafsky and then Feigele and Fanny Lindner and finally, Aliza Rudinsk in case the young woman had reverted to the name her parents gave her. She wasn't listed there or in the volumes for 1894 or 1895 either. That evening when I opened the diary, I felt torn between belief and skepticism.

ꕥ

Fanny's Diary, on the train to Seattle, Washington

Finally I have the leisure to record my thoughts even if the bumps of the train are making my pen do a hora on the page. I have had no time for recording anything during these past busy months, but there has been much to record. May this pen turn into the writhing serpent that tempted Eve if what I am writing next did not happen. One evening after work Bernie finally invited me to meet his brother Jake, so I agreed to go to their room. My friend Bridget often accompanies Sean to the room Sean shares with his brothers. Jake was late getting back. While we waited, Bernie spoke of his love for me and asked me to marry him. I have loved Bernie for a long time, so I was happy to learn that he felt the same. He said that we were betrothed and that he was sure both of our families, may they rest in peace, would have blessed our upcoming marriage.

Then he kissed my mouth over and over until my lips burned under his. Before I could stop him he was stroking my breasts and my buttocks until, beneath his hands, the fabric of my dress seared my flesh like the flames that had consumed Papa and Mama and Little Yitzak. I heard their voices from the pyre of Gnilsk calling to me, Aliza, to resist. But Fanny did not hear them. Their screams were once again consumed by fire, the fire that burned in me.

I backed onto the bed, lifted my skirt, and opened myself to Bernie. When he entered me I felt a knife, but then it was as if all the burning places on my body had fused, and I was one flame. I recognized our groans of pleasure as the same sounds of love Mama and Papa had made in their bed on the Sabbath, and tears blurred my view of Bernie's face. My tears washed away any shame I felt, and when I realized that, like Mama and Papa, Bernie and I would know this bliss again and again, I felt only joy.

We waited for Jake a little longer, and when he did not come, Bernie walked me home. As if his proposal and our love were not excitement enough for one night, right there on Orchard Street among the roughnecks, prostitutes, and carousers who made the street their own after dark, Bernie told me of his dream that we go west to marry! I swear these were his exact words, "Fanny, let's leave behind this desert that is New York and make our way west to the real America, to the real Promised Land." He sounded like Moses.

Bernie spoke next of his cousin, Sam Olafsky, in Seattle, Washington. This cousin wrote him that there are Jews there too and rabbis to marry us. Sam also wrote that in Seattle, Washington, there are good jobs for smart salesmen and accomplished seamstresses. He would help us get work and an apartment of our own with room for a family even. I was so happy when Bernie said, "Fanny, picture us getting married in the Promised Land, a place worthy of our love!" My Bernie is a poet, but he is also a man and now he is hungry, so I must stop writing and get out the bagels I brought along to sustain us on our journey.

Fanny's Diary, Seattle, May 11, 1893

Oy. I am so grateful to Meier Horowitz, may he live a long and happy life, for giving me this diary. If I could not write of my misery, it would claw at my insides until I died of the pain and you who come after me would never know of my struggle. I am in Seattle, Washington, but I am not Mrs. Bernard Olafsky. Mama and Papa, may they rest in peace, will never know that I spent a night in jail like a criminal. I will never forget how alone I felt in that cell on my first night in this remote town perched on the edge of a vast sea and surrounded by forests and mountains of ice. Luckily I now have a safe place to stay for a while, and I will make a wedding dress, but, alas, not for myself.

I should be turned to stony salt like Lot's wife if every word I write about what happened on that train is not the truth. On the first day of our journey Bernie and I kept our eyes out the window, watching America. After we left New York behind, there were fields, farms, forests, and some big towns and little ones. That night Bernie slept, but I watched the stars and the moon, and sometimes I saw a light on in a farmhouse. By the second day of our journey, I grew sleepy and dozed off beside Bernie.

I slept for many hours. When I awoke, Bernie was no longer on the seat next to me. No more was his canvas bag on the floor at our feet. I waited for him to return from the privy, but after an hour, he had not appeared. Two pretty and well-dressed women in the seats across from ours noticed my distraught state and spoke to me in English. With the help of my dictionary and many gestures, they made me understand that when the train stopped in a town called Chicago, Bernie got off with his bag, and when the train started he had not returned.

I told myself that he missed the train, but when I searched in my own bag, I found my savings were gone. Bernie waited for me to sleep and then took all the money I had left after buying our train tickets, every penny! That moment, bent over with my hand still groping among the bagels and underwear in my bag, I realized that there had never been a betrothal. Or a letter from cousin Samuel Olafsky. There was no Samuel Olafsky. There had probably never been a brother Jake either. And there was no apartment waiting, no work. And there had been no love, only lies. At that awful moment, I wasn't even sure there was a Seattle, Washington. I looked through my tears at my ticket stub and made out the S and the W. I would arrive in Seattle alright, but alone. Bernie was as bad as Boris, a real nogoodnik. And I was still a blockhead greenhorn girl.

I could feel the broom handle hole in my stale bagel heart grow bigger. The women across from me offered me some of their food, but, ghost girl that I am, I had no appetite. By the time the train reached the Seattle station, I was dizzy and my arms and legs shook with fright. When I got off the boat in New York I had Gitl with me and Herman and Chaya waiting. But in Seattle, Washington, I arrived alone and no one waited to greet me. I tried to summon the courage and the English words to ask a passerby to direct me to the Jewish Quarter where I might look for work and shelter.

But before I could utter a syllable, I was herded into a wagon along with the two nice women who had tried to help me on the train. The uniformed woman holding the reins of the wagon horses seemed to be expecting us, but I was not expecting her. She hollered some English words at us. In a matter of minutes we stopped at what I soon realized was, I swear, a jail. We were herded off the wagon and inside. I heard the heavy door with the tiny barred window slam shut behind us.

The other two women did not appear either surprised or upset to find themselves there, and soon a man arrived who seemed to know them, and they were released. Before they left, the one with the hair more red than mine took my hand and said something kind to me that I did not understand. After the door banged behind them, I stared out the little barred window and wept as I watched them walk away. But now, the bride is here for her fitting. I will continue my sad story another day.

ꙮ

I resisted my temptation to edit Feigele's understated description of Bernie which I translated as "a real nogoodnik." To my mind, Bernie was a nogoodnik like Henry VIII was a bad husband. But I let her hybrid description stand.

The diarist's decision to take off with the feckless Bernie proved rash, but her guileless sexual capitulation to him struck me as an even bigger mistake. God knows it wasn't that I didn't like sex. Pleasing Harry had excited me, and, when I occasionally enjoyed a blissful spasm of my own, I figured it was a happy byproduct of our intimacy, a strictly connubial perk. I shuddered at the risk the motherless girl had taken in that perilous pre-Pill time by giving in to Bernie before tying the knot. What if she got pregnant? Unbeknownst to Harry, I had a long talk with Marsha before she left for Vassar, told her about the Pill, and reminded her that even in 1965 an unwed mother was still a girl in trouble.

Although I found no trace of Feigele in the Polk Directories, I felt compelled to call Tim Hunter with news of Feigele's reported relocation, news that confirmed his conviction that the bones were hers. I would also tell him I had to renege on my offer to translate for free. "Tim, Rachel Mazursky. Sorry to disturb you, but . . . "

"Hi, Rachel. I like being disturbed by you."

His blatant flattery made my face warm. "I wanted to tell you that you're probably right."

"Being right is almost as good as being disturbed by you. What am I right about?"

"The bones. The diarist writes of coming to Seattle." I hesitated. "So the bones really could be hers, and I wanted to tell you that. But I checked a few Seattle Polk Directories in the library, and I didn't find her listed." I added that just to let him know that I was earning the pay I hoped to get.

"Well, those directories are useful, but not infallible like me and the Pope." I heard his chuckle. "Thanks for keeping me posted."

"One more thing." I steeled myself to tell him that I wanted to change the terms of our agreement. "Tim, I know I told you I wouldn't accept any pay, but . . ." I hesitated long enough for him to interrupt, offer compensation, but he didn't. "Something's come up. My lawyer gave me some bad news. I'd like to be paid."

If Tim thought I was a money-grubbing Jew, he didn't let on. "Sorry you've had bad news. Of course we'll pay you. But as I mentioned in our first conversation, we can't offer much. I think there's a hundred dollars in the department slush fund I can put in for. Will that help?"

"Yes. Thank you." Silently I thanked God that I had other work.

"Glad we can do it. I'll let you know when those artifacts get here."

I wasn't scheduled to work at the store the next day, so I could go to Yetta's. Bess ushered me into the house and down the corridor to the room where I first met with my newest employer. I was pleased to find the maroon velvet drapes pulled back. Sunlight revealed ornately carved furniture and metal file cabinets where there had been only shadows and cream-colored walls where there had been dark corners.

The sunlight also revealed hats. To my amazement, almost every piece of furniture was bedecked with hats. There were Jackie-inspired pillboxes and floppy-brimmed fedoras that would have suited Marsha's heroine Bella Abzug. There were tams, berets, straw hats, feathered hats, flower-covered hats, Panamas, turbans, and even a couple of fur numbers. The room looked like a milliner's shop, a mad hatter's trove.

"Here she comes." We could hear Yetta tapping her way along the hall. Bess moved to the window and quickly unhooked the drapes so that, once again, they shut out the sun. "Glaucoma. The bad kind. And cataracts. The doc says it's the cataracts that make the light bother her." I appreciated Bess's unsolicited explanation of Yetta's eye problems.

"Hello, Rachel." Yetta tapped her way to the table and sat down, once again hooking her cane over the back of her chair. "Even though I don't work nights anymore, I still sleep late, so Bess is going to bring me some breakfast. Would you care for an omelet?"

My stomach rumbled a yes. "I'd love one. Thank you."

"Good. Bess, an omelet for Rachel too, please." Bess left. "After we eat, I'll go back upstairs so you can let in the light down here and take a look at the files. My accountant says he's not going to need to see them until summer's end, so our arrangement should work out." Yetta didn't seem to expect a reply, because she immediately lobbed questions at me. "How's your translation work going?" Sam must have told her about my project. "Who was the poor Jewish girl who wrote that diary? And how did she end up in that hellhole?"

I was still talking when Bess brought our omelets. Yetta listened in silence until I got to Feigele's arrest. "It figures. Back then *seamstress* was just another word for *hooker* and the damn Seattle police actually hired a lady cop to meet the trains and intercept working girls hoping to set up shop here. So the cop figured your Feigele for a hooker like the two lovelies she was traveling with. The madam they were going to work for probably paid off a cop to let them out. Maybe your Feigele was a hooker too. Ever think of that?" I bridled at Yetta's crass suggestion and didn't dignify it with an answer. But the ex-madam's annotation of the diary corroborated at least a part of Feigele's account.

It took me all afternoon to survey Yetta's many drawers of jumbled files and plan a sorting and refiling strategy. When I got home, I scanned the messages of sympathy still coming in the mail and envisioned vast tracts of trees donated in memory of Harry greening the Israeli desert. I tossed the notes into a large basket that had held fruit from Bobby Gradstein, the same Bobby Gradstein who, long ago, filched my diary and the same Bobby Gradstein I'd once literally rescued from the very jaws of death. I grinned at my own hyperbole.

Decades ago on the way to school Bobby was bitten by Latke, the Smolinski's dog. Poor old Latke thought the ten-year-old was after his fresh bone and took a chunk out of the boy's ear. A few steps behind Bobby, I heard him yowl and saw blood spurt from his head. I shoved my clean hanky into his hand and jammed that hand over his earlobe before I dashed past Latke and banged on the Smolinski's door for help. I sighed. That was a long time ago. I'd have to get Bobby's New York address from his mother.

Chapter 10

. . . vu Goht flegt zain . . .

. . . where God used to be . . .

Fanny's Diary, June 10, 1893

It is the Sabbath and I have put aside my sewing for now. But Ava's husband goes to his store on Saturday, so who's to say I cannot write? I must finish writing about how I came to be freed from jail, to be here in this house. Not until Ava Weiss arrived did my lungs take in air freely. Ava is a small woman with watchful eyes, and she talked to my jailer in English and then she spoke to me in Yiddish. "Come with me. You can't stay here," is all that she said, but this stranger's use of Yiddish made those simple words a love song to me. So when the jailer opened the door to my cell, I walked to Ava's side and followed her.

While we walked, Ava explained that she was a Jew who had heard about me from her rabbi who heard about me from the lawyer who arranged the release from jail of the other two women. Unlike God, those kind women had not forgotten me! May they lead long and happy lives. Ava then said that she was taking me to the home where she lives with her husband Nathan and their two little children and where I might recover from my ordeal.

We rode up a big hill in what Ava said was a cable car. Tired as I was, I stared out the window. Off to the right I saw a massive mountain of shining ice. I swear it is higher than Sinai and rounded like the skirt of a satin wedding gown made for a giant golem bride. In New York there are only tall buildings, but Seattle has the sea and hills and mountains and trees along with houses and stores. Ava says there are lakes nearby too. The streets here are muddy like in Gnilsk, but they are not crowded and noisy like Orchard Street. The people we passed appeared well-dressed, and they did not shout. I sat alongside Ava in a trance.

Ava says the home she lives in with her husband Nathan, their little ones, and several servants is not in the Jewish Quarter because when they arrived in Seattle many years ago there were few Jews and no special provision for us. The house occupies three floors and is as clean as Meier's house. When we arrived, she insisted that I bathe and put on a night dress she provided. No one had used the bath water before me, and the night dress was worn but clean. Then Ava stood over me in her kitchen while I ate a bowl of chicken soup that the maid Kathleen brought to the table. I wasn't hungry but Ava said I had to eat. Once I had a few spoonfuls of soup, I became hungry and Kathleen refilled my bowl. While I ate Ava stared at my fingernails, and I wished that they were cleaner and less ragged. Finally Kathleen led me upstairs to a small room on the top floor where I fell asleep in a real bed with a real mattress. Kathleen said I did not have to share this bed with anyone. The room either. I slept for many hours.

When I awakened, I remembered all that happened and felt again the emptiness in my chest. But then I saw on the chair beside the bed a clean dress and some underclothes. These garments were not new, but they smelled of soap and trees like the kind that grow in Gnilsk. I dressed and went downstairs to the living room where Ava waited. For the next hour she threw questions at me. Where was I from? How long had I been in America? How old was I? Where was my family? Had a young man seen my photo and sent for me to be his bride? If not, why had I left New York and come to Seattle? Could I speak any English at all? Had I had any schooling? Any money? What work had I done in Gnilsk? In New York? And last, why was I traveling with those low women?

Ava nodded her head at some of my replies and shook it at others like when I told her what had happened to Mama, Papa, and little Yitzak. She made clicking sounds and a sour face when I told her about leaving New York with Bernie. And she rolled her eyes when I got to the part about how he stole my money and got off the train. I could not bring myself to tell Ava that Bernie Olafsky had known me as a husband knows a wife, but I think she suspects. I did not tell this stern woman of the hole in my heart where God used to be either. She finally smiled when I told her how

I can sew by hand and machine and that I can make dresses, pants, skirts, shirts, and coats and that I am eager to work and save up to rent a room somewhere. That's when she asked me if I could make a wedding dress, and I told her yes.

And may my dirty fingernails fall off if this is not what she said next. "You can work for me to start. My family came to America from Germany many years ago and God has been good to us. So my friends and I try to help greenhorns like you who need to learn how to keep yourselves and your homes clean. We see to it that you learn English and how we do things in America." At her words, my cheeks reddened with shame, and I curled my fingers in my clenched fists to hide my grimy nails. Ava Weiss might as well have called me, "Dirty Jew" like the wop boys on Orchard Street had. But shame or no shame, I am glad of her help. And she is honest. I have had enough of lies and liars.

"Now listen, Fanny, I have promised to make a wedding for a young Jewish couple from Russia." That's when Ava told me about Devorah Pinsker, a picture bride just off the boat who arrived here last week and is living with Ava's sister. Myron Warshavsky, Devorah's fiancé, has been here for a few months working as a house painter. He lives with some other young Jewish men in a boarding house. The Weiss's rabbi is going to marry the couple in the Weiss's living room. Ava asked me, "Can you make this girl a simple wedding dress? I can get you a sewing machine from my husband's store and my sister has some leftover fabric." I nodded glad to finally please my new benefactor. And now the bride has come, and I must meet with her. I will swallow my tears, so that this Devorah Pinsker does not guess that the wedding dress I make for her is the one I planned to make for myself.

Fanny's Diary, Seattle, June 20, 1893

I have had no time to write down my thoughts because Ava has me working like one of Pharaoh's slaves. Hanele was my school for sewing. Ava Weiss is my school for America. She speaks to me only in English now and has commanded her husband to do the same. She makes me buy from the German, Italian, and Swedish peddlers who come to the back door selling fruits and vegetables and fish. I mostly point at what we need, and then I laugh with the peddlers at how this stinking language tangles all our tongues.

Last week Ava loaned me a book that belongs to her little boy so I could learn the English ABCs and learn to read and write English. This morning she made me read aloud letters and words I recognize in the newspaper ads. When I speak English, I still feel like there is a frog jumping on my tongue, but I do as Ava tells me. She makes me go to an English class. It is better than the class I went to in New York because the teacher is a woman and is not cranky and there are not so many students. Our teacher wants us to learn the words to use in stores and if we are sick. This class is more advanced. Ava says I have to run errands for her in the gentile shops. She says I will never learn English if I only go to the Jewish shops on Jackson Street. On Friday nights I listen to the conversations Ava and Nathan have with her sister and her husband during dinner. They laugh and argue a lot, and I do not understand much because they speak English fast. You, my little ones, will not struggle to master this language as I do but will be born speaking English like the Weiss's boy Abraham and his sister.

Ava is helping me a lot. But ungrateful girl that I am, this afternoon, I snuck off to tell fortunes. Ava would not approve because she would think only ignorant people do this. But maybe she would not mind because I read palms now in English. I waited outside a coffeehouse near the wharf where there are many Greek sailors, and I read their palms. These newcomers know less English than I do, so they do not know that I too am a greenhorn or a Jew. The owner of the coffee house is a nice man. He gave me free coffee and invited me to sit inside because he said I was good for business. So there I made a few extra pennies to put towards renting a room. I will go back.

Even though I have my own nice room here, I do not belong. I am not a paying boarder or a servant or a real guest or a relative. And I feel as if Ava can see through the walls, can read my thoughts. She is always correcting my English and telling me how to fix my hair. When I said I wanted to make myself a dress, she insisted on choosing the fabric. But, she paid for it too, so what could I say? As soon as Ava's husband Nathan lets me sew in his big store, he will pay me wages, and I will be able to rent a room elsewhere.

Fanny's Diary, Seattle, July 25, 1893

It is hard to find time to write, but I have a full heart. This afternoon while I was telling the fortune of a fisherman outside the coffeehouse, the red-haired woman I met on the train walked by! We recognized each other, and she waited until my customer left to approach me. I spoke to her in English, thanking her for helping to get me out of jail and for her kindness and that of her friend. She told me that her name is Desiree and said how good my English had become. After I told her that I made a wedding dress in return for my board, she asked me if I wanted to make dresses for her and some of her friends.

She was only trying to help me, but of course I said no. Ava told me that Desiree and her friend were prostitutes, low women, just like those pathetic creatures on the stoops and in the alleys of Orchard and Hester Streets, only much better dressed. Seattle may be the Promised Land, but there are many dance halls and brothels here where these women find work. The police arrest them and the brothel owners bribe the police to let them out of jail. When Ava told me that the policewoman had thought that I was such a lowlife, my face turned the color of borscht. As long as I live under Ava and Nathan's roof, I can have nothing to do with Desiree.

But she and her friend had been more than kind to me, so I offered to tell her fortune as a way of repaying her. She laughed and held out her palm. After studying her long index finger and her prominent Mount of Venus, I told her that there was much gold in her future and happiness with a good man. She appeared pleased with this information, and we parted. I am grateful that our paths crossed again so I could thank her.

Fanny's Diary, August 18, 1893

Last week on the Sabbath, Ava Weiss and her husband invited me to attend synagogue with them and their two children. They go to Temple Ohaveth Sholum. It is the first synagogue to be built in Seattle and what I write next is the truth. The men and women were sitting together! They sat side by side, men and women, boys and girls, the rams next to the ewes. I saw a few girls my age there in fancy dresses and hats sitting right behind a row of boys. When I saw one of the girls looking at me, I smiled but she did not return my smile, so I turned my attention to the huge instrument, a big piano with tubes attached. I saw it and heard it myself. And the rabbi spoke as much English as Hebrew and the prayer book too is mostly in English. And the entire service lasted no more than two hours! In Gnilsk and on Orchard Street, two hours is barely enough time for opening the Torah.

I wanted to thank the rabbi there for sending Ava to me in jail. I had prepared a few words to say to him, and after the service Ava approached him with me behind her. I said my thank you. Ava seemed pleased that several of her friends were standing nearby listening as I spoke of her many kindnesses. But I will never forget what happened next. And, may I drown in the sea at the bottom of the hill if it did not take place exactly as I write it. The rabbi took my hand in his to bless me! A real rabbi would never touch the hand of a woman lest she be unclean, as on that day I happened to be. The evening before I had placed between my legs the worn towel I use to absorb my monthly flow. My face grew hot. The rabbi and Ava probably thought I reddened out of shyness, but it was really from my shame at what I knew to be the rabbi's sin, a sin that I had caused and that would remain my secret. But as I write about this I realize that I was not totally unclean because I had used the little nail brush Ava gave me. The nails on the hand the rabbi took in his were freshly scrubbed.

Right after the service ended, Nathan left us to go to his store. What kind of Jews are the Weisses and their friends? They work on the Sabbath. They do not keep kosher. They do not pray daily. And they sit together in the synagogue, the men and the women. But they excel in charity. Every week, Ava and her friends carry baskets of food and used clothing to the homes of poor Jews. Mama, may she rest in peace, used to say, "It does not matter how long you pray if you have no heart for the poor and the sick."

The work Ava and her friends do is important because Seattle has few Jews and most of us are poor. I have never lived in a place where there are so few Jews and so many Christians. There are many more Americans here than in New York. And Jews like Ava and her husband and their children act more American than Jewish. They were all born here, went to school here. Even Ava went to school. They are all citizens. My children will be like them.

Fanny's Diary, October 4, 1893

So much has happened since I last had time to record my thoughts. A few weeks ago I moved into this room at the home of Devorah and her pious husband Myron Warshavsky. I came here as soon as I began to do alterations at the big store of Nathan Weiss. I am comfortable renting a room here. The Warshavskys keep a kosher home, observe the Sabbath, and speak Yiddish. Devorah is a good cook, and I take meals with the family. The only chore I sometimes do is watch little Leah for an hour or two. She is a dear baby, and I like to take care of her.

At the store I speak English all day, fitting customers. Weiss and Company is a big and busy store. Nathan pays me well and the work is easy, mostly alterations. During my lunch hour I take walks and watch the loggers, construction workers, businessmen, and housewives shopping on the downtown streets. I often run into Desiree and Suzanne. They are always wearing the latest fashion, always glad to see me, and always trying to persuade me to make dresses for them. Always I say no.

Each week I deposit all but my rent and a little money for the poor in a bank. And if what I write now is not true, may my hard-earned savings yet again disappear. The bank is owned by a Jew, a man named Jacob Furth! I heard there was once even a Jewish mayor here. Maybe Seattle really is the Promised Land, the real America, because here a Jew can be mayor or head a bank. And in Seattle, a greenhorn girl can learn English, earn good money, keep it safe in a bank, and sleep in a real bed in her own nice room. And I do not go to that bed hungry. But I am watching little Leah and she awakens.

I pushed the diary away, lit a cigarette, and savored the dual pleasures of relief and recognition. I marveled at the utterly American conspiracy— Irish hookers, their employer's lawyer, a rabbi, and a wealthy do-gooder German-Jewish housewife— that proved to be Feigele's get-out-of-jail-free card. If that seems implausible, it really isn't. Not if you know the Weisses, and I do. They're still a prominent local Jewish family. Abe Weiss, Nathan and Ava's son, is a founding member of the exclusive Seattle Athletic Club, one of several private clubs where local movers and shakers eat, drink, and do business. And Nathan and Ava Weiss were my friend Arlene Weiss Golden's paternal grandparents.

Arlene was a relatively new friend, one I'd known only since college. The Weiss mansion was on Capitol Hill, a ritzy outcrop still occupied by a few of Seattle's wealthy Jews, descendants of that English-speaking vanguard of German-Jewish merchants and bankers who helped settle America's frontier. Capitol Hill wasn't far from Madrona, the neighborhood of modest one-family houses nestled close to one another on narrow hilly streets, where I grew up. Arlene racked up her A's at Broadway High while I was earning mine at Garfield. German-Jews and their Eastern European brethren rarely mixed socially, so as kids Arlene and I met only in Temple de Hirsch's Sunday school which welcomed girls.

That's why it wasn't until we began college and joined Hillel that the cashmere-clad Arlene and I, in my cousin's cast-offs, really met. Of the eight coeds in our freshman class at the U in 1940, we were the only Jews. This dubious distinction and our mutual appreciation of history fostered our friendship, as did the fact that junior year we both became engaged to young Jewish men not native to Seattle. We used to commiserate about how hard it was to integrate our fiancés into our completely separate but equally xenophobic circles of friends, mine the offspring of humble Eastern European refugees, hers the progeny of high falutin' German pioneers. And our bond intensified when we both lost our mothers. Even so, after graduation and marriage, it was understood that we wouldn't socialize as a foursome. Instead Arlene and I met occasionally for catch-up sessions in a luncheonette just off campus, not far from the Hillel office where she worked. So Feigele's mention of the Weisses was indisputable validation of her tale.

Once Feigele arrived in Seattle, I found myself reading her words differently. The girl's unhappy sojourn in a tenement and sweatshop on New York's Lower East Side mirrored, in many ways, the sojourns of lots of other poor, homesick, and exploited immigrants. But once she got to Seattle, I experienced another, more immediate, sort of recognition. I'd been in the very rooms the diarist described. My friend Arlene and her husband Joe Golden had lived in the house her grandparents, Nathan and Ava, once occupied. After Arlene had her first baby, I visited her there bearing a wee blue cap for the infant. Feigele's encounters with a family I knew in a house I'd been in and her first impressions of my hometown and "my" mountain resonated with the charm of the familiar. I was eager to tell Arlene about her grandmother's kindness to the jilted and penniless stranger.

When I reached my friend at the Hillel office where she worked, she suggested lunch outdoors at the U on Monday. We arrived at the same time, hugged, and settled ourselves on the low wall surrounding the circular fountain at the heart of the campus. Mount Rainier was clearly visible in the cloudless sky. Its massive hump looked benign beneath the blanket of snow that concealed the crater at its summit and the volcano at its core. The sight prompted me to share a memory. "When I was a child, I heard the rabbi say that God appeared to the Israelites in the desert as a smoking cloud above the Ark, so I always pictured Him as Mount Rainier, a huge cloud-covered volcano. Then when I learned in school that some Indians worshipped the Mountain, I thought maybe they were Jewish."

Arlene smiled and opened the bag she carried. When she had offered to bring sandwiches, I didn't protest, knowing that her cook would make them. Arlene was the only friend I had with both a maid and a cook. "Tuna on white, okay?" I reached for a foil-wrapped packet. "God, it's good to get out of that office." Her grin belied the whine in her words. "I swear Rabbi Moscowitz lives to rile the Christians. He refuses to understand that Sunday is sacred in Seattle, so he keeps pushing to get graduation moved from our

Sabbath to theirs." The Hillel Rabbi's highly publicized commencement crusade was troublesome to many of Seattle's attention-averse Jews.

"Oh stop complaining. If you didn't love your work, you wouldn't have been doing it all these years." I often envied Arlene, not for her money or good looks, but because she spent every weekday from nine to three at the U keeping the Hillel office and events running smoothly while mothering homesick Jewish students. She didn't need the money and donated her small salary to the organization she served, but Arlene Golden had a job worth doing, and she loved it.

"So tell me, who was this diarist and what did she have to do with my grandmother?"

I summarized what I'd read of Feigele's immigration and life in America and the events leading up to her arrival and imprisonment in Seattle. "So your grandmother sprung her from jail, took her home, fed and clothed her, taught her English, and gave her work sewing. Even introduced her to Reform Judaism. And when her English was good enough, your grandfather gave her a job doing alterations in his store. Who knows what might have happened to her if Ava and Nathan Weiss hadn't come along?"

"I never knew my grandmother, but you make her sound like a one-woman Settlement House, like your mom." I attacked my sandwich. "Manya Wilenski's been dead for over twenty years and people still talk about how she greeted refugees when they got off the train and how she tossed their luggage into a wheelbarrow and pushed it all the way up First Hill. What was it they used to call her?"

My cringe was reflexive. "Manya the Mule." There with Arlene, I spoke those three words without shame, but when I was a child this crude tribute to my frumpy yenta mother's stubborn strength had plagued me. I hated trudging along behind her with those tired and scared people. I could still hear her gasping for breath and cursing at each puddle, see her calf muscles knot with every step.

"Right." Arlene was quiet a moment. "It seems fitting somehow that Manya Wilenski's daughter should be translating this poor dead immigrant girl's diary." After a pause, she asked. "Is it hard work, the translating?"

I was pleased by Arlene's interest in aspects of my project other than those having to do with her family. "It is hard. I use a magnifying glass. Sometimes I have to steam pages apart over a tea kettle. And I'm doing a transliteration too. But you know what the hardest part is?" Finishing her last mouthful of tuna and bread, she shook her head. "Not editing out her repetitions. She keeps insisting she's telling the truth over and over. It's as if she feared her diary would be read by someone who doubted her."

"Maybe she can't believe what's happening to her herself." Arlene's voice with its furry undertone made her speculation sound mysterious, secretive almost. "Those Holocaust survivors you interviewed had that problem, remember?" I'd discussed that project with Arlene over lunch too. "You said the survivors were afraid people wouldn't believe what they went through. Their worry sounds foolish to us. Who would question the Holocaust?"

She had a point, but before I could say so, Arlene continued. "Speaking of those survivors, I heard some women from the Jewish Federation and the librarians in the manuscript section of the U Library are teaming up to create an archive for Jewish historical documents." My friend's voice hummed with satisfaction. "Your translations of the survivors' stories and this diary and the diary itself could be preserved there."

"The tapes and transcripts I made of those interviews with survivors are moldering in my attic. And I was wondering what would become of the diary when I finished translating it."

"Things are changing." Arlene spoke as she opened her thermos. "There's also been talk about interviewing and taping some folks from our parents' generation before, you know . . ." She sighed and passed me the thermos of iced tea.

I figured she sighed because of her father. Like his father before him, Abe Weiss had benefited from Seattle's early affinity for German-Jewish money and business acumen. The son had parlayed the profits from his father's successful dry goods store into a lucrative network of investments and, of course, that founding membership in the Seattle Athletic Club. But times had changed. The Queen City's private clubs hadn't admitted any Jews in decades, not even the sons of their own Jewish founders. Early in the century when so many Eastern European Jews came here, anti-Semitism in the form of exclusion became a fact of life in Seattle, like the rain. But Abe Weiss refused to resign from the SAC publicly to protest. My father's usually mild tone had been laced with contempt when he added, "Abe Weiss says he prefers to fight the SAC's anti-Semitism 'from within.'"

But when Arlene spoke, it was of her own father's well-known philanthropy. "My dad will tell the interviewer all about his pet projects, cancer research and the United Jewish Appeal. He's being honored this year at the UJA dinner. Last year his cousin, old Daniel Meyer, got the same award, so Joe and I had to go to the banquet. Looks like we'll have to go again this year." She sighed once more.

Then, perhaps realizing that attending a boring banquet was not really a big problem, Arlene shifted gears. "So, what made you decide to take a job at Frederick & Nelson? Was it to take your mind off losing Harry?" I was tempted to tell her what Harry had done, why I had to go to work, but I hadn't told Sam or Marsha, so I couldn't possibly confide in Arlene Weiss Golden, make her privy to the financial woes of the ragtag Wilenski-Mazursky clan. I was relieved when she added a question I could answer. "I thought you wanted to teach again. Did you change your mind?"

"No. I filled out an application with the Board of Ed. They've probably done all their hiring for the fall, but it doesn't hurt to try."

"Good. I remember how much you liked teaching. And who knows? Maybe over the summer some young history teacher will get pregnant or move and voilá, an opening!"

There in the sunshine with the Mountain in full view, I dared to hope that Arlene was right. "From your mouth to God's ears."

"Would you like me to speak to my father, ask him to get one of his friends in the SAC to give God a little push?"

Touched by Arlene's wish to help me, I was tempted to say yes, but the prospect of benefiting from her father's membership in a club that wouldn't accept other Jews was distasteful. "Thanks, but I'll take my chances."

If Arlene was offended by my refusal, she didn't say so, but shrugged and murmured, "I wish you luck." Her coolness, if it had been there at all, dissipated while we caught one other up on the doings of our kids and, when we parted, it was with the usual promise to get together again soon. Little did I know that before long I'd be kicking myself for calling Arlene, for having shared Feigele's story with her.

Arlene wasn't the only one interested in Feigele's adventures. Yetta asked for updates whenever I visited. I tried to oblige the housebound invalid, but bringing order to her files demanded most of my time and attention. It was slow going. The woman was a packrat with a special penchant for paper. She'd saved receipts, news clippings, and assorted correspondence, mostly with the IRS. And for years Yetta had been "filing" these items without being able to read either the papers themselves or the labels on the existing folders. I sorted the messy detritus of her life into categories including Legal Matters, Loans, Home Expenses, Business Expenses, Medical Expenses, and Registration. This last was the euphemism I attached to the ledgers in which Yetta had tracked the comings and going of the "guests" at her "hotels." I began subdividing each of these categories. After only a couple of hours, my back ached, my eyes blurred, and the table was blanketed with heaps of documents. Before I left, I topped each pile with one of Yetta's hats. They made handy paperweights.

I didn't have to work at the store that evening and resolved to go to bed early. I warmed up a can of Chef Boyardee and was downing the contents when Tim Hunter called. "Rachel, sorry about the short notice, but can you stop by tomorrow? That detective finally dropped off the artifacts found with the bones. His timing couldn't be worse. Summer school ended yesterday, I leave for vacation the day after tomorrow, and I've got to keep these doodads locked up here, so could you come on over and have a look? Otherwise you'll have to wait until I get back."

I was scheduled to work until four. "Not until after four. Is that too late?"

"Nope. Summer school grades are due, so I'll be putting in a long day. A visit from you will be a bright spot." He'd probably need a break. We'd examine the artifacts together and discuss them, perhaps over a cup of coffee. There was no harm in having a cup of coffee with a colleague.

Chapter 11

. . . est mit bayde hent **. . . . . . eats with both hands . . .**

That afternoon, before I left the store, I freshened my lipstick, smoothed my French twist, and reached under my skirt to yank down my blouse so it clung just a little. When I knocked on the door of Tim's office and stepped in, he looked up from the exam he was reading. "Hi, Rachel, you're a sight for sore eyes." He raked his hair with his fingers. "I keep forgetting that many of our grad students can't put a decent sentence together, and some haven't heard a word I've said all semester. Two more sets of these confounded treatises to plow through before I say *sayonara* to this place for a few weeks." Shaking his head, he unlocked a lower desk drawer, took out a manila envelope, and, without ceremony, handed it to me. "Here. See what you make of these. You can look at them in Carston Horner's office down the hall. He's up in British Columbia recording Indian dialects. Roberta will unlock it for you."

My disappointment at Tim's brush-off was tempered by curiosity about the objects found with Feigele's bones. I gently shook the dead girl's keepsakes out of the envelope onto the green blotter on Carston Horner's desk. There was her locket, no bigger than a quarter, brown with tarnish, and battered shut. It didn't yield to my efforts to pry it open with my nail file, but I was sure that inside I'd find Feigele's tresses twisted together with those of her little brother. On the blackened chain with the locket was a thimble, also tarnished and mis-shapen. I stared at Feigele's mother's parting gifts, the locket a talisman whose power was ancestral, and the thimble a small shield against the pricks endemic to the needle trade. Even though these trinkets had provided little protection in the New World, Feigele wore them around her neck until the end. Then and there I resolved to send Manya's wedding ring to Marsha.

The only surprises to emerge from the envelope were a few niblet-sized nuggets of what looked like gold and a small red gemstone with enough scratches visible to my naked eye to make me pretty sure it was glass. Against the green blotter, the gold bits and the fake ruby gleamed as if on display in a jewelry shop. I'd read nothing about them in the diary, and I'd brought the little book with me, so I unwrapped it and found my place. The next entry followed four jagged page edges, giving the volume's spine the feel and look of the frayed inside seam of a cheap skirt. The entry itself was undated. I scanned it as rapidly as I could without translating, hoping to find some reference to the nuggets and the crimson bauble.

Feigele's Diary, Seattle

I turn to this book as I once turned to God for comfort. If I write what happened, maybe the memory will become less painful. Even though it happened months ago, I remember every beautiful moment and every hateful word. Daniel Meyer, the son of Nathan Weiss's sister, came from San Francisco to work at Weiss and Company. He is living with Ava's sister and her husband in their big house on Capitol Hill. The moment I saw Daniel I felt my heart, the very same heart I thought Bernie Olafsky had stolen along with my money, beat once again in my chest. Daniel is polite and educated like Meier Horowitz, but maybe a little quieter. Daniel came to the Weiss's for dinner on Friday nights. I sat at the table as usual with a giant frog on my tongue and said only my pleases and thank-yous.

I did not dare to hope that Daniel would notice me at the store, but without my telling them to, my feet started walking out onto the sales floor when he was there. He began to converse with me. Soon he was finding reasons to appear in the back room where I sewed. Then one day when I went out to walk at lunchtime, he joined me.

And then every day at lunch we strolled together. Daniel taught me words for the items in the shop windows. He spoke to me of his parents. "My mother is very smart and educated, like her sister-in-law Ava. She also helps others less fortunate." I liked how proud he was of his mama. He said his father owns a big store like Weiss and Company, only it is in San Francisco. He was proud of his papa, too. Daniel spoke to me of his dreams. "I want to go into the family business, to start more stores, perhaps in Tacoma and Spokane. I came here to learn from my uncle." Then, I swear, he stopped walking and looked down into my eyes and said, "I'm glad I came."

He asked me all about my childhood, where I lived, how I became such a good seamstress, and what brought me all the way to Seattle where I have not a single relative. I answered his questions with care, especially the last one. I did not know what Ava and Nathan told him about me, if they told him anything, but I said nothing of Bernie Olafsky.

Instead I told him most of the truth. "I came to Seattle because I have no family in New York either and never will. Besides, I was unhappy with my cramped living arrangement and my work. I made the same section of a garment over and over. This boring repetitious work was beneath my ability and did not allow me to advance." He seemed so interested and wanted to know why I chose Seattle over say Chicago or Detroit or Philadelphia. Again I told him most of the truth, that I heard Seattle had lots of room and plenty of work. I told him about George Washington.

Daniel Meyer listened as if every word I said was important and this made my English words flow easily, made me hope. I hoped that he was beginning to care for me as a man cares about a woman. On the last day we walked together I told him that someday I would like to have my own dressmaking shop like Hanele's. Until I began to walk and talk with Daniel, I had not even told myself that I had this ambition. It was inside me but I did not know. Daniel said I was very brave. These are his exact words, "You are so courageous. I've never known a girl like you. All the girls I grew up with think only about what they're wearing and what party they're going to next. Your English may not be perfect yet, Fanny, but I've never had such interesting conversations with a girl before." When I heard that, I allowed myself to believe that instead of keeping us apart our different positions in the world would draw us together like my curved magnet draws in the straight pins.

The very next morning, I arrived at the store a little early to take in a jacket. Soon I heard talking in the office. I recognized Nathan's voice. But when I heard Daniel's voice I pressed my ear to the wall and listened hard. Nathan was talking. "I'm telling you, Daniel, you can't get involved with Fanny. Be reasonable, son. Ava found the girl in jail." I couldn't hear what Daniel said in reply, but Nathan kept on. "She got picked up by the police along with two other whores. Come on, Daniel, how do you think that makes the rest of us Jews look?" Again I could not hear Daniel's reply, but Nathan was quiet only a second or two so Daniel could not have said much. Then came Nathan's sharp voice again. "Fanny was one of Ava's most challenging projects. She practically scalded the clothes the girl had on and taught her to bathe." Why didn't Daniel defend me or get up and walk out? Nathan still wasn't finished. "Daniel, your parents will never forgive me if you get involved with her. Like the rest of those kikes pouring into the country now, she has no education. She's a greenhorn from some Godforsaken Eastern European shtetl that I can't even pronounce. Her real name is Feigele, and she eats with both hands, like a peasant."

I was numb all the rest of that day, could hardly stitch straight. Is that who Nathan Weiss really sees when he looks at me? A kike? A peasant? An ignorant greenhorn? A dirty Jew? A whore? A jailbird? Is that what I am? If that is what he says I am, what is the high and mighty Mr. Nathan Weiss but a Jew hater? And a man who speaks out of two sides of his mouth. I know Nathan and Ava Weiss think I am a good seamstress. That's why he paid me so well. And how many times did he say I am a quick learner because I improved my English so fast? But my sewing and my intelligence were not what he chose to speak of to his nephew.

And I did not hear that nephew utter a single word in my defense. Not one. And he did not stomp out of the office either. That awful morning with my ear to the wall was when I realized that Daniel Meyer would never be the father of my children. I would look for work elsewhere. Even now it hurts me to recall those words and after writing them in this book, tears sting my eyes. I can write no more today.

Fanny's Diary, Seattle, November 5, 1894

I've been too busy to finish my story, but no one is home now and I have an evening to myself. I could not work anymore for Nathan Weiss. I told him only that I had an opportunity to sew somewhere else for better money. He was angry and called me an "ungrateful little trollop." I looked that word up later in my dictionary. I left the store right after that without seeing Daniel Meyer again.

With my savings I bought a sewing machine and three weeks ago I made a bridal gown for Devorah's friend Shoshana. She could not pay much, but Devorah and Myron did not mind if Shoshana came to my room for fittings. Shoshana told her friends about me, and now I have other brides to sew for and sometimes a Jewish palm to read after a fitting. I am not making too much money, but I have no boss! My room at Devorah and Myron's is my shop. I buy fabric and make gowns that suit each customer and charge what is fair.

When I am not sewing, I read palms at the Greek coffeehouse near the water or take care of little Leah. I like the feel of her in my arms and the way her small soft body gets even softer when I sing to her and she falls asleep against my chest. With a comfortable place to live and enough work, I should be content; but the memory of Nathan Weiss's cruel words still pains me and the memory of Daniel Meyer's silence does too. When I am not remembering the pleasure I took in his company, I remember that silence, can hear it in my heart.

Nathan Weiss, Arlene Golden's grandfather, was an arrogant and snobby bastard, a Jewish anti-Semite. It was as if the man took Feigele's bruised but still-beating heart in his fist and squeezed it until her dreams dripped red between his fingers. Was I over-dramatizing? Harry said I had a tendency to do that. But Nathan Weiss badmouthed and belittled the latest wave of Jewish refugees while professing concern for how poor Feigele's awful night in jail reflected badly on Seattle's assimilated Jews. His indictment of her was an indictment of me and my family.

It had been drilled into me that Jewish self-hatred was a reflection of the hatred of others, but I still couldn't forgive the man. It pissed me off that even in 1965, Seattle's German-Jews, well born, educated, and Reform, still felt superior to shtetl-born, pious, poor, pogrom-plagued Yids like Feigele, like the Wilenskis and Mazurskys for that matter. I taught Irish and Italian kids who spurned less assimilated classmates. And Bess described the Southern black girl who worked for Yetta's neighbor as a "know-nothing field hand." So it wasn't only Jews who let accents, table manners, and education divide us. Still, I wished I hadn't told Arlene that her grandparents had taken Feigele in and nurtured the girl. That was only half the story.

The other half was that Arlene's own father had been raised by a man who called his fellow Jews *kikes.* Given who raised him, it was no wonder Abe Weiss refused to make like a Jewish Martin Luther King and demand equal access to the whole American dream, membership in the damn Seattle Athletic Club, for Seattle's Jewish businessmen. The man was a bigot like his father. And what if Daniel Meyer continued to see Feigele after all? Was it possible that Nathan Weiss, my friend's grandfather, was not just a bigot but also a murderer? Horrified anew, this time by my own suspicions, I re-read the offending passage.

Finding references to the nuggets and the red gem could wait. Talking with Tim Hunter could wait. I wanted to talk with Daniel Meyer, a man who had actually known Feigele. Arlene mentioned a cousin of her father's named Daniel Meyer being honored by the UJA last year. He must be the one, must be nearly ninety. What did this old man remember about Feigele? I carefully closed and repackaged the diary and returned the artifacts to their envelope.

I knocked on the door to Tim's office. There was no answer. I tried turning the knob. The door was locked. Damn. I'd missed him. I headed down the corridor to the desk where the department secretary was typing. "Roberta, I'm sorry to bother you, but Tim's door is locked. I have to return this envelope before he leaves for vacation. The artifacts that turned up with that diary I'm translating are in it. May I leave it with you to keep for him?"

"I thought Tim was still here."

"The door's locked. I knocked and there was no answer, so . . ." I put the envelope on Roberta's desk.

"Those things should be under lock and key. I can't keep them here. My desk drawers don't lock." Roberta was on her feet. "Come with me. I'll open his door and you can leave this on his desk yourself." She handed the envelope back to me, and I accompanied her down the corridor. "I'm telling you, Rachel, the professors are worse than the kids. They leave everything for the last minute. Grades are due tomorrow. Tim's probably just locked himself in to finish up."

She inserted her key in the lock, turned it, and pushed. Almost at once Roberta backed out trying to pull the door closed behind her. Determined to leave the artifacts, I pushed by her. It was only then that I saw Tim, his back to the doorway as he bent over the desk, his naked butt jack-hammering away. I saw all that before I even noticed the girl's slim bare legs tangled in his trousers, heard his grunts.

I dropped the manila envelope on a chair, pivoted, and left, yanking the door shut. Tim Hunter hadn't brushed me off earlier because of all the work he had to do. The only thing busy about him that afternoon was his butt. One glimpse of that bare professorial behind going at it served as an instant antidote to my infatuation.

As we hurried back up the corridor, Roberta was the first to speak. "That Tim Hunter. I swear they must put something in the water the way some of these professors carry on nowadays. And the students!" Her keys jangled as she raised her hands to hold her head, her gesture reflecting my own dismay.

But the dismay I felt had more to do with my own narrow escape than with the sexual turbulence of our times. And it also had to do with Tim Hunter as reader of Feigele's diary, an ongoing preoccupation of mine. After seeing the professor in action, I wondered how sympathetic he would or could be to the young woman's outpourings. An adulterer on the prowl in my once-staid alma mater, Tim himself preyed on girls like Feigele or, for that matter, like my Marsha. And he would have preyed on me, but having seen him going at it, I knew I just wasn't that lonely.

Chapter 12

. . . il lidlle iz in mein hartz . . .

. . . her song in my heart . . .

Driving home I focused on the conversation Feigele claimed to have overheard between Nathan Weiss and Daniel Meyer. Perhaps because Feigele insisted so often on the truth of what she wrote, I wondered if she invented the exchange between the two men to explain Daniel's lack of interest in her. Almost before I'd fully conceptualized this possibility, I dismissed it. Everybody knew that German-Jews thought they were better than the rest of us, just like we Eastern European Jews, except for my father of course, figured we were better than the Sephardics. But even more convincing were the splotches on the pages recounting Nathan Weiss's harangue. I was sure they were tear stains.

I found Daniel Meyer listed in the phone book. I was glad because I dreaded having to ask Arlene where to reach the old man. Again I wished I'd never mentioned her family's role in Feigele's life. Arlene preferred to see her own father as a generous philanthropist rather than as a coward who kept silent about anti-Semitism at the SAC. She'd probably never speak to me again after I exposed her dead grandfather as an anti-Semite or worse.

But I was getting ahead of myself again. That's why as soon as I dialed Daniel Meyer's number, I put the receiver down. I'd talked to Arlene before I read all Feigele had to say about the Weiss family, and I regretted it. I didn't want to make the same mistake twice. So I resolved not to contact Daniel Meyer or Abe Weiss until I finished reading and translating the diary. I needed to know as much as Feigele had to tell me about the rest of her truncated life before I started accusing my friend's relatives of being Jew-haters let alone murderers.

At the top of a sheet of loose-leaf paper, I wrote "To-do" and jotted down Daniel Meyer's name and phone number. Abe Weiss came next. I'd add the names of any other people Feigele mentioned who might still be alive or have descendants living locally and, after I finished translating, I'd try to contact them. The familiar format that I used for listing my domestic chores reassured me. Resolute, I opened the diary again.

But before I resumed reading, I ran my fingers very gently along the three narrow and jagged edges of paper protruding like sepia stained rickrack from the spine of the little book. Again I wondered what Feigele had written that she regretted enough to rip out. Had there been more to her relationship with Daniel Meyer? Or had she written of something else entirely and excised that? The next entry appeared over a year after the last dated one. A lot could happen in a year. A woman could get pregnant and give birth. Had Daniel Meyer gotten Feigele pregnant? On my list I jotted "Baby with Daniel Meyer" and added a question mark. Most likely I was, as Harry used to say, "imagining things."

When I told Yetta of Feigele's latest heartbreak, I heaped scorn on Nathan Weiss. "According to Feigele, Abe Weiss's father was a Jew who felt, articulated, and acted on contempt for other Jews. Worse yet, he passed his bigotry on to the next generation."

"I don't see why you're so surprised. Jews who come here want to fit in, to be American. That's why we came. Those who can do that when they arrive have two choices. They can stay away from the *Yids* whose English isn't so good or who don't keep clean. Americans worship cleanliness. A pious man with BO is out of luck here." She chuckled.

"What's the other choice?" I asked, but I knew.

"To do what Ava Weiss did, what your mother did, what all those do-gooder Jewish women's groups try to do, clean us up, teach us English, get us jobs. But even then the German Jews still don't want their kids to marry us." There was something touching about the way Yetta included herself among the unwashed.

"Speaking of jobs, I better get to work."

"I can take a hint." Yetta stood. When I could no longer hear her cane tapping, I threw open the drapes and turned on the lights.

I pored over many documents I'd only scanned before. Some of them were so intertwined as to defy the neat categories I'd invented. Stretching and arching my aching back, I wondered if I'd have to revise the filing system that, I had hoped, would accommodate her messy and intermingled records of deals, doctors, and purchases. That evening it was a relief to turn to Feigele's relatively straightforward and usually chronological account.

Fanny's Diary, Seattle, February 12, 1895

Nothing bad has driven me to write in many months. I live a busy life sewing and reading palms and being like an aunt to little Leah. But one day a few weeks ago I was on my way to the coffeehouse when I met Desiree and Suzanne. This time when they asked me to make them dresses, I agreed. I am tired of making bridal gowns for others to wear.

But I knew Devorah and Myron would not want two "fallen women" or "soiled doves" coming to their home, so I arranged to meet my newest customers at their rooms. Where they live is brick and so fancy that a king should live there. The letters on the door read *Lou Graham*. Suzanne told me that she and Desiree work for Lou, and that Lou's girls cater only to powerful local officials, businessmen, and visiting dignitaries. Desiree said Lou runs a clean house and watches out for her girls. "Working for Lou is a lot better than entertaining roughnecks in some crummy crib on Skid Road." That is what they call Yesler Street where the logs skid downhill to the mill. There are a lot of lowlife places on Skid Road.

A male servant answered the bell and escorted me through a huge parlor, bigger and fancier by far than the Weiss's. I noticed a piano at one end of the room and drapes made of red velvet. When we passed a dining room with walls of gold, my mouth fell open so wide my chin nearly hit my toes. The servant took me upstairs. Suzanne's room was also very fancy, with wallpaper of rose silk and a big bed that looked like a rose-colored cloud.

After I measured her, she gave me the fabric she had sent for, a roll of shimmering silk, the same green as her eyes. Suzanne asked me how I thought the dress should fall, and while we were talking Desiree came in with a roll of black satin that set off her red hair. I measured her. Again my toes were in danger from my chin when Desiree said, "Charge what you will, Fanny. Lou pays for her girls' clothes." There was no sign of this Lou, but Desiree told me to be on Main Street on Sunday afternoon when I could see Lou's carriage driving back and forth over several blocks with a few of her girls waving at bystanders. Desiree and Suzanne planned to wear the dresses I was making for them on a Sunday drive with Lou.

Desiree was laughing about how she was going to "initiate" the son of one of the City's most important families that evening. They had to cut our visit short because the doctor who comes regularly to check on their health arrived. As I lugged the bolts of fabric back to my plain little room at Devorah's, I marveled at the luxury and good cheer I had glimpsed.

Desiree and Suzanne paid me more for each dress than I made in a month at Weiss and Company. Desiree said, "Why, Fanny, this dress is as stylish as any I've had from Paris." And Suzanne said, "This is the most becoming dress I've ever owned, Fanny." Now the other girls at Lou's want dresses, so I have a lot of work and my savings account is growing again. I enjoy designing their dresses and making the patterns to suit each woman. My brides want white dresses in the current modest style, but these women dress in many sparkling shades and welcome designs that are unusual. Their conversation, too, is exciting.

But last week Devorah saw the lush and colorful fabrics I was sewing sequins on and realized that I was making dresses for women who were "less than respectable." A kind and well-meaning woman, Devorah worries about me. Now over and over she says, "You need a husband, Fanny. When you have a husband and a baby and your own home to take care of, you'll have no time for making dresses for those no-good women." Then she pats her stomach, once again swollen with a child. Like Chaya, Devorah is content with her husband, her babies, and her endless domestic chores. I do not answer her. Maybe she is right.

ꟹ

Fanny's Diary, April 8, 1896

Today I had an argument with Devorah which has left me upset. What if she and Myron decide I am no longer fit to live in their home? It started as usual when Devorah saw me stitching beads on the bodice of a green silk negligee for Desiree. Devorah started in again on how my customers are low women not fit to associate with. "Leah is getting older. What if she realizes you're making clothes for prostitutes? What will I tell her?"

Usually when Devorah talks like this, I talk about something else or remind her how well I am paid. But this was the first time she brought little Leah into the discussion and that made me angry. I tried to explain. "Desiree and Suzanne are my friends. If not for them, I might still be in jail. They went out of their way to help me get out of that lousy cell. And they did it not because my being in jail made them look bad but because they saw how sad and frightened I was and took pity on me. You could tell Leah that Desiree and Suzanne are my good friends, and they are kind."

"Kind does not matter if they are bad women. And if you take their money, maybe you are no better than they are. You need a husband. Myron thinks so too. Then you would not have time or need to sew for them." Devorah, with her big belly, who vomits all morning and scrubs her kitchen floor all afternoon, thinks a husband is the solution to all of my problems. I did not argue more with her because she loves her Myron and they too have been kind to me. They treat me more like a friend or a relative than a roomer. But what I did say was maybe worse. "Devorah, if Lou Graham herself hired Myron to paint all the rooms in her big house, would he go to work for her?"

Devorah did not have to stop and think for even one second before she answered. "Of course he would. What a question!"

"Well, then, what is wrong with me making dresses for her employees? It's the same thing, isn't it?"

I swear Devorah's answer was this. "No it is not the same, Fanny. Myron is a man with a wife and child to feed and another one coming. He cannot turn away work and stay in business." Then she stomped out of my room. I wonder who she thinks is putting food in my mouth and keeping this roof over my head. But I hope this fight does not lead to anything because I have no desire to look for a room elsewhere. Whatever family I rented from would feel as Devorah does.

ꝏ

Fanny's Diary, Seattle, January 4, 1897

I haven't had time to write because my work keeps me busy all day and Devorah's brother, Avram Pinsker, visits almost every night since he got here a few months ago. He is a greenhorn from Poland, a housepainter. He speaks slowly and with a slight stammer and stares at me with hungry eyes, like Yekel, may he rest in peace. Devorah asked me to help Avram learn English, but I suspect she has other reasons for wanting him to know me. If he is not too tired from painting houses all day and if it is not raining, we go walking in the evening.

The other night I spoke for the first time of Mama and Papa and little Yitzak, may they rest in peace. I spoke of how Mama used to sing us to sleep, how I still hear her song in my heart. When he saw my tears, Avram took my hand in his right there on the street. I did not pull my hand away. This is America and the man has a kind heart. With my hand still in his, his calloused thumb moving over my knuckles, he stammered, "I mean no disrespect."

ꝏ

Fanny's Diary, Seattle, July 10, 1897

I come here once again to sort out my thoughts. They are thoughts about Avram. There is much to admire about this Avram Pinsker. He works very hard and has his life planned out. He hopes to earn enough money to buy or rent a small building and open a paint store. He wants to marry and live in an apartment over the store. Perhaps his wife's dowry will help him get started. Someday his wife and children will help him run the store. Tonight was the first time he mentioned his hope of a dowry. I thought of my savings account in Mr. Furth's bank. After Bernie's betrayal, with Mr. Furth's help, I have guarded my savings carefully.

Then Avram asked me about my plans. This question tangled up my tongue. Even though I am a palmist who predicts the future of complete strangers, I could not find a single word for my own. Finally I said that I am no longer in the habit of planning far into the future. When he heard that, Avram stopped walking and faced me, so I stopped too. Those eyes of his stared into mine, and he spoke without a trace of a stammer. He said that he wants me to plan on becoming Mrs. Avram Pinsker.

Do I want to marry Avram? Ava and Nathan Weiss would say he's an uneducated Yid, a stuttering peasant with crude table manners, coarse clothes, and paint under his fingernails. But Mama and Papa would speak of how hard Avram works, how regularly he prays, and of the good reputation of his family. And I have grown fond of Devorah and Myron. We have our disagreements, but they are kind-hearted and pious. Like them, Avram does not approve of many of my customers, but if we married, maybe I could change his mind. Besides, I am getting older. If I don't marry and have children, who will read this diary? I should marry Avram.

It had taken pride and guts to leave the employ of Nathan Weiss and the aura of his appealing nephew. Feigele's hardships had made her more thoughtful, more calculating, more observant. She'd learned to guard her money and weigh the pros and cons of big decisions. Even so, I was relieved that she was about to make a marriage promising stability if not romance, and material comfort if not excess, kind of like what Marjorie Morningstar ended up doing. Then I remembered that my marriage to Harry had also promised stability and modest comfort. I hoped Feigele had better luck. I hoped the girl enjoyed many good years before her killer struck, that she and Avram had kids and grandkids.

No sooner had I imagined these progeny then I resolved to track them down. With the name of a head-of-household, Avram Pinsker, I might actually find Feigele listed in the Seattle census for 1900 when those figures finally became available in 1972. While I added Avram's name to my list, I pictured a graying version of myself placing the diary and translation into the hand of Feigele's grandson or granddaughter. I envisioned this grateful descendant at last saying *Kaddish* for the diarist and reading the words she wrote.

But in the meantime I'd resolved to include Feigele in the growing list of those for whom I already said the Mourner's Prayer. Counting my mother and now Harry, and, of course, the Holocaust victims, Feigele would be the six million and third dead person I thought of when I stood and joined the congregation to recite the ancient words of praise. So when I entered the spacious new sanctuary of Temple De Hirsch that Friday evening, I was a woman with a mission.

But the Sabbath is a time for rest and reflection. So while I scanned the pews for an empty seat, I reviewed events in my own life since the damn quake killed the steady provider I thought I'd married, leaving me to mourn instead a deceitful and irresponsible stranger. No longer was I a bored housewife. Now I had two jobs and no husband. I filed for a woman who had profited from selling the bodies of other women, and I sold fancy flatware to debutantes and dowagers. Thanks to that quake I was translating Feigele's diary, seeing Seattle's Jews through her outsider's eyes. That quake had spun me into the orbit of the predatory Professor Hunter, a married student-*shtupper* who wasn't even Jewish. Plus I hadn't heard from Marsha for a few days. And I hadn't heard from the Board of Education at all.

Halfway down the center aisle I froze mid-stride like a bride having second thoughts. A glimpse of the side of a man's head, his ear, stopped me in my tracks. I would know that ragged flap anywhere. It belonged to Bobby Gradstein. I slid into an empty seat on the aisle directly behind him just as the congregation stood for the opening of the ark containing the Torah. I reached out and tugged at the remains of Bobby's left ear lobe. He swiveled as he rose, and I started at the scowling face nearly hidden behind a flowing silvering beard. It was the face of a prophet, stern and sharp-featured, eyes ablaze. But when those eyes met mine, they softened, and, behind his facial hair, I saw the scowl also soften into Bobby's familiar smirk. What was he doing back in town? At our class reunion, before he became incoherent, Bobby spoke of New York as the be-all and the end-all in that smug way that New Yorkers do. Besides, wasn't he at the wrong synagogue? His mother belonged to Orthodox Bikkur Cholim, now relocated to Seward Park.

The rest of the service was a pastiche of familiar Sabbath songs and prayers, and I allowed the traditional melodies and words and the proximity of old friends, including Bobby, to soothe me. Like Feigele, I needed a Sabbath, a respite from grief, worry, and work. When Rabbi Glick invited the congregation to rise for the Mourners' Prayer, I stood, and when he read the names of those congregants who had died during that week in years past and asked for any additional names, I fudged the dates only a little, and whispered my mother's name and then Harry's and after him I flashed on The Six Million. Then I pronounced the names, "Feigele Lindner-Aliza Rudinsk," adding the twice dead girl's real name just to make sure. I chanted the guttural tongue-twisting Aramaic syllables in practiced unison with the rest of the congregation and so said *Kaddish* for Feigele. When the prayer ended, I sank once more into the pew and muttered a few words to God. They came out in Yiddish. "*Brengen tsu keyver yisroel.*"

"What's this about you bringing somebody to a Jewish cemetery? My mother told me your husband was buried at Temple De Hirsch's boneyard. And who the hell are Feigele Lindner and that other woman?" As we made our way up the aisle at the end of the service Bobby took my arm in the same brusque and proprietary way that I'd tugged at his ear. He was firing questions at me as if he had seen me yesterday and had a right to instant answers.

"I'll tell you later," I promised. Our arm-in-arm march up the aisle made me feel like a bride, heady after that first married kiss and eager to greet well-wishers with my groom at my side. When we reached the vestibule, Bobby did indeed stay close while we each chatted with old friends.

"You're a hard woman to get on the phone, Rachel." The reporter's knowing glance took in the man at my side. I recalled Jake Heller's note nestled among the rugelach: *I've been down the road you're on. I know all the potholes . . . .* "Are you ready to tell me about that book you're translating?"

I shook my head. "Not yet. I'll call you." He smiled politely and left.

My own lips had arranged themselves in a smile that was more than polite. It had been a while since I smiled spontaneously at friends, and that night it felt smooth and easy like that first sweet swallow of ice cream after a tonsillectomy. Even as I accepted belated condolences and put off dinner invitations, I felt more like a newlywed than a widow. When Bobby and I finally broke away, I asked him, "Do you need a lift? I've got my car. I'll drop you at your mom's."

"Only if I can buy you a drink first."

Chapter 13

In minutes Bobby and I were in a booth at Victor Rossellini's, a popular downtown restaurant Harry had taken me to only once, on our twentieth anniversary. Harry made light of the expense, saying he'd earned a big commission that week, but now I wondered. Maybe he'd really paid for our extravagant meal with poker winnings. This possibility sullied a warm marital memory.

Bobby sniffed the garlicky air. "So when did people on the frontier start dining instead of just eating?" I didn't answer but looked across the table at him and shook my head.

"What are you shaking your head about? Is it this?" He tugged at his beard. "It's a real timesaver."

"No. It's just strange for us to be sitting here together, all grown up." I sighed. "We used to sit around in your room while our parents were downstairs listening to the news. We had our whole lives ahead of us then. Now we're in a fancy restaurant, and your father and my mother are gone. We've had two more wars. You're divorced and I'm widowed. I have a daughter." I paused for breath. "God, Bobby, my daughter's older than we were then." Still shaking my head, I wound down. "It feels strange. I've seen you exactly twice since you left for the military . . ."

"Yeah, I know. My old man's funeral and then that damn reunion when I got loaded and puked in your car. Maybe you're the only one who's grown up."

I looked my old friend in the eye. "No. You've changed. You've been through so much. I mean the War and all that schooling and your hospital work." Bobby, who in high school rarely got a grade higher than a C minus, rode the GI Bill through NYU pre-med and then earned his MD there. He'd been directing the emergency room at Mount Sinai for years. I didn't mention his marriage and divorce again when listing the catalytic events in his life, but I was hoping he'd bring them up. "Now it's like here we are, '*tsvey mesim geyen tantsn.*'" For the second time that evening, a Yiddish phrase slipped out unbidden.

His eyes narrowed before he translated, "'Two corpses go dancing,' right?"

"Right."

"Speak for yourself. I'm very much alive. And I'll bring you back to life." He shrugged. "That's what I do these days."

Our waiter materialized before I figured out if Bobby was being arrogant or flip or simply describing his work in the emergency room.

"Hungry? Of course you are. What are you drinking?" After he ordered our drinks and an antipasto platter, he cocked his head and looked at me. "So how the hell are you? My mom says you're coping, but your husband's death like that had to be quite a shock, quite a loss. How are you really?" He reached over and placed his hand, palm up on the table. I was about to reach for a cigarette, but instead I placed my hand in his and felt his fist close around it, warm, natural. I didn't even think to look around to see if anyone we knew was there and noticed the recent widow holding hands with the bearded stranger. "And how's your daughter? My mom says she's in New York at your cousin's. Maybe when I get back, I can take her out to dinner, show her around."

Bobby's offer touched me. "Marsha would like that. She's heard a lot of stories about you."

"I bet she has." Bobby didn't relinquish my hand when the waiter brought our drinks. "I'll give her a call."

"*L'chaim*, to life." Lifting my glass, I imagined the hand holding mine soothing fevered brows and binding terrible wounds.

"To your resurrection." Bobby clinked his martini glass against the one holding my scotch. He sipped and nodded his approval. "So who is this Feigele Lindner you're saying *Kaddish* for? That name doesn't ring a bell."

I explained in some detail how Feigele's bones were discovered and about translating her diary. I told him about her struggles and that she was murdered. Two more scotches and several glasses of wine as well as my anger over Feigele's sorry fate inflamed my storytelling. By the time I finished, Bobby was digging into a plate of veal Marsala and I was savoring lamb chops. "So tonight I said *Kaddish* for her, and I'm going to arrange to have her buried at Temple De Hirsch's cemetery."

Naming the synagogue triggered my earlier curiosity, so without waiting for Bobby to reply or signaling a change in subject, I asked, "Speaking of Temple De Hirsch, what were you doing there? Your mother . . ."

"I know. My mother belongs to Bikkur Cholim, so I should be over in Seward Park with her, right?" Bobby's Yiddish-inflected singsong response made audible the contempt he felt for those outgrown filial expectations.

"Right. But you don't go to services. Your parents practically had to tie you up to get you to go to your own bar mitzvah. Have you gotten religion in New York?"

"Are you kidding? New York is wall-to-wall Jews. I don't have to work at being Jewish there." Bobby grinned. "You know what Lenny Bruce says?"

I shook my head. Harry had not approved of the notoriously foul-mouthed comic.

"He says in a big city like New York, everybody's a Jew, even if they're Catholic. But if you live in, say, Butte, Montana, you're going to be *goyishe* even if you're Jewish. The man's a genius, a prophet, really."

I nodded, but, at that moment, my interest in why Bobby had shown up at the wrong synagogue was far greater than my interest in Lenny Bruce. I persisted. "So did you just want to see our new building?" Seattle's recently dedicated Reform temple, a descendant of the synagogue Feigele had visited, was second in size only to New York's Temple Emanu-El.

My question flitted over the table between us during the long seconds it took for Bobby to push his empty plate away, light a cigarette, take a drag, and speak. "I figured you'd be there saying *Kaddish* for your husband and for Manya. So I grabbed a cab at the airport and went straight there." He paused. "I went there looking for you, not God. I'm back here just to see you, Rachel."

Maybe it was the scotch and wine that enabled me to hear the urgency that made Bobby's explanation a confession. His intensity was both gratifying and disorienting. I sipped my wine and sought refuge in the mundane. "But your mother . . ."

"Doesn't know I'm in town yet unless some yenta we met tonight calls to tell her . . . but she won't answer the phone on the Sabbath, so . . . Anyway I don't have to get my mom's permission to pay a belated condolence call on an old friend, do I? I really have grown up, and I came back here to see you." He offered me a drag on his cigarette.

I shook my head and giggled. I felt giddy and young and pretty, like that Puerto Rican girl in *West Side Story*. "You may look like Moses now, but behind all that fuzz you're still a nut." As I spoke of his beard, I imagined it against my skin. So I was not at all taken aback when I heard my own voice proclaim, "Screwing you would be practically incest."

Bobby, however, greeted my alcohol-inspired pronouncement with raised brows and a grin that quickly became a frown, both barely discernible behind the beard. His only other response was to signal our waiter for a check.

But wine glass in hand, I had more to say, a last slurred hurrah from my super ego before it drowned in alcohol. "I didn't stop taking the Pill when that son of a bitch died." My wine glass fell to the table as a sob tore its way up out of my gut, ripped through my chest, and left my mouth as a long, low moan. That's all I remember.

To hear Bobby tell it, I was still sobbing when he paid the check and, carrying my purse, propelled me out onto the street. He didn't steer me to my car, but instead held me up against him and marched me, weeping and wobbling, around the block, uphill and downhill, too many times to count. Every now and then he wiped my nose with his handkerchief. Eventually he fumbled through my purse for the car keys, poured me into the passenger seat of the Chevy, and got me to name my street.

After he maneuvered me up the steep steps and into the house, Bobby filled a glass with water and insisted I drink it. Then he insisted I drink two more. I did, even though I kept trying to get to the sofa so I could lie down. Bobby had other plans for me. He nudged me up the stairs ahead of him and into the bathroom. "Strip, please." As he recounted later, I stood on the red bath mat and then, leaning against the sink, began to fumble with the buttons of my blouse. He claimed I stood there glassy-eyed like a "boozy bathroom Botticelli" until he took my hand, assuring me safe passage over the side of the tub. Then, with my hand still in his, he turned on the cold water in the shower full force. That part I remember. I snatched my hand away. "Shit! Shit! It's cold. What are you doing? Shit! Jesus!" And then, "Bobby Gradstein, I hate you!"

"That's more like it." I heard him on the other side of the shower curtain counting, a steady bass line beneath my shrieks and curses. I reached for the tap, but he grabbed my hand before I could turn off the water. Finally he turned it off himself, handed me a towel, and watched me scale the side of the tub. Only then did he leave the bathroom. I heard his footsteps on the stairs. For a terrible moment I feared he might leave.

But as I crossed the hall to the bedroom, I heard noises from the kitchen. By the time I threw on a pair of jeans and one of Marsha's old tee shirts, I smelled coffee. Harry never learned how to work our coffee pot, could make only instant. Why was I thinking of poor Harry instead of feeling sheepish and embarrassed about my drunkenness? I'd never been that drunk before. God only knew what I'd said in that state. Had I thrown up? I shuddered and returned to the bathroom to brush my teeth.

"All better?" Bobby was seated at the kitchen table sipping scotch and smoking a cigarette. When I came in, he poured me coffee. "Milk? Sugar?" I shook my head, sat down in front of the steaming brew, and put a cigarette in my mouth. Bobby offered his lighter.

"Bobby, I'm so sorry. I've never . . ."

"No, you probably haven't. Relax. Now we're even, but you didn't puke in the car." He grinned. Then the grin disappeared. His eyes darkened. "So tell me, what did your late husband do to make him a 'son of a bitch?' Did he . . ."

I felt my face flush, realizing that under the influence, I must have bad-mouthed Harry. "No. No. Nothing like that. Did I say that? Harry never hit me or Marsha either." I sipped my coffee and steeled myself to explain out loud what to me still seemed inexplicable. "We had a savings account for Marsha's college tuition. Not too long before he died, Harry played in a high stakes poker game, and he lost. I didn't know. Our lawyer showed me a notarized IOU for nine thousand dollars that Harry signed. When he died so suddenly"— I snapped my fingers — "the guy he owed demanded payment and Bruce said to pay him, so I had to use Marsha's college money." I lowered my eyes. "Harry also borrowed on his life insurance. I'm working at Frederick & Nelson now."

It was Bobby's turn to shake his head. "Harry sounds more like a *schlimazel* than a son of a bitch." He sipped his drink and cleared his throat. "Listen, Rachel, we docs make out alright, so even after alimony I've got a few coins in the bank and a few shares of some decent stock. I can take care of that tuition for you."

"Thanks, but I'm pretty sure I've got it covered. But really, thanks." I reached across the table and stroked Bobby's bearded cheek. He took my hand and held it as I continued to talk. "It's just that I feel so stupid not having known about it, not having known what Harry was up to." I paused to find words for feelings I had never said aloud. "It's like Harry was a stranger, or two people. If I'd known what he did before he died, I'd have hated it. He had to know that. That's what's so terrible."

"If he'd lived, your husband might have paid back that debt without you ever finding out about it. He was a real go-getter at the reunion, even tried to sell me a policy." My eyes widened at this revelation. "He tried hard. That's the last thing I remember before I got loaded. But, on the other hand, had Harry lived, he might have tried to win the nine grand back and gone even deeper in the hole."

Bobby wasn't telling me anything I hadn't told myself, but it was a relief to speak aloud of Harry's betrayal. Since Bruce told me about it, Harry's misdeed had felt like a secret stain, soiling my memories and threatening to blacken Marsha's future. I was glad I confided in Bobby.

"You're not making big bucks at Frederick & Nelson. So tell me, Rachel, what the hell are you doing to earn that kind of money? I mean you're still looking good, but . . . ."

I felt my face flush as I remembered the shower and then laughed and laughed some more. Bobby could always make me laugh. He smiled too and held onto my hand. When I stopped laughing, I answered. "I'm organizing the files of a wealthy blind woman."

"Well that figures. You always had all those tabs in your loose leaf. You got really pissed off whenever I switched them around." He locked eyes with me across the table, and when he spoke next, his voice was low. "Have you forgiven me? Don't you think it's time we kissed and made up?" In less time than it took for me to fathom the several implications of his query, his lewd wink turned it into a joke.

I smiled, but I didn't answer. I had another secret to divulge. "But Bobby, the blind woman used to be a madam! She earned all her money running whorehouses."

"But is she Jewish?"

Leave it to Bobby to reduce my shame to a punch line. "Yeah, in fact she is. But, she's not exactly someone I'd run into at a Hadassah meeting. Bobby, please don't tell anyone about me working for a madam. I've applied for a teaching job, and it wouldn't look good if . . ."

"Your lurid secrets are safe with me." Bobby pushed his chair away from the table and was on his feet. "In fact, before I go back to New York, I intend to ply you with alcohol again and hear more of them. But right now I'm going to go break into my mom's house, scare the hell out of her, and catch her in the act of watching Johnny Carson on the Sabbath. I'd call her, but she won't answer the phone." Rolling his eyes at the inconvenience of his mother's selective Orthodoxy, Bobby pulled my car keys from his pocket. Can I borrow your car? I'll bring it back first thing in the morning."

Sad to see Bobby leave, I walked with him to the door. "Thanks for dinner and for getting me home in one piece and for letting me cry on your shoulder. I'm sorry I was such a bad drunk."

"I'll give you another chance. Have dinner with me tomorrow night."

"Sam is eating here. Why don't you and your mom join us? It'll be like old times." I would check my freezer for string beans and stop at the store for a chicken and potatoes.

"It won't be like old times, but I'd like to join you and Sam. And I'll ask Harriet." He rolled his eyes again. "Your kitchen probably isn't kosher enough for her. But maybe for you she'll make an exception like she does for Carson. I'll tell you in the morning. Till then, get some sleep." The kiss he planted on my forehead was chaste. My disappointment startled me.

Chapter 14

. . . mehr menner vee shnayflecks oyben darten . . .

. . . more men than snowflakes up there . . .

Fanny's Diary, July 25, 1897

Last week everything turned upside down! A ship called the Portland carrying over a ton of gold sailed into Seattle, and the whole of America went crazy. Almost overnight Seattle is like New York with people from every state and even Europe rushing to get here. From here they are preparing to sail north to a place called the Klondike where all this gold was found to look for more gold. And the ones who are not going north themselves are staying here to sell provisions to the others. They are saying Seattle is the "gateway to the Klondike." Men rush everywhere. It's like a stampede, so they call these men stampeders. They hurry to buy food and clothes and tools for the trip. Goods and customers line the street outside Weiss and Company and the other stores, so First Avenue looks like Orchard Street, only with less shouting and fewer women. Hotels and rooming houses are full, and saloons never close.

Today I wanted to be in the center of all the excitement, so I spent hours at the Greek coffee house near the wharf reading palms at fifty cents each. This fortune telling is another activity the Warshavskys would not approve of. They would object because only God can know the future and also because almost all of my customers are Greek men and because, of course, I must take their hands in mine when I read their palms. But Devorah, Myron, and Avram do not know that I go regularly to the coffeehouse to do this work and that my business cards stay on the counter there and clients await my coming. Avram and I are not yet married, and already I have a secret from him. But I wonder how he would feel if he knew that today I was charging more than triple my usual fee. My clients were glad to pay it, and not one of them noticed that I foresaw the appearance of the same pile of gold in every hand I studied!

Fanny's Diary, On the boat to Skagway, Alaska

Once again I write sitting on the crowded deck of a ship at the start of a journey to a strange place. Once again I disappear like the ghost I have become leaving behind only two notes and a week's rent. And once again I take my savings on a trip to a faraway place. But this time, my money is hidden beneath my skirt in a pouch fastened securely around my waist. No one will steal these earnings from me while I sleep. And my hard-earned money will not finance Avram Pinsker's dream either. This time I do not travel with a boatload of starving and frightened Jews or with a nogoodnik, lying thief, but with my friends, Desiree and Suzanne.

Last Friday when I delivered a cape to Suzanne, I was surprised to find both women packing. Suzanne took the cape and, without even trying it on, folded it into a trunk. She was talking all the while. "Why should we stay here and work for Lou, who takes most of what we earn, when we can go to Alaska and make a whole lot more and maybe even catch ourselves husbands? There are going to be more men than snow-flakes up there, most of them young and single, not like some of these old coots Lou sends up."

Then Suzanne said, "Why don't you come too, Fanny? You can keep us and the other showgirls in fancy gowns and tell fortunes and find yourself a rich, good-looking husband too. There will be more lonely single men up there than you can count, all with pockets full of gold." She looked at me hard and added, "You can use our friend's ticket for the boat. She was going too, but her ma back in Idaho got kicked by a horse, and Ellen's got to go home." Once again I would board a ship in place of another.

Desiree pulled my chin around so I was facing her and said, "Maybe getting away will put a smile on that sad little face of yours, Fanny." Still talking, she turned back to her packing. "It'll be easy. I'll pay Ellen for the ticket, and you can pay me back on the boat. She was going to sell it for three times what she paid, but she won't do that if I buy it. She owes me a favor. We leave Tuesday. Meet us at the dock at eight. We three will share a cabin. Bring your sewing machine. Desiree and I will be the best dressed actresses in Alaska."

"Yes, and bring warm clothes. I hear Alaska is colder than a witch's teat in a peat bog at Christmas, but we're going to warm it up, right?" And Desiree grabbed me and Suzanne, and we three hugged and laughed.

Hearing the unfamiliar sound of my own lost laughter, Aliza Rudinsk's laughter, I knew I would go with them. Sitting here on this boat, I think yet again about my decision and tell myself I was right to leave. Avram Pinsker will find someone else to marry and pay for his paint store. Devorah and Myron will rent to another roomer, one they do not find so much fault with. I am fond of Devorah, but she has become more like a mother than a friend, and long ago I learned to live without mama. I will miss little Leah, but she will not remember me. Besides, if Suzanne is right, maybe in Alaska, I will find a good husband and have a child of my own.

ℵ

I wasn't sure what to make of Feigele's rejection of Avram Pinsker. Would she have begrudged him her hard earned savings if she loved him? I doubted it. I admired her for avoiding a loveless marriage, if not for the way she did it. Feigele's hasty decision to run off to Alaska explained the gold nuggets in the bag with her bones. But Alaska . . . I worried about the vulnerable young woman going to Skagway, especially in the company of two prostitutes no matter how nice they were.

Having never known hunger, I didn't understand having sex for money. Raised in America by two people totally besotted with one another, I couldn't even imagine having sex with someone I didn't love, or at least think I loved— until I'd found myself drawn to Tim Hunter. My grip on the wheel tightened as I cringed. Even the private memory of my recent and short-lived infatuation with the prurient professor was an embarrassment. And after what I'd seen, our next encounter promised to be, at best, awkward. Lighting a cigarette, I resolved to finish working on the diary before he returned from his vacation. But that morning I abandoned Feigele after translating only two entries. Saturdays were busy at Frederick & Nelson, and I couldn't be late for work.

I was looking forward to dinner at Harriet Gradstein's with Bobby and Sam. Harriet had offered to host the evening meal herself rather than forgo it or risk insulting me by bringing her own kosher food and eating it on her own paper plates. As Bobby put it, "She threatened to defrost stuff she's probably had since the War ended, but don't worry, I'll cook. For this I went to medical school?" The prospect of dinner at Harriet's sustained me and enabled me to be pleasant with the customer who dithered for an hour over whether her daughter would prefer a string of pearls or pearl earrings for her birthday.

The evening did not disappoint. Over cocktails Harriet and Sam relived every one of Bobby's boyhood exploits and then she recapped her boy's military career including how he 'ate Spam for Uncle Sam.' With a catch in her voice, she told of how he attached one of her letters to a stick to make a white flag to surrender to some enemy soldiers who, thank God, turned out to be British. She illustrated her narrative by pointing to photos of the prodigal in uniform with three laughing buddies outside a London Pub.

During his mother's retrospective, her son-the-doctor himself was in the kitchen putting the finishing touches on spaghetti sauce and a salad. At the dinner table that night there were only happy memories. Harriet bragged, "My Bob is some cook." She'd been calling him Bob all evening.

"Am I supposed to call you 'Bob' now?" I posed the question while he rinsed dishes and I loaded them into the dishwasher.

"I answer to anything but Shithead. But, come to think of it, I've been known to answer to Dr. Shithead."

"Seriously," I pressed.

"Seriously, I've been Bob since I left here except in the army where for the first few months I was 'DirtyJew.'"

Just then Harriet called from the yard. "Come on! It's getting dark! It's time to make *havdala*." I hadn't lit a candle to mark the end of the Sabbath and the return to the workaday world since Manya died. So I was startled when Harriet handed me the candle and matches.

As I lit the candle, I willed the long unsaid Hebrew words to my lips and Sam poured the requisite glass of wine. He made sure to fill it to overflowing to symbolize prosperity so great that we need not worry about wasting a few drops. I sighed at both the timeliness and the futility of this hope.

But when Harriet passed around a tiny silver box of mixed spices and the sweet scent of cloves and cinnamon filled the air, my bitterness dissipated. In an old folk tale, Jews were granted a second soul during the Sabbath and the fragrant aroma was intended to fortify the body as it bid farewell to that second soul at the end of the holiday. It occurred to me that Bobby had materialized on the Sabbath, like my second soul.

After I dropped Sam off, I went home. It had been a long day following a late night, and I was tired. But I was neither surprised nor sorry when, while I was brushing my teeth, the doorbell rang. Bobby stood there with a bottle of Cutty and a single pink rose, obviously plucked from the bush just outside my door.

"Thought you could use a nightcap. I polished off all your scotch last night." He offered no other explanation for his late night arrival.

"Thanks, but I'll make some decaf. I learned my lesson. You help yourself." In the kitchen, I took the rose and stuck it in a glass of water. "That was a lovely evening. And you make excellent spaghetti sauce."

"Like they say, a man's gotta eat. So should we discuss what I'd like you to call me now that I'm not a kid anymore?"

I had a different topic in mind, one that seemed more important. "Bobby, why did you stop answering my letters? I've always wondered."

"I'll tell you if you'll answer a question for me." His tone was light, but his eyes were serious.

"Deal. Answer mine first."

"Okay. Here goes. I fell in love with you one night junior year." In an effort to deflect the impact of this unsettling declaration, I struggled to recall any evening that stood out from the many we had whiled away together.

"We were up in my room, and you were trying to drum the plot of *Great Expectations* into my head so I could pass a test. You were all fired up as usual, but I had to take a leak. When I came back, you were drawing moustaches on the naked ladies in my favorite porno magazine."

I grinned. "Right, I did. But that was because you stole my diary the week before. Remember?"

"That was a letdown, Rachel. The most interesting events in your diary were the fights you had with Manya." He mimed a yawn, but his grip on my hand tightened and his words came slowly. "Anyway, by adding those moustaches, you somehow insinuated yourself into my fantasies. I fell in love with you that night." He paused. "Or maybe I'd always been in love with you and didn't know it until then." Resignation was implicit in Bobby's sigh. "So when you wrote that you were seeing someone and getting engaged for Chrissake, I decided I didn't want to be the GI Jew you corresponded with out of friendship and patriotism."

Was that really why I'd written to Bobby? And if so, was there anything wrong with friendship and patriotism? He poured himself a couple of inches of scotch and raised his eyes to meet mine. "You're the reason I stayed away, and you're the reason I'm here now."

I sat still, stunned into silence by Bobby's repeated revelation, the same revelation that, at Rosellini's, along with the drinks, had made me giddy with pleasure. I reached for a cigarette. As he held the lighter, his eyes were on my face. The look my old friend fixed on me exposed us both.

When Bobby spoke, his tone was light, the voice of a man who saw some humor in his own vulnerability. "My turn now, right?" I nodded. "Last night, at the restaurant, when I was trying to declare my undying love, you announced that screwing me would feel like incest." My eyes widened, but I kept quiet. "Then you said that after your husband died, you didn't stop taking your birth control pills. So who are you screwing?"

I was on my feet reaching across the table and slapping Bobby in the face with all my strength. He seized hold of my wrist before I could hit him again, but not before I exploded into sobs. I spoke in the intervals between them when I gulped air. "Nobody, you asshole. I'm still taking those pills because to stop would be like . . . like I don't know . . . like killing part of myself. I don't want to be dead at forty-five."

Bobby's mouth twisted in sympathy or empathy or, perhaps, relief. But his voice was strangely stiff when he replied. "I'm sorry if I've offended you. I had to know." He released my wrist, and I sank, still sobbing, into my chair. He waited a moment before standing and walking around the table. "Jesus, Rachel, I'm sorry. Now, if you'll promise to stop assaulting me, what do you say we move the party into the living room?"

He picked up his glass and led me out of the kitchen to the sofa where he sat and pulled me down close to him. He put his arm around me and held me while my sobbing intensified and then, gradually, abated. He handed me his handkerchief. "Keep it. I owe you a handkerchief anyway, Rachel. Remember?"

"Of course, I remember." I blew my nose.

"I never told you, but that day you stuck your handkerchief onto my bloody ear is the day I decided to go into emergency medicine." He fingered his jagged flap of a left ear lobe.

I followed his conversational lead. "So tell me the real reason you opted for emergency room work. Your mother thinks it was the War, the awful things you saw."

"Yeah, it was pretty bad." He didn't elaborate.

I tried another approach. "You must love your work. Your wife thought you spent too much time at the hospital, right? At the reunion you seemed very sad about her leaving. I'm sorry."

"At the risk of beating a dead horse, it was you who drove me to drink at the reunion, Rachel, not my ex-wife." Once again, Bobby surprised me into silence. I pressed even closer to him. "But you really want to know about my divorce, right?" I nodded, wishing I'd been more direct. "Well, to tell the truth, I was mostly relieved when Judy left. She's a nice enough girl, a terrific nurse. But we didn't get along very well after she stopped working."

"She's gorgeous." I resisted the temptation to trace the ridge of my nose with my index finger. Emboldened by our proximity, I pressed. "Is that why you married her?"

"It helped that she's a knockout. But that wasn't the only reason. You were taken. I was well into my thirties and screwing too many nurses I didn't want to wake up with. You're not the only one taking that pill, you know." Bobby grinned. "Anyway, Judy came along and seemed like the answer. Like I said, she's a nice woman, a great nurse, and she's actually Jewish." He shrugged. "But if you'd been single . . ."

"Bobby, if you really were in love with me back in high school, after high school, why didn't you tell me?"

He took a deep breath and inspected his empty glass before putting it down on the end table. "I was such a fuck-up and a dud in school and shorter than you, and you were such a . . . a . . . brain and a prig too. You weren't impressed by my only talent which was playing basketball. Christ, you wouldn't even let me cheat off you on those friggin' history tests." He tugged at his beard as if reliving his frustration. "But I figured if I went into the Army and came back a war hero, you'd see me in a whole new light." He glanced over at his empty glass. "Would it have made any difference if I'd told you?"

I shrugged, enjoying how his arm moved with my shoulders. "Who knows? I've always felt close to you." I hesitated. When I spoke again, my voice was low, confessional, my eyes averted. "But I guess I wasn't really close to you, because I never knew, never even suspected how you felt about me. Kind of like I never suspected Harry was gambling. I am so obtuse."

"Well, I don't know about Harry, but I hid how I felt pretty well." I appreciated his attempt to minimize my self-flagellation. "So tell me, how did you meet Harry? It was at the U, right?"

"Right. He was a transfer student. His dad was the kosher slaughterer in Spokane, and they didn't get along. When Harry showed up late for work in the butcher shop one afternoon, his dad yanked a knife out of a chicken and went after Harry with it. That same night Harry hitched a ride over the mountains to Seattle. I thought he was a bold adventurer, a hero." I sighed. "Anyway, the next day he showed up at the U, at Hillel. That's where he first spotted me. He didn't know a soul."

"You never could resist a guy in trouble, could you?"

"The rabbi got him a job in a shoe store off campus and a room over the store. Harry saved his money and the next semester he registered for classes."

"I knew he was a go-getter. I hope you had a good run with Harry."

I tensed. It was important for me to remember the way things were with Harry and me. The way they really were. In the aftermath of the earthquake, Harry had been canonized. Even Marsha seemed to have forgotten the many beefs she had with her dad. That was okay for her. Harry was her father. But I was an adult, and Harry had been my husband. I spoke slowly. "Things were okay while Marsha was young. But as she got older, Harry and I fought more." Before Bobby could ask, I explained. "He didn't understand teenagers, treated Marsha as if she were still a child. And then, after she left, Harry wouldn't let me go back to teaching."

In light of Harry's literally earthshaking death, these complaints sounded petty, bitchy. To give them heft, I added, "On top of that he voted for Nixon in 1960." I shook my head at what I still saw as Harry's impossible political views. "He couldn't stand JFK. Wanted everything to stay the same. Sam steered clear of talking politics with him. Everybody did. Except Marsha. She used to take her father on.

"You know, Bobby, I miss being married. I miss it a lot. And I miss Harry." I hesitated to articulate the new confession forming in my mind, and then out it rushed. "But I don't always miss him." Uttering these words aloud felt blasphemous. Then I reminded myself that, unlike many of my friends, Bobby could be counted on to keep his mouth shut. Besides, he'd soon be gone, taking my sad secrets with him.

"If Harry had lived, would you have divorced him?" Bobby's even tone made divorce sound normal, like having breakfast.

I hesitated. Perhaps in New York divorce was more accepted, easier, but it sure wasn't a popular option among my friends. "I don't know. Maybe when I found out about the gambling, the debts . . . But God, then everybody would have known what he did." On the verge of tears again, I shook my head. "Sam and Marsha would have hated that. Me too. I just don't know."

Bobby squeezed my hand. "Let Harry rest in peace, and tell me what's with this madam you're working for? You wouldn't let me cheat off you, but now you're working for a madam?"

Relieved to change the subject, I explained my arrangement with Yetta, trying to make the bizarre series of events that led me to her and the work I was doing for her sound logical. "So I'm kind of like a seeing-eye secretary. It's just a summer job, but it will pay most of what I need for Marsha's last three years at Vassar. Now if I can just get a teaching assignment . . ."

Half way through my story, Bobby released my hand and began twisting a lock of my hair. He tugged at it gently when I stopped talking. "You're going to be okay, Rachel." He let go of my hair and turned my chin towards him. I felt the kiss coming, parted my lips, and reached up to pull his mouth down to mine. He tasted of Scotch and cigarettes and I drank him in.

He pulled away. "Rachel, what do you say this time we move the party upstairs?"

Chapter 15

. . . Ich bin der eintziker Yid, un es iz nish do gezetzen.

. . . I am the only Jew and there are no laws.

What had I done? This accusatory question drove me out of the bed where Bobby still slept and into the shower. The streaming hot water would either cleanse me of my folly if that's what having sex with Bobby had been or enable me to classify it as something else. Bobby or Bob, or whoever he was now, and I barely knew each other as adults. Was he really still in love with me? Was I in love with him? How could that be? It was too soon after Harry's death for me to get involved with someone new. My brief but intense interest in Tim Hunter proved that. But what if that someone wasn't really new, was someone I'd been close to before I ever heard of Harry?

Harry. Sex with Harry had been mostly a matter of keeping his insecurities at bay. On the very morning he died, I screwed him silly, so he'd go off to meet his big deal prospective clients feeling like a mensch. In spite of everything, I still felt good about that.

Of course Bobby was a different sort of lover. But what I hadn't expected was that I too would be different, that I would lose myself, the self I recognized. The thought of having an identity crisis at my age was disquieting, so after I toweled off and while Bobby still slept, I turned to Feigele. She too was second guessing a recent decision. I read fast leaving the translating until later. Yiddish, a language bred of dislocation, suited my own mixed-up mood and hers.

ᗱ

Fanny's Diary, On the boat to Skagway, Alaska

What have I done? Why did I leave a clean room in a comfortable Jewish home where I was treated kindly? Why did I flee a beautiful town where Jews are free to pray and be bank presidents? And why have I chosen to sail away from a marriage Mama and Papa would have blessed many times over? Suzanne has just brought a gentleman she knows to our cabin, so I will write no more now.

Fanny's Diary, On the boat to Skagway

I didn't mind leaving our cabin yesterday, because I was hoping to read the palms of our fellow travelers. I thought getting outside would make me feel better. So I went up on the crowded deck where Desiree offered me a sip from a flask of whiskey. She said it would cheer me. The sharp tasting liquid burned my throat but made my body glow with sudden and welcome warmth. It loosened my tongue too, and I told Desiree about Avram.

She said, "Fanny, Fanny, Fanny, Skagway has 15,000 stampeders and 300 women! You'll meet hundreds of men who'll want to marry you. And they'll have their own money, buckets of it. Just wait. Meanwhile have something to eat." Desiree handed me the flask again and offered me some of the food she brought. I was very hungry, so I took the chunk of meat she held out and bit off a piece. It was flavorful and tender. She smiled and said, "Isn't this ham good?" I gagged and rushed to the ship's rail to vomit up the unclean meat I had unknowingly eaten. Even the Weisses do not eat pork. But at the sight of the forests and peaks of the shoreline growing smaller, I swallowed my bile and the ham.

Beneath the vast and darkening sky, I stared at the endless waves lapping against the sides of the ship, like a watery quilt tucked around a sleeping child. For a second I thought I saw the face of the real Feigele Lindner, the drowned girl, white against the black water, but her features soon became my own. Who would miss a godless, greenhorn, orphan girl, a ghost of a girl, really? Disturbed by my dark thoughts, I began to hum the tune I used to sing to little Yitzak to help him find sleep. I still held the remaining chunk of ham and thought of tossing it into the sea. But instead I put it in my mouth and savored its forbidden salty taste.

When I returned to where Desiree sat, she had been joined by a curly-haired young man named Ryan O'Neal whom she seemed to know. I read his palm, where I saw a golden future, and he paid me more than I asked.

I accepted a drink from his flask and then one more from Desiree's. I am not used to whiskey, and soon I felt dizzy and wanted to return to the cabin. Ryan helped me down the narrow staircase. When we got to the cabin door, Suzanne and her friend were leaving. Ryan held the door, and when I heard it slam shut, I was surprised to find Ryan behind me in the tiny space. "I'll help you out of your things."

Then he picked me up and laid me on the bunk bed. The next thing I knew, I was half undressed and Ryan was on top of me, inside me, and I could feel him moving in rhythm with the motion of the boat. Like when I was with Bernie, I heard Mama and Papa calling from the flames that radiated from where Ryan and I were joined. To silence their voices, I threw my legs around Ryan and rocked with him until I felt the flames circling us subside.

After he left, I looked at my shoulder. Imprinted in my bare flesh was a cross. I had eaten pig and let an uncircumcised stranger have me. I was marked. Then I remembered that around his neck Ryan wears a silver cross like Bridget's. When he pressed himself into me over and over, his cross left this bruise. It was fading already. My tears of relief tasted salty, like the ham.

Fanny's Diary, Skagway, August 1897

Our ship is approaching Skagway, so everyone else is on deck looking for the shore and I have the cabin to myself for once. Desiree was right. Last night, our final one on this ship, I had a marriage proposal from Ryan. He is generous and can make me laugh when he tells me stories. In that way he is like Papa. And he has big plans. Even before I read Ryan's palm, he expected to strike gold in the Klondike and become rich.

I was happy Ryan asked me to marry him, because my monthly flow was late and I was very worried. I had not slept for two nights. I hardly know Ryan, so I was not sure he would make a good husband and father, but if I was going to have a child in Alaska, that child would need a father. I told him I would think over his proposal and tell him in the morning. Ryan was not happy with this response, but I remained firm. Then later last night Ryan beat another stampeder just because the man asked me to read his palm a second time. I tried to stop Ryan from hitting this man, but he would not stop until the man lay still on the deck. So Ryan is jealous and violent. He is also a Catholic. He says religion does not matter, but I suspect he did not mention me in the letter he wrote yesterday to his parents.

Again I spent a sleepless night. When early this morning my monthly flow stained the sheets, my first thought was that perhaps God has not forgotten me after all, has forgiven me. My second thought was that God is telling me not to marry Ryan.

I was glad Feigele had avoided marriage to a hotheaded and brutish man she hardly knew and unwed motherhood. Once again I wondered if she'd gotten pregnant by Daniel Meyer and had either a baby or a nightmarish backroom abortion. If so, would she have been so quick to risk another pregnancy with Ryan? But Feigele wasn't used to drinking, had been feeling alone. Again I thanked God Marsha knew about the Pill. Hell, I thanked God I was still taking it. Because of the Pill, there was no need for me to make a big deal out of sleeping with Bobby. He lived on the other side of the country and would leave soon. When I heard him in the shower, I closed the diary and started the coffee.

In the morning light across the kitchen table from Bobby in his wrinkled day old clothes everything felt different than it had the night before. It was as if our charged reunion that led so naturally to the twin bed in Marsha's room never happened. Over the English muffin I was buttering, I felt as if I were on a blind date. I reached for the grape jelly. Bobby reached for the Smirnoff in the cabinet behind the table and poured some into his orange juice. "Want a slug?"

I shook my head. "Thanks again for letting me cry on your shoulder." I thought I saw his eyes cloud at my formal tone, my clichéd euphemism, and my obvious omission, but he didn't speak. I directed my eyes to my plate. "Listen, I've got to be at Yetta's by nine." This was only a little lie. But I didn't have time for anything but earning back the *kishke-gelt*. I really needed to complete that project and get paid. I'd cut my hours at Frederick & Nelson in order to spend more time on Yetta's files.

Cocking his head, Bobby managed to catch my eye. "I'd like to have dinner with you tonight, Rachel. Alone." I lowered my eyes again. "But we don't have to screw. Not if you don't want to." I couldn't prevent the corners of my mouth from curling into a rueful smile. I never could keep a straight face around Bobby Gradstein.

If Yetta wondered why I was so animated that morning, she didn't ask, but she did pay me a rare compliment. "You must have been a wonderful history teacher. You really know how to tell a story." Because she couldn't see my gestures or facial expressions, I used my voice and vocabulary to make my recaps of Feigele's adventures as lively as I could. "You make me feel like I'm right there, aboard that ship with that girl." Yetta herself sounded unusually lively. "I didn't think she had it in her to leave Seattle! But now she's headed for trouble."

"I think she left trouble behind. Remember I told you a year went by after she overheard that conversation between Nathan Weiss and his nephew and her next diary entry? And there are pages missing too. Maybe Feigele got pregnant by Daniel Meyer and had an abortion. Was it hard to get an abortion back then?"

"Exactly how old do you think I am?" Yetta sounded more amused than hurt. "In a boom town like Seattle, there's usually some doc willing to help, to do it right for a price. Last I heard Dr. Mamie McLafferty was doing abortions in her office right across the street from Frederick & Nelson." This was news to me. "Lou Graham's girls would have known a doc, maybe several."

Yetta had a question of her own. "So Rachel, don't tell me you still believe your Feigele was going to Skagway to sew and read palms. That's like a guy going to Lou Graham's to admire the decor. Skagway was the wildest place up there except for Dawson. And she went with two hookers!" I did think Feigele planned to support herself sewing and telling fortunes in Skagway, but I didn't have time to argue, especially if I wanted to make a dent in the filing before joining Bobby for dinner. I felt a twinge in my back at the prospect of hunching over those drawers all day.

At first the work went well. I easily separated medical and grocery receipts from the many Grunbaum's and Frederick & Nelson receipts. She'd bought whole rooms of expensive furniture at Grunbaum's. And Yetta had been one of my other employer's better customers. Over the years she'd purchased china, silver, glassware, clothes, shoes, jewelry, and gourmet foodstuffs. Every year at Christmas she'd bought a slew of gift items—silver pitchers, trays, candy, and dozens of monogrammed flasks, cufflinks, and tie tacks. Picturing every cop in Seattle sporting fancy cufflinks, I found myself smiling as I worked. It wasn't that Yetta's gifting cops amused me, but rather because I was getting so much done. I didn't even stop filing when Bess placed a chicken sandwich and a glass of iced tea on an empty corner of the table.

Only after I'd filed every last medical bill chronologically in the appropriate folder did I stretch and scarf down that sandwich. Energized by the progress I was making as much as by the food and tea, I attacked the bound ledgers containing guest registries for the Seattle-area "hotels" Yetta had owned. I flipped through page after page of "guests' names," assigned rooms, dates, and rent or rentals. I scanned the dates and stashed the five ledgers, earliest first, in the designated drawer in a labeled section of their own.

It was the La Salle registries that flummoxed me. They were like the others, except for an extra empty rental column. Also there appeared to have been fourteen "permanent guests" at the La Salle, many more than at her earlier places. Beside all that, a couple of the later La Salle ledgers were missing. Maybe the building had been sold sooner than I thought. Among the other legal papers in a pile on the table under a gray fedora feminized by a nosegay of pansies, I found the closing documents for the purchase of the La Salle. It had been known as the Outlook Hotel until 1942 when Yetta bought it from a family named Kodama and Frenchified its name. But it wasn't the building's new Gallic identity that threw me. It was the Japanese name linked to the year of the Internment.

To some Americans, the post-Pearl Harbor punishment of Japanese citizens may have been an abstraction, but where I came from, this purge was personal. Our Seattle neighborhood, the Central District, was one of the few in The Queen City where Jews and Japanese and other newcomers could buy property, and our proximity made friendships inevitable. In fact, the only friend I ever had who wasn't Jewish was Michiko Himitsu. We were both bookish little girls. As soon as we could write English, we sat on each other's front steps chronicling the mundane minutia of our daily lives in painstakingly neat print in the black and white notebooks we pretended were diaries.

I was in college when her family and lots of others had to go. I'll never forget the frenzy, the rush-rush of their leaving. Manya and I were helping Michiko and her mother bundle the few belongings they could take with them. Sam was running around helping Mr. Himitsu to find a buyer for their little house. That afternoon when I came back from the U, the Himitsus were gone. After revisiting memories of their hasty leave-taking, I was certain that Yetta Solomon's purchase of the Outlook Hotel from the exiled Kodama family had literally been a steal.

Sighing, I stretched and focused once more on the pieces of paper in front of me. After the earthquake, another Japanese family, the Ikedas, bought the La Salle from Yetta for $17,500. The closing documents, describing the four-story, fifty-seven room hotel built in 1909 at 83 Pike Street and listing its guest load and furnishings, seemed unremarkable. But the sale date was, in fact, over a year after the dates in the most recent ledger. Unless the building had stayed vacant for a year, one or maybe even two ledgers were missing. I turned back to those that remained, running my index finger down the lists of Joeys, Juans, Seans, and Sals.

Hadn't the Ikedas wondered why no women stayed at the La Salle? Not if they were greenhorns like Feigele or my parents or the Kodamas had once been. Not if they had spent years in the internment camps like the Himitsus.

What would they have known of Seans and Juans? Of whorehouses? I was willing to bet that Yetta had deceived the Ikedas, letting them believe that all those men were, in fact, legitimate overnight guests in a legitimate hotel.

How could Yetta, herself a daughter of immigrants, cheat other immigrants? What need had the wealthy madam to profit from the Kodama's forced evacuation or to outright cheat the Ikedas? And would I have the guts to ask her? After all, she was paying me to put her files in order, not to accuse her of greed and dishonesty. Besides, at this late date, what good would it do to confront her? But I wanted to know. Maybe I would find out when I asked her about the missing ledgers. I went looking for her, but I found her busy in the living room with her accountant. I left a little early, eager to read more about Feigele's Alaskan odyssey.

Fanny's Diary, Skagway, September 12, 1897

Now I am really alone. Ryan, Desiree, and Suzanne have all left Skagway for Dawson, a Klondike town closer to the fields of gold. Desiree says there are more dance halls there and more stampeders. Even though Skagway is supposed to be the "gateway to the Klondike," Suzanne says it's nothing but a tent town and that Dawson is more built-up and civil.

But to get there they must climb the steep and rocky White Pass Trail with all their provisions tied to pack animals. I told Ryan I would not marry him because I was afraid of climbing this trail. That is most of the truth and he believed me. Suzanne and Desiree wanted me to go with them, and I told them the same thing. A Tlingit woman told me that this trail was blazed long ago by Tlingit hunters. But at the camp where the trail begins, I heard terrible tales from gaunt and wild eyed men returning without pack animals, provisions, or gold. They told of a toll taker tossed into the gulch below. They spoke of horses losing their footing on the White Pass, even in summer. People are starting to call it "Dead Horse Trail." I really am afraid of the trek over White Pass. I cannot lose my sewing machine. And the Klondike is in Canada, not America. Who knows if the fierce and vigilant Mounted Police at the border permit Jews to enter their country? I do not know what it would take to bribe them. I prefer to stay in America.

But Ryan, Suzanne, and Desiree are not afraid. They plan to go over the Pass and then they must make rafts to carry them down the wild Yukon River to Dawson. They spent all the money they saved buying provisions and pack animals, and on hiring a Tlingit guide. The provisions cost much more here than they do in Seattle, but those three don't care. Like the others, they expect to become rich. I am saving my money for winter, when I will want more than a tent over my head. I am not sad to see Ryan leave, but I will miss my two good friends. I fear for their safety.

Fanny's Diary, Skagway, September 18, 1897

Ryan was not gone two days when another stampeder, a young fellow with soft hands and a voice that still cracked, proposed to me while I was reading his palm. He asked me if I saw a bride there, and when I said no, he invited me to marry him and join him on his quest. I laughed and told him to ask me again on his way home after he struck gold. I think he was lonely and homesick, and I did not charge him for the reading.

Skagway does not seem entirely strange to me. Except for the gunfire and ragtime music, it reminds me of Gnilsk, another poor little place full of flies, mud, and people who dream of a better life. But the dead dreamers of Gnilsk were law abiding Jews, while here in this remote village on the edge of the sea, I am the only Jew, and there are no laws. There are not many women either. Skagway is not really civilized.

But it is more civilized than the snow covered woods beyond. At the camp where the White Pass Trail begins, I share a tent with Hattie, my lame Tlingit friend, who does laundry. In nearby tents there are saloons, cooks, and a barber. So before setting out, a stampeder can get his last drink, meal, clean shirt, haircut, and have his palm read. There are even prostitutes and fiddlers. The men are not afraid to spend money because, like Ryan, they all think they will find gold.

℘

Fanny's Diary, Skagway, October 15, 1897

I have had no time to record my thoughts. Stampeders eager to pay me well for predicting that they will reach the Klondike safely and strike gold keep me staring into their palms. Some of these palms are coarse and rough from farm, ranch, or kitchen work. Some are soft and smooth from writing or dealing cards, and others are red and weathered from life at sea. But I see almost the same future in all of them — a safe journey to a riverbed or hillside made of gold. Many pay in nuggets they won in cards or at the blackjack tables.

Here I feel as if I am the only Jew in the whole world. I have never lived in a Jewless town, a village really, with no synagogue, no ritual bathhouse, no kosher food, no Yiddish. Not a single soul here cares if my fingernails are clean or what I eat or don't eat or that I speak English with a "European" accent. No one cares if I write in this book or read palms or sew on the Sabbath. And in Alaska a woman does not have to be married to use the bathhouse. No one cares that I choose for friends a Tlingit laundress and several prostitutes. I enjoy the free and easy camaraderie at our camp. In this outpost at the edge of the wilderness I have found the real America. But as a daughter of the Ukraine where in November the air bites your lungs and snow buries whole villages, I have respect for winter. The days grow cooler, and I must look for better shelter in town where I can earn money sewing dresses for the girls in the dance halls and shows.

℘

Fanny's Diary, Skagway, November 20, 1897

I write in my room where I await a customer who is late for a fitting. She has a room just down the hall. Several entertainers live here over the saloon where they dance. Sawyer's Stage Door Saloon is the fanciest bar and brothel here. It took me a while to find this small room with barely enough space for my bed and a table for my sewing machine. But I have more privacy than I did in New York. And it is warm and close to my customers, to the town's few restaurants, and to the bathhouse. One of these customers, Theresa, a showgirl whose stage name is Texas Terry, talked the saloon's owner, Alan Sawyer, into renting to me. "It'll be good to have our dressmaker handy," is what she told him. But it was only after I offered to pay three times what the other girls pay that he agreed. I was lucky to get a room anywhere. Skagway is growing. Wooden buildings have already replaced many of the tents, and boards have been laid over the mud in the streets just like in Seattle.

I too have found work in the saloon downstairs. I read palms there. Alan Sawyer says I'm good for business. I've heard that before. He says if I read only in his saloon, he'll charge me less rent. I like telling fortunes here because the men pay so well and many of them are very nice. Last night one of them, a stampeder from California, proposed to me right after he won at poker. He said he thought my reading brought him luck. He is good-looking, strong and generous, but I hardly know him. I did not turn down Avram Pinsker to marry a stranger. Besides, what would happen when my handsome gambler lost at poker? His bad luck would be my fault too. And he isn't Jewish. Do I still care if I marry a Jew or not? Mama and Papa, may they rest in peace, will never know if I do not. Anyway, there are no other Jews up here. I do not think about this often, but when I do I remind myself that if I wanted to marry a Jew, I should have stayed in Seattle.

Fanny's Diary, Skagway, November 30, 1897

May this pen turn into a pickle and rot in my hand if what I am about to write is not so. The dress I finished making this morning measures no more than ten inches from shoulder to hem. Here in this gold rush Gomorrah where there are no children I am sewing doll clothes. Terry and the other girls wear proper dresses for dancing with stampeders and getting them to buy drinks. Then the girls change into costumes and sing and dance in the show. And later the girls entertain clients upstairs. Each girl usually wears dresses of a particular color. Theresa's are blue to set off her yellow hair and match her blue eyes.

On a shelf behind the bar, Mr. Sawyer keeps six dolls, each one dressed in a different color. When a stampeder comes in and wants to see Terry, he goes to the bar and points to the doll in blue. The bartender lays that doll down to show that Terry is busy and sends the man upstairs.

When the stampeder pays her the five dollars, Terry drops the coins or nuggets down a pipe to the bar where the bartender keeps track. When the customer leaves, Terry taps on the pipe to signal the bartender to stand the doll in blue up again. The dresses on the dolls were torn and soiled, so the girls offered to pay me to design and sew new ones. I have finished three, and several men admired them and asked me about making dresses for their wives when they arrive here in the spring.

ꟸ

Chapter 16

I looked forward to sharing Feigele's latest adventures with Yetta prior to tackling her piles of paper. I also wanted to ask her about the missing La Salle ledgers. When I pulled up, a locksmith's truck was in her driveway and a young fellow, an apprentice I figured, was working on the side door. Yetta told me she had the locks changed every three months, so I wasn't surprised to see him. I parked down the street in the welcome shade of a Bigleaf Maple and approached the front gate.

It was Martin, not Bess, who parted the curtain upstairs and then came down and let me in. His hair was tousled, his face gray, and his words rushed. "Yetta had another heart attack. The doctor just left."

"Oh no! Is she alright?" I was surprised at how alarmed I was.

"Won't go to the hospital." Martin gave me a knowing look as if he expected me to understand his consternation at Yetta's stubbornness, as if he and I had a history of complicity. "She's in bed. She was getting dressed when it happened. Doc Lancaster says she has to stay in bed. Can't even get up to pee." He shook his head. "I took her cane away so she doesn't try any of her tricks." He waved his hand at the stairs where Yetta's walking stick dangled from the coat tree like an outsized candy cane. "The doc'll be back tomorrow morning. She's asleep now."

"Where's Bess?"

Martin threw up his hands. "At her sister's place in Tacoma. Minding her nephews. Her sister's at a cousin's funeral in Portland." His piqued tone made it clear that Martin considered this cousin's death ill-timed. "Bess left here yesterday. But her sister's coming home tonight, so later on, around eight, I'm going to Tacoma to bring Bess back here where she belongs. Yetta needs her." He hesitated and raked his thinning hair with both hands. "Rachel, can you stay until I get back? I can't leave Yetta here alone. I'll pay you."

I kept my voice even when I answered. "There's no need to pay me, Martin. Of course I'll stay." His chin quivered. He was really a wreck. "Has she had lunch? Should I fix something for her? A little soup maybe?"

"The doc said not to give her anything but broth and toast if she wants it." He smiled indulgently. "Yetta likes her meals."

"I'll get it ready just in case. Let me see what's in the kitchen." I found a can of chicken noodle soup I could strain and got out a loaf of bread. "Just let me know when she wakes up, and I'll fix a tray and bring it to her." I looked at him again. "Martin, have you eaten today? Do you want me to scramble you some eggs?"

After Martin and I ate, I called Bobby and left word with his mom that I wouldn't be meeting him for dinner that night. Then I attacked yet another pile of paper, one connected to the money Yetta lent. I was amazed at the numbers and names on receipts I kept finding for loans she'd made. The sums were substantial and the interest she charged varied. The names of the borrowers, some Jewish some not, were familiar— a jeweler, several other merchants, two city councilmen, three builders, and quite a few lawyers, including one of those Harry was going to pitch a policy to when the earthquake hit. Most of the receipts bore relatively recent dates. Although Yetta, blind and ill, no longer presided over a house of ill-repute, she had by no means retired from the business world. Half of Seattle was in hock to her.

I'd been sorting and filing for several hours when Martin popped in to say that Yetta was awake and would appreciate a bit of soup. In the darkened room, the diminutive woman lay prone, her slight frame further reduced to a narrow ridge in the bedclothes. Her voice was a whisper. "So sorry to trouble you, Rachel. But Bess . . ."

Before I could reply, Martin spoke. "Don't worry, Toots. Bess will be back tonight, I promise. I'm going to get her myself. While I'm gone, Rachel's going to stay here with you. She'll take good care of you. She's fixed you some lunch. Here, let me get you propped up so you can eat."

When Martin finished fussing with the pillows, I handed him the tray and squeezed Yetta's hand. "So sorry you're not well. I'll get back to work now. Martin will let me know if you need anything."

No new mother leaving her infant with a sitter for the first time gave more careful instructions than Martin gave me that evening before he left. He drilled me on Yetta's medications, which included a sedative, and he left the doctor's home phone number. After Martin drove off, I abandoned the files and took his place in the easy chair he'd pushed to Yetta's bedside. By nine, Yetta was nodding. I warmed the bedpan under hot water before sliding it beneath her. It wasn't until I was removing it that I glimpsed the purplish scars striping the back of her slim thighs. Fearful of upsetting my patient, I didn't remark on them or ask about them. In a few minutes she had dutifully taken her pills and fallen asleep.

Sitting there in the dark, I worried. I worried about my faraway and fatherless daughter, about the stricken and scarred woman in front of me, about what was with me and Bobby Gradstein. Then I stewed over the fact that the summer was passing and I'd not yet heard from the Board of Education. In spite of the breeze from the Sound coming in the open window, I felt suffocated, short of breath, helpless, the way I felt years ago at the bedside of my dying mother.

A creak from downstairs cut short my time travel. Who was that? Had Martin forgotten something? Seconds later, I heard another sound, one I knew well, even with Yetta's gentle snores making it hard to hear. It was the squeak of metal on metal. Someone was opening a drawer in one of the file cabinets in the dining room. My heart froze in my chest. No one but Martin had a key to the gate and house. Was all his concern for Yetta only a pose? Had the son of a bitch returned to rob the enfeebled woman? Not on my watch.

I slipped out of my sandals, rose from my chair, and tiptoed noiselessly down the stairs. At the bottom, I stood listening and looking. I'd left the vestibule light on for Martin and Bess, so I could see the front door. It appeared undisturbed since I'd locked it behind Martin. Was I imagining things? I was about to return to my post at Yetta's bedside when I heard another drawer squeak slowly open, saw a light flicker in the doorway to the dining room. I grabbed Yetta's cane from the coat tree and weighed it in my hand. Then, hugging the wall, I crept stealthily towards the sound and the light.

From the doorway, I saw the young locksmith kneeling beside the bottom drawer of a cabinet, not two feet from me. He was so close I could see the acne pustules dotting his cheeks. The drawer gaped open and the burglar's flashlight illuminated stacks of banded bills inside. No wonder Yetta told me not to bother with the "junk" in the bottom drawers of her file cabinets. She'd said she kept money in the house, but I hadn't suspected a cache like this.

The sight of the thief busily cramming Yetta's ill-gotten gains, into his tool bag enraged me. This punk had no more right to Yetta's stash than Harry had to gamble away Marsha's college money. In fact, some of those bills the kid was stuffing into his bag were Marsha's college money. I had to stop him before he looked up and saw me. I lifted the cane with both hands and put all my weight and rage into bringing it down on the burglar's head. I felt the lumpy crook crash into his cranium, heard him grunt, and watched him crumple at my feet.

I stepped over him and, still clutching the cane, made my way to the phone.

Lightheaded and shaky, I asked the operator to get me the local police station. The officer who took my call sounded bored until I gave Yetta's name and address. Then he assured me he would dispatch men there right away. I asked him not to use sirens.

After I put the receiver down, I wanted to go upstairs and check on Yetta, make sure she was alright, was still asleep, but I was afraid to leave the young man on the floor. He'd opened his eyes. He raised his hand to his head where blood, mingled with Brylcreem, matted his greasy black DA. He was coming to. When he turned his head and saw me standing over him, he grimaced, and rose to his knees. Without thinking, I whacked him with the cane again, aiming for the same spot I'd hit before. Again he grunted and fell, this time on his face, one arm still extended as if reaching for the bills he'd dropped earlier. Staring at him, it occurred to me that Yetta might not want her drawer of hundreds exposed, even to the police, especially to the police. So I quickly stuffed all but one of the banded stacks back into the cabinet drawer and closed it.

Clutching Yetta's bloody cane and too scared even to smoke, I stood over my victim. I was terrified that the kid would come to again before the police arrived. But I was equally terrified that he wouldn't. After I'd hit him the first time, I'd seen his chest rise and fall. But after I crowned him the second time, he lay inert, sprawled on his stomach, a little blood oozing onto the floor. Harry had died from a head injury. Feigele too. Was this kid dead? Was I, Rachel Mazursky, a murderer? I stared at the cane without seeing it. What had I done? I put in a quick word to God.

After the police arrived they lugged the inanimate intruder into the empty garage and turned the garden hose on him. When the kid I feared I'd killed cursed his way back to consciousness, I was giddy with relief. He needed stitches in his head but appeared otherwise unharmed. He was pissed off to have been knocked cold by a woman. The young man's humiliation amused the police. He confessed to them that earlier in the day he had walked by the dining room en route to the bathroom just as Martin was taking cash out of a drawer to pay him. That was when the apprentice glimpsed the stacks of bills. Later, knowing that Martin would be away and not knowing I was still there, he decided to return and burgle the place. He entered by way of the side gate and door.

When Martin returned with Bess, he was beside himself with guilt. "Yetta always pays in cash, but she never lets anybody know she keeps it here, in the house. I got careless. I got distracted by Yetta being so sick, by Bess being away."

"How did this mess get to be my fault when I wasn't even here, Mr. Martin?" Bess stomped off to see to Yetta. At the foot of the stairs, she turned and looked at me. "You're a fighter like your daddy."

When I finally made it home, the phone was ringing. I thought it might be Bobby, so I was taken aback to recognize my cousin's voice. In New York it was five o'clock in the morning. This was not good. For the second time that night my heart iced up in my chest. I hoped God was still paying attention.

"Miriam, what's wrong? Is Marsha okay?"

"She's fine. Where the hell have you been? I've been up all night trying to reach you." Miriam was two years older than I, but we'd always been close. Long ago she'd earned the right to be cross with me. I missed her after she fell for Jay and defected to New York.

"I've got another part-time job. I was working late. Is it Susie? Jay?"

Miriam snapped out her response like Dragnet's fact-hungry Sgt. Friday. "No. We're all fine. But Marsha's moving out. She says you'll approve. I'm checking. Do you?"

"What?" I thought I heard wrong.

"I figured. That's why I'm calling." Miriam sighed. I knew my cousin was piqued by having to explain something as complicated as the decision of an adolescent at five in the morning. "She wants to move into a rattrap apartment in the Village with a friend from Vassar, Trish Dubois, for the rest of the summer. Says it's closer to her job. Says she can pay her share of the rent out of what she's earning at the Strand."

"I didn't know she wanted to move. I do know who the friend is though." Trish Dubois was an older Vassar friend, a recent grad.

"Marsha's hanging out at bars and jazz clubs downtown, staying out late. Susie goes with her most of the time. Marsha invited Susie to move in with her and this Trish, but Jay put his foot down." I pictured Jay exploding at the thought of his daughter living anywhere in Manhattan but home. He'd see such a move as both extravagant and insulting. That's how Harry would have seen it too. That's how he saw Marsha's going east to college.

But Feigele's migration to New York probably saved her life. Her move to Seattle forged her into an American. And her relocation to Skagway offered adventure and escape from the Weiss's sabotage and a loveless marriage. Right now, an apartment in bohemian Greenwich Village with friends might be just the thing for Marsha. "Thanks for letting me know. The only part of this that bothers me is that Marsha didn't tell me herself."

"Probably didn't want to worry you. I figure she'll call you as soon as she actually moves. I just wanted to make sure you don't want us to try harder to stop her."

I was grateful to Miriam for her common sense and concern and for staying up to call me. "Thanks, but no. Let her go. It'll be good for her to see what it feels like to pay rent and utilities on what she's making. But tell her to call me." My own recent brush with a burglar prompted me to add, "And tell her to keep her door locked."

Before locking my own door for what was left of the night, I opened the mail. To my delight, there was a letter from the Board of Education requesting an interview. God wasn't only paying attention, He was working overtime. I reread it several times before I collapsed into bed where I slept really well. I wasn't sure if it was because of the letter or because bopping burglars over the head agreed with me.

Soon after Yetta learned there had been an attempted robbery and that I thwarted it by clobbering the felon, the sightless and weakened woman took my hand. "I told you I was getting a bargain when I hired you, Rachel. You're your father's daughter. Thank you."

I enjoyed the praise, but I dreaded any mention of my exploit in the newspaper. I didn't want Seattle's Board of Education members to learn of my association with Yetta. "So far there's been no story about the robbery in the paper. Do you think there will be?"

"Are you worried that playing bouncer to a madam will cost you your teaching career or your sales job?" Yetta's voice was stronger now, and there was a note of sharpness in it. I didn't answer. "Well, relax. I told Captain Swenson not to report the incident. I don't want more punks trying to rob me. Of course he agreed." She rubbed her thumb against her second and third fingers, a gesture she used often. Seeing it, I understood why the police responded so quickly, why the officer in charge was so solicitous.

Dressing for my interview with the principal of Franklin High offered yet another chance to be grateful to Miriam, this time for the very clothes on my back. The gray-and-white plaid sleeveless cotton sheath I was zipping up was a hand-me-down from my clothes horse cousin. She had flown in for Harry's funeral with a suitcase full of outfits she'd tired of or outgrown. I cajoled my hair into a French twist, pinned it securely, and applied a touch of lipstick. When I checked my image in the mirror, I was pleased. The boxy cut of the bolero jacket was flattering without making me look like a floozy. The skirt was a decent length. I told myself I looked mature, not old. Driving along Rainier Boulevard to Franklin High, I saw the mountain that gave the Boulevard its name looming ahead, white and lovely, a good omen.

But, as I told Yetta later, the interview did not go well. "Principal Jankowski began by saying there are no openings in the history department. He called me in only to decide if I was worthy of adding to a waiting list of applicants, people he can call on to sub."

"And what did you say?" Yetta was sitting in a chair in her bedroom recovering from the welcome exertion of her first shower since her heart attack.

"I thanked him. I told him I was disappointed though." I'd struggled to remain composed in the face of my letdown. "He wanted to know if I'd be willing to substitute if he ever needs someone." I made no effort to purge the exasperation from my voice.

"And what did you say to that?" Yetta's own voice was regaining strength every day.

"I said I would."

"Did he ask you about your experience?"

"Yes. And he liked the fact that I had some, wasn't right out of college. But he also said things had changed a lot in twenty years because today's students didn't respect teachers the way they used to. He went on and on about how badly prepared the kids are when they get to high school. I made him laugh when I said that hadn't changed."

"Well, if you really want to teach, sooner or later, something will open up. Be patient."

Chapter 17

Vas toot a fayner Yiddishker maydel in uza platz?

What's a nice Jewish girl like you doing in a place like this?

Fanny's Diary, Skagway, July 2, 1898

I have made a big mistake, and now I live and write in fear. I was reading palms at my table in the back of the saloon when Soapy Smith entered with his gang. Soapy is the most important man in Skagway, a big shot, but he is also a fast-talking con artist who leads a band of thieves. They prey on townspeople and stampeders alike. Terry told me that in Seattle he sold soap by tricking people into thinking each bar of soap was wrapped in a fifty dollar bill. That's how he got his name. Here in Skagway he ran a fake telegram service for a while. Another business of his, The Reliable Packing Company, promises tenderfoot stampeders to pack their goods for the trip to the Klondike, but Soapy's men just steal the goods and sell them. Terry says he even sells used clothes behind the mortuary. But Soapy gives generously to widows and orphans, so some here do not mind his thieving ways. He is going to lead our parade July 4th. This is an important American holiday, like Passover, so leading the parade is an honor. Skagway was a lawless place before Soapy Smith and his friends arrived, but since they came, it has become even worse. I stay away from him, even though he is a good-looking man, with money in his pocket and an eye for the ladies.

One of Soapy's gang is Red Jackson, a repeat customer of mine. Red has asked me to marry him several times, but I will not marry anyone who is an associate of Soapy Smith. I don't say no though because I don't want to make Red angry. I just tell him I'm considering his offer and then I pray that the gang will leave Skagway soon. But last night Red brought Soapy to my table. I examined his big hand, prepared to predict he would come into more wealth in Dawson. But when I saw how short his lifeline was and pressed the swollen pad of his Mount of Mars, I stammered and hesitated. “What is it? What do you find there?” His loud voice startled me, and I blurted out that I saw his life cut short by a violent death.

As soon as those words left my big mouth I wished I had swallowed them, but it was too late. Soapy snatched his hand away and stormed out of the saloon, taking his hooligans with him. Now Alan Sawyer is angry with me. He scared me more when he told me Soapy strangled his own mistress and took her money. What if I had married Red? But Red does not seek me out any more, and I am glad. I pray for protection, but I have little hope that the God who deserted my pious family will hear my prayer.

Fanny's Diary, Skagway, July 10, 1898

Yesterday Soapy Smith was shot and killed. And if that is not the truth, may all my hair fall out and my teeth too. Yesterday morning in broad daylight his men robbed a stampeder of his poke in Soapy's bar, and the Marshall formed a posse to take them down. There was a shootout between Soapy and the Marshall. Soapy was killed, but the Marshall was badly wounded. I pray for his recovery.

I know it is not right to rejoice over the death of someone, but I was afraid of Soapy Smith, and, may God forgive me, I am glad he is dead. I am not the only one who is glad, because he was a bad man. Only the few widows he gave money to will miss him. One of them, Maria Delores, told me that without Soapy's charity she fears she and her infant will go hungry. But the rest of us are relieved that he is gone. Papa would say it is not right to find pleasure in his death. Mama would take food to the mother and child. So I will give Maria some money for food each week until she can work again. I am doing well here, but Skagway is a hard place for a mother and baby.

Before I predicted Soapy's death, my fortune-telling business was good, but now it is even better. Now even those few who doubted my ability to read their future in their palms are lining up at my table in the saloon. I am beginning to imagine that perhaps I really do have the ability to foresee events. I predicted to Terry that Red Jackson would high-tail it out of town after the posse took down Soapy, and he did. I am grateful God watches over me in this remote and dangerous place in spite of my many sins.

Fanny's Diary, Skagway, September 1898

A woman arrived here from Seattle last week selling ready-to-wear dresses, so there is a little less demand for my work. But I can still earn $8 for making a plain wool skirt, $10 for a fitted blouse, $12 for a plain dress, and $15 for a fancy dress. If I provide the fabric, I can earn more on each item. Skagway is like Seattle, always growing and changing with the times. They are building a railroad over the White Pass Trail! When it is finished, maybe Suzanne and Desiree will visit me here. I can pay the fare to Dawson. I earn $1 for each palm I read. But I still do not want to leave America.

Now that there is less sewing for me, I dance with stampeders and encourage them to buy me drinks. I like to wear my pretty dresses and I have learned American dances, but I do not like to drink, so I usually pour half of the whiskey they buy me into a bottle or spittoon under the table. Alan Sawyer tells all the dance-hall girls to do this or to drink colored water because then the stampeders buy us more drinks. My dance partners pay me in ivory chips which I can cash in at the end of the night. I get one dollar for each dance and a 25 percent commission on each drink I sell. Terry says I should steal from my partners when they get drunk, but I do not choose to break this commandment. Even so, with many partners in one night, I make good money as a dance-hall girl, and it is a change from sewing and reading palms.

I almost married one of my dance partners, a handsome man named Clark Reston. He was on his way home to Indiana with what he said was a fair amount of gold and "no wife to spend it." He was a big man and sure of himself. And because he was on his way home, I would not have to climb the White Horse Trail with him. He kept after me. But one morning my Tlingit friend Hattie was limping along just ahead of him carrying a heavy basket of clean laundry. He shoved her aside so hard she fell to the ground and all those clothes went into the mud. He didn't even stop to help her gather them or throw her a coin to make up for the damage he did. A bully with no feelings would not make a good husband or father no matter how much gold he has.

Besides, I have money of my own. I have two strongboxes now behind the wall boards in my room. They are filled with bills, nuggets, and coins because my treasure is now too great to carry easily at my waist in a poke. When I go out, I lock the door and the key stays on a chain around my neck with the thimble and locket Mama gave me. I wear this chain even in the bathhouse. My treasure is a big comfort to me, but it is not much company when I feel alone.

ꕤ

I closed the diary reluctantly. It was interesting to me that Feigele was not about to "settle" for just any husband. And Soapy Smith sounded a lot more intimidating than the Katzenjammer kid I'd beaned. I hoped Marsha wasn't running into any thugs in New York, especially now that she had left the comfort and security of her Aunt and Uncle's Upper West Side apartment. When she'd called to announce her move and ask for my chicken salad recipe, I warned her again to keep the apartment door locked. I repeated that advice every time we talked.

Yetta was still confined to the bedroom floor of her house, but she had begun to recover, so after giving her the usual update on Feigele, I broached the subject of the missing La Salle ledgers. "I can't find them anywhere, and I've looked through every drawer of every cabinet."

"Well, I know exactly where they are." There was an edge in Yetta's voice.

"If you tell me, I'll get them and file them where they belong."

"You can't. They took 'em. Toby Cutworth, an asshole Seattle cop I kept in cufflinks and turkeys for a thousand Christmases, had the gall to walk into this house one morning with some Jap lawyer and a search warrant. If I hadn't told Martin to let them have those goddamn ledgers, they'd have gone through every drawer and closet." Yetta sighed wearily and turned her head away.

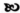

When she faced me again, her voice was low but every clipped syllable was distinct. "It was that damn lawsuit. The Ikedas sued me! When my manager and I went over the guest cards with them, there were thirty-four permanent guests. I didn't mention that some of those were me, my business manager, my porter-chauffeur and my girls. And if a guy stayed a week, I called him a permanent guest." I could make out Yetta's shoulders rising in a shrug.

When she continued, her tone was martyred. "Even though my health was poor, I met with the Ikedas and their realtor in my suite. I explained that there were so many one-night guests at the LaSalle because I had a good advertising program abroad and it drew merchant seamen to the place. That's the God's honest truth." The aging madam's insistence that she was telling the truth reminded me of Feigele's, and the missing ledgers brought to mind the pages torn from the diary. Before I could think through the implications of these similarities, if there were any, Yetta continued. "And while the Ikedas were in my apartment, I opened a drawer or two, so they couldn't help but see some of my cash." I pictured Yetta grinning. "They bought the La Salle."

Yetta sipped from the glass of water on her nightstand. "But guys kept showing up there looking for girls. That fool George Ikeda and his big shot law student son kept telling them, 'No girls.' They even put up a sign. It took a while before the Ikedas figured out that my 'guests' were sailors and lumberjacks looking for love who stayed only as long as it lasted. Under their ownership, the hotel's popularity declined drastically." Neither time nor crime nor her recent illness had squelched Yetta's sense of humor. In spite of how appalled I was by the fact that she deliberately deceived the Ikedas, I smiled.

"Those bastards took me to court! Can you believe that? They actually sued me for fraud. And they won. They got over seven grand plus interest out of me. But I showed 'em. This is America. I appealed to the State Supreme Court." From Yetta's triumphant tone you'd have thought she'd secured an audience with the Pope. "Lost there too. But I made all the papers." Yetta sounded pleased by the newsworthiness of her fraud conviction.

I asked her the only question her narrative left unanswered. "Don't take this the wrong way, Yetta, but since your own parents were immigrants and since you didn't need the money, why did you go to such lengths to cheat those greenhorns?"

When she replied, her speech was rapid-fire staccato, her voice raw. "Rachel, you and I live in two different worlds. I'm a businesswoman. I ran a whorehouse, not a damn welcome wagon."

Fanny's Diary, Skagway, November 17, 1898

I did not write for a long time because so much dancing to ragtime music was leaving me too tired to lift my pen. But the events of the last few weeks have made me so happy that I must record them. One night about three weeks ago a soft-spoken young man named David asked me to dance, and afterwards he bought me several drinks. In his slightly accented English he told me he was not a stampeder but had come here all the way from New York to open a cigar store. I shared with him my impressions of Skagway. I advised him of the cleanest bath house, the most skilled barber, the best restaurant and laundry. He was very attentive to my words, and I felt drawn to him. I was pleased when he came back every night for a week and danced and drank only with me.

One night he said his new store was nearly finished and invited me to see it. I walked with him to the shop. And may my pen become a length of rope binding my hands and feet if what I am about to write is not true. As we approached the shop, I saw his sign on a board in the window: *D. Minsky, Cigars*. I had not asked his last name before, but now that I knew it I became very curious. Could David be a Jew like me?

Before I could figure out how to pose this touchy question, we went inside. David's store is a small wooden building with a front room where he will display cigars and candy and greet customers and a back room where he is already living. Although he has only a bed and a trunk, I noticed a bottle of whiskey and two glasses on the trunk. He opened the bottle and poured whiskey into each glass. "I'm only giving you a little so you don't have to pour it out," is what he said with a smile. I blushed. I was ashamed that this nice man knew I had been cheating him. Then we drank to the success of his new business.

It began to rain hard, and we waited out the storm. For lack of chairs, he invited me to sit on his bed, and when I did, he leaned over and kissed me. I returned his kisses, and soon he had put out the candle and begun to undress me. I offered no protest. He makes love the way he speaks, gently and with great attentiveness to what will give me pleasure. It was this pleasure that made me reveal my secret. As his lips and hands awakened my body, I moaned and muttered a few words . . . in Yiddish.

To my delight, he replied in Yiddish. His own deep breaths divided his question, but I understood it. "What's a nice . . . Jewish girl like you . . . doing in a place like this?" As I realized that he was indeed circumcised, my pleasure grew, and I answered him freely in Yiddish. All night each of us cried out in Yiddish so that our shared mother tongue became a part of our pleasure and our bond. We are together every night now and I am so happy.

When no one else can hear we speak Yiddish. Even ordinary words like "Would you like to dance?" or "Your friend Hattie did a good job on my laundry" in Yiddish bring great pleasure, great comfort to me. My English is quite good now, so I did not realize how much my tongue and my ears missed my own language. David is a Jew more like the Weiss's than like Mama and Papa, but he says his parents are very pious. He says he wants the best of both worlds. He says I remind him of his sister but that I am more adventuresome. She would never come to Alaska. I give thanks again to God for sending David all the way to Skagway for me.

Fanny's Diary, Skagway, May 5, 1899

I have been too busy to write in this book until right now when there are no customers in the store. I have also been so happy that I have not felt driven to record my thoughts. Several months ago David asked me to marry him! A customer paid for several boxes of very fine cigars with a large nugget. David had Kirmse the jeweler make it into a ring for me and gave it to me when he proposed. It is beautiful. We will be married by a rabbi in Seattle after we have saved enough money to return there and invest in land. David visited Seattle on his way to Skagway, and he thinks that city will expand. Since that night I have been living with David in the room behind his shop. I fit customers and make dresses in our cozy back room and read palms in the store. David says my palm-reading attracts customers.

Gradually more women have been arriving in Skagway. Some come on business, some seek adventure or love, and some are the wives and daughters of the stampeders and shopkeepers already here. Those who can't fit into the ready-to-wear dresses or who want something finer need my services, so I still have some dressmaking work. Although David keeps the shop open on the Sabbath, we usually make time to go to the bathhouse and for me to light the candles and say a blessing before we go to bed. My cup runneth over.

Now that I am no longer dancing, I am gaining back some of the weight I lost. When Terry visited last week, she thought I looked the better for it. "A few pounds and a smile do wonders for a girl" was how she said it. She looks thin and tired and one of her front teeth is black. I promised her I'd make a new blue dress for her doll. I won't charge her for it either. She is a good friend.

Fanny's Diary, Skagway, June 16, 1899

I have seen a ghost, a ghost that drives me to write. David often receives packages from New York. Most of them contain merchandise, but sometimes they are from his sister. She sends him vials of the ointment he uses when his feet ache and two boxes of the headache pills he favors, all carefully wrapped in newspaper and then packed in a carton.

One of these packages came yesterday. David exclaimed when he unwound the pages of newsprint. They are not written in English. They are from a new Yiddish paper in New York called *The Jewish Daily Forward.* We smoothed out the pages and read every word. This paper, all in Yiddish, is full of news about Jews and advice for greenhorns.

It also has ads for jobs and photos of husbands who have run away. It was in one of those photos that I saw the ghost. My heart raced. May the earth open beneath my feet and swallow me if what I am about to record is not the truth. The face of Boris Lipschitz stared out at me from the newspaper, the same Boris Lipschitz who employed me in his sweatshop in New York the minute I stepped off the boat. My heart still making like a drum, I read the words beneath the photo. "Boris, please come home. All is forgiven. Your wife and four children need you. Without you we have nothing. I beg of you, we all beg of you, Boris, please come home. Your wife, Oodle Lipschitz."

I was so surprised to see Boris's face that I looked at the photo carefully to be sure my eyes were not telling me lies. I saw the familiar narrow eyes and pinched mouth. I read twice more the sad message from Oodle. I was not surprised that Boris found himself a wife because men with work who wish to marry have little trouble finding wives. Also I was not surprised he and this wife had four children. I would have had sisters and more brothers if Mama had not lost the babies she carried between me and Yitzak. Chaya probably has about ten little ones by now and Devorah wanted a houseful. And I was not surprised that Boris needed forgiveness from this wife because he was already a criminal like Soapy Smith. Maybe Boris got caught and went to jail and lost his shop. But it surprised me to see a Yiddish newspaper in Skagway and it surprised me even more that this particular paper with Boris's face in it is the one David's sister wrapped his medicines in and sent all the way to Alaska. I thank God I did not marry Boris or it would be me, not Oodle, writing those sad words.

Bored, restless, and still confined to the bedroom floor of her house, Yetta continued to find Feigele's experiences diverting, if occasionally less than credible. I wasn't surprised when she found the last few entries hard to swallow. "I'm sorry, Rachel, but I have a hard time believing that among the thousands of guys in Skagway, Feigele ran into the one other Jew."

"That's because you're a cynic." I tried to sound bemused, not accusatory. Actually I was pleased Yetta felt up to arguing. "Not so long ago you told me you were sure Feigele was prostituting herself."

"Of course she turned tricks. I may be a cynic, but you're naive. I don't care what she wrote down. That whoremaster in Skagway wouldn't have rented a crib over his saloon to a seamstress even if she was Betsy Ross. He could make too much off that room to let her have it without turning tricks for him. Besides, in my business, cynicism pays." I made out Yetta's fingers moving on her tray. The familiar gesture encapsulated perfectly the retired madam's jaundiced world view: everything and everybody had a price. "Read between the lines. The girl's writing a fairy tale."

"Earlier in the diary Feigele wrote that her father was a good storyteller. You think she takes after him?"

"I sure do. That's probably what made her such a popular fortuneteller. Or do you also believe she was really clairvoyant?"

I ignored her sarcasm. "Yetta, if you don't believe what Feigele writes about David, don't you also doubt her when she writes that her sweatshop boss's photo turned up in *The Forward*? In the very same issue that David's sister just happened to wrap his medicines in? I'm no cynic, but I wondered about that coincidence myself."

"That I believe. *The Forward* was full of those ads. Back then lots of marriages were arranged in the old country, and they didn't always work out here. Lots of those couples had too many kids and not enough money. In the land of the free, some Jews with more kids than schooling and who couldn't get work left their wives, left their kids, just took off. And if Boris went to jail, he probably came out with no moola to start over . . . In Canada I came across quite a few of those deserters myself." Then, as if to clinch her argument, Yetta added, "Besides, why would she bring up Boris if she didn't really see *The Forward*, see that picture?"

I had no answer, but I was enjoying our chat. The files could wait a few more minutes. I stretched. "Did I tell you I saw the artifacts that were in the bag with her bones?"

"No, but I bet the cops took anything worth stealing."

"You're impossible. Nobody took anything except the person who killed her. Remember, her ring finger bones are missing." Whenever I remembered Feigele's missing bones, I shuddered. "Professor Hunter thinks she was killed for a ring. Maybe it was that big gold one David gave her."

"So what did they find with her?"

"Corset stays, some little nuggets, a fake ruby, and a beat-up silver locket passed down from Feigele's grandmother to her mother. I told you how Feigele's mother gave the locket to Feigele along with a silver thimble when she was leaving home, remember? The thimble's there too. So Feigele didn't make up the locket or the thimble." I barely refrained from adding a childish, "so there." Next thing I knew, I'd be sticking out my tongue. "That girl treasured those beat up old tchotchkes all her life."

To my surprise, I got no argument from Yetta. She was reaching over to the side table and groping among the pill bottles and Kleenex. "What is it? Can I get you something? Do you want a tissue?" I couldn't imagine hardhearted Yetta being moved to tears by Feigele's attachment to a couple of worthless baubles.

"There should be a comb here, a small wooden comb. It's always right here." The urgency in Yetta's voice troubled me. She wasn't supposed to get upset.

"I see it. Here." I handed her a comb that had been nesting in her silver-backed hairbrush. "But Bess already did your hair."

Yetta didn't raise the comb to her hair but handed it back to me. "This belonged to my mother." Her voice was suddenly childlike. I studied the small, worn, wooden comb as best I could in the limited light. It looked to be a homely object, especially in comparison with the luxuries Yetta possessed. Opposite the comb's teeth, on the handle, I felt the vestiges of a design, its outlines muted into unintelligible but still symmetrical nubs. Yetta fidgeted in her easy chair, and I saw her hand reach out, a moving shadow. "Give it back."

As soon as Yetta's fingers closed around the little comb, she began to talk. "My mother's father was a wood carver. In the Ukraine he decorated the wooden synagogues. He made, you know, the lions at the side of the Ten Commandments over the Torah arks. He carved this comb with the same two lions on it for my mother. When they came to this country, he got a job in a woodworking shop on Coney Island making horses for the carousel. That's where my mother was raised. Coney Island." Yetta's voice sounded far away. "That's where she met my father." She sighed. "When they met, she was already in her twenties and frail. I think she had heart trouble like me." I made out Yetta drawing the hand holding the comb to her chest.

I leaned forward, not wanting to miss a whispered word.

"Anyway, to get her married, her father gave a small dowry with her, and my father used the money to travel west." Yetta's loud 'tsk tsk' was accompanied by vigorous headshaking.

Why would a woman who amassed a fortune selling female flesh be bothered by the traditional financial transaction that had enabled her own sickly mother to marry? Or was it the trip west that bothered Yetta? Or marriage itself? She and Martin did not share a last name. I waited for her to continue.

Yetta's next words rewarded my patience. "My mother never wanted to leave Coney Island." Yetta sighed again, troubled anew by the memory of her mother's forced migration. "But my father talked big about striking it rich and buying a ranch. I remember him singing that old vaudeville tune, "I'm a *Yiddishe* Cowboy." Do you know it?" Yetta began to tap her fingers on the bedside table. This faint percussive fusillade was only the overture before the former madam burst into song, her voice a pitch-perfect alto, her usually unaccented English exaggeratedly inflected. There in the darkened room Yetta continued tapping her fingers even after "tough guy" Levi uttered his final giddy up.

I clapped. "No, I never heard that one. Maybe it never got past Montana."

"Like my parents. They only made it as far as Butte." Lenny Bruce claimed that a Jew in Butte would be goyish, not Jewish. Maybe that's why Yetta could pass so easily as Edna Douglas or Nellie Curtis. "Right after I was born, my father got a job there as the jailhouse janitor, and, for all I know, the son of a bitch died doing that." I recalled the scars on Yetta's thighs. Had her father beaten her?

"He was a hanger-on, kowtowing to all the big shots." Yetta's summary of the man's career was snarled rather than spoken, making her contempt for him clearly audible. "Didn't do him any good though, because we never had anything nice, never lived anywhere decent. In fact, we'd have been better off if he'd up and left us." I fingered the raised design circling the rim of my empty Wedgwood coffee cup and pictured the polished floors, Persian rugs, ornate furnishings, and overflowing closets of Yetta's home. "That bastard worked and screwed my mother right into her grave. She died giving birth to my sister. But between labor pains she gave me this comb." I should have given Marsha Manya's wedding ring before she left for college. I would send it to her.

The little wooden comb had acted as a Rosetta stone, making Yetta's memories accessible. It was her own memories, not Feigele's that had moved the professed cynic to tears. She was groping for a Kleenex just as Martin, back from his daily trip to the grocer, entered the room. "You're not supposed to tire yourself out yakking." He turned to me, "Let her get some rest now."

I handed Yetta a tissue, leaned over, and, without thinking, kissed her cheek. I wanted to stay, to hear more. Yetta's girlhood was more interesting to me now than her myriad financial dealings, the iffy records of which I was attempting to arrange in sensible categories and a plausible sequence. But Martin was right. Yetta needed her rest.

I went home a little early determined to straighten up before showering and getting ready for what felt like a first-time fix-up. My body opened eagerly to Bobby, but my brain was still having trouble with the idea of having a lover at all, let alone having that lover be my old friend. After Harry's death, my life changed so fast that I felt sometimes as if the quake that killed him had picked me up and plopped me down in someone else's life. This was one of those times. When the doorbell rang, I was stepping out of the shower. I threw on a robe and ran downstairs.

"I'm sorry, Bobby. I'll only be a minute. Fix yourself a drink." I heard myself talking like a hostess welcoming a casual acquaintance. Should I have greeted Bobby with a hug? Told him how very glad I was to see him?

I rummaged through Miriam's recent cast-offs until I found a black linen sleeveless shift with pleats down the front. Even though it was black, to me the dress screamed *New York* not *Recent Widow*. I shimmied into it and checked the mirror. My bra strap showed, recalling Feigele's whalebone stays that, in the end, outlasted the flesh they had constrained. With a shrug, I pulled the dress over my head, unhooked my bra, slipped out of it, and tugged the chemise down into place again. It was short, just hitting my bare knees, but not mini like the dresses in magazines.

My hair had dried into a bush, so I brushed it away from my face and confined it there with an arced tortoise shell comb. I put on a bit of Cherry Red lipstick, my old black patent pumps, and a pair of faux pearl earrings. The outsized earrings drew people's eyes away from my nose. As I descended the stairs I acknowledged something that would have been unthinkable even a week ago. I wanted to look really, really good for Bobby Gradstein.

Chapter 18

. . . Ich daven fahr a mahn . . .

. . . I pray for a husband . . .

ꟗ

Fanny's Diary, Skagway, July 30, 1900

Now I must write or I will do worse. Last week when David was at the bathhouse, another package from New York came for him. Like always I was excited to read the Yiddish newspaper his sister wraps his medicines in, so I opened the box. On top inside there was a flat object wrapped in *The Forward.* I carefully removed the paper. The object was a framed photograph of a pretty young woman and three small boys, all with David's features. In one corner above this picture were the words "To my David" and in the opposite corner on the bottom I read, "Your loving wife Selma and your sons, Morty, Saul, and Max." David is already married, the father of three.

I did not know, did not imagine. I stared at that picture for a long time, not caring that my tears fell on it. They blurred the glass face of David's "loving wife" staring out at me with her big eyes. But even through my tears, I could see that she is real. The children are real. God help them all. "Her" David is a liar and an adulterer. Our "engagement" was a cruel tale he made up to keep me in his bed, in his store. To him I am just a foolish dancehall girl who believed his talk of being married by a rabbi. But even dancehall girls have hearts that break and bleed. I can write no more of this now.

ꟗ

Fanny's Diary, Skagway, August 5, 1900

Once again I write from this room above Sawyer's Stage Door Saloon. After seeing the picture of David's wife and children, I could not bear to set eyes on David again. I wanted to be gone from the store before he returned. I jammed my fingernails into the palms of my hands to make myself stop crying. Then I packed my things quickly, took my strongboxes from beneath the floorboards and paid a boy with a cart to haul them to the saloon. I followed close behind him. Then I sent the boy back to the cigar store to get my trunk and my sewing machine. I left no note, just the photograph atop the opened package. I did not allow my tears to fall again until I was once more alone in this little room.

I am grateful to Alan Sawyer for taking me back even though business is slow. I have no place else to go. A lot of people are leaving town and going to Nome because the Klondike fields have no more gold. I heard David is one of those leaving. Very likely one day I would have awakened to find him gone, like Bernie Olafsky, like a ghost. Bernie Olafsky stole my heart and my money. David Minsky took only my heart. I am glad I left first. He came last night to see me, maybe to beg forgiveness, but I would not stop dancing to talk with him. And I was not spitting out my whiskey either.

Fanny's Diary, Skagway, August 20, 1900

My old friend Desiree came to Skagway yesterday. She asked for me at the saloon and came up to my room. At first I thought Desiree was a vision brought on by strong drink, but she is real. Her face is thinner than I remember, and her eyes no longer dance, but she is still beautiful and still the same good, dear friend, even though she is a married woman now.

We talked for many hours and I told my friend how David lied and broke my heart. I held nothing back. She wiped away my tears and gave me wise counsel. Her practical and sensible advice made me feel much better, as did her understanding and the way she listened to me. Desiree does not sit in judgment on me.

Later she told me about her husband, Ralph Thurston, a stampeder from Iowa. Ralph is one of the few lucky ones who struck gold. They are going to Seattle because Desiree is not happy in Dawson anymore. Most of the stampeders have gone to Nome and Suzanne left with them. Dawson is becoming respectable, so there are churches now, and the other married women, the church ladies, do not invite the Thurstons to their parties. And their husbands, men she has known for years, do not say a word. Desiree says those bastards deserve the bitches they married. So Ralph went ahead to Seattle to look at property. They plan to buy a boarding house there.

It was hard to say goodbye to Desiree. When I saw her waving from the ship's deck, I wept. She promised to write when they are settled, and I will answer her letters. I am glad for her good fortune. But I would be a liar if I did not write that my friend's happiness with her husband makes me yearn for David and the future I thought we would share.

Feigele's Diary, Skagway

I do not know what to do. Skagway is quiet now with most of the stampeders gone, the tent city torn up, and just a few folks stopping by on the way to Dawson, Juneau, or Nome. Now that selling liquor is legal here, there is a big licensing fee. $1500 is what I heard. So a lot of the saloons have closed. Terry went back to Texas a few weeks ago. There's nobody to dance with anymore but the colored soldiers stationed nearby, no more showgirls wanting fancy dresses. The church ladies here do not want dancehall girls at their balls. I have few friends left. Even the Jap girls on Yokohama Row are leaving. Now I get by on what I have saved plus what little I make reading the palms of the few tourists who pass through on the train. It frightens me to be living off my savings. I pray for a husband.

Maybe I should go back to Seattle. With the port and the army base and the loggers, there is entertainment and money to be made. I could sew again. And it is warmer. Devorah and Myron would not want me boarding with them after I ran off. I am sure Devorah's brother Avram has married. But Desiree is there and she wrote me that she and her husband would welcome me if I chose to return. She wrote that Seattle is still growing, not shrinking like this place. Skagway is like a ghost town now. I feel like a ghost.

I reread the entry in which Feigele described her discovery of David Minsky's duplicity three times before I even tried to make the woman's anguish, so wrenching in Yiddish, palpable in English. At first I was angry with her for not suspecting David was married, for not getting the truth out of him right away. But I know an Orthodox upbringing stays with you no matter where, or even if, you worship. In spite of what she wrote earlier about not expecting to find a Jewish husband in Alaska and about how her parents, the only people who would care if she didn't marry a Jew, were dead, Feigele really did want that Jewish husband. So when she learned David was Jewish, she probably believed that, unlike some of her other suitors, the man was, literally, heaven sent and so above suspicion. But the diarist wanted a Jewish husband of her own, not somebody else's.

Before I passed judgment on her for being naive, I recalled also that the two-timing cigar salesman had fooled me too. And at forty-five in 1965, I'd almost fallen for the married Tim Hunter's seductive flattery. And I'd never suspected that my own husband of twenty years was gambling away our savings. It seems no matter how smart we women are, when it comes to men we believe what we want to believe.

Driving to Yetta's, I thought about Feigele's return to her room over Alan Sawyer's saloon. Yetta just might be right. In all likelihood, Feigele was a prostitute. She probably chose to exclude this from her diary because she still hoped to marry and envisioned her children reading it someday. I'd come across a few references to these yet unborn readers. The diarist even addressed them directly once or twice. Or maybe Feigele was just ashamed and left her whoring out so she wouldn't have to confront it herself. If that were true, what else had she left out? Or changed? Or written about and torn out, the tattered edges of those excised pages the only testimony that they had ever been there. Who knew? Who would ever know?

And what if Feigele was a hooker? So what? That wasn't all she was. Similarly, Yetta Solomon could not be completely defined by her former profession any more than by her failure to join a synagogue or observe the Sabbath, additional "crimes" for which my mother had undoubtedly shunned her. Even poor Harry's complexity couldn't be measured only in poker debts any more than Bobby could be dismissed as an underachieving cut-up. And what about my mother? There had been more, much more, to Manya than her old country Orthodoxy and accented admonitions.

I pictured the people I knew stepping out of my labeled boxes. I resolved to think about this some more, perhaps because, like those church ladies Desiree and Feigele talked about, I sensed that freeing people from their boxes posed a real threat to my own well-entrenched sense of moral superiority, my conviction that I, Rachel Mazursky, was somehow better-behaved than most. Was this why Bobby used to think of me as a prig? But since Harry's death I'd lusted after a married man who wasn't even Jewish, bashed in somebody's head, had sex without marriage, and worked for a madam. Did these decidedly unpriggish acts make me a bad person? My daughter thought so.

My heart constricted at the memory of Marsha's telephone call early that same morning. I was in the bathroom when the bedside phone rang, awakening Bobby who reflexively answered it. At the sound of his voice, Marsha figured she had the wrong number and was about to hang up when he assured her that she had reached the Mazursky household. Rachel would be on the line in a minute. By the time I raced to the phone, Marsha's tone was accusatory and her rapid fire questions a shrill barrage of condemnation. "Mom? Who was that? Who's there? How could you? In the bed you and dad . . . . No wonder you don't want me to come home." Before I could answer, I heard the receiver click. Marsha hung up on me, a first. To my daughter I was not only a bad person. I was a bad mother too.

Later that day after Marsha didn't take or return my many calls, I phoned my cousin Miriam. Her daughter Susie had already briefed her. "Marsha told Susie you're 'desecrating' her father's memory." Miriam paused and then her cousinly curiosity got the best of her. "So, Rachel, does that mean you're seeing someone?"

"Yes. Bobby Gradstein. Remember him?"

"Mo and Harriet's son?"

"Uh huh. He's in town visiting his mother. He lives in New York now. He's divorced." I took a deep breath. "He answered the phone early yesterday morning when Marsha called here."

"*Oy.*" For some Jews, this monosyllabic Yiddish exclamation had degenerated into a grunt of mere frustration or impatience, but Miriam could still put more existential angst into that single syllable than anyone I knew. "His timing stinks." She shifted quickly from angst to advice. "Keep calling. The kid just lost her father. She's probably afraid of losing you too. And she's angry that she has to grow up. But don't worry. She's fine. We're keeping tabs on her."

I didn't have to tell Miriam how much I missed talking to my daughter or how guilty I felt at what Marsha saw as my premature betrayal of Harry's memory. But even the Orthodox are required to abstain from sex for only thirty days after the death of a spouse. Then they're free to remarry, not to screw around. But, the men who framed the Talmud didn't know about the Pill. And, as Bobby pointed out, it wasn't as if I planned our reunion. Maybe I should have bought a new bed, but, unbeknownst to Marsha, we did avoid the connubial bed on our first night together. Still, I wished Bobby had not picked up that phone.

Guilt eroded my self-confidence, turned the affection and desire I felt for Bobby into distrust. Was I being naïve like Feigle? What if he was just using me as a diversion during a long-overdue visit to his mother? Soon he'd return to New York and his harem of nurses, all willing and able to bed him with, as he had put it, no strings. With my stretch marks, my schnozz, and strings like umbilical cords reaching back to our shared playpen, how could I compete with this line-up of undoubtedly nubile and pug-nosed nurses?

I was too old to be part of the mini-skirted, marijuana-mad, sexually-liberated set, but too young to resign myself to long days keeping house, planning fundraisers, and selling flatware, and even longer nights going to bed alone. I needed a teaching job and a husband. Since Harry's death, just as Feigele envied Desiree I envied my married friends. I envied their settled lives and the companionship and sex they took for granted. I even envied their petty gripes about their spouses' sharp toenails and loud snoring. Since the mourning period ended, I'd avoided these coupled friends, the only ones I had. Did other widows envy their married friends? Did widowers? Had Jake Heller? Was this jealousy of the married one of those "potholes" on the path of instant bereavement he mentioned in his note?

I was still pondering the complications of contemporary widowhood when I pulled up at Yetta's. I was surprised to find the convalescent seated at the kitchen table. In honor of Yetta's first descent since her heart attack, Bess had poached and chunked a slab of salmon and presented it along with lemon wedges, lettuce, tomatoes, and fresh rolls. "Sit down." Yetta's voice was girlish. "We're really celebrating tomorrow night. I've invited your father for dinner. Rachel, that man's been calling every single day since you told him I took ill." Her tone was accusatory, but it was clear that she relished Sam's attention.

"I know he'll be relieved to see how well you look. Just don't overdo it." Like Martin, I feared for Yetta's heart.

"To make sure that I don't, I'd like you to join us. You and Martin can take turns monitoring my behavior. And, Rachel, invite your doctor friend. I'd like to meet him."

I was no longer astonished that the sequestered blind woman knew so much about what went on outside of her dark and limited orbit. Clearly, Sam spilled the beans about Bobby and me. "Thanks, Yetta. I'd like you to meet him too."

"Good. Martin, please pass the rolls. They won't be this fresh at dinner." Yetta turned back to me. "So tell me, what's our Feigele got herself into now?" Then in a voice that was lively and sure, Yetta answered her own question. "I bet my favorite hat that her precious Hymie knocked her up and took off with somebody else."

I was too startled by the possibility of Feigele's being pregnant to be put off by Yetta's crudity. I'd focused on the girl's heartbreak, not her anatomy. "You get to keep your hat, Yetta. You're half right. Feigele doesn't say anything about being pregnant, but she learned that the son of a bitch had a wife and three kids back in New York." Yetta didn't find this revelation or my own strong language startling enough to warrant more than a nod. She'd thought David was too good to be true anyway. "Yetta, I can't stay late today, so I'm going to take my plate with me and hit those files."

"I'll ask Bess to wrap a couple of pieces of pound cake for you. And, Rachel, before you go home, take your check. Martin will leave it with the cake. You're due half of what I owe you, and I figure you probably need to send something to your girl's college."

"Thanks, Yetta. I appreciate not having to wait for all of it." In a few hours, I would hold in my hands a check for four thousand dollars, almost half the missing *kishke-gelt.*

When I got home, tired and bleary-eyed, I opened the mail. Along with the electric bill was an envelope from the Seattle Board of Ed. The secretary to the president of that exalted body wished to inform me that an unexpected vacancy had occurred in the history department at Franklin High School and Principal George Jankowski recommended me for the position. Was I still available? Standing in the kitchen with that letter in my hand, I gave God points for coming through with a teaching job and half the *kishke-gelt.*

Then I asked Him nicely for a little help with Marsha. Taking Miriam's advice, I phoned my long-distance daughter to tell her I would be teaching in the fall. Her roommate answered, and through the muffled receiver I heard that same daughter say, "Tell her I'm not here."

Chapter 19

Lomir chasuna, Roiter.

Let's get married, Red.

ஐ

Fanny's Diary, Skagway, September 20, 1900

God did not forget me. Not a week after Desiree left for Seattle, Ryan O'Neal returned to Skagway. Women are no longer allowed in the saloons, so the woman who bought the cigar shop from David, Bea Smithers, may her life be for a blessing, lets me read palms there like I did before. When Ryan came in, I almost didn't recognize him. He was thin and pale, a ghost of the young stampeder who proposed marriage to me on the boat to Alaska. But he greeted me warmly in front of the other customers. He said meeting me again meant his luck was turning.

Ryan spends his days looking for work and his evenings dancing and drinking with me at Sawyer's. He is still a good storyteller, and he tells me of his adventures on the Dead Horse Trail and in the goldfields. I listen with both ears as if I have not heard a thousand such stories. Like many others, he struggled hard and left there with nothing but a few nuggets to show for his efforts. But not many men return from the goldfields unchanged by the hardships they lived through there. Ryan seems less cheerful, less hopeful. But in one way he has not changed. He still wants me. He begs me to move into the room he rents above the bakery. I have not agreed yet.

Then last night Ryan proposed to me again! "Let's get married, Red," were his exact words. He calls me Red because of my hair. This time I accepted his proposal with a glad heart. My fiancé wants to postpone our wedding until he finds work. I am less eager to wait.

ஐ

Fanny's Diary, Skagway, October 1, 1900

I am Mrs. Ryan O'Neal. My friend Craig, the station master at the train depot where I sometimes read palms, gave Ryan a job selling tickets. Ryan won't make much money, but the job is easy, and there is no other work to be had here. He started this morning, so yesterday we were married.

Ryan and I met on a ship, so it is fitting that we were married by a ship captain named James Olsen on a boat moored in the harbor at Skagway. The sun shone, the sea was calm, and I wore a pretty dress and warm cape. But there was no rabbi and no wedding canopy, no priest or cross. And there were no relatives. I felt their absence even though none of our parents would have blessed our patchwork American wedding anyway. But it is legal. Tom O'Shea, a friend of Ryan's, and my friend, Bea Smithers, bore witness to our little ceremony. The ring Ryan gave me is a simple gold band, melted down from a small nugget he won at poker. When Captain Olsen pronounced us man and wife, tears of joy came to my eyes. Afterwards we celebrated with our friends over dinner in the dining room of the Pullman Hotel. I am Mrs. Ryan O'Neal, but Ryan still calls me Red.

Fanny's diary, Skagway, January 18, 1901

Months have passed since Ryan and I were married. They have been busy months with little time to record my thoughts. Now in my spare time, instead of writing in my diary, I sew tiny garments because soon I'm going to be a mother. In October when I told Ryan he would be a father, he was thrilled and went off to the depot the next day a proud and happy man.

I remember when Mama, may her life be for a blessing, was pregnant with little Yitzak, may he rest in peace, she used to talk with other ladies who were also expecting babies. Those who were already mothers would give advice and tell stories about birthing and talk of how to be a mother. Chaya and Devorah also had many other women to talk with about these matters. But here in Skagway I have not any friends who are mothers except my Tlingit friend Hattie who still does not speak a lot of English.

Bea Smithers has no children and little advice even though she is kind. There is no midwife here.

Ryan hopes for a son. He does not know that I pray for a little girl, because it will be difficult to arrange a circumcision here in Alaska. Besides, a baby boy would remind me of little Yitzak and my heart would break every time I looked at him.

Fanny's Diary, Skagway, 1901

Yesterday a Jewish woman stopped for a night in Skagway on her way back from Dawson. I was delivering a dress I made for the owner of the Pullman Hotel when the Jewish woman arrived there. Her name is Becci. I recognized her accent, and we talked for a long time. Her husband remains in Dawson running the hotel they started, but Becci cannot bear to be separated from her three little ones any longer. She is on her way home to New York to see her children.

It was good to talk with another Jewish woman, especially one who is a mother, and I asked her many questions about birthing and caring for an infant. Becci was generous with her knowledge and told me many things about what my new baby would need. Of course I saw in Becci's palm a joyous reunion with her children.

Fanny's Diary, Skagway, June 11, 1901

Once again God answered my prayers. In March with the help of Bea Smithers and Hattie, may the lives of these good women be filled with blessings, I gave birth to a baby girl. When Bea put my baby into my arms, I forgot the pain of a thousand pitchforks piercing my gut during the long hours I struggled to expel her. And I thank God that even though she was born a month or two early, my baby is perfect.

Even Ryan smiled when he first saw her, and he had not smiled often those last weeks. Ever since the station master fired him for returning to work late after lunch once too often, my husband's mood has darkened. Ryan wanted to name the baby Rose after his mother, and I agreed because my own mama, may she rest in peace, was named Rivka, and the initial is the same. My dear one stirs in her cradle now. I must feed her. I will resume writing later when she sleeps again, so someday my Rosele can read of the joy she brought us. Meanwhile I pray that Ryan finds work.

She is sleeping now, but I have little time to write because since I became a mother I am busier than ever. And my sweet Rose does take a little bit of time when she is hungry or wet or cannot fall asleep. But Rose is not to blame for my being so busy. I must be the breadwinner because again Ryan has no work. And even though my husband does not earn money, he still spends it at the saloon. He says he goes to Sawyer's in the hope of hearing about a job and that he cannot sit there without ordering a drink or two.

He tried to get a job as a bartender, but there are few bars left and none need help. No stable owners need help either. So I must earn money to pay the saloon, the baker who rents us our room, and to buy food. I do not want to use my savings. But there is very little dressmaking work now, so I bring my little Rosele with me to the cigar store and to the train station where I tell fortunes. Ryan does not like it that I go to the train station, because the stationmaster fired him, but there are few other places to read palms, so I must. I don't talk about it with Ryan and hope no one mentions seeing me there to him.

Fanny's Diary, Skagway, September 23, 1901

Ryan was drinking more, and I was starting to despair. We three were still living in Ryan's room over the bakery, but it was noisy and small. We needed a place of our own, and Ryan needed a job and there was no hope for either. And then our luck changed or God remembered us. Or maybe we just have Bea Smithers to thank for the relief she provided. May God bless my dear friend Bea with good fortune in her next venture. Last week she mentioned to me that she would soon leave for Nome and wanted to sell her well-stocked cigar store. In less time than it used to take me to blow out the candles on Friday night, I arranged to buy the little shop from her with some of my savings. It is fitting that my Rose should live in a house that David built.

At first, my husband, who is nothing if not proud, did not like the idea. But I knew how to win him over. I told Ryan I was depending on him to run the store and that I would read palms there and that we three could live in the back room, and he agreed to give it a try. I also reminded him that the cigar store had sentimental meaning to me because it was there that he and I met once again. So last Thursday, as soon as Bea moved out, with the help of the baker's delivery boy, we moved in.

Ryan was at the cigar store already at work, so I stayed at our room over the bakery to supervise the loading of our few things. Bea agreed to do me one last favor before she left the store. At my request, she asked Ryan to deliver several boxes of cigars to the Pullman Hotel. While he was gone, I paid the baker's boy to bring the locked strong boxes containing my savings in his wagon from our room over the bakery to our new home. After he left, I quickly unlocked and emptied the two large boxes into four smaller ones that I could lift. I locked these, and, with Rosele and Bea as my only witnesses, I lowered each of the boxes into their old hiding place beneath the floorboards, stashed the keys in my poke, and put the old too-big boxes where Bea's things stood awaiting a boy to take them to the train station.

I feel strange living and working once again in this little nest I shared with David. Sometimes I see his face in the window glass or hear him speaking to me in Yiddish. But these memories will fade, and we will be happy here. Bea left us Goldie, her yellow kitty, so Rose has a playmate. Ryan has been behind the counter less than a week, and already he is very good with customers. David talked with them mostly about the qualities of different cigars and about where and how they are made, but Ryan tells them stories and jokes, and they seem to like that. If one of the customers has a serious question, I answer it. My husband is surprised by how much I know about the cigar business and about cigars. I told him I learned by watching Bea.

Only when Ryan takes a break for lunch at the saloon do I venture behind the counter. Then my Rosele sits on a blanket on the floor and plays with the empty cigar boxes and the blocks Ryan carved for her. When he returns, Ryan sings her Irish love songs and makes her laugh. At night, when he goes again to the saloon, I sing her Yiddish lullabies that make me cry. She is my angel, my life.

Fanny's Diary, on the boat to Seattle, April 5, 1902

Once again I write in this little book from aboard a ship. I am in a cabin and beside me Rosie sleeps, her chubby fingers still sticky from candy. Her round face is peaceful and her perfect eyelids move with her dreams. I could stare at her forever, hide my nose in the folds of her neck forever, and breathe the sweet smell of her forever. I have my savings in my strong boxes on the cabin floor beside my bed, but this little girl is my real treasure. Someday she will read these pages and understand why we had to leave Skagway and Ryan. But today she asked for her dada several times and I had no ready answer. It is the same when she asks for her kitty.

I see only now what an optimist I was to think Ryan would take well to marriage, to fatherhood. Few will have trouble believing the problems that came from my desperation. Things grew so bad between us that, for a long time, I could not bear to write of them, as if putting them down on paper would seal our fate. But now, on our way to a new life, I can explain. Ryan drank more and more, stayed out longer every night. Once when he came home he accused a good customer of an ungentlemanly interest in me and, when I protested, Ryan hit me. Blood poured from my nose. I can still hear my Rosele's scream. My nose has not returned to its real shape.

What little money I took in, Ryan spent on drink. When he came home to sleep, he was angry if my Rosele made even a peep. Once he raised his hand to her for singing a little ditty to her doll. I stepped between them and he backed off, but I became afraid for us both. Then last week Ryan was arrested yet again for brawling over a bar tab, but this time when I heard I felt relief. This time I paid the police chief to keep him in jail an extra few days, and while he was gone I booked passage to Seattle for Rosie and me. I left Ryan the store, the gold wedding ring he gave me, and some cash. With a roof over his head and money for the saloon, maybe he will not come after us. Perhaps God punishes me for marrying a non-Jew. But tonight, on this boat, I will sleep without fear beside my Rosele.

That Feigele suddenly found the previously unacceptable Ryan O'Neal a good catch and had a baby born "a month or two early" forced me to realize that, once again, Yetta was right. The young woman was pregnant when she married. I should have figured that out. After all, condom shmondom, before the Pill and after each miscarriage, my own fear of pregnancy climbed into bed with Harry and me every single night. That same fear must have shadowed Feigele and finding herself pregnant by the deceitful and despicable David Minsky would have been a decidedly mixed blessing. Unless she married somebody, her child would be a bastard, but at least a Jewish bastard.

To Feigele, marrying a non-Jew, a jobless, unsuccessful stampeder she knew to be jealous and prone to violence, was preferable to giving birth to a bastard. "Marry the next guy who asks" was probably the "wise counsel" Desiree gave her. Because the supply of men in Skagway had dwindled along with the vein of gold in the Klondike and because she was pregnant, Feigele lowered her standards. How many pregnant women during the pre-Pill millennia made similar compromises? Should I applaud Feigele's flexibility or bemoan her concern with propriety?

But even though Feigele's shotgun marriage to a hard-drinking and hard-up lapsed Catholic failed, I had to hand it to her. She'd wanted a husband to make her child legitimate, and she'd found one. Ryan wouldn't marry without a job, so she got him one through a friend she'd cultivated. Later, when Ryan needed another job and their little family needed more room, she bought him a business that included living quarters. Finally, when Ryan became violent, she acknowledged that marrying him was a mistake born of her own "desperation."

So rather than remain in thrall to a brutish sot, Feigele made a well-planned escape. Hers was a getaway that took more than smarts. It took money. And thanks to her hard work, frugality, and developing business acumen, she had money. Perhaps she'd figured from the start that one day they might need to leave and safeguarded the savings that would fund their escape. Nonetheless, the young mother's return to Seattle filled me with foreboding. According to Tim Hunter, a fatal bludgeoning awaited her here.

But I was glad the intrepid diarist had a daughter, even if the child's birth did confirm know-it-all Yetta's cynical speculation that Feigele had been "knocked up" well before her marriage. Feigele's daughter, Rose O'Neal, born in 1901, would be in her early sixties and might have children and grandchildren of her own. And these descendants just might have ideas about who killed Feigele. I resolved anew to find them, query them, and put her diary into their hands myself. Feigele's family would also want to claim her remains and arrange her burial. But if Rose had married, she'd have a different name. Would she have remained in Seattle? Or gone back to Alaska? Or migrated to Canada? Or California or New York even? Before I could seek her out, I needed to finish the diary. Maybe it would offer a clue as to where Feigele's daughter was now.

Before doing more translating, I met again with Franklin High Principal George Jankowski. He greeted me cordially and assured me that, pending routine approval by the Board of Education, the job teaching history and social studies at Franklin was mine. He presented me with well-worn copies of the textbooks I would use, the school calendar, and the name and phone number of the chairman of Franklin's history department. My teaching job secure, I reported to work at Frederick & Nelson and, before I left that day, gave notice.

Sam's reaction to my phoning with the good news was predictable. "I figured you'd get the job. Who better?" I could imagine my father's stoop-shouldered shrug and the pride it failed to mask.

Bobby's reaction was equally predictable. We were barely seated at Rossellini's when I told him. "Mazel tov!" He signaled the waiter. "A bottle of Asti, please."

"Oh no. You don't have to do that." I was gratified though. I really did feel like celebrating.

"Rachel Mazursky, getting this job is a message from God. Now you have to come to New York this summer before you start teaching. If I send you a ticket, will you?"

I didn't expect this invitation. "Part of me wants to stay here and get used to being a widow, to living alone, to being single."

"My timing sucks."

"That's what my cousin said when I told her about how you picked up the phone that morning when Marsha called."

"You mean the day your daughter found out her mother wasn't a virgin?"

For once his flippancy rattled me, so I put my index finger to his lips. His kiss on my fingertip was odd punctuation for my next words. "That same part of me wants to keep you as my old friend, somebody I can confide in like, like a brother."

Over the rim of his glass I saw his eyes roll. "Okay. So tell me about the other part of you. Maybe I can get her to come to New York."

"The other part of me wants to feel free and alive but . . ."

"But what?"

I played with my fork. "I wonder if you're just using me. Why do you need me in New York if you've got all those nurses?" My voice was low. My insecurity and jealousy embarrassed me.

"Rachel, don't take this the wrong way, but what the hell would I be using you for? Do you seriously think I came all the way back here just to get laid? Look at me, dammit." His order was really a plea.

I looked up and into his glowering eyes. "Well. . . ."

"Rachel, haven't you heard anything I've said? I've been in love with you for most of my life. I came back here to tell you that, to see if, now that you're free, you could feel that way about me."

I looked up and spit out the question that, until that moment, I'd been asking and answering myself. "So what if I could? What's the point?"

Bobby blinked as if blinded by the light bulb flashing on in his head. Then he grinned. "Are you proposing, Mrs. Mazursky?"

I felt the blood warming my cheeks. In the era of *Sex and the Single Girl*, Bobby's taunting one-liner exposed me as a middle-aged throwback to, God forbid, the Fifties. He was accusing me of husband hunting. My desire for strings to tether Bobby to me was pathetically retro.

He wasn't through. "The thing is, Rachel, you're nuts about me too, and that's got you worried." When I offered no argument, didn't look away, he continued. "We should see as much of each other as we can and play it by ear. If it turns out that we're both still crazy about each other in a year or two, we'll work something out. Maybe, if I play my cards right, you'll propose again, who knows?"

"And the nurses?" I couldn't help myself. I pictured a stacked siren in a skimpy white uniform, a perfumed acolyte of Helen Gurley Brown, bending over a gurney in the ER, drawing a scalpel from between her ample breasts and handing it to Bobby. Harry, he should rest in peace, may have been disastrously reckless at the poker table, overprotective of Marsha, and a Nixon supporter who really believed slaves were happy on the plantations, but he'd been faithful. As far as I knew.

"Dammit, Rachel, the nurses were a phase, and it's been over for a while. No nurses. I swear." Bobby raised his right hand in a simulated oath. "I'm not going to ask you to make any promises. But if someone else comes along, I want to know."

I nodded. Bobby's gruff assertion reminded me I wasn't the only one with monogamy on my mind. I felt we reached some sort of *cockamamie* modern agreement, an agreement to "play it by ear" and to play only with each other. On impulse I twisted off my wedding ring. But when I put it in my change purse with my pennies, stamps, and paperclips, I realized that although Bobby had rushed back to Seattle too soon, I was the one rushing things now. "I can't go to New York this summer. I have the diary to finish translating, a murder to solve, and lessons to plan. Besides, my daughter is not ready for me to show up in New York with a lover. "

"Then I'll come back here in the fall." Booby reached for my newly naked hand and covered it with his. With the other hand, he raised his glass. "*L'chaim.*"

And he agreed to come with me and Sam to Yetta's for dinner. "Sure. The only madam I ever met was unconscious." I raised one eyebrow. "Car accident. Concussion and multiple fractures."

When Martin greeted Sam, Bobby, and me at the door, the downstairs windows were uncurtained. The late afternoon sun blazed in like stage lights illuminating a set, a Victorian parlor furnished in period pieces upholstered in lush mauve and silvery gray. Like props, Yetta's sterling tea set and her Royal Copenhagen figurines awaited the players. Martin mixed drinks while Bess presented a tray of oysters on the half shell arranged around a mountain of Dungeness crab meat. After we dug into the shellfish, Bess bustled around drawing drapes.

Only then did Yetta make her entrance at the top of the stairs. Resplendent in a green taffeta sheath and matching turban, she was Norma Desmond incarnate. She hesitated for a moment and then, head high, began her perilous descent. Again my heart went out to the frail and blind older woman, overdressed prima donna and ex-madam though she was. Martin and Sam stood like sentinels at the foot of the stairs. Softly, so as not to startle, Sam began to sing, "Here she comes, Miss America" and Martin joined in and then Bobby and I. Bess's rich contralto sounded from the doorway. Yetta took our chorus as a cue to stop every few steps and blow movie-star kisses to her fans. None of us knew the rest of the song, so we repeated the first line several times until our hostess tapped and kissed her way to the bottom of the stairs.

Later at the table, recurring references to the build-up of troops going to Viet Nam kept the overall tone grave. Perhaps to lighten the mood, Yetta addressed Bobby, seated at her immediate left. "I bet our heroic vet has had enough of war to last a lifetime. Am I right?"

"Yes, Yetta. That's one of the reasons I'm divorced." We all laughed.

"Tell me, Doctor, if men refuse to fight, do you think we'll draft women?"

"I hope not. What makes you ask?"

"Lately I've been thinking our Rachel would make a good soldier. Has she told you about how she flattened a burglar here last week?"

I had, but Bobby didn't let on, so Yetta and Martin took turns telling the story, each interrupting the other to add a detail. The pimpled punk became a burly thug and I was an Amazon warrior. Yetta ended their recitative by exclaiming, "So she crowned the Palooka again, and he went down for the count."

Bobby grabbed my hand and held it above my head as if I'd just won a boxing match. "The woman's a force to be reckoned with. That's why I try like hell to stay on her good side."

"Sounds like Yetta and the cops. She tries to stay on their good side too."

"Damn right I do. After over twenty years in business in this neck of the woods, I've only been arrested twice. In all that time, I spent just one night in jail!"

"Ever think of writing a book?"

That Bobby knew how to charm didn't surprise me, but Yetta's reply did. "I thought about it a lot before my eyes went. I've got a title, *Madam Shmadam: The Story of a Jewish Entrepreneur.*"

While Yetta shared her literary aspirations, Bess carried a cut-glass bowl brimming with chocolate mousse into the living room. "I've got coffee and brandy in there, too. Go on in and help yourselves."

Unhooking Yetta's cane from her chair, Martin handed it off to Bobby, bowed deeply, and offered our hostess his arm. "Allow me to escort you to the parlor, Toots." We all stepped aside to make way for the pair.

"So this is what you knocked out that burglar with?" Bobby leaned over the table and studied the crook of the cane in the flickering light of a candle. "Looks like somebody carved this by hand, right, Sam?"

"That's what I told Yetta. When she bought her first place here, there was a lot of stuff in the rooms and the basement, junk most of it. So I told her I'd cart it all away gratis if I could have it, and we made a deal." Sam's tone was self-congratulatory. "But when I came across this cane, I brought it back. 'Keep it,' I told her. It might be worth a few bucks someday. It's hand carved.'"

Sam's voice became mournful. "Never thought Yetta would ever need to use it." When he spoke next, I felt his eyes on me and could see him shaking his head. "Never thought you would either, Rachel. Thank God I spotted it." It was good to see my father, usually modest, claiming credit for saving me from disaster.

Chapter 20

. . . ober zei redden nisht Yiddish . . .

. . . but they speak no Yiddish . . .

Fanny's Diary, Seattle, Spring 1906

I have been busy since Rosie and I arrived in Seattle. But today I am done with my dressmaking and a hard rain keeps me from dragging the child out to the Greek coffeehouse. Rosie is content pretending to feed one doll and reading the palm of the other. And this diary waits for me like an old friend.

I am lucky to have other friends here too. Leo Patsakos, the coffeehouse owner, welcomed me back. God forgive me, I told this kind man my husband got sick and died in Alaska. I now wear the large ring David gave me and claim it is the wedding ring from my late husband. Leo and his customers are sweet to my Rose. Just yesterday a sailor bought her a pastry and, while she ate, he carved a little boat out of a piece of driftwood. She watched him with big eyes. When he finished making the boat, he gave it to her. I could make more money telling fortunes in this town's many taverns on Skid Road than I do at Leo's, but I do not want my Rosele in those Godless places. In Leo's coffeehouse she sometimes plays with his son. Leo Jr. is older than Rose, but he makes nice with her and even tries to teach her letters. Yesterday when his mother Melina came for him, I tried to talk with her of those things that mothers talk about, but again she did not speak to me. She never speaks to me. Leo says she is very reserved.

Now the rain comes down so hard it sounds as if the Tsar's army is stamping on the roof. I thank God for our warm and dry room at Desiree and Ralph's boarding house. I wrote to tell dear Desiree we were coming, but we left Skagway in such a rush that my letter arrived after we did. But

Desiree opened her arms to us and her home too. With their savings she and Ralph bought an old hotel downtown above the water and made it into a boardinghouse which they live in and manage. They rent our room to us cheap in exchange for dresses I make for Desiree and grocery shopping I do when the servant is away.

I had a business card printed about my sewing, and Ralph visited the dance halls and taverns and gave it to the showgirls. I also had cards printed about my fortunetelling and, once again, Leo keeps a pile of them on the counter in the coffeehouse. I keep my savings once more in Mr. Furth's bank. Someday I will buy my little girl a piano. But just now she pushes a story book onto my lap, so I will read it to her.

Feigele's Diary, Seattle, Spring 1906

During the years I was away, Seattle changed. May I be forgiven for saying that here in America men do what in Gnilsk was the work of God. They make big hills flat like potato pancakes and, with the dirt from the hills, they turn the sea into dry land! Tall buildings grow out of the ground now. Seattle is growing like my Rosele. The other day when I passed by Avram Pinsker's paint store it was filled with many customers. It is a good time to sell paint.

But another change has taken place here, one that I could not have imagined. Just last week I met some new foreigners, men from Greece, at the coffeehouse. These men are not like other sailors who come, even though Leo speaks to them in Greek. He told me they claim to be Jews! But when I asked them in Yiddish if they wanted me to read their palms, they did not understand one single word of what I said. So how can they be Jews? But why would they pretend to be Jews if they are not? I cannot explain how strange these new Jews seem to me.

Leo introduced me as a Jew and he translated my questions. "I did not know there were Jews in Greece. How did Jews come to be in Greece?"

The man they call Azaria, the most talkative, answered. "A long time ago our forefathers lived in Spain and Portugal but Jews had to leave there." He shrugged and looked at me but said nothing of why. I assumed there were pogroms in those countries. "We were welcome in Greece and Turkey."

This Azaria spoke Greek to Leo, but to his friends he spoke another language. "What language is it that you speak among yourselves?" I never heard of Jews who do not speak Yiddish, our mother tongue. How could this man be a Jew? Leo did not need to translate Azaria's first reply. It was as if the newcomer read my mind, understood my suspicion. He reached under his shirt and tugged until I could see the fringes Jewish men wear to remind them to pray. Then I had to explain this custom to Leo. Certain that he had proved to me that he really was a Jew, Azaria answered my question. "Many of us know Greek and Turkish and Spanish too. But to each other we speak Ladino. It is Spanish mixed with words from Hebrew and also from Greek and Turkish."

My heart went out to these greenhorns who know no Yiddish or English. "Why did you come to Seattle?" was my next question.

Again Azaria answered for them all. "Life on Rhodes is hard now. And we heard there was work here. Seattle is by the sea like Greece and Turkey, and we are familiar with catching and selling fish." Later Leo told me that a couple of rabbis helped them find a place to board. They stay for now in a shed behind a synagogue. In return they help to clean the synagogue. The men found work peddling fish and vegetables on street corners. And just yesterday Azaria himself asked Leo to assure me that even though they do not speak Yiddish, they keep kosher and wear not only fringes but also phylacteries. They worship with the most pious. I believe him, but the more Azaria tells me, the more astonished I am. Even in Alaska where I met people from many lands who spoke many languages and Tlingits too, I never met any people like these strange Jews. Leo and I will help them learn English.

Fanny's Diary, Seattle, Spring 1906

There is only one woman among these greenhorn Jews, a girl really, and I met her. Her name is Tzipporah Peha, and she is betrothed to Azaria Salazar, my best pupil. This girl's mother remains in Rhodes with terrible pain in her fingers, so she could not finish sewing her daughter's wedding dress. When I heard this from Leo, I told him to tell Azaria I would finish Tzipporah's gown for her at no cost. It is rare that I get to do a favor for another Jew.

Azaria took me, my Rose, and Leo to the rabbi's home where Tzipporah is staying until they marry. Tzipporah does not speak any Yiddish or English either, but she has a smile like an angel and she gave my Rosele a cup of milk. Then we two and Rose went into the bedroom and the bride tried on the wedding dress. She is slight, more like a girl than a woman about to be married. How alone she must feel as the only woman among these men. How it must pain her not to have her mother here. I recalled my motherless wedding. While I pinned the hemline and the cuffs of her bridal gown in silence, I wondered how well Tzipporah knows Azaria, if she loves him, if he loves her. I wondered if she cries herself to sleep yearning for her mother, her family so far away. I go now to sing my own precious girl to sleep.

ꙮ

Although I was charmed by Feigele's discovery of the Sephardics, I was riveted by her mention of Leo's surname, Patsakos, and by the appearance of Tzipporah Salazar in the diary. Feigele hadn't written Leo's full name earlier, and knowing this last name might enable me to track down Leo Jr. Perhaps he would recall the little girl he taught the ABCs at the coffee house and her mother. Of course the young bride Feigele described had to be old Tzipporah Salazar née Peha, the woman I'd met outside Yetta's. But when I remembered our silent car ride back to Seattle that day, I decided to try to find Leo Patsakos Jr. first. He wasn't listed in the phone book, so before going to the store, I visited the library.

On the way, I reprised Feigele's readjustment to life in Seattle. Even though she left here abruptly, she was still welcome to read palms at the coffeehouse and had the foresight and savings to arrange for comfortable lodgings and a socially acceptable, albeit false, identity as a widow. She was determined to shield her Rosie from bars and dance halls and to keep her safe among friendly respectable people. Like lots of American Jewish mothers, Feigele dreamed of buying her child a piano someday. Immigrant parents worked long and hard for their children, not for themselves, and Feigele was no different. Who would want to kill such a hard-working and devoted mother?

I was disappointed when I couldn't find Leo Patsakos in the most recent Polk City Directory, the one for 1964. On a hunch, I checked to see if he'd been listed in 1940 and there he was. Patsakos, Leo Jr. had been living with Melina and Maria Patsakos on 29th Avenue, not far from where I grew up. Leo Jr. had probably been killed in World War II. I lowered my eyes just long enough to thank God that Bobby had survived that same terrible war. And while I had His attention, I gave God a little nudge. Maybe, just maybe, Maria, Leo Jr.'s wife, was stubborn like my dad and still lived in the house on 29th Avenue and maybe her mother-in-law, Melina Patsakos, had spoken of Feigele and little Rose. I added Maria Patsakos's name and address to the list of those I would talk with after I finished reading the diary.

But after finding the Patsakos listing I was impatient with my own damn resolution, so during my lunch hour I looked up Maria's number and dialed it from the pay phone in the employee break room. Telling her only that I wanted to ask her about a long dead friend of her husband's family, I kept the excitement out of my voice so as not to frighten the woman. She agreed that I might stop by late that same afternoon during her brother's customary visit. In lightly accented English, Maria explained, "Louis comes here for coffee before he goes to work."

The next three hours of dusting, polishing, and chatting up shoppers dragged more than usual. In between customers, I planned how I would approach Maria, exactly what I would ask her. Finally, at four I left Frederick & Nelson and drove to the Patsakos's home. A barrel chested, smiling man greeted me with a nod, introduced himself as Louis Photopoulos, brother of Maria Patsakos, and ushered me in.

Maria herself, dressed entirely in black, awaited me in her parlor, a dark, formally furnished room where, I imagined, plastic slipcovers usually protected the plush maroon velvet upholstery. She was probably in her forties like me, but her somber, outdated clothes and severe features gave her the appearance of a much older woman. She took in my dark skirt and white blouse approvingly before she spoke. "We'd like to express our condolences." Her eyes misted. "I lost my husband too, in the War." She pointed to a photo of a boy with prominent features and a generous smile wearing a white uniform. I gaped at the doomed young sailor who had been little Rose's playmate. Rose and Feigele had known that very smile.

"Thank you. I'm so sorry."

Louis interrupted our commiseration. "My sister says you have questions about Leo's mother." Had Maria misunderstood me? I'd explained on the phone about Feigele, her diary, and how she frequented the coffeehouse. I'd not mentioned Melina Patsakos.

"Actually, I wanted to ask you about a woman named Fanny O'Neal. I'm translating her diary. As I mentioned, she was a fortuneteller who read palms at the coffeehouse your father-in-law owned. So she knew your in-laws."

"Fanny O'Neal was my husband Leo's real mother." Maria's voice was solemn, authoritative. Having delivered this pronouncement, my hostess disappeared into the kitchen leaving me wondering what she was talking about. Had Leo and Melina Patsakos adopted Leo Jr.? I pictured those tattered pages torn from the diary. Picking up the photo of the smiling sailor, I stared into his clear brown eyes. Could it be? Had Feigele borne a son to Daniel Meyer and given him to Leo and Melina Patsakos to rear? Had Leo Jr. been Feigele's son, Rose's half brother?

I sank into the nearest chair, and Louis seated himself on the sofa. "Maria's getting coffee. That'll fix you right up." Apparently discomfited by my inability to utter a word, he attempted to make conversation. "Are you related to Leo's mother?"

There it was again. I made an effort. "No, I'm not. In her diary, Fanny O'Neal wrote that Melina Patsakos was Leo Jr.'s mother."

"Aha." Then, perhaps having decided that I was too simpleminded to pose a threat to his sister, he stood. "Maria will explain. I have to go." He stuck his head in the kitchen, said goodbye to Maria, and left without ever having the cup of coffee he ostensibly came for.

By the time Maria returned with a tray of pastry and espresso and poured our coffee, I'd recovered somewhat. I began questioning her. "Maria, was your husband adopted?"

My hostess, it seemed, was not inclined to simple answers. "After Leo Sr. died, his wife Melina came to live with us." Maria sighed. I wondered if she missed her mother-in-law or regretted their years of togetherness. "Melina Patsakos was the only mother my husband ever knew. No one could have cared for him better. She's been gone five years now." Maria sighed again.

Perhaps the woman was beating around the bush to prolong our visit because she was lonely. Resolved to be patient, I sipped my coffee. "This is so good." I accepted the flaky pastry she offered. It was drenched in honey and filled with nuts. "Mmmmm. This is delicious, too. Did Melina ever talk about adopting Leo Jr.? Did she ever let on about where he came from?"

"Not exactly. But when we learned he wasn't coming home from Europe . . ." Maria teared up before continuing. "She got a little, you know . . ." Maria circled her index finger alongside her ear to illustrate. "Over and over, day and night, she kept saying that God took their son to punish his father for his sins. It was terrible. Finally I got her to take some of the pills the doctor gave me, and she calmed down a little."

"So Melina did not actually give birth to Leo Jr.?" She shook her head. This time I let my raised eyebrows do the questioning.

"I know this because years later when my mother-in-law herself was dying, the poor woman became delirious and raved about how she was barren." Maria's next words were a mumbled aside. "You know, it's always the woman's fault." She gave me a look as old as Eve.

I nodded, hoping she wouldn't get sidetracked, would go on with her story.

"From all her carrying on I put together that one day Leo Sr. came home and told her that a man he knew had an unmarried sister who just had a baby boy and wanted to find him a good home. Like he was a kitten." Maria shrugged and paused. "Leo Sr. was so happy. Melina was young and innocent then, so at first she didn't suspect anything." Maria gave me another woman-to-woman look. "She kept saying how the baby was a gift from God, how God finally smiled on her." As if imitating the benevolent deity, Maria herself smiled and her severe features softened. "It didn't hurt that the infant was a boy baby either. At his christening they named him Leo Jr." My hostess put down her coffee cup and opened her hands in front of her. "That's all I know about my Leo. They never told him he was adopted. But they raised a fine son. My husband was a good man."

I feared my next question would be too personal, but I had to know. "Forgive me for asking, but was your husband circumcised?"

It was not modesty that reddened Maria's face, but indignation. "No! My husband was no Jew. He was a good man."

The honeyed morsel in my mouth soured. I heard my own voice as if from a distance. "I'm a Jew." I put down my coffee cup and stood.

My hostess reddened again. "Oh, I'm sorry. I didn't mean . . ."

"Fanny wrote in her diary that Melina was a very good mother and that Leo Jr. was kind to her own little girl." I paused. "But she also wrote that when she and Melina met at the coffeehouse, Melina wasn't friendly to her, didn't want to chat."

Maria shrugged, cocked her head, and looked up at me. The last words were hers. "Do you blame her?"

I drove home upset by Maria's anti-Semitism, by her barbed final sally. But I was also excited by the possibilities her revelations posed. Had Feigele and Leo Patsakos Sr. been lovers? If so, had she borne his child and given it over to him and his wife to rear as their own? And had that wife killed the diarist out of jealousy? Or had Leo told his wife the truth and was Leo Jr. really the son of a friend's unwed sister? If so, had Melina snubbed Feigele, not out of jealousy, but rather for the crime of being Jewish? Snubbing was a far cry from murder.

But when I envisioned again the jagged remnants of the torn out pages of the diary, I spun an alternative scenario. Could Feigele and Daniel Meyer have been lovers until, under pressure from his uncle, Daniel spurned her? If so, could she have had Daniel's baby and given the infant to the childless Leo and Melina Patsakos to rear? But would Feigele have allowed her son to remain uncircumcised? To be christened?

Surely Tzipporah Salazar could answer some of these questions. The old lady would not have forgotten the seamstress who finished her wedding dress. Tzipporah might even know what really happened to little Rose, if Feigele had other children, grandchildren. She might even know whose baby her husband's friend Leo Patsakos adopted.

Then I remembered how Tzipporah and I had sat in silence on the drive back to Seattle from Alki. How on earth would we communicate? I'd consult my father. Sam would know which of Tzipporah's relatives could act as an interpreter. I'd also ask Yetta. She must have talked to somebody to get Tzipporah out to Alki to minister to her.

Yetta's response was disappointing. "Your father arranged for Tzipporah's visit. It was his idea to have her come. Thought it might help my eyes. Talk to him."

"Will do." I remembered my manners. "Yetta, I enjoyed dinner the other night. We all did. The food was delicious and you and Martin made us feel at home."

"We enjoyed ourselves too. I've always worked nights and for years now I've been sick, so we haven't had many dinner guests. Besides, I'm better at making money than friends." I heard wistfulness rather than self-pity in Yetta's voice.

To lift her spirits rather than because I wanted or expected a useful answer, I asked what I considered a rhetorical question. "So tell me, what do you think of Bobby?"

"You really want to know?"

"Yes, I do." Suddenly I really did.

"He drinks too much." Yetta spoke softly as if certain that her four word assessment would be unwelcome.

"What? We were all drinking. It was a party. And how would you know how much he drank, anyway?" I made no effort to hide my indignation, my rage. No wonder the bitch had few friends. How dare this old flesh peddler say that Bobby Gradstein, a veteran and a doctor at Mount Sinai Hospital, drank too much?

"He sat next to me at dinner. He refilled his glass of Chivas four times while we were at the table. I heard him. I can't see, but I'm not deaf." Yetta hesitated. "Remember, Rachel, you asked."

"And you're telling me this for my own good, right?" I was still angry, but I had to admit that after running whorehouses in two countries for four decades, it was very likely that Yetta knew something about men who drank. More than I did anyway. Harry had enjoyed a little wine on the Sabbath, a beer or two on Saturday night, and a shot of slivovitz at weddings and bar mitzvahs. "Thanks a lot. I'll keep it in mind."

I had to, because I couldn't get Yetta's unwelcome words out of my head as I drove home. They triggered memories that I'd downplayed. After Bobby got really drunk at our high school reunion, I figured he probably wasn't the only guy who threw up after that event. When he spiked his orange juice with Smirnoff in the morning, I figured he was on a long-overdue and well-deserved vacation. Besides, maybe his wartime experiences made a drinker out of him like Hilda Bloom's husband, Joe. But even in my besotted state, I knew these excuses were just that, excuses. Maybe his drinking was the reason Bobby's wife left him. But the man held a very responsible job. And he was such an enthusiastic lover which, even I knew, he wouldn't be if he drank too much. Besides, everybody knows that, poor Joe Bloom aside, Jewish men are not lushes.

That night Bobby drove his mother to visit a friend on Mercer Island, and Sam came for dinner. He stood watching me jam chicken parts into a mound of crushed cornflakes, so I handed him a can of cream of mushroom soup and the can opener. That's when he asked, "What's new with Marsha?"

I recalled Marsha's phone call, her angry accusations, the click of the receiver when she hung up on her Jezebel of a mother. If he knew about that, knew I hadn't heard from her since then, knew she wouldn't take or return my many calls, Sam would worry. And I was worried enough for both of us. "She's fine."

"Good. I miss that girl. And I don't like it that she's not at Miriam's." He handed me the opened can.

"I talked with Marsha this morning, and she's just fine." This half-truth left my lips as easily as the mushroom soup plopped into the casserole with the string beans.

The only relative I'd talked to that morning was Miriam whom I had taken to calling every day for news. According to her, "Marsha's fine. She and Susie and Trish went to a jazz club in the Village last night. Some guy Marsha went to high school with was playing down there. Hendrix his name is."

I arranged the frozen onion rings on the string beans, shoved the casserole into the oven next to the chicken, and summarized Miriam's report. "Marsha's enjoying Greenwich Village, Dad. She and her roommate and Susie go to jazz clubs after work."

This tidbit apparently satisfied Sam who was rinsing the lettuce he'd brought from Manya's garden. His back was to me when he introduced another charged topic. "You and Bobby. Who knew?"

Miriam knew. And my cousin thought it was too soon. "Don't make any big decisions for a while, Rachel," was how she put it whenever we spoke.

I didn't want to hear Sam's opinion of my relationship with Bobby. Marsha thought her mother was a slut, Yetta thought Bobby was a lush, and Miriam thought we were both rushing things. God only knew what Sam thought about his recently widowed forty-five-year-old daughter sleeping with her old friend, the son of his own old friends, a divorced doctor who not only drank heavily but also smoked and lived three thousand miles away. But if Sam was worried, for once he was keeping it to himself.

Grateful, I changed the subject. "Dad, remember your friend Tzipporah Salazar, the old Sephardic lady? The one I met at Yetta's?"

"Yeah. What about her?"

"Feigele knew Tzipporah when she was a girl, when she first came here. Feigele finished making her wedding dress."

"How could that be? To this day Tzipporah don't speak English and she never knew a word of Yiddish." Sam shook his tufted head. The well-known Yiddishlessness of the Ladino-speaking Sephardic Jews still flummoxed him. Over dinner, I explained how Feigele frequented the Greek coffeehouse, a gathering spot for Sephardic men when they first arrived in Seattle. "Surely Tzipporah will remember her. But who will translate?"

Sam thought for a minute. "Where you dropped her off in Seward Park, that's where she lives now with her oldest daughter. I forget this girl's name, but she's the one you should talk to. Ladies gab more than men. You'll sit around with Tzipporah and the daughter and drink coffee, and she'll talk."

"Let me know as soon as you remember the woman's name." Sam nodded. I reminded myself that only after finishing the translation would I know the scope of the questions I'd want to ask. "I'm getting near the end of the diary. I'd like to finish before I start preparing to teach."

Chapter 21

The night before he flew back to New York, Bobby insisted we have dinner at Canlis, reportedly Seattle's most expensive and romantic restaurant. He looked relieved when the waiter brought our drinks. "Here's lookin' at you, kid." With that boost from Bogart, Bobby raised his glass and, with his free hand, reached into his pocket and withdrew a small beribboned package. I recognized the Frederick & Nelson wrapping paper. He pushed the little box across the table. "It's for you. Open it." He downed his martini while I struggled with the ribbon. Inside was yet another box, this one of dark blue velvet. I took it out and opened it.

The diamond inside was as big as Yetta's. "Oh, Bobby!" I stared at the brilliant stone and blinked.

"You like it? I'm tired of waiting for you to propose again, so I'm jumping the gun. Try it on."

"Propose?" Had I heard him right?

"Yeah." Bobby signaled the waiter for another drink and then, in a rush of words, made what I recognized as a pitch, a good one. "With my experience I can get a decent job at a Seattle hospital. I'll make less, but the cost of living here is a helluva lot lower than in Manhattan. I'll get that ball rolling right away, and as soon as I get a job here, I'll give notice at Mount Sinai. Then I'll sublet my place until my lease expires, move back to my hometown, marry the girl of my dreams, and take care of my mother." He stopped for breath. "Go ahead. Put it on."

"I can't." It took all my strength to push the little velvet box back across the table. With fingers that trembled, I pried a cigarette out of the pack.

"What are you talking about?" Bobby's grin gave way as his lips began to twitch and he blinked repeatedly. His face was that of the frightened ten-year-old boy with the bloody ear. Fighting tears of my own, I left the cigarette unlit.

"It's too soon." Miriam's sensible cousinly advice sounded trite even as I echoed it. I forced myself to catch Bobby's eye, to look at him, as if my gaze could shield him from the pain I was inflicting.

"That's bullshit, Rachel, and you know it. I thought . . ." He shook his head. "Christ, it's not as if we just met. And I thought you loved me. You do love me. So what's wrong? Enough already with the bullshit. Tell me." He lit our cigarettes with a hand so unsteady the flame of his lighter wavered. The waiter delivered Bobby's martini. Fortified by its arrival, he didn't wait for my reply. "I can't believe you'd be humping me if there was somebody else."

"No. That's not it."

"So what the hell is 'it'?" His shoulders straightened. Reassured that he had no rival, Bobby braced to rebut whatever explanation I offered.

I forced myself to look straight at him, but my words were less direct than my gaze. "Feigele married a real *shikker*." At the sound of the disparaging Yiddish word for a heavy drinker, his eyes narrowed and he leaned back in his chair. I lowered my voice but not my eyes. "By the time she left him, he was hitting her and threatening their child. She had to pay off the sheriff to keep him locked up."

Bobby glared at me before he said anything. "I wish you'd never come across that damn diary." He sounded like Harry when he damned my scrapbooks. But when Bobby spoke next his tone was patient, his arguments practiced. "Look, I hold down a very responsible job in a big hospital. I also do pretty well picking stocks. And I perform in the bedroom. Does that sound like a guy who drinks too much?" When I didn't contradict him, didn't reply at all, he stopped defending himself and attacked. "You're the one I had to pour into the shower sloshed, remember?"

"I was a mess when you got here. I told you. I felt dead." I shivered. "But then you showed up out of the blue on the Sabbath, and then after dinner at your mom's I realized you were my second soul." I reached across the table and took Bobby's hand. "I was so glad to see you again, so happy to see what a mensch you turned out to be. And you made me feel like a kid, a pretty kid. And then you said you loved me." I lit my own cigarette. "I've always felt close to you, probably always loved you." I shrugged. "So I told myself you were drinking so much because you were on vacation, because we were celebrating...."

"And now?"

"I'm not a kid anymore, Bobby. And neither are you. We're in our forties, plenty old enough to know better."

Bobby withdrew his hand from mine. "Did someone put this crap about my drinking into your head? Sam? Does your father think I drink too much? Is he worried about it?"

"If he is, he hasn't mentioned it." When I acknowledged this fact, I found it surprising. But it was probably hard for Sam to find fault with his old friends' son, a boy he'd watched grow up, a veteran, a doctor. And Bobby was as anti-war and pro-civil rights as Sam. So he had a few too many once in a while . . .

"So who the hell was it?"

"Yetta commented on how much you drink." Bobby winced. "But sooner or later, I would have acknowledged it myself." I heard the resignation in my voice.

When Bobby spoke next, his voice had an edge I'd never heard. "So, Rachel, when were you planning to tell me this? If I hadn't shown up like a jackass with this goddamn ring, would I have left tomorrow without your telling me that a blind madam yenta for Chrissake convinced you I'm a lush?" He picked up the blue velvet box, crammed it into the larger one, and stuffed them back in his pocket.

"I'm sorry about not saying something before, but I didn't want to believe it. And I didn't want to ruin our time together. I needed a chance to think, to figure out how to bring it up. And I thought we had time. But seeing that ring, hearing you actually proposing . . . ."

"I really don't drink too much, but, to humor you, what if I cut back to wine or a couple of beers with dinner and a nightcap?"

My shrug hid how, for a moment, my heart lifted. Married to me and living and working in slow-paced, low-key Seattle, Bobby just might drink less. But he might not. It would be a gamble. When I shrugged again, he tilted his head and glared at me through still narrowed eyes. "So this is it? You stay here to teach school and play detective, and I fly home and drink until my liver gives out?"

My rage at Bobby's manipulative ploy took me by surprise. "You've got the first part right. I do stay here and, thank God, I have a job." I ignored his slur on my sleuthing. "As for you and your liver, Bobby Gradstein, you're the hotshot doctor." We were having our first real fight.

"Forget it. Right now I feel about as married to you as I want to be." He raised his glass in a defiant, wordless toast, chugged the drink, and signaled our waiter for a check. Fatigue and sorrow displaced my anger. I just wanted the evening to end. Apparently Bobby did too. Later that night I awoke to find him propped on one elbow, his wide open eyes staring down at me. I held him fast until I dozed off.

When I woke again, it was barely light. I saw Bobby's face, haggard from sleeplessness, and heard his voice, flat and sorrowful. "Want me to make coffee? We've got over an hour before we have to leave." I nodded while the events of the night before replayed in my head. I got the marriage proposal I'd thought I wanted, and turned it down, turned down Bobby. Our honeymoon was over before it began. He was leaving.

"Thanks." Seated opposite him at the kitchen table, I eyed the bottle of Smirnoff towering over the salt and pepper shakers and the sugar bowl. I didn't know if Bobby had had a drink yet, and I didn't ask. Instead, figuring I had nothing to lose, I nodded at the bottle and posed a bigger question. "So when did you start drinking like this? What happened?"

"World War II happened." His sigh was a wordless whisper of regret and loss. "Hell, you remember what a know-nothing I was before I enlisted. I'd never been east of the Cascades, never held a gun, never even eaten a goddamn pork chop." He lit one cigarette for us both. "Once we got over there, the guys in our unit, we all got pretty tight. There aren't any anti-Semites in trenches. We saved each other's asses over and over again. We were damn lucky. Then, near the end of the war, our luck ran out."

His eyes narrowed. "We were mopping up in some godforsaken field in France. Four of us got separated from our unit. We found an empty farmhouse and figured we'd hide out in there until it got dark. But there were still a few Krauts in the area, and one of them must have seen us go in. That son of a bitch threw a couple of grenades in the window." Bobby's voice dropped. "Tony was sleeping on the floor. He never knew what hit him." Bobby turned his head away and handed me the cigarette. "Louie was right next to him. He was bleeding from one eye and holding his head. He was babbling." Bobby took a deep breath and rubbed his own eyes before going on. "Al's foot blew across the room and landed under another window. He could see it from where he fell."

When I returned the cigarette, Bobby looked at me. "I was the only one unhurt. I held Louie's bloody head in my lap. The poor bastard was delusional, thought I was a priest, wanted me to take his goddamn confession. He cheated on his wife with some English broad. Angela. It was eating him up. I couldn't do anything for his eyes or his head wound, so I played along." Bobby shrugged. "I heard his confession and muttered some made up Latin phrases. I tried to sound like those priests in the movies. Louis died right after I made the sign of the cross." With the hand holding the cigarette, Bobby made the familiar motion.

"It was worse with Al. I couldn't stop the bleeding or the pain." Bobby shook his head. "After Louie died, Al asked me to bring him his friggin' foot, and when I crawled over and got it for him, he sat there holding that goddamn bloody boot with a piece of his own hairy leg sticking out of it. He just kept looking at that boot. I figured it was better than looking at what was left of his leg. Then he begged me to shoot him."

Bobby looked up abruptly. He sounded perplexed, as if once again pondering his dying friend's request. "Would that have been murder? Who knows? But if I fired my gun, any Krauts still in the area would know we were in there. But, Jesus, Al was in a lot of pain. While I was trying to decide what the fuck to do, he lost consciousness. I stayed next to him on the floor with my rifle in my lap until he finally stopped breathing." Bobby lowered his head into his hands.

I recalled his mother's photo of Bobby with three other GIs in London. Were those laughing boys Tony, Louie, and Al? I wanted to reach over and stroke his hair the way I used to stroke Marsha's after a nightmare awakened the child. Instead I asked a question. "How did you get back to your unit?"

He lifted his head. "That night I started walking through the woods in what I hoped was the right direction. I hid during the day. Finally, after what seemed a goddamn lifetime but was really only a few days, some British scouts spotted me. They thought I was a Kraut and started shooting. I figured they were Krauts." Bobby shook his head, still bugged by the craziness of what he remembered.

"I didn't have anything white except a letter, so I opened it up and poked a stick through it to make a flag." The smile he managed was twisted. "Then I held the stick up in front of me with both hands and walked out into the open. I figured I was a dead man, but I got lucky again." Once more he shook his head, as if the memory of his good luck was hard to believe. "They spoke English, and I answered. They gave me some of their grub, and they had a working radio. They helped me to reconnect with my unit. I walked another two days, but by then the territory really was ours."

"That's the letter from your mother, the one she always tells about?"

There was that twisted smile again. "That's what I told her. But actually, Rachel, the letter was the last one I got from you, the one telling me you were engaged."

"You kept that?"

"Yeah." Bobby's voice lowered again. "See, I still daydreamed about coming home to you, so I needed something to remind me that wasn't going to happen. I reread the damn thing whenever I started thinking about you. But I wasn't about to tell my folks that. Besides, my mother just loves thinking her letter helped save my sorry ass."

Bobby told his mother the story she wanted to hear. Had he twisted the facts in the tale he'd just told to wring sympathy from me? To make his drinking somehow okay? Had Yetta's cynicism rubbed off on me? Then I chastised myself for questioning Bobby's honesty. When had he ever lied to me? It wasn't his honesty that worried me. It was his drinking. I wanted to help him. "Have you seen a psychiatrist?"

He grimaced. "Rachel, why should I see a psychiatrist?" When I didn't answer, he explained, his tone the long suffering drone of a man repeating a familiar argument. "I'm not crazy. Anybody would be haunted by the memories I have. If they didn't keep me awake, then I'd see a psychiatrist."

In a few minutes we left for the airport, driving most of the way in silence. At the gate, he kissed me goodbye, wiping away my tears with his handkerchief. Then he flicked open the white square, and waved it. "You win. I surrender. Here." He pressed the wet hanky into my hand. "Take it. I'll come back and reclaim it whenever you say, Rachel. I'll give you time, but I'm not giving you up again without a fight."

Chapter 22

Maya hartz hot gemacht a tumul vee a bahn in mayn broost.

My heart made a noise like a train in my chest.

Fanny's Diary, Seattle, November 1906

A few days ago I saw a ghost. Rosele, my little dancing shadow, was with me in a shop buying groceries for Desiree and Ralph's boarders. As we left the store, a delivery boy stopped his wagon there. He works for one of the wholesalers who buy crops from the farmers and sells them to the shop owners. Rosele wanted to share her apple with his horse, so we stopped. Then I saw that the delivery boy was not a boy at all. He was a cripple who leaned on a cane to walk the few steps to the back of the wagon. I saw his face. My heart made a noise like a train in my chest. It was Boris Lipschitz. I pulled on Rosele's hand and hurried her away before the ghost looked up.

Last night I dreamed I was back in Boris's shop working as fast as I could, but each time he yelled, the seam I was sewing unraveled. He hooked his cane around my arm and pulled me over to where he sat. Rosele awakened when I cried out. I knew I would not sleep well until I learned where Boris lived so I could keep clear of him. I asked Desiree's husband Ralph to follow Boris when he left the wholesaler's at the end of the workday. That turned out to be an easy job. Ralph said that when Boris returned from the stable after making his deliveries, he went upstairs to rooms above the warehouse.

Today Desiree went there, climbed the rickety stairs, and knocked on the door. The woman who answered the door was fat and wore a dirty apron. And she had a black eye and a cut on her cheek and two little girls hanging on her apron. Desiree told this woman she heard rooms there were for rent. The woman got mad. She said she was the wholesaler's sister and that she lived there with her husband Boris Levin who worked right downstairs and they weren't going anywhere.

So Boris is married again and to his boss's sister. For sure poor Oodle and their four children wait for him still in New York. Did he ever go to jail or did he just run away? Now the arsonist is also a lousy no-good bigamist with a new name and a new wife and more children. It looks like he beats his new wife. Who else would give her a black eye? Now that I know where Boris lives and works, I will avoid him. But if our paths do cross and he recognizes me and bothers me, I will threaten to let his boss know that the husband of his sister and father of his nieces has already one wife and four little ones in New York and maybe a jail sentence too. Last night I slept soundly. I am grateful for good friends like Desiree and Ralph.

Fanny's Diary, Seattle, December 10, 1906

Boris is not the only ghost in Seattle. Not long after Desiree talked to Boris's wife, I saw Daniel Meyer leaving his uncle's store on First Avenue. I walk by the store often, and I have never seen him. But on that day he came out with a woman on his arm. She was well dressed and held a little boy by the hand. They walked right past us. A lifetime has passed since Daniel and I used to walk and talk together on that same street. He looks older, heavier, but he is still handsome. I stared straight at him, but he looked through me as if I were not there. Maybe he did not recognize me. I fix my hair differently and dress nicer now, and, since Ryan hit me, my nose has a new bump. Maybe Daniel Meyer did not expect to see me also holding a little girl by the hand. I have aged. Maybe he thought I was a ghost. Sometimes I feel like a ghost.

Fanny's Diary, Seattle, May 1907

It is not surprising what Desiree just told me. I have been expecting it. This afternoon Natalia, a customer of mine, made a special visit to Thurston House to see me. I was out, but she told Desiree to tell me that in the bar where she dances, a man named Ryan admired a very elaborate gown I made her. He asked for the name of her seamstress. Natalia did not like the looks of him, called him a "fast-talking, hard-drinker with fox eyes." She gave him a false name.

I knew that sooner or later Ryan would drink up the money I left and whatever he could get for the cigar store. And then he would come after us. But I know how to deal with this ghost of a husband. If he lays claim to Rosie, I will tell him the truth. He is not her father. And I will give him money to go away. I am sure that is all he wants. I am not afraid if I meet him where there are people around.

There may be ghosts here in Seattle, but there are kind people too and plenty of work. I have several good customers for my dresses now, and my savings grow. Our room is large, with good light, and Desiree feeds us well. She and Ralph are childless, and they dote on my Rosele. Our nightly meals together are pleasant. The other boarders are older men. Two of them work at the nearby Pike Place Market, and one is a cook on a ship, so his place at our table is often empty. They are not Jews, but they are respectable and hardworking and like uncles to my Rosie. Leo and the other Greeks at the coffeehouse are also kind to us.

I do not have to go to a synagogue to thank God that I returned here with my little girl. In Skagway I learned to live without Jews, and here I do the same except for Azaria Salazar and the other Sephardics. Azaria told Leo *Sephard* is Hebrew for *Spanish.* Because their ancestors once lived in Spain that is how these new Jews are known. Even though Azaria himself never lived in Spain, he thinks of it often. While he learns English and sips coffee, he carves a wooden statue. It is a figure of a woman exactly like the woman the Catholics call Mary. Seeing him carving this Mary day after day, I became suspicious again. Today I got Leo to translate my question. "Azaria, if you are a Jew, why do you carve a Christian idol?"

I will never forget Azaria's answer. "A long time ago when my ancestors lived in Spain, Jews were forced to convert, to become Christians, if we wanted to stay. But, many of these *conversos* did not change their beliefs and practiced Judaism secretly. Of course they weren't allowed to have *mezuzahs* on their doors . . ." I had to explain to Leo that a *mezuzah* is a small box that holds the Hebrew commands to love God and live according to His law when we are at home and when we go out. Then Azaria told us more. "Statues of Mary were allowed, so we hollowed out one of her legs and put the little scroll with the commandments inside." He makes the Mary-*mezuzah* as a reminder of his ancestors' time in Spain.

Are Azaria's ancestors not Rosie's and mine also? These new arrivals do not know that I once was a greenhorn too, an ignorant girl with dirty fingernails who ran off to Alaska with two prostitutes and a sewing machine. Azaria told Leo to tell me that after he and Tzipporah marry and have their own place, they will invite Rosele and me to Sabbath dinner. Rosele has never known a real Sabbath meal. Azaria invited us to their wedding. I am making Rosele a pink dress.

Fanny's Diary, Seattle, August 17, 1907

Today Seattle went crazy. Not since that day ten years ago when the Portland sailed into the harbor loaded with gold has this town been the scene of such madness. But this rainy morning there was no ship full of gold, only farmers in wagons full of vegetables and fruits. These farmers came to Pike Place to sell their crops directly to housewives and restaurant owners.

Who knew the opening of a market would be unsafe? I should not have brought Rosele. It was no place for a child. There were housewives everywhere, each with her basket, and they rushed those wagons like stampeders. Those ladies were crazed. They lifted their skirts out of the mud, climbed onto the wagons, and stripped them clean, leaving coins behind them. I think I saw Devorah among these women, but before I could be sure, I stepped back for fear that Rosie and I would be trampled. We joined the many onlookers gathered to watch the spectacle.

Because of the early morning rain, there were not many farmers, but there were wholesalers with cartons of fruits and vegetables pretending to be farmers. As if vegetables grew in cartons! The women avoided them, preferring to leave with empty baskets than to buy from these thieves. Boris was among these fakers. There was no mistaking his mean face. A chill came over me and we left. I pray that he did not see me or recognize me.

This public market will leave the greedy wholesalers with few goods or customers. Desiree heard that later in the morning a Japanese farmer approached Pike Place on a wagon filled with produce. An angry wholesaler went after the unlucky farmer and yanked him out of his own wagon with a cane. Then all the wholesalers threw the Jap's fruit and vegetables onto the ground and stomped on them. I'm glad little Rosie and I left before that.

In spite of the "ghosts" who materialized in Seattle, Feigele seemed content, and as I neared the end of her diary, my eagerness to rush to the final entry was more than ever at odds with my desire to read on and on. But there were only a few entries left. Before I talked to Tzipporah I wanted to track down a descendant or someone else who might have known of Feigele, might suspect who killed her. So once more I headed to the library. I would look for traces of Ryan O'Neal, Boris Lipschitz, and Rose O'Neal.

Finding the directory for 1907 right there on the shelf was a promising start. I lugged the bulky volume to a nearby table where I searched the alphabetical list for O'Neal, Ryan. He wasn't there. I checked an alternative spelling, O'Neil. He wasn't there either. Damn. I returned to the shelves and helped myself to directories from 1906 and 1908 and looked through them to no avail. Apparently Ryan had not stayed in Seattle or, if he had remained, he'd managed to evade the record keepers.

I'd come up cold. As if to emphasize how cold, the air conditioning turned the library into a giant refrigerator. Discouraged and eager to feel the sun on my bare arms, I quickly opened the 1907 directory again, rapidly flipping pages and scanning names in search of Lipschitz, Boris. I wasn't surprised not to find him. With little hope and less reward, I looked under Lipschutz, Boris. Then I tried Levin, Boris. Nothing. On a long shot I ran my eyes down the page looking for Levine, Boris. That's when I saw it. Not Levine. LeVine. *LeVine, Boris whol J.B. Bowles & Co. Inc. b 819 Western Ave w Mabel.* I felt like hollering. According to the list of abbreviations, "b" meant "boards" as in "boards at" and "w" meant wife. It had to be him. Not content to merely Anglicize his name, Boris had gone Gallic. So Feigele was guilty of misspelling, not misrepresentation. And she had feared Boris.

I flipped through the list of businesses and found *J.B. Bowles & Co Inc Comm 819-23 Western Ave cor Marion St.* On a roll, I scanned the directories for 1900-1906 and 1908-1910. Boris LeVine's name didn't appear until 1903, so in all likelihood he arrived in Seattle, found work, and remarried while Feigele was still in Alaska. In 1908 he was listed as residing on Stewart Street, and there was no mention of either employer or wife. After 1908, he was no longer listed. I scribbled down his last address.

Pushing my luck, I looked for Desiree and Ralph Thurston and found them registered as living on Virginia Street. The only Thurstons listed, they were the proprietors of Thurston House Room and Board, at the same address. That the Thurstons were, in fact, included in the directory and ran a boarding house further validated Feigele's account of her life in Seattle.

No longer aware of the chill, I leaned over the directories again, this time in search of five different names: Aliza Rudinsk, Feigele Lindner, Fanny Lindner, and Fanny O'Neal or O'Neil. Like Yetta, Feigele had quite a few names. That not one of them showed up did not really surprise me or detract from the pleasure I took in having corroborated Boris Lipschitz/LeVine's presence in Seattle. Feigele, cleverer by far, and intent on eluding Ryan, had taken pains to avoid having her own name or her daughter's listed. Or, perhaps, like Yetta, she had invented yet another alias.

At the other end of the wall of books, I found the Polk Directory for 1964, the most recent one available. Without taking time to return to the table, I cradled the big book in one arm and flipped through the pages. No Rose O'Neal or O'Neil. Dismayed but not defeated, I checked a few other volumes covering random years between 1907 and 1965. No Rose. The girl probably married, so was listed under another name. Perhaps she moved. For a scary moment, I wondered if Ryan found Rose and took the little girl back to Alaska. I dismissed that possibility as unlikely on the basis of Feigele's certainty that Ryan really wanted only money, not a child who wasn't even his. But Ryan had crooned Irish lovesongs to Rose at bedtime. Worried, I went home to translate the last few entries.

Fanny's Diary, Seattle, October 1, 1907

There is nothing that gives me more joy than my Rosele's smile, and today my little one smiled many times thanks to Basil and Leo. Basil is a Greek who visits the coffeehouse when his ship is in the harbor. The other day passing one of the stairways leading to the streets below ground, he saw a yellow kitten no bigger than his fist. It was at the top of the stairs blinking in the light. Basil felt pity for the little runt, so he picked it up and carried it to the coffeehouse.

Basil hoped I would take it for Rosele. But Desiree and Ralph do not allow pets in their boarding house. When Leo, may his life be for a blessing, saw how taken my Rosele was with this little creature, the same color as her cat Goldie, he agreed to keep it so she could visit it. "We need a cat here to catch mice" was how this good man hid his kindness. "And since he's so small, I'll give him a big name, a big Greek name. We'll call him Aristotle." I had never heard this name, but I laughed with all the Greeks. Such a little cat, such a long name.

Leo let Rosie put out a bowl of milk which the hungry kitten lapped up. Then little Aristotle, no more than a skeleton covered with fur, climbed into her lap and purred as she stroked him and sang to him. Now each day my daughter is up and dressed without nudging, eager to go to the coffeehouse to feed Ari. That is what she calls him. I told her that "Ari" means lion in Hebrew, and that someday her little kitten would grow up to be big and strong like Goldie, like a lion. I have not seen my Rosele so happy in a long time.

Fanny's Diary October 9, 1907

Yesterday my Rosele awoke hot and without her smile. We did not go to the coffeehouse for Azaria's lesson. Leo sent a boy to see what happened to us. When he got here, Rosele was hotter and crying. The boy told Leo of Rosele's illness, and he told Azaria. Last night after work Azaria came with his Tzipporah. He said Tzipporah's mother is a healer on Rhodes and that Tzipporah has stolen her mother's gift and brought it here to America.

Whispering in her language, she put some cloves she had brought with her into a spoon. She moved the spoon over my Rosele where she lay in her little bed. Then Tzipporah lit a match and put the flame beneath the spoon. As each clove exploded, she uttered words in Ladino. Before she left, she poured the contents of Rosele's little chamber pot on the doorstep and said more Ladino words.

I am grateful for Tzipporah's kindness, but I told Desiree that if Rosele is no better by tomorrow, I will take her to the hospital. My child has never been sick like this before. Tonight I sit up with her, putting a cool wet cloth to her little head, praying to God for her fever to break. I pray in Yiddish in case God did not understand what Tzipporah said in her language.

Feigele's Diary, Seattle, October 1907

The Sabbath, a day the same now as all the others. I went below seeking my Rosele's killer. There was a dead rat in the trap I set yesterday. He was big, heavier even than that damn Ari, now also dead by my hand. I opened the trap and yanked the dead rodent out by his long hairless tail. "Are you the one? Was it one of your fleas that killed my Mercada?" Mercada was a lie. I spoke Yiddish to my victim. English is not strong enough for me down below. I will not cut off his tail and take it to the health department. I do not want their stinking reward. This rat is the sixth I have killed. Goddam Ari . . . Tomorrow I will go down there again to kill with the ghost. Tomorrow my own sweet Rosele, may that most precious child rest in peace, would have been six . . .

I pushed the thick square book away lest my own tears mingle with Feigele's and further blur the doomed diarist's disjointed and truncated final entry. I'd braced myself for the end of both the woman's story and her life. But the child? May the poor little girl rest in peace. It was too much. After a life of hard work, dislocation, loss, and betrayal that Feigele should lose her precious little girl to the plague was just too much. Clearly she had no worrywart father to warn her, "*Az m'kusht di katz, kusht meyn oykh di fley*," when you kiss the cat, you also kiss the fleas. I doubted I could survive losing Marsha. This grim prospect made so real by Rose's death galvanized me. I rushed upstairs, plucked Manya's wedding ring from my jewelry box, wrapped it, drove to the post office, and finally mailed it to Marsha. The little silver circlet would serve as a talisman if not a peace offering.

When I returned, I reread that final diary entry, hoping I'd misinterpreted because Feigele's handwriting was even harder to decipher than usual. Her scratched scripted characters were crammed together in erratically spaced rows that collided with one another before careening into the spine of the little book. And because Feigele's distinctive and by now familiar voice "sounded" ragged and raw, her words were harder to translate.

It was as if one of God's note takers had literally descended to hell where, doing the devil's bidding, she sought revenge by slaughtering rats and the child's cat. Pulling the book close to me again, I reworked my translation to be sure I understood her references to killer rats and killing rats. When I finished, I had no doubt that little Rose's illness and death had left her mother maddened in Seattle's nightmarish netherworld, the same place her own bones were found, babbling in Yiddish to dead animals she herself killed. I shuddered.

Who the hell was Mercada and why was she "a lie"? And who was the "ghost" Feigele mentioned killing rats with her down below? My brain awhirl with questions, I fingered the two yellow legal pads, their sheets covered on one side with my own schoolmarm script. Blank, the tablets had been slender. Now they were swollen with Feigele's sad and maddeningly unfinished story. Maybe one of the people still alive and mentioned in those pages would know how her tale ended. It was time to seek them out.

Starting at the top of my list, I found Daniel Meyer's number in the phone book and called him. A woman answered. "Mr. Meyer isn't taking calls. Do you want to speak to his son, Joshua Meyer?"

I did. I'd heard Joshua Meyer's name, read of his philanthropy in the Jewish newspaper, but our paths had never crossed. His voice was low and receptive. "You say my father knew this girl?"

"Yes. She lived with your uncle and aunt, Nathan and Ava Weiss. Fanny worked at Weiss and Co. at the same time your father did." I didn't mention the possibility of romance.

"Well, Dad's been ill, but I'll ask him. Tell me her name again."

"Fanny Lindner."

I was disappointed when, after a few moments, Joshua returned to the phone only to say, "Sorry to keep you. I ran the name by him and it didn't seem to register. Sorry."

I'd barely had time to open a can of tuna fish when Joshua Meyer called back. "I pressed my dad again, and this time he seemed to recognize that girl's name. Would you like to meet with him?" I agreed to visit the old man the following afternoon after work.

Chapter 23

My shift at the store dragged more than usual. When I finally left, I drove straight to Capitol Hill and parked on a broad tree-shaded street. The Meyers' stately mansion and elaborately landscaped grounds dwarfed Yetta's brick bastion with its scrap of yard. A uniformed maid answered the door and ushered me into a high-ceilinged foyer at the foot of a flight of stairs. "This way please."

I followed her down a carpeted hallway. The eyes of Meyers and Weisses in portraits lining the walls tracked my progress until a wedding photo stopped me short. A young groom and his white-gowned bride stood ramrod straight behind an older, seated couple. The names on the golden oval beneath were Nathan and Ava Weiss and Abe and Sarah Weiss. I was actually looking at a photograph of Feigele's slanderer. I hurried to catch up with the maid.

A graying man in his late fifties, wearing a satin-cuffed brown corduroy smoking jacket, was seated behind a desk, smoking. He stood, introduced himself as Joshua Meyer, and pointed to a chair. No sooner had I taken it than he offered not only condolences and a cigarette, but advice. "After I lost my wife, I got involved with planning the Jewish Community Center. Keeping busy is important." I nodded but kept one eye on the door. Where was Daniel Meyer?

"I'll get Mr. Meyer." The maid left us.

Joshua prepared me for his father's arrival. "You know, my dad's had a stroke. He isn't up to much conversation." He lowered his head for a moment. "But, as I told you, the second time I asked him about that girl, he nodded as if her name rang a bell."

"I understand. Thanks for asking him a second time." Because I'd not stopped eyeing the door, I was the first to see Abe Weiss stride into the room and greet his cousin with a handshake. I'd not seen Arlene Golden's father in years, but every time he donated to any cause his cherubic face appeared in the *Transcript*, so I recognized him. What was he doing there?

Joshua explained. "You mentioned that the girl lived with the Weisses, so I asked my cousin to join us. Abe Weiss, Rachel Mazursky." I didn't know whether to be glad that Joshua's invitation had saved me the trouble of contacting his cousin separately or worried that Abe Weiss's presence would inhibit Daniel Meyer.

Josh stood, offering his older cousin the chair behind the imposing desk. Before he sat, Abe Weiss extended his condolences. Then, like the busy man he still was, he got to the point. "Arlene told me you're translating the diary of a girl who stayed with my family and that she's the same woman whose bones turned up recently downtown. So when Josh called, I was curious. And maybe I can help." He leaned back in his chair as if struggling to remember. "But I'm not sure. That had to be a long time ago, when I was very young. There were always people staying at our house." His tone was somewhere between martyred and nostalgic.

To jumpstart his memory, I said, "You were old enough to have an alphabet book that she shared." He shook his head. I tried again. "Fanny Lindner was an impoverished immigrant girl from the Ukraine. She kept a diary and, according to her diary, your mother got her out of jail where she had been held by mistake. Then your mother took Fanny into your home and helped her learn English. She lived with your family for several months." Abe Weiss's polite smile became expansive. He clearly relished my account of Weiss largesse. "Fanny was an accomplished seamstress, so your father gave her work in his store." I turned to face Joshua. "That's where your father met her."

As if on cue, the maid returned pushing a wheelchair in which a skeletal old man wearing a patch over one eye sagged to the left like a piratical scarecrow in a high wind. There was no trace of the handsome charmer who had captivated Feigele. During the next few minutes I gave up any hope of gleaning information from him. As if I needed convincing, the other two men enacted a noisy charade. Abe stood and shouted Fanny's name into his cousin's "good" ear while Joshua waved one arm around and around in what I realized was his attempt to mime the act of sewing. Then he wrote **FANNY LINDNER** in block capitals on a piece of blank stationary and stuck it within range of Daniel's "good" eye. When a tear of frustration or maybe something else formed in that eye, Joshua waved Abe away and stroked his father's head repeating, "It's okay, Dad. I'll take you to Mom."

My pity for Daniel Meyer did not diminish the curiosity I felt after Josh wheeled him away, leaving me alone with Abe Weiss. Had Abe really joined us just to revel in my retelling of his family's generosity? I wouldn't put it past him. He relied on that generosity to make up for his failure to resign from the anti-Semitic Seattle Athletic Club. He spoke first. "Arlene is pleased that you have such an absorbing project to occupy you during this difficult time in your life."

"It is a difficult time, especially with my daughter away."

"Yes. And speaking of daughters, it's quite a coincidence that you and my daughter are friends and that this diarist lived with me and my family. Small world, isn't it? And I know all about your mother. My mother was the same way. Never knew how to say no to a refugee."

Wary of even indirect flattery, I used Abe Weiss's own phrasing to refocus the conversation. "Your father knew how to say no, though. When Daniel Meyer took a romantic interest in Fanny, your father objected."

Abe Weiss smiled, seemingly unperturbed. "Well, of course. When Daniel came from San Francisco to work at Weiss and Company, he was as good as engaged to Meryl Schwartz. Their romance is a legend in our family." He shook his head as if this legendary love still awed him. "Their parents were old friends, so those two met in San Francisco when they were children. They've been married over sixty years." His smile had grown so wide it threatened his ears.

It was time to flesh out Abe Weiss's fairy tale version of the past, to confront him with Feigele's. From my purse I pulled the loose-leaf page on which I'd copied the translated conversation Feigele overheard between this man's own father and Daniel Meyer. I pushed it across the desk where it lay while Abe extricated an eyeglass case from his jacket pocket, took out a pair of thick-lensed specs, and put them on. When he picked up the sheet of paper, he held it in liver spotted hands that trembled so the page quivered like the wing of a giant white moth struggling to stay airborne.

As he read, his face flushed and his mouth clamped shut imprisoning his inverted lips as if he had ingested that big smile. I waited for Abe Weiss to crumple the damning paper in his fist, but he didn't. Instead he rolled it into a scroll and jabbed it in my direction repeatedly as he spoke. "This is claptrap. She even says my mother got her out of jail. Do you expect me to take the word of a dead jailbird?" He gestured dismissively at the scroll unfurling in front of him.

"If you believe your mother got the diarist out of jail, why do you doubt the rest of what Fanny says?" Abe Weiss wasn't used to having his pronouncements questioned. Watching him absorb my hostile rejoinder was like watching the sun burn away the clouds hiding the snowcapped Cascades. His eyes flashed like shards of ice reflecting light. He took off his glasses and directed his unobstructed glare at me. Then, to my consternation, he smiled as he might smile at a slightly retarded child.

"Rachel, my father had many faults, and if he really did say those things, I'm not proud of it."

His patronizing smile and iffy acceptance of Feigele's words nullified the effect of his quasi apology. I added something that might jog his memory. "Fanny may have had a child by Daniel."

Abe Weiss leaned back in his chair, considering his reply. "My dear girl, you're distraught now and with good reason." He smoothed his bald pate with one hand. "But, whether there's a word of truth in that diary or not, Joshua wouldn't want his mother to hear people talking about poor Daniel's premarital fling with some little gold digger. Meryl Meyer doesn't deserve that."

I hated hearing him discredit Feigele's tear-stained testimony as the unreliable word of a "jailbird" and relegate Daniel's interest in her to a "premarital fling with a little gold digger." What was he getting at?

"So I'd like you to expunge this from your translation." He flipped the paper scroll back across the desk. "I'm sure you'll agree there's nothing to be gained by upsetting Meryl."

Suddenly I understood. The words of the dead diarist still had power, still spoke to the living. Otherwise, why would this big shot want me to censor them? "The truth is often upsetting."

"The truth is also elusive." He paused. "Rachel, suppose this girl's ravings are true, and there was an affair, even a child. The girl would have asked for money, and my father or Daniel himself would have paid the girl to go away." He shook his head. "But I don't believe it ever came to that. Believe me, if there were a bastard Meyer running around, the kid would have showed up at Daniel's door long ago looking for a handout, and I'd know about it. My cousin and I have no secrets. I'm telling you, this is all claptrap and you do no good by repeating it."

"I won't leave a single syllable this woman wrote out of my translation."

Not many people said no to Abe Weiss. He blinked once and then leaned back again and began fiddling with his glasses, no doubt considering how to respond. He'd played on my sympathy for Meryl Meyer, Daniel's unwitting and aged wife. He'd offered an alternative scenario. What other argument could the old fox possibly make?

When he stopped toying with his glasses, he raised his head and his eyes met mine across the desk. His gaze was benevolent, the bemused look of one listening to the gibberish of a crazy person. "Arlene admires you, Rachel. She tells me you hope to teach." I nodded, my stomach suddenly constricting. He went on, his voice paternal, honeyed with phony concern. "Do you really think you're up to such demanding work right now? Maybe you need a little more time to recover from your loss before you take up that challenge." The man was trying to blackmail me. Outraged, I stood and muttered a barely civil good bye. Without waiting for Joshua Meyer or the maid to escort me out, I left.

As I walked back to my car, my thoughts fed my fury until I could hear my heart pounding. Abe Weiss had barely bothered to veil his threat to prevent me from getting a teaching job unless I agreed to excise the conversation Feigele overheard between his father and Daniel Meyer from the translation. Arlene had offered to speak to her father about helping me get a teaching position. How much easier it would be for him to prevent me from getting one. His associates at the SAC surely had connections on the Board of Education. When my name came up for what Principal Jankowski had called "routine approval," a Board member would simply declare the grieving widow too "distraught" to teach just yet. If I didn't agree to censor the diary, maybe I'd never teach again.

Yetta actually shed a tear or two when I told her how sadly Feigele's diary ended; so, hoping to get some of that sympathy for myself, I poured out the details of my chat with Abe Weiss. But my listener had run out of sympathy. "You were naïve to think Abe Weiss would want his family's name dragged through the mud, especially after the whole mess with the SAC."

"I'm just doing what I think is right and censoring my translation of the diary isn't right." I took a breath. "United Jewish Appeal is giving Abe Weiss an award this year. Do you think they'd do that if they knew he was the son of a Jew hater?"

"Maybe. Jews haven't held sons accountable for the sins of their fathers since we left the old country." I was taken aback to hear a retired madam mouthing Jewish teachings about Torah. Yetta sounded more herself when she added, "Besides, the man's generous." Then she hesitated. "Listen, you have no reason to believe Feigele's relationship with Daniel Meyer didn't end when she says it did and no proof there was an affair, let alone a kid. And Rachel, about those missing pages, for all you know, she spilled soup on them and ripped them out. Even you can't translate what isn't there."

I pictured the remnants of the three pages torn from the diary, recalled the many months between crucial entries, but I kept quiet. Yetta was right. Missing pages hinted at much but proved nothing. And the diary was filled with long gaps between entries.

Yetta wasn't done defending the man who disparaged Feigele and threatened me. "Abe Weiss is also right that, if pressed, his father would have bought off Feigele, and she would have taken his money." Her next words were small comfort. "But it would be wrong of Abe to keep you from getting that teaching job just because you didn't kowtow to him."

"I'll live. I stopped by the personnel office at Frederick & Nelson and they'll take me on again. Selling china and silver isn't my dream job, but I'm pretty good at it, and it pays the bills."

"That has to be a relief. But you must be disappointed at losing that teaching position."

I didn't want to talk about it anymore, so I told Yetta my visit with Tzipporah Salazar was arranged for the next day. "She lives with her daughter Lilli and Lilli's husband, Judah Ovadio, in Seward Park. Tzipporah not only met Feigele. She remembers her."

Chapter 24

I wanted to read up on Seattle's bubonic plague outbreak before I talked to Tzipporah, so when I left Yetta's, I hurried to the library's Newspaper Room. Bound copies of the *Seattle Times* and the *Post-Intelligencer* from October of 1907 were in cabinets there. But the bound copies of the *Seattle Star* for that same time period were stored in the basement of the West Seattle Branch library, so I filled out a form requesting them and left it at the service desk. Immersing myself in the minutiae of Rose's premature death would distract me from the fact that my daughter wasn't talking to me, my lover was gone, and my teaching career was over.

The reading was not as grim as I expected, even though graphic ads for rat traps accompanied accounts of the scourge's lethal course. Thanks to aggressive action by a newly appointed Director of the Office of Public Health, Seattle's outbreak, far less severe than the one in San Francisco, claimed only seven victims. Feigele's Rose was not listed among them.

In more than one history class I'd learned that the dreaded black plague, once blamed on the Jews, was actually spread by fleas from infected rats on ships plying trade routes. Thousands of flea-infested rodents made their way from the harbor to the subterranean streets that not long before had been tidal flats, alive with shellfish and Suquamish encampments. Too late for little Rose, these rats were exterminated and the muddy underground streets cemented over and declared off limits.

I combined this information with what Feigele wrote and reconstructed the chain of events that led to her little girl's sad end. Rose's runty kitten, probably born below ground, hosted these fatal fleas and transmitted at least one to the child who nuzzled him. Soft, furry little Ari turned out to be a Trojan horse, and no history teacher ever warned Feigele to beware of Greeks bearing gifts. But surely somebody in Feigele's circle must have known rats carried the Plague. I resolved to return to the library to read the

Seattle Star's accounts of the outbreak. Meanwhile I would ask Tzipporah Salazar what she recalled.

Eager as I was to talk with the old woman, I was also anxious. Growing up I'd had no Sephardic friends, and I still didn't. I'd never been inside a Sephardic home even though there had been several in our neighborhood. Just as Seattle's pioneering German Jews considered themselves too good to socialize with us "huddled masses" from Eastern Europe, so we considered ourselves above the late-arriving, dirt-poor, and religiously-suspect Sephardics. Marsha's friend, Sandy Yellin, slept at our house for a week after her parents threatened to disown her if she continued to date a Sephardic boy she'd met at the U. It was as if, long excluded ourselves, we American Jews needed to exclude somebody, so we excluded each other. Go figure.

Also, I was used to being the translator, the one who understood and interpreted a speaker's every word, vocal nuance, and facial tic. Having to depend on Tzipporah's daughter, someone I didn't know, for this service worried me. As I reached for the doorbell I reassured myself. After all, like me, Tzipporah's American-born daughter was probably used to translating for her mother.

"I'm Lilli Ovadio. Please, come in." She looked like her mom, but while age had wrinkled Tzipporah's face and whittled her down to elfin proportions, the years had not yet marked or diminished Lilli. I figured her to be about forty. She carried enough weight to keep her cheeks smooth and her buxom torso rounded beneath her striped apron.

Unlike Ashkenazic Jews who name children after dead relatives, Sephardics bestow the names of living ancestors on their offspring. Sam had warned me that among the Salazars, this custom, together with the matriarch's insistence on surviving so long, had resulted in a cornucopia of cousins all named Tzipporah. But only one came to the door to greet me. "My daughter, Tzipporah." Lilli nudged the teenager who offered a smile.

"Call me Cookie."

"I'm Rachel Mazursky. My father . . ."

"Yes. Sam talked to my brother at the Market and he called mom. She's all excited. She remembers that woman who wrote the diary. She's waiting. Please come in."

The Ovadios' living room was elegantly furnished with sleek Scandinavian pieces framed in light wood and upholstered in several shades of green. "How lovely!"

"Thanks." Lilli cocked her head at the little figure perched on the green sofa like a bug on a leaf and addressed her in Ladino. I flinched when I heard how loudly Lilly spoke so that her mother could hear. To my American ear, the stream of Ladino words, had the music of Spanish and the solemnity of Hebrew. I couldn't understand a word. My Hebrew, long bolstered by transliterations in the Reform prayer book, didn't include the homely Hebrew words intertwined with the ones in five-hundred-year-old Spanish.

"I'm glad to find you looking well. Thanks for agreeing to see me." I spoke directly to Tzipporah, sensing that Lilli would pitch in and translate without my having to ask. The old woman grasped at a turquoise charm around her neck and made what seemed like a long serious response to my greeting.

Lilli translated at once: "When I saw you last, I wanted to offer you my sympathy because you lost your husband, may he rest in peace." I nodded and Lilli added, "Of course you have my sympathy too." I muttered a thank you.

Cookie plopped down beside her grandmother on the sofa and helped herself to one of the pretzel-like confections piled on a tray on the glass coffee table. Tzipporah playfully slapped the girl's wrist, and Lilli rolled her eyes before she spoke. "Cookie, offer some *biscochos* to our guest. I'll be right back with coffee. The girl passed me the tray, and I took a circlet of dough. It was crunchy, only slightly sweet, and very good. The coffee Lilli served in espresso cups put Maxwell House to shame. There were ashtrays on the table. I took out my cigarettes and raised my eyebrows in the direction of my hostess. Lilli's nod was a relief.

Tzipporah spoke: "When we first came to the Central District, a Sephardic man opened up a coffeehouse next to a Sephardic grocery store. The owner of the coffeehouse used to go to the grocer and buy a hundred-pound bag of coffee beans, and the grocer would grind the beans for him so he could make Turkish coffee for his customers. All the men used to hang out at that coffeehouse on Sundays."

I nodded. The affinity of Sephardics for coffee was well known. Seattle's Sephardics knew how to relax. Sam credited this talent to the mild Mediterranean climate they had enjoyed and the fact that part of their Ottoman interlude, between the Inquisition and the Holocaust, had been mostly free of pogroms. "The diarist wrote that the Sephardics who first came here went to a Greek coffeehouse near the water. That's where she met Azaria. She told fortunes there. She . . ."

Lilli motioned me to stop and relayed my statement to her mother. Tzipporah's reply was brief: "That coffeehouse would have been the Golden Door."

"Well, she —Fanny O'Neal was her name— Fanny wrote of meeting Azaria and his friends there. And she also wrote of meeting you, of your kindness. Fanny offered to finish making your wedding dress. She died soon after that." After Lilli repeated my words, Tzipporah lowered her head and again fingered the turquoise amulet at her neck.

"Uh oh. You got her with that one. She only grabs that thing when she's worried about the evil eye." The ridicule in Cookie's interjection was softened by the hug she gave her grandmother.

The concentric circles of Cookie's tie-dyed tee-shirt formed a halo above her grandmother's head when she spoke again and pointed to a shelving unit across the room: "Look at my wedding picture. You can see the dress." There were many pictures arranged beneath what looked like a framed family tree, and in a prominent position was a black and white snapshot of a beaming young woman with dark curly hair next to a strapping young man. She wore a long-sleeved and high-necked white gown and he a dark three-piece suit. It was hard to see the details of the dress, but it was clear that the bride wore it with pride. Her smile was immediately recognizable as Tzipporah's.

From the sofa, the matriarch spoke again, her voice surprisingly strong for someone of her age and tiny stature: "That's the photo I sent back to Rhodes, to my parents. Azaria and I were married by Rabbi Genss at his house. Back then we all got married in homes because we had no Sephardic synagogue."

Lilli added a thought of her own. "Rabbi Genss wasn't Sephardic and didn't have his own congregation, but he helped all the immigrants find work, find places to live just like your mother."

I was pleased by this reminder that my mother's good works lived after her, but I didn't want to lose focus. I sat down again, lit a cigarette and, looking straight at Tzipporah, carefully worded an open-ended question. "Fanny's diary ends abruptly after her daughter died. She wrote of killing rats, and then she stopped writing. What do you remember about that time of Fanny's life?"

I was unprepared for the old lady's reaction. She grabbed her amulet with both hands and began to rock back and forth and spoke until Lilli held up her hand to silence Tzipporah while she translated: "I only met Fanny twice. We Sephardic women did not frequent coffeehouses. We didn't even go downtown to shop." Lilli ignored Cookie's exaggerated sigh. "The men worked downtown, and they brought groceries home on the streetcar. So Azaria knew Fanny better than I did. Fanny helped him learn English at the Golden Door. I met Fanny when Azaria brought her to see about my wedding dress. Fanny wouldn't take any money."

Lilli paused and nodded to Tzipporah, who continued to clutch the chunk of turquoise at her neck and sway. Cookie cradled her grandmother in a hug and rocked with her. When Tzipporah resumed speaking, her voice was softer and her words came in spurts. I realized that she was crying although no tears were visible: "When Azaria told me Fanny's little girl was very sick, I told him to bring me to the child's bedside to perform an *espanta*. . . . "

Lilli explained the Ladino word. "That's a healing ritual. My grandmother was a highly respected healer on Rhodes. There were no doctors on the Island until 1908. The older women did what they could."

I directed my response to Tzipporah. "Fanny was grateful for your help. She was so worried about her daughter."

"I was too young then to be a healer. Most healers were older women."

Again, Lilli explained. "Younger women, those who might have been, you know, having their periods when they performed a ritual, were considered unclean." Beneath our raised brows, our eyes met. Cookie shook her head.

"Fanny wrote that Tzipporah stole her gift of healing from her mother. I don't understand what she meant."

Lilli didn't need to consult Tzipporah. "The rituals involve communicating with the spirits, with God. They were too sacred to teach, so younger women observed in secret what herbs their mothers used, what words they said. My mother was very young when she left home, but she tried to absorb what she could before going." Lilli shrugged. "It was a different time, a different place."

Tzipporah resumed speaking: "I tried hard to save the child. I visited her house and tried to drive out the evil spirits by burning cloves and pouring her urine on the doorstep."

Lilli interrupted her translation. "Urine was thought to purify."

"Also our family bought the little one. Azaria gave Fanny some money for her, and I renamed her Mercada." Hearing this, I understood Feigele's claim that "Mercada was a lie."

"But Fanny would never have sold her little girl."

Once more Lilli didn't translate but enlightened me herself. "They didn't really buy and sell the kid. It was a sham transaction to fool death. They believed that if she was sold and renamed, The Angel of Death wouldn't know her by her new name, wouldn't be able to find her." The Angel of Death had not been fooled by the exotic name. Bubonic plague was not like

American anti-Semitism. It couldn't be staved off with a name change. "My mother did what she could."

"I know. Your mother is a very kind woman. She went out of her way to try to heal my mother too. And to this day my dad and I are grateful." Lilli smiled and repeated this praise to Tzipporah who slowed her rocking and favored me with a nod. But one bony hand still gripped her amulet, her knuckles white against the turquoise stone.

"I figure Rose contracted bubonic plague from a pet kitten. I guess Fanny didn't realize that the cat, born in the underground streets, had fleas that could spread the plague." Lilli translated while pouring another cup of coffee for each of us.

Then Tzipporah barraged her daughter with a storm of words. Lilli repeated a few of them verbatim. "'*Quando besas el gato, tambien besas las pulgas.*' When you kiss the cat, you kiss the fleas." She continued translating: "When the city's health workers finally told people about the fleas, it was too late for that little one. She was already sick. Until the swellings darkened, Fanny thought she just had a fever. By the time Leo, the Greek who owned the coffeehouse, carried her up the hill to Providence Hospital, she was too far gone." Providence used to be the only hospital in Seattle that treated Jews. Marsha was born there: "The little girl, may she rest in peace, died there."

Tzipporah did not wait for another question: "Azaria got Rabbi Genss, and he convinced the nuns to release the child's body, promised that she would be buried right away. He arranged for her burial in Orthodox *Bikkur Cholim*'s cemetery. He was a member there, not the rabbi. He brought together a *minyan*." Tzipporah paused for Lilli's translation.

I was relieved there had been a funeral. Feigele would have wanted her Rosele's body to lie in consecrated ground. "What do you remember about the funeral?"

Tzipporah closed her eyes and lowered her voice. Lilli leaned towards her to catch her words: "It was in the section of that cemetery set aside for Sephardics before we had our own. On Rhodes, Jewish women did not go to the cemetery until a month after a funeral, so I didn't go. I stayed at Rabbi

Genss's house with his wife. Azaria and the other two Sephardics from the Golden Door took off from peddling fish that morning. They went with Leo."

"Did Azaria tell you anything about the funeral?"

Tzipporah, her eyes still shut, hesitated. When the old woman did speak, she sounded hypnotized, her voice low and her words halting: "It was a long trip to the cemetery. The three of them from the Golden Door were the only Jews Fanny knew at the burial. Rabbi Genss brought some others to make the *minyan*. Fanny came with her Christian landlord and his wife. Azaria said Fanny looked like a ghost."

"The poor woman must have been crazed with grief." I spoke so softly that Lilli had to lean over to hear me.

"Rabbi Genss offered to bring a *minyan* to her boarding house to pray with her, but Fanny refused. She never went back to the coffeehouse. After a while, Leo and Azaria went to her rooming house, but she wasn't there. Leo talked to her landlady. She said about a week after the child died, Fanny started going out every day and one day she didn't come back."

I pictured Feigele alone in her room sitting *shiva* for her little girl before descending to Seattle's historic rat hole to take revenge on the rodent who transferred the flea that killed her Rose to the child's kitten. And on the hapless kitten too.

I worded my next question carefully and hurled it from left field. "This Leo adopted a baby boy. Did Azaria ever mention whose baby he was?"

Understandably this non sequitor caught Tzipporah off guard: "I didn't know Leo's son was adopted. What does that child have to do with Fanny?" I told her what I'd learned from Maria Patsakos, what I suspected.

"So you think Feigele and Leo might have been lovers? Had a child together? Azaria never mentioned any romance between Leo and Fanny. After her little girl died and Fanny disappeared, Leo told Azaria he thought she threw herself into the Sound." The old lady reached for her amulet: "We were very sad."

I refuted Leo's dire speculation with the equally dire truth. "There is evidence that Fanny was robbed. And the anthropology professor who examined her bones says Fanny died from a blow to the head."

Lilli gasped and Cookie's eyes widened, mirroring those circles on her t-shirt. She pulled her grandmother close while Lilli translated. As she listened, the old woman clutched her amulet and, within her granddaughter's embrace, resumed rocking. Her wordless response needed no translation.

Chapter 25

My conversation with Tzipporah outlined her efforts to save little Rose and clarified Leo Patsakos Jr.'s paternity, but the old woman had shed no light on who might have killed the child's mother. I wasn't optimistic when I returned to the library to read the *Star's* coverage of plague-related events. But this paper's reporting proved more detailed than that of the *Times*. In their wrap-up article listing known plague victims, I came upon the name *Mercada Salazar*, the alias given to little Rose O'Neal by Tzipporah in her vain effort to mislead the Angel of Death. I also learned that the child died on October 9 of what was, only in hindsight, thought to have been the plague. Ministered to by the Sisters of Charity at Providence Hospital and destined to lie under an alien name in a Sephardic graveyard in Washington State, Feigele's little girl died weeks before life-saving prophylactic serum from San Francisco and Chicago arrived in Seattle.

And it wasn't until the end of October, far too late for Feigele's Rose, that Seattle's Office of Public Health began a massive effort to contain trash, rat proof buildings, and exterminate rats. Editorials warned the public to be vigilant in their war on the deadly rodents. It was when I read that the Office of Public Health paid a bounty of five cents for the tail of every dead rat trapped and brought in by a citizen and that later officials raised the bounty to ten cents a rat tail that my pulse quickened. This had to be the "stinking reward" Feigele spurned.

But according to the *Star*, others welcomed the money, and several *Star* reporters described successful bounty hunters. Surely some of them stalked their prey in the rodent-infested underground streets. Was it one of these bounty hunters Feigele referred to when she wrote, "I go down there again to kill with the ghost?" I read on. The bounty seekers certainly were a creepy lot. One man brought in a barrel filled with dead rats. A zealous teenaged boy proudly produced a bloody string of fourteen rat tails tied end to end. A night duty police officer carted his quarry in a wheel barrow, and a peddler with a bad leg hobbled in, his sack full of the lifeless critters. Straightening in my chair, I ran my finger over the words "peddlar with a bad leg" as if to make sure I wasn't imagining them.

Could this hobbling peddler hauling a sack of dead rats have been Boris LeVine aka Boris Lipshitz? Feigele often referred to Boris as a ghost. Could the lame bigamous bully have been reduced to killing flea-ridden rats for a living after the opening of Pike Place Market destroyed Seattle's wholesale produce business? Had Boris run into Feigele in that creepy rat-ridden catacomb and killed her for her ring, for rejecting him years ago, for threatening to blackmail him? Why not? He had more motives than most murderers. Even though I was pretty sure I was right, I felt no elation. Without a witness or some other proof, I was, as Bobby had said, just "playing detective." I'd never be certain. And I better get used to that fact. I closed the large volume. It was time to bury Feigele and, with her, my unverifiable suspicions.

Perhaps keeping my promise to bury Feigele would enable me to literally let the poor woman rest in peace. As a first step, I called Tim Hunter. I expected our conversation to be awkward, but he was his silky-smooth Southern self. "Rachel, I've been thinking of you. We just got back from the San Juans yesterday. I can still feel the boat rock under my feet." He paused, perhaps expecting me to inquire how his sailing odyssey was. When I didn't, he went on. "I was going to call you. I assume you finished translating that diary. Would you recap it for me over coffee one morning next week? I'm considering including it on my syllabus as supplemental reading."

"I did finish the translation, and I'll give you a copy. But the reason I called is . . ."

"You want your check, right?"

Was there a sarcastic undertone to his drawled question? "Not until I give you the translation. No, I'm calling because I'd like you to arrange for the University to release the diarist's bones to the funeral home. Someone from there will contact you. I'm having her buried in a Jewish cemetery after a graveside service."

"Oh yes. You said you wanted to do that. Getting the bones released shouldn't be a problem." He paused. I knew what was coming. "But I doubt if there's any money in our department budget . . ."

"Her funeral expenses are covered." How many serving spoons and platters and gravy boats would I have to sell to pay for Feigele's burial? I didn't care.

"That's good. Listen, Rachel, I've dug up my share of bones, but I haven't buried many, so I'd like to come to that funeral. Will you let me know when it is? You can give me the translation and the diary then, and I'll bring your check."

"Don't bring the check to the funeral. You can mail it to me later along with the artifacts."

"You want the artifacts too?"

"Yes. I'm turning them over to the Jewish Federation along with the diary for inclusion in the Jewish archive they hope to found at the University library. Anyone interested in seeing them can visit them there."

"Okay, I'll get the artifacts and the diary released. It's not as if they're leaving the University. Anything else I can do for you, ma'am?" Now there was no disguising his twangy sarcasm. But his voice was serious and his cadence less cloying when he spoke again. "Rachel, before you judge me, remember those Old Testament heroes of yours. They weren't exactly saints." If Tim thought I was going to prolong our conversation by refuting this half-assed non-apology, he was wrong. He was literally a loose end I was tying up.

Tying up loose ends usually cheered me, but after I put the phone down I was still glum. I offered no argument when Yetta phoned. "I'm ready to pay you the rest of what I owe you. I'm not putting a check that size in the mail. You'll have to pick it up. Come tomorrow." Maybe a chat with Yetta and her check in my hand would distract me from my daughter's silent treatment, my failure to prove Boris killed Feigele, the mess with poor Bobby, and the end of my teaching career.

I was glad to hear Yetta tapping her way into the darkened dining room. Because I had no more of Feigele's adventures to report, Yetta looked to my own life for diversion. I was about to tell her about Bobby's premature proposal when the phone rang. Elsewhere in the house, Bess took the call and hurried in, slightly out of breath. "It's your accountant again. He's all riled up."

"I'll talk to him." Yetta sounded resigned, put upon. Bess moved the phone from the buffet to the dining room table and placed the receiver in the hand her employer extended. The phone's long cord caught in the crook of Yetta's cane, dislodging it from the back of her chair.

"I've got it, Bess." I bent down and picked up the walking stick and sat there cradling the lumpy crook once again in my hand. The heft of it transported me back to that awful night when, for just a few seconds, in that very room, I wielded that piece of wood as a weapon. I felt again the adrenaline coursing through my body, heard the thwack of the cane connecting with the burglar's skull.

Sam took credit for this cane being handy. With his eye for "good junk," he spotted it among the rest of the things he hauled away from Yetta's place. How had he seen a hand-crafted antique where I saw only a lumpy stick? What caught his eye? Intrigued, I touched Yetta's arm and whispered, "I'll be right back." Still attentive to her caller, she pressed my hand to show that she understood. I went no farther than the kitchen where I stood blinking for a moment in the afternoon sun blazing through the window.

When my own eyes became accustomed to the light, I looked at the cane and saw it through my father's eyes. The crook crested in a rippled knob the size of my fist. A small scratched red stone was embedded in it like the eye of a Cyclops except that the red gem wasn't centered. There was a slight circular indentation about half an inch away where, perhaps, there had been another fiery eye. In the newly opened eye of my own mind, I envisioned the fake red jewel found in the leather sack along with the bones and the book. The bit of red glass fixed in the cane in my hand appeared the twin of that one.

I recalled Feigele's earliest mention of Boris's walking stick. "As a joke, Boris calls his cane Ari." The intimidated girl had misunderstood. Boris wasn't joking. He called his cane *Ari*, Hebrew for *lion*, because its crook, like Yetta's comb, was actually carved in the shape of a lion's head with a rippling mane and two fierce red eyes of gleaming glass. Did Boris Lipschitz also have a relative or family friend back in the Ukraine who carved lions to guard Torah arks? And had this relative or friend crafted this cane for the crippled boy in the hope that the lion would guard him on his immigrant's journey? If I believed in *bashert,* or fate, this scenario would be a great example. It was too bizarre to even consider.

But I couldn't help considering it. If the *Seattle Star* reporter was to be believed, Boris could, in fact, be the "peddler with the bad leg" killing rats underground. In that case were the last words of Feigele's diary, "Goddamn Ari," a curse directed not, as I had assumed, at Rose's diseased kitten already dead by Feigele's own hand, but at Boris's cane? That cane was a weapon her old nemesis used against her in New York. Feigele still had nightmares about Boris and that cane. So were the fortuneteller's final words really a clue hidden in a curse? Was I holding in my hand the weapon that killed Feigele? That possibility was way beyond *bashert.*

But was it really? Stunned, I returned to the dining room where Yetta was still immersed in her phone conversation. Sitting once more in the darkened room with the cane in my hand, I remembered that according to Polk's Directory, Boris LeVine boarded on Stewart Street in 1907. That was just twenty-five years before Yetta bought her first Seattle "hotel" on the same street. I remembered coming across the paperwork for that transaction in a folder marked "Medical Expenses" and refiling it. Could Boris's last listed street address be that of Yetta's Stewart Street property?

I rested the cane carefully in my lap and rummaged in my bag for the notes I took at the library. If the number of Boris's rooming house on Stewart Street was the same as that of Yetta's property, Yetta's cane could have once belonged to Boris and Boris could have left it behind when he fled the area. His landlord might very well have stowed items left by roomers in an attic or cellar. My own father made a living carting away and reselling stuff like that, had, in fact, relieved Yetta of the "junk" left behind by the Stewart Street building's previous owner.

Excitement was making my hand fumble inside my purse, so that I groped among its familiar contents without finding my notes. I emptied my bag onto the dining room table. In the dim light I ferreted among my keys, wallet, change purse, Kleenex, and makeup until I came across the small scratch pad where I'd jotted down the information from the Polk Directory.

Damn. In the semi-darkness, I couldn't read my jottings, wouldn't be able to read Yetta's files. I'd have to wait until she got off the phone and ask her the address of her Stewart Street place or look it up later. But I couldn't sit still. Once again, I whispered to Yetta that I'd be right back and returned to the kitchen. There I glanced at the pad and noted the jotted address: 96 Stewart Street. Yetta was still yakking on the phone when I returned. I willed her to finish her conversation.

When she finally did, she was furious. "Damn IRS. The bloodsuckers won't be happy until I'm in the poorhouse. They want over a hundred grand from me."

I ignored her fuming. "Yetta, do you remember the address of the property you owned on Stewart Street?"

"Of course I do. I'm not senile." She rattled off the address. "96 Stewart Street."

"Yetta, that's where Boris lived. That's the address he's listed under in the Directory." When she didn't answer, I figured she had forgotten who Boris was. "You remember, Feigele's old sweatshop boss? The groper and arsonist who deserted his wife and kids and came out here? He married again and worked for a wholesaler. That man once lived in a building you bought."

"So?" Yetta still sounded mad. My discovery had not displaced her preoccupation with the IRS.

"So, I think this cane that Sam found in the stuff he hauled out of there belonged to Boris. I think he killed Feigele with it."

"So?" My revelation wasn't having the desired effect on my listener. In fact it wasn't having any effect.

"Feel." I placed Yetta's fingers over the glass eye and the adjacent indentation on the knob of the cane, and tried to keep my words from tripping over each other as I explained.

At first Yetta seemed oblivious to my torrent of words. "When he found this cane and gave it to me, your dad didn't even know my grandfather was a woodcarver. Sam just knew it was hand carved." She ran her fingers over the crook of the cane again. "This stone falls out once in a while. But Bess always finds it when she vacuums and glues it back in." Yetta was quiet for a moment. "Seriously Rachel, you can't prove this cane is the murder weapon."

"I can't. But if you're willing to part with it for a few days, Tim Hunter can. You can use the cane with the silver crook, okay?" Yetta handed me her cane.

I picked up the phone and soon had the professor on the line. "Hi, Rachel. I just wrote you that I arranged for the release of the bones, the artifacts, and the diary. What else can I do for you?" Again, his breezy greeting offered no suggestion that the last time I'd seen him he'd been half naked violating at least one commandment.

"I'd like you to reexamine the skull and the artifacts."

"Yes ma'am. I'm happy to oblige, but tell me, what should I be looking for this time?"

"I'll be there later this afternoon, around four, and I'll explain. If you're not too busy that is." I wasn't trying to be sarcastic. I just wanted to make sure I didn't catch him with his pants down again.

"I'll be expecting you this time." When I heard him chuckle at his own attempt at humor, I didn't bother to say goodbye, just put down the phone.

"Your professor can have a look at my cane. But I'd like it back." I was itching to go, to take the cane to Tim Hunter. But when Yetta spoke next she sounded both childish and bossy. “Rachel, before you rush out of here, tell me about your doctor’s leave-taking, how you’re holding up.” I wasn’t going anywhere right away.

“I miss him.” This was a masterpiece of understatement. After I watched Bobby’s plane take off, I’d felt bereft. I pressed my lips together every few minutes as if doing so would preserve the memory of his goodbye kiss, and I had a juvenile urge not to launder the sheets and towels that smelled of him. But gradually Bobby’s absence became bearable, like a wound that only hurts when you touch it, like Harry’s death come to think of it. The project I’d taken on to distract me from Harry’s absence was now distracting me from Bobby’s. I was too busy to think much about either one of them. “We had dinner at Canlis, and he proposed.”

“And?”

“Relax. I said no.” Yetta grabbed my hand and squeezed it. “I’ll give you a blow-by-blow, I promise, but not now. I’ve got to get this cane to Tim Hunter.”

“Go. But don’t forget your check, Sherlock.”

I drove straight to the University. The door to Tim’s office was wide open. “Good to see you, Rachel.” He glanced at the cane. “Either you’ve been injured or you’ve come armed.” He grinned. “Nothing serious I hope.”

It felt good to be impervious to that grin. “See this?” I pointed to the bit of red glass embedded in the crook of the cane. “I think it’s the same as the red glass in the bag with the other artifacts.” I pointed with the cane itself to the familiar lumpy manila envelope on his desk. “I want you to compare them.”

“You think you’ve actually turned up the murder weapon? After all these years?” His disbelief bordered on scorn.

“I’m not sure. But it’s possible that a blow from this cane killed the diarist. After you compare the two bits of glass, if they match, I’d like you to see if the bit found with her bones fits into the indentation in the cane and into the dent in her skull.”

The man was still too incredulous to even feign cooperation by reaching for the manila envelope right in front of him. Annoyed, I picked it up, opened it, took out the piece of glass, and placed it on his desk. Next to it I placed the cane. "Please compare them and see. The stone in the bag was probably already loose." I remembered the blood-matted hair and Brylcreem my blow left on the head of the burglar. "I think the force of the blow embedded this red stone in the diarist's scalp and it stuck there. As her flesh deteriorated, this gem was dislodged into the sack." When the anthropologist still didn't move, I picked up the bit of red glass myself and held it next to the lion's eye in the crook of the cane. They looked identical to me.

Finally obliging, the professor pulled a magnifying glass out of his desk drawer and scrutinized the two phony rubies.

"They're identical except for the scratches." He shook his head. "After you called I went up to the fourth floor storage closet and brought the bones down." He reached for a carton on the floor behind him. "I'll take a look." I was relieved not to have to personally disturb Feigele's brittle bones again. Tim Hunter dealt badly with living women, but he respected the dead ones, would handle the diarist's skull with deft, careful hands.

He gently withdrew Feigele's cranium from the box and set it on his desk. We looked down at the crack and the dent. Impatient still, I picked up the loose red eye and handed it to him. Wordlessly he took it and reached into his desk drawer for what looked like an outsized tweezers. He bent low, peered into his magnifying glass, and, gripping the stone with the tweezers, rotated it above the dent. At last, with surgical precision, he inserted the red eye into the impression in the bone. It fit. "Looks like you're onto something." He retrieved the red bit and placed it into the indentation in the cane where it immediately became a second eye. There was no mistaking the astonishment and grudging respect in the professor's drawled queries. "Where on earth did you find this cane, Rachel? How did you make the connection?"

Having gotten what I came for, I didn't feel like sticking around to explain. "It's a long story. I'll summarize it in writing and give it to you and the police along with the translation." Before he could ask, I added, "And I'll let you know the burial date when it's firm." I thanked him and left the office, taking Yetta's cane with me.

Now that I knew who struck the fatal blow and with the murder weapon beside me on the seat of my car, I reconsidered Boris Lipschitz/LeVine's motives. Perhaps Feigele told Boris's wife that her husband was already married and a father of four. Or maybe Feigele had only threatened to inform on him. Losing his job could have made Boris crazy. Boris and Feigele might have argued underground where he thought she was poaching, killing rats in what he saw as "his" territory. Perhaps when they met, he made advances that she repelled yet again. Or, as Tim said early on, Boris might have killed her for her ring. I'd never be certain.

I hadn't felt like talking to Tim Hunter, but I did want to talk to Rabbi Glick and Jake Heller. I visited the rabbi and after we set a date and time for Feigele's burial. I loaned him my translation so he could compose her eulogy.

Feigele's burial service should be announced in the *Transcript.* And it was time for the story of Feigele, her diary, and her murder to appear there as well. I called the reporter.

"Hi, Jake, it's Rachel Mazursky."

"Rachel, how are you?" His serious tone made his question more than a formulaic greeting. "I've been trying to reach you. Want to buy you a cup of coffee."

"I've got quite a story for you."

"About those bones and that Yiddish book? I'm listening."

"It's a long story."

"Good. You can tell it to me over that cup of coffee. I like long stories. Not for nothing, I'm the Ears of Jewish Washington."

I smiled. That was the name of Jake's weekly column in the *Transcript.* The reporter was the first person I invited to Feigele's funeral.

It was after six when I opened the day's mail. There was an envelope from the Board of Education. I was sure the Board secretary was writing to inform me that, regrettably, at its August meeting members did not approve my teaching appointment. This reminder of the price I was paying for preserving Feigele's words as she had written them dampened my spirits. I had to force myself to open the envelope and read the letter. Then I read it again. It was from the Board Secretary alright, but she was writing to say that at their August 22nd meeting the Board voted unanimously to approve my appointment to the faculty of Franklin High School.

I recalled my earlier discussion with Yetta, her roster of influential "business associates" all indebted to her. The blind woman had made good on her promise to watch my back. What a fool I'd been for assuming that my connection with her, if known, would prevent me from getting a teaching job. The opposite was true. Yetta had made it happen, perhaps over the objections of Abe Weiss's less powerful cronies.

I was about to pick up the receiver and dial Yetta's number to thank her when the phone rang. Startled, I grabbed it.

"Rachel, Abe Weiss here." I tightened my grip on the receiver. What on earth did he want? "Arlene suggested I phone you. I've done some thinking since we talked. May I drop by one evening this week?" He paused and when I didn't answer, he padded his request. "I have something to tell you about the woman who kept that diary." I agreed to see him the following evening. After I put down the phone, I reread the letter from the Board of Ed several times to make sure I'd really gotten the position. That night I commended God for His help of late, but I gave Him what for again about Marsha.

She called the next morning. "Mom?"

"Yes? Are you alright?" I figured only a life-threatening injury would prompt her to phone her harlot of a mother.

"I'm fine. Listen, thanks for Manya's ring. I love it, but it's a little small, so Duke bought me a chain for it." Her voice gave no hint of the misery that made her refuse to speak to me for weeks.

"Duke?"

"Trish's brother. He's been staying with Trish and me for a while."

"Oh. It was nice of him to get you a chain for the ring."

"He's a really cool guy. But I gotta go now. I just called to say thanks."

As my cousin said when I phoned her with the news, "Stop crying. Thank God you sent her Manya's ring. That gave her an excuse to call." Miriam hesitated. "Trish is a nice girl, but I don't know her brother."

"What's to know? He's probably nice too. So he's a *goy*. I don't care as long as she called." That night I thanked God and told Him pretty much the same thing.

I doubted that Abe Weiss would have anything to say that would change my mind about who killed Feigele, but I was very curious about whatever it was he wanted to tell me. When he rang the bell, I greeted him and invited him to sit down.

"Before I sit, I want to apologize. I owe you an apology. In fact, I owe you more than one apology." He frowned. I waited. "Rachel, I'm sorry that I threatened, even implicitly, to prevent you from teaching." He shook his head as if to stress his disapproval of his own behavior. "Thanks to my daughter, I didn't act on that threat." That meant that Yetta hadn't had to use her influence on my behalf either. "When I mentioned our chat to Arlene, she gave me a piece of her mind." His lips twitched in an awkward attempt to smile, perhaps at the role reversal he was describing. "So, Rachel, I was glad to hear you have a teaching position. I'm sure you'll be a credit to us."

"I accept your apology and I appreciate your honesty."

"That makes my next apology harder." He hesitated and then sank onto the sofa. "I lied to you that night at my cousin's house." I was all ears again.

"Do you remember Fanny?" I sat down in the rocker opposite him.

"No, I don't. As I told you, I was very young and we had many visitors. That was true." He hesitated. "But my cousin, Daniel Meyer, did speak to me of Fanny once."

Abe's smile was gone, replaced by a moustache made of beads of sweat.

"Oh?" I remembered the glitter of what might have been a tear in the old man's eye the evening of my visit.

"It was years before Danny's stroke, not long after his grandson, Josh's boy, eloped with a girl he met in college in Chicago, Julie Savasta." Abe pronounced the bride's name slowly and precisely, as if each Latinate syllable were part of an incantation that, said correctly, would ward off her dangerous spell. "Danny and Meryl were devastated. Danny asked me what I thought he should do. I told him to cut the boy out of his will."

His round eyes blinked rapidly. "But my cousin didn't take my advice, didn't really want it. That night Danny told me how, when he was young, he fell hard for a greenhorn from the Ukraine, a seamstress at my dad's store." I pictured Feigele's scrawled script covering the diary's pages. She might be dead, but her words still had power, power to move the living.

"My father and Danny's parents threatened to cut Danny out of the business if he continued to see her, so he dropped her. But that night Danny confided that for years he hated himself for giving her up, and he resented his family for asking him to. I'd never have known. Meryl doesn't know." Abe sighed and shook his head, apparently silenced for the moment by empathy for his cousin. When he spoke again, his voice was resigned. "So Danny wouldn't disinherit his grandson for falling in love with a Catholic. 'That's what happens in a melting pot,' he said. 'Borders melt.' And he never mentioned the seamstress to me again."

Abe took out a handkerchief and mopped his face. "When I explained this to Arlene, she insisted that I come clean to you. So, Rachel, I regret misrepresenting my poor cousin and I regret the way I spoke about the dead girl." He pocketed his handkerchief. "I hope you'll forgive me. But this Seattle Athletic Club mess has me seeing enemies everywhere."

"Again, I accept your apology." I decided to push what I saw as my advantage. "But tell me something. If you're so troubled by the way we feel about your continuing membership in the SAC, why don't you just resign? That would be a way of protesting the Club's anti-Semitism. You'd be a hero."

When he answered, I could tell he was repeating something he'd said before. "Rachel, I don't delude myself that my resignation will change the

SAC's policy. That will only happen when the state or federal government makes all the private clubs stop discriminating." When I gave no sign of agreeing with him, he offered an explanation. "It's like with the Negroes. The slaves were freed over a hundred years ago, but Negroes didn't get the right to vote until just this past year, and half the country's still not happy about it. Meanwhile, as long as I'm a member, the other SAC members can interact with me and see that we Jews don't wear horns. Besides, Rachel, I'll tell you the same thing I keep telling Arlene. I'm a businessman, not a hero."

Chapter 26

The small coterie of invited mourners clustered around the coffin next to the waiting grave. I took my place between the rabbi and my father. Standing between Yetta and Abe Weiss, Tim Hunter was donning a skullcap with all the grace of a man balancing a used rubber on his head. I turned toward Rabbi Glick as he welcomed the mourners and then gave thanks for the dry, bright, late summer day.

The rabbi made the transition from blessings to eulogy with a story from the Talmud about a member of Joseph's generation, a very old woman named Serah bat Asher. Serah remembered where in Egypt Joseph's remains were and told Moses. Thanks to her, Moses found his ancestor's bones and, as Joseph had wished, brought them out of Egypt during the Exodus.

I smiled, expecting the rabbi to pay tribute to Tzipporah Salazar. After all, like Serah, Tzipporah was the only one among us who not only knew but also remembered the deceased. But he didn't. Instead, Rabbi Glick likened me, Rachel Mazursky, to Serah. "By remembering where Joseph's bones lay and directing Moses to them, Serah linked Moses to his ancestor so Moses could honor Joseph's wish and keep his history, the history of Israel, alive. In the same way, by translating Aliza Rudinsk's diary, solving her murder, and arranging for her burial, Rachel has both preserved Aliza's story and reconnected her with us and our own complicated history."

I was relieved when the rabbi began to make Aliza herself the focus of his remarks. "At first, she was typical of the immigrants fleeing persecution who arrived in this great country with only their work ethic, their wits, and their God to help them make their way." He went on to say that, in spite of her talent and her determination, Aliza became "one of those often unsung immigrants whose sojourn here ended, not in the American Dream, but in misfortune, madness, and a violent death.

"As I read Rachel's translation of Aliza's diary, I was reminded of another immigrant woman driven to madness here in America. Her name was Naomi Ginsburg, and she was Alan Ginsburg's mother." I was surprised to hear the Rabbi refer to the controversial beatnik poet. "Like Aliza's death, Naomi's death went unsung. There were not enough Jewish men at her funeral to say *Kaddish*." Rabbi Glick paused to let this communal failure sink in. "So Naomi's son wrote *Kaddish* for her. In this moving poem, Ginsburg sings of his mother, of her arrival in America, in New York. Ginsburg tells how fifty years ago when his dead mother was a scared little girl just off the boat from from Russia, she struggled to find her way in the crowds of Orchard Street." The Rabbi sighed and drew himself up. "Where was she going?"

Rabbi Glick then drew himself up until this man of unimposing height appeared to tower over those around him. When he spoke next, his usually sonorous voice was stern, even harsh. "*Where was she going?* is a good question. Naomi Ginsburg went a little south, from Orchard Street to New Jersey. But Aliza Rudinsk came west, to Seattle. Along her way and upon her arrival, Jews and Christians alike helped her; but there were others, among our own people even, who deceived her, defamed her, shunned her, and preyed on her. One of us murdered her."

He touched on the highlights of Aliza's life, making no mention of the possibility that she fabricated any part of her diary or wrote and then excised a dark secret. Instead, he spoke of her determination and hard work, her love of her family, her adaptation to cruel circumstances, and of how she helped the Sephardics and was welcomed into their midst.

I started at the sound of my name. "Rachel thinks Aliza kept this remarkable record of her American odyssey for her children, certainly a valid speculation. Perhaps, like many diarists, Aliza also wrote to better understand herself and what was befalling her. But both Rachel and I also believe Aliza told her story and preserved it on her own person to the end" —here Rabbi Glick patted the front of his dark suit jacket as if he, too might have a diary stashed beneath it— "as a cautionary tale, a story that others, not only her children, might learn from." The Rabbi stopped speaking and looked around him, deliberately making eye contact, first with me beside him and then with the others ringing Aliza's grave. "Finally, I suspect the diarist had yet another Reader in mind." At this Rabbi Glick raised his eyes heavenward. There was no mistaking his meaning. "This young woman —so talented, so hard working, so cruelly cut off from her roots— wanted to explain herself to God, to keep faith with the Covenant." When Rabbi Glick began to chant *Kaddish*, I was quick to add my voice to his and the other Jews there joined in.

When we had all shoveled earth onto Aliza's coffin, I invited the mourners to my home for a simple and abbreviated shiva. Early that day I'd rushed to Brenner's for rugelach, filled the coffee pot, scoured the downstairs bathroom, and asked Sam to bring some of Manya's dahlias to put on the table. At the last minute, I remembered to leave a pitcher of water and a roll of paper towels beside the front door so mourners arriving from the cemetery could keep the tradition of rinsing the taint of death from our hands before coming in.

This shiva-cum-coffee klatch was a lively affair. Jennie Larson, Royal Townsend, Detective Lombardi, Tim Hunter, Lilli and Cookie Ovadio, Arlene Golden and Abe Weiss, and Jake Heller, scribbling, encircled my father. Delighted to have an audience, Sam described how he found and preserved Yetta's cane and how I'd determined it to be the murder weapon. Jake broke away long enough to schedule an interview with me. And that cup of coffee.

I took Tim Hunter and Detective Lombardi aside and handed Tim a manila envelope. "Here's my translation of the diary. Please ask Roberta to type up carbon copies and send one to Detective Lombardi, one to the Jewish Federation along with the artifacts, and the original back to me." I looked at the detective when I continued. "I've also included a note identifying the diarist's murderer and describing the weapon he used." I turned back to Tim. "As we agreed, Professor, I'm turning the diary over to the women at the Jewish Federation who hope to establish a Jewish archive at the University library."

"Thank you, Rachel. I'll have Roberta put your check in the mail." Tim walked out the door with my translation in his hand. Soon I'd give over the little leather book itself, but I took comfort in the thought of the transliteration upstairs in my desk drawer.

After everyone left, I drove to my father's house and went straight to Manya's garden. The parsley had gone to seed, but dahlias and a few ripe tomatoes still flourished. I sat down on the bench. It was not enough to have translated Feigele's diary, figured out who caused her death, and buried her bones. I needed to make sense out of the diarist's life, out of my own. Rabbi Glick agreed there were lessons to be learned from Aliza's sad story.

But what could I, a mature modern American woman, an educated and assimilated Jew, learn from this young, unlettered, turn-of-the-century Orthodox immigrant? Struggling to find some message in Aliza's short and sorry life, to translate all that pain into purpose, into a reality relevant to my own, I closed my eyes and thought for a while, like a rabbi trying to tweeze a life lesson from the tangled tales of Torah.

Aliza Rudinsk changed her name several times, traveled across two continents and an ocean, learned a new language well enough to teach it, and fled America's Jewish ghettoes when they threatened to suffocate her. She practiced a forbidden art, married a *goy*, noshed on ham, named the Deity, and avoided synagogues where, either because she was too Jewish or too un-Orthodox, members disparaged her. In other words, she became an American Jew.

And like other Americans, she reinvented herself often. But no matter what identity she assumed, in her diary as in her heart, she was always Aliza. Just before her death, she looked forward to sharing a simple Sabbath meal in a Jewish home, to introducing her little girl to one of the great pleasures of Jewish family and social life. As best she could, Aliza kept faith with the Jews' Covenant with God, but she also kept faith with herself. Often unsure of where she was going or even where she was, Aliza never lost sight of whom and where she came from. And she valued the truth of the story she told and the Jewish tongue she told it in.

Manya too had loved Yiddish. I looked around. The fruit and flowers my greenhorn mother willed from the wet, rich Seattle dirt were her memorial. But someday this garden will go to seed. The generation of people who remember valiant Manya the Mule will die. But contrary to what Rabbi Glick said, Aliza survived. One of God's least likely note-takers, Aliza Rudinsk lives on in the splotched pages of her diary.

There in my mother's garden I resolved to help get that oral history project started. And next summer, while school is out, I'll help Yetta write her autobiography. I stood, stretched, and twisted the nearest tomatoes off the vine. They'd go with the tuna fish salad I promised to make Sam for supper. In the morning I'd begin reading the history textbooks Principal Jankowski gave me. I had lessons to plan.

Selected Resources

Writers' Organizations: Authors Guild; Mystery Writers of America National-Rebound Grant Committee; Mystery Writers of America Pacific Northwest Chapter; Sisters in Crime, National and Puget Sound Chapters

Forensic and Medical Mavens: Janet L. Barrall, M.D.; Rick Boettell, docent, Seattle Underground Tour; Detective Mark H. Hanf, Seattle P.D. / C.S.I Unit; Annette Hollander, M.D.; Gil Kerlikowske, Seattle Police Chief ; Detective Brian Stampfl, Seattle P. D. / C. S.I Unit; Katherine Taylor, Ph.D., Forensic Anthropologist, King County Medical Examiner's Office

Jewish History and Culture Mavens: Kathy Barokas; Marge Graham; Yechezkel Kornfeld, Rabbi, Shevet Achim; Natan M. Meir, Ph.D., Assistant Professor of Judaic Studies, Portland State University; Murray Meld, President, Seattle Yiddish Group; Mike Meltzer; Mimie Meltzer; Anita Page; Daniel Weiner, Senior Rabbi, Temple De Hirsch Sinai

Seattle History Mavens: Mary Leeds; Paul Malakov; Marge Shawn; Barbara Royalty; Art Siegal; Alice Siegal; Emily Shaffer

Mensches Who Listened and/or Critiqued: Deborah Adams, Editor, Oconee Spirit Press; Susan Babinski; Jules Berger; Evelyn Blatt; Lyn Bolen; Carolyn Broomfield; Barbara Carole; Liv Cartwright; Larry Cheek; Robert Christenson; Karye Cottrell; Jennifer Fisher; Daniel Isenberg; Miriam Isenberg; Susan Jensen; Pat Juell; Larry Karp; Stephen Kiesow; Paul Malakov; Rebecca Mlynarczyk; Jeannie Moscowitz; Laura Peterson; Joan Rabin; Arnie Robins; Myra Rothenberg; Judi Schraeger; Barbara Slovin; Brian Stoner; Rachel Stoner; Katherine Sylvan; Sol Sylvan; Ruth Tait; Phil Tompkins; Kim Turner; Ellen Turner; Shilyh Warren; Frances Wood; Joyce Yarrow

Libraries: King County Library System, King County, WA; Seattle Public Library, Seattle, WA; Temple De Hirsch Sinai Libraries, Seattle and Bellevue, WA; University of Washington Library, Washington State Jewish Historical Society Jewish Archive, Seattle, WA

Museums: The American Folk Art Museum (www.folkartmuseum.org); The Klondike Gold Rush National Historic Park, Seattle, WA, and Skagway, AK; Rhodes Jewish Museum (www.rhodesjewishmuseum.org); The Seattle Police Museum, Seattle, WA; Seattle Underground Tour, Seattle, WA; The Skagway Museum, Skagway, AK; The Tenement Museum, New York, NY

Cultural and Religious Organizations: Endless Opportunities, Jewish Family Services, Seattle, WA; www.historylink.org; Jewish Genealogical Society of Washington State, Seattle, WA; The Montana Historical Society, Helena, MT; The National Yiddish Book Center, Amherst, MA; Temple De Hirsch Sinai, Seattle, WA; Washington State Holocaust Education Resource Center, Seattle, WA; Washington State Jewish Historical Society, Seattle, WA

Periodicals: *The Jewish Transcript*; *Lilith*; *The New York Times*; *The New Yorker*; *The Seattle Times*; *The Seattle Post-Intelligencer*; *The Stranger*; *The Seattle Star*; *www.skagwaynews.com*; *www.tabletmag.com*

Bibliography: *Born to Kvetch: Yiddish Language and Culture in All of Its Moods* by Michael Wex; *Daughters of the Shtetl: Life and Labor in the Immigrant Generation* by Susan A. Glenn; *Digressions of a Native Son* and *Once Upon a Time in Seattle* by Emmett Watson; *Family of Strangers: Building a Jewish Community in Washington State* by Molly Cone, Howard Drucker, and Jacqueline Williams; *Good Time Girls of the Alaska-Yukon Gold Rush* by Lael Morgan; *I Remember Rhodes* by Rebecca Amato Levy; *On the Harbor: From Black Friday to Nirvana* by John C. Hughes and Ryan Teague Beckwith; *Pioneer Jews: A New Life in the Far West* by Harriet and Fred Rochlin; *Rites of Passage: A Memoir of the Sixties in Seattle* by Walt Crowley; *Ritual Medical Lore of Sephardic Women: Sweetening the Spirits, Healing the Sick* by Isaac Jack Lévy and Rosemary Lévy Zumwalt; *Sephardim and the Seattle Community* by Albert Addatto, MA Thesis; *Skid Road: An Informal Portrait of Seattle* by Murray Morgan;

Songs for the Butcher's Daughter by Peter Manseau; *Sons of the Profits* by William C. Speidel; *The Forging of a Black Community: Seattle's Central District from 1870 through the Civil Rights Era* by Quintard Taylor; *The Jews of Rhodes: The History of a Sephardic Community* by Marc D. Angel; *The Jews of Sing Sing* by Ron Arons; *The Journey Home: Jewish Women and the American Century* by Joyce Antler; *The Joys of Yiddish* by Leo Rostand; *The Pike Place Market: People, Politics, and Products* by Alice Shorett and Murray Morgan; *Women of the Klondike* by Frances Backhouse; *You Never Call! You Never Write! A History of the Jewish Mother* by Joyce Antler

About the Author

Jane Isenberg wrote the prize winning memoir *Going by the Book* (Bergin & Garvey) and *The Bel Barrett Mystery Series* (Avon/HarperCollins). She earned degrees from Vassar College, Southern Connecticut State College, and New York University and taught English for nearly forty years, first in high school and later in community college. Now retired from teaching, she writes in Issaquah, Washington where she lives with her husband Phil Tompkins.

Visit her web site: www.JaneIsenberg.com
and her blog: www.notestomymuses.wordpress.com.

CPSIA information can be obtained at www.ICGtesting.com
Printed in the USA
LVOW081440200912

299635LV00010B/6/P